EXSANGUINATE

WORLD OF BLOOD: BOOK ONE

I0665067

KILLION SLADE

A Division of Draconian Publishing

Cover art: Ravven Kitsune http://www.ravven.com/

Published by Spirit, an imprint of Draconian Publishing.
P.O. Box 1000
Conrad, MT 59425

Disclaimer: This book is a work of fiction. Any references to real events, people, or places are used fictitiously. Other names, characters, places, and incidents are products of the author's imagination. Any resemblance to actual events, places, or people, living or dead, is entirely coincidental.

First Edition:

6x9 paperback ISBN 13: 978-0-9859381-5-4

Exsanguinate is a standalone reading experience, containing interactive content. Please visit WorldofBlood.com to explore cut scenes, character dossiers, and extended versions. We encourage you to access and discover our complimentary "second screen" addition.

If you are familiar with how QR codes work, you can scan the above code to access the page. We hope you join us in this interactive adventure.

Acknowledgments

It is well said launching a book takes a village, and I for one, advocate that thought. They say if you want something done well, then you need to surround yourself with people who are smarter than yourself to get the job done right. For without the amazing professionalism, dedication of time and resources from some of the most beloved people in our lives, this book series simply would not exist.

Our deepest appreciation goes out to our editors, Mary Ann Peden-Coviello, Virginia Smith, Rhonda Carpenter, Devon Ellington, and Wendy Schirmer. For without their tireless efforts, this novel would never have seen the light of day or helped our dream come true.

Our heartfelt thank you goes out to Ahnah Jenkins, Alicia Wood, Amy K. Marshall, Apple Ardent Scott, Bill Crane, Billie Sue Mosiman, Chantal Noordeloos, Cindy Kersey, Diana Holdsworth, Faith Dincolo, Jaime Johnesee, Jeannine East, Kelly Whitley, Kimber Rowe-Samborki, KT Wagner, Leigh Lane, Lin White, Lisa Schmidt, Lisa Weir, Nina Benneton, Pamela Toler, Ravven Kitsune, Robyn McCleary, Roma Lee Fuson, Roxanne McHenry, Theron Lalla, Tirsea McNeal, Vix Kirkpatrick, and Watson Davis. Each and every one of you has had delightful impact on either the planning, brainstorming, marketing, or overall creative fun for this novel. You are held in our deepest and sincerest gratitude! Thank you for joining us in our journey :)

Dedication

And last, but certainly not least - we dedicate this book to my fathers, Dr. James Paul Kersey and Edward Brant Smith. We have missed them now for too many Thanksgivings from our table. We will cherish you forever in our hearts.

Contents

Prologue

The The pain gave clue it might be time to pray for death – that would be easier than remaining alive. My eyelids, heavy as cast-iron skillets, made it difficult to see through the haze. Prying them open revealed intense, bright light bouncing off shiny surfaces, forcing me to close them once again. When I found the courage to peek, the penetrating, painful light made it difficult to focus. My hand ventured out to help me understand my surroundings. I discovered warm skin at my fingertips.

"Cheyenne? I'm here, baby. It's ok-kay. You're in the hospital. Everything is g-gonna be just fine."

I followed the welcome sound of my father's voice, managing to focus enough to see his swollen, tear-streaked face. His lips trembled as he bent forward and kissed my forehead. His stutter and affection hinted he had terrible news or I was dead. Considering the amount of pain I was in, I would have preferred the latter.

The last time I saw him openly cry was when my mother died. Not a good sign for me.

I looked around for the morphine vending machine everyone loves when they're in the hospital, but what I found instead was bloody ooze seeping through gauzy bandages all over my body. My right arm was pierced with an IV and blood shunt, while a pressure cuff inflated on my upper left arm, cutting off the circulation. The amount of tape holding down my bandages reminded me of the mummy costume I'd been wearing before waking up in here.

With every heave of my chest, I heard the crack of micro-fractures in my ribs. The torturous pain kept me at the crossroads – on the brink of another black-out. A percussion section of hums, beeps, blips, and pings harmonized the soundtrack of the intensive care unit behind my head.

My father let out an oppressive breath which smelled as if he hadn't exhaled for days. Quietly, he choked on his words. "I came as soon as the p-police contacted m-me."

Police?

He grabbed my hands to help quiet my confusion. "Shh. It's all right, Cheyenne. J-just relax now, honey."

Questions seared my mind more than the pain scoured my nerves and nothing made any sense. I sank farther back into the bed to rest in safety.

Through clenched teeth, I tried to say my sister's names. "Da..ko..ta. Sher..dan"

My father swallowed hard. I watched his lips try to form words. His voice choked and stopped. His face creased with worry. He reached for a newspaper on my rolling bedside table and held it to his chest. I stretched out my fingers to indicate I wanted to see. He unfolded the front page of the *Orlando Sentinel* for me to read.

12 Dead, 16 Injured, 3 Missing in Horror Night Massacre

Daddy's trembling fingers pointed to the number three. My sisters were missing!

I looked up at him. My heart skipped a beat. Machine alarms screamed out my misery – everything my mouth couldn't say. My mind recoiled in denial and recollection. Hoarfrost retreated into my bones as a flood of blood left my brain with the speed of a torrential downpour.

I remember. Oh Dear God... I remember!

I tried to breathe, but it caused more pain in my chest as the ribs cracked. I searched for the little red morphine button and pushed it.

I must be one of the sixteen. Sweet Jesus. Twelve people were killed in that horrible room? There was no way out – how did I survive?

The morphine elixir bathed my nerves as my head grew fuzzy. I wondered which was worse – dead or missing. If they're dead, they're gone and there's nothing I can do about it. If they're missing, I can find them. After what I saw that monster do to those people in that chamber of horrors, there's no telling what freakish atrocities could be happening to them right now - if they're still alive.

The fateful pull of the reaper beckoned me to join him once again. Sinking into the welcoming arms of Morpheus, I whispered into his ear, "I'll find you ... I pinky swear promise, my sisters ... I'll ... find ... you."

Chapter One

Part One

The Penthouse

Twenty Four Hours Earlier

N ormally I loved Friday nights. This Friday however, was a different story. My presence was mandatory at one of the scariest places on the planet – Halloween Scream Nights. Scheduled to arrive at Global Studios for their annual fright fest with both my sisters, I had a backstage pass to watch, record, and study fear. I needed to analyze the types of things that cause grown men and women to run out of buildings while screaming and pissing their pants. This fear data would help us develop the next rollout of "ExsanguiNation", our online role-play simulation game. According to my boss, my older sister, Sheridan, it was my professional responsibility to research what frightens people, regardless of whether or not it frightened me.

I thought about how three sisters should have had better means of entertaining and employing themselves than finding new and improved ways to scare the beegeezus out of one another. No wonder we were the weird ones. The Irish, redheaded, horror-obsessed O'Cuinn sisters. We knew horror movie trivia better than other people knew baseball. I wouldn't trade my sisters for anything in the world. I never knew why the three of us couldn't be all up into guys, shopping, or something else mundane like that.

Lying in bed before starting the day, I often questioned my sanity and choice of profession. Why did I become a software programming engineer for online game simulators powered to scare the hell out of people, when I personally was the biggest chicken-shit on the planet?

The alarm clock beamed seven-thirty a.m. onto the ceiling as *Celebration* by Kool and the Gang blared out the speakers. I stared at the numbers as if they were an omen. Not wanting to wake up, I held the pillow over my face. The day I had been dreading since last Halloween had finally arrived.

"You have an online chat message from Sheridan O'Cuinn." PADME – my Personal Automated Domicile Management Executive walked into my bedroom and announced my sister was online. It had taken a few months getting used to the idea of a holographic person in the house, but PADME had become something I relied on for almost everything.

I rolled over and groaned. Knowing the inevitable was coming, I said, "Okay, put her on." I sat up in the bed.

Beano, my sixty-five pound Boxer puppy, jumped onto the bed and dropped Mr. Pooh bear into my lap. "Good morning, my big, handsome fella. How are you today?" He licked my face. Beano's grin always brightened my mornings.

My bedroom wall changed from the serene beachfront with breaking waves to the face of my older sister, Sheridan.

"Good morning, Cheyenne. Time to wakey wakey. Eggs and bakey."

"Sher, it's not even eight o'clock." I hated morning people. "I was up past three this morning with Roxas."

"What you do on your time off with Rox is none of my concern." Sheridan changed her tone and singsonged at me. "Today's the big day. Just wanted to make sure you got Dakota's surprise for our big event tonight."

I blinked at her. Sheridan was always way too cheery for this early in the morning. "Surprise? I've barely opened my eyes. All I know is Dakota said something about picking up costumes this morning after class." I looked around the room. Sure enough, a card and a small cylinder lay next to the iPod alarm clock.

"Yeah, it looks like she left me something. I wonder what else she did in here while I slept. I'll check it out in a bit."

"Excellent. Yeah, you better check your tooth paste. She once changed mine out for that Preparation H stuff."

"Ewww."

"That's all right. I put hair remover in her shampoo, so it's all good." Sheridan picked up a small doggie carrier which held her little Pomsky puppy, and set her in front of the camera. "I also wanted to see if I could drop off Stormaggedon before we go to the theme park this afternoon. You know how she loves to play with Beano. I don't want her to be all alone." Sheridan ended her request in doggie baby talk.

"Sure. What time?" I placed my feet solidly on the floor and scratched my back. My elbow creaked from all the computer time. I looked over at the screen and Sheridan had Stormy dressed in a University of Florida Gators cheerleading outfit.

"I should be there around four. I have to arrive at the park early to coordinate equipment checks with the tech one supervisor."

Stormy pulled at the costume with her teeth.

"So ... have you decided about tonight?"

"Decided what, Sheridan? You know I can't even think straight without coffee. Padme – could you please start the coffee pot in my office?"

Padme responded, as always, with polite charm. "Absolutely, Cheyenne. Would you like the pumpkin spice eggnog creamer or the Bailey's in your coffee this morning?"

"Bailey's definitely. The chocolate kind."

"You put Bailey's in your coffee?" Sheridan grabbed a miniature pom pom.

"Yeah – why not? If it's a great after dinner drink, then I figure it oughta be even better before breakfast."

Sheridan put a pom pom on one of Stormy's paws. Beano picked up Mr. Pooh bear and nudged me. I grabbed the teddy bear and played tug-o-war with my puppy.

"Seriously, Sher? You're gonna give that poor little dog a complex. She's not a toy. Why do you dress her like that?"

Stormy shook her little paw, most likely trying knock the pom pom off her, making it shake.

"What? This is her Halloween costume, of course. Didn't you get something for Beano?"

Beano stopped his tugging on Mr. Pooh and cocked his head to the side as if he were waiting for my answer. "Uh ... that would be a no. Besides, I'm sure he'd take my arm off if I tried."

"Boo. You're no fun. This is supposed to be an exciting day. I have the hugest surprise for you."

"I bet you do."

She grinned at me. "Have you decided to face your biggest fear and go in the haunted house alone, tonight?"

"Hold that thought. I've gotta pee. Why don't you let the pups talk for a sec."

My favoritest pair of capri jeans and tank top lay at the foot of the bed where I had shed them mere hours before. I grabbed them and shuffled into the bathroom. The mirror mocked me when I looked at my disheveled auburn curls and bloodshot blue eyes. Serious nerves of wrought iron steel were needed to help me get through this night and there was only one person, or rather one avatar, who could help me.

Beano stood protecting the bedroom fortress, and barked at Stormaggedon until I re-emerged from behind the bathroom door. Stormy's tiny bark was entirely too cute. I bet she thought she was as big as a standard sized Siberian Husky instead of the miniature Pomsky cross that she was.

"Look, I have to tell you. I don't have a problem programming scary things for the game, but I don't like haunted houses. Ya know?" I sat on the bed and grabbed my leather sandals. "It's going to be a challenge for me to face this fear alone. Watching horror movies is always safe. The worst thing that happens is spilled popcorn, right, but being live and in person at the haunted houses – that's a totally different story."

"Oh, didn't I tell you?" I watched as she took the cheerleading costume off Stormy and pulled on a ballerina's pink tutu.

"Tell me what? That tonight is canceled?"

"No, silly. Since this is the 25th anniversary event of the Halloween Scream Nights, Global Studios is allowing the park-goers to dress up in costume. Isn't that fantastic?"

"What? Are you serious? I thought the only reason we're dressing up is 'cause we're part of the guest cast. I can't believe Global Studios would do that. Consider the liability. The security risks. They've never done that before. We won't be able to tell who works there and who doesn't. It'll be a virtual serial killer Las Vegas buffet."

"Exactly, it totally rocks. Don't worry. There will be tons of extra security guards and off duty police dressed up in costumes as well. It'll be the best opportunity for research."

I didn't acknowledge her.

Yeah, research of the worst kind.

Sheridan danced Stormy on her back feet to show off her pink tutu. "What do you think of this one?"

"Cute. Better than the cheerleader."

Beano nudged my arm. I stroked his furry, sweet face.

"It's those damn scare zones that bother me the most, Sher. I can't get to a bathroom without being accosted by the preternatural, undead, creepy crawlies."

Beano woofed at me. I looked at him and said, "I wish I could take you to the park with me, big fella. You'd be my scary protector, wouldn't cha? No ghoulies would dare come after me with you by my side." He wagged his nub at me.

"I'm so excited, Cheyenne. I can't wait to see the costume Dakota is getting for you. You're gonna freak."

"Lovely."

"I'll have you know - I am privy to information that the movie studio has built truly perverted concoctions with extra creepy weirdos for the big anniversary event."

Any moment I thought for sure Sheridan was going to break out into a cheer herself.

"We're gonna see things we've never experienced to scare the living hell outta us. There's so much to do to get ready. Don't you just love half-day Fridays?"

"Take a breath, Sheridan. You're gonna hyperventilate before the day even begins."

Her morning energy always made me wonder how we were related. She was always one of those people who got up at 4:30, ran a 5k, and milked a cow before the rooster crowed.

"Okay – sounds super. See you this afternoon. Laters." I waved goodbye as I exhaled with mock excitement to get Sheridan off the line.

"Okay, see you then." She waved goodbye with Stormy's paw.

"End transmission."

Padme resumed the screen to its former calm constant feed of waves onto the shore. "C'mon Beano. Gawd only knows what she'll make her kids dress up in one day. At least she didn't get you a Gator outfit."

The temperatures were gonna top out into the nineties today in

Orlando, and the humidity level was already at eighty-five percent. I put my unruly dark auburn curls into a floppy ponytail.

Washing my face, I turned on the news in my mirror to watch the daily headlines. Traffic was already jammed up on I-4. Good thing I knew the back way to the theme park.

My eyebrows were in desperate need of a good grooming. There were so many stray hairs on my face, it looked as though I hadn't been out of the house in a decade. It always hurt like hell when I had my eyebrows waxed. I hated plucking because I would pluck out the hairs whose nerves were attached to my toes and would shoot sharp shards of pain down my body and make my eyes water. I learned a long time ago you never ever pluck after applying mascara. Inevitably, you'd have watery eyes and have to redo your makeup from the streaks of mascara down your cheeks. What a nightmare.

Picking up the tweezers, I held them up to my mouth like a microphone. "Hey, Beano, what do you think of this one? I could call myself *The Monobrow*, the super villainess of all those who fear the dreaded tweezers. Striking horrific fear into the hearts of persons afflicted with pluckophobia. Coming to a bathroom mirror near you. Video at eleven."

Beano looked up at me and cocked his ears in curiosity. Forgoing the plucking, I gave him a kiss and grabbed his leash. "C'mon, Beano. I know, your momma is the weirdest."

Chapter Two

I grabbed the little card off my bedside table and the small cylinder with a chain on it. It was a little key chain container of pepper spray with tape over the label. Dakota had written on the tape, *Vampire Repellent.*

After feeding Beano, I grabbed a quick glass of orange juice from the kitchen. Wonderful aromas of coffee awaited me while I walked my ten second commute into my home office.

The sun shone through the windows with true-to-form Florida intensity. Even for October, it seemed unseasonably hot for Orlando.

"Padme, could you please adjust the tint opacity in the infrared sensors to fifteen for the office windows and close the blinds?"

"Certainly. Would you like for me to adjust the internal thermostat while I'm at it?"

Padme's program automagically closed the blinds, changed the electrocoating on the exterior glass, and blocked the sun's infrared heat, immediately cooling the room.

"Padme, what is the current temperature?"

"The ambient house temperature is 72 degrees, Fahrenheit. Outside, it is a balmy 94 degrees with a UV index of a nine. Be sure to wear your sunscreen today, Cheyenne."

"Thank you. No, we don't need to lower the internal temperature. The blinds and window changes should take care of the heat. Thanks for the heads up on the outside temps. I hope it cools off before tonight."

Padme scanned the weather forecast. "Tonight's low is 75 degrees with a thirty percent chance of rain mid-afternoon and evening showers."

I opened the card from my sister Dakota.

It read –

Cheyenne,
Thought you might want to add this to your collection of mace, garlic, pepper, and bear sprays to ward off any rabid forest animals or would-be vampires tonight.
Love ~ Kota.

Lovely. Gotta love their sense of humor. I put her card in my in basket and attached the little canister to my keychain. I'd have to think of something equally creative to get back at her.

Preparing for beta tests with my senior programmers, I stared at the computer console. The monitor cursor blinked at me with the impatience of a toddler waiting for Santa on Christmas Eve. As I pondered which avatar to log into the ExsanguiNation gaming portal, my fingers scrolled down the vertical glass and paused over a name – Lady Cazenove. A double tap later and the database immediately delivered my shot of courage packaged in a vivacious avatar who preferred to carry a katana or a crossbow over a gun any day.

Lady Cazenove was my edge, my escape to the dark side. My alternate personality built into my virtual avatar. My Alt. Based on Casanova himself, Lady Caz gave me a sense of unbridled, romantic seduction against fear. Terror succumbed to her every whim. Just as in *Silence of the Lambs*, she ate trepidation with fava beans and a nice bottle of Chianti. Since my own uneventful life reflected the opposite, Lady Caz always delivered just the right amount of snark and kickassery against anything or anyone who threatened her safety – my safety.

Perking perfection wafted promises of consciousness as I poured the first cup of coffee. The morning schedule had four hours blocked out to complete the final boss sequence for the next roll-out in the game. Then it would be time to get the truck loaded with our gear for the night's misadventures. If only it were as easy to load an avatar like Lady Caz in real life as it was online. I needed an avatar who wouldn't be afraid of the crazies, the ghoulies, the monsters hiding behind the sandbag curtains tonight, because I already knew I was gonna scream like a little girl. I needed her nerve, her katana, and her ability to run in stilettos.

How do I get myself into these situations?

"C'mon Beano. Let's get to work." He padded into the office and lay down in his doggie bed.

One would think I was running Disney World from where I sat in my home office. Mission control had nothing on me. Several ginormous monitors hung on my walls. Two rolling, floor-to-ceiling holographic touch panel displays had helped me develop ExsanguiNation with my crack team of coding ninjas. One of my favorite toys was a 3D rendering counter which allowed me to program actual fight sequences from a green room.

I envisioned the monstrosities of horror I would need to construct on this machine after tonight. It was one thing to write code for fighting off vampires and werewolves inside a game. It was an entirely different thing to walk alone through a pitch black insane asylum while you knew crazy people were going to jump out at you.

Setting it atop my head, I grabbed the wireless headset and turned it on over my ears.

"Padme, please open up the group conference line and set me as the moderator of the call."

Any time now, my virtual team would arrive to greet the virtual workday. I watched on the monitors as my team teleported into our simulated - SIM - office as their own avatars.

"Hey Caz? That you? Morning." Tony Briggs' deep voice resonated over the conference line. He always sounded like Barry White to me. "Mind if I run tank this time?"

"Yeah, I'm ready. Still tryin' to wake up though. Sure, you can run tank. I'd rather run the Shaman princess today so we have a healer in the group."

Briggs' avatar rezzed into our virtual admin simulated office inside the game. He joined Lady Cazenove by the water cooler. Her avatar script allowed her to grab a water glass, fill it up, and drink it in a steady, natural rhythm.

It might have been rude, but I forgot to mute my microphone and yawned, "Who else is on the line with us?"

"I'm here." Harris Archer, my old college roommate, popped in to the office. "Sorry, I'm a couple minutes late. I just finished my latest virtual geo-cache on the sim."

I loved Harris; he was one of my best buds on the planet. We spent most of college together. The brother I never had. Total geek, total cutie, total cyberchondriac. If there was a new ailment to have, Harris was convinced he had it every full moon.

Enjoying the warmth from the coffee coursing through my veins I said, "Slow down. Not running a marathon here this morning, Harris. No worries, I'm still on my first cup. It's all gouda." I put the guys on speaker through my wireless headset. "Briggs and I were just suiting up our avatars for the roles we're gonna play on the Battle Kroc boss sequence. I have a few new alternate endings I want to test out on you guys."

"Hey, Briggs, did I ever tell you about that time Cheyenne and her sisters got grounded for a month because of a geo-cache?"

"Seriously? What the heck did they do? Plant the cache in a cemetery or something?"

"Bingo."

"Yeah, all right, Harris. Thanks for reminding me of that fantabulous time. It wasn't my fault Sheridan wanted to hold a séance at ole man Flannery's grave. I was only a sophomore in high school."

"That's a story I'm gonna have to hear one day, Cheyenne," Briggs said.

Roxas Morgwain rounded out the roll call. "Good morning, peeps. What's the craic?"

Roxas spawned his avatar into the office. My breath hitched in my chest. Memories of last night's virtual simulation play with Rox in the adult underworld playground sent heat up my face.

"Top of the morning, Cheyenne. Are you awake?"

"Barely. If it weren't for a call from Sheridan earlier, I might have missed this one. She woke me up."

It was fun dating in an online virtual simulated environment with

Roxas. We had the world at our fingertips. One night we might walk through the Louvre museum in Paris, the next night we might go dancing on the bow of the Titanic. Dating in a simulator gave us freedom to explore the world and each other. He always kept me guessing as to what our next date night would encompass.

I swallowed a sip of coffee and exhaled an *Ahh* as the caffeine surged through my arteries bringing animated consciousness back. "Hey, guys. Dakota says she's gonna be late from her editing post-production recording class this morning. Something about picking up our costumes for Halloween Scream Nights tonight."

An "Ah, man,"sounded from Briggs. He had the major hots for Dakota and made it crystal clear to her and everyone else just how hot. She only had morning classes on Fridays, but Briggs always seemed to like it when she was available to game with us.

Roxas' avatar walked over to Lady Caz. I watched as Roxas typed [/hug Lady Cazenove] into the public chat window. His avatar opened his arms wide and embraced Lady Caz in a huge hug.

After about five seconds, Harris started to groan. "Get a room already."

Briggs purred in that *Can't Get Enough of Your Love* sort of way. "That's all right, allow the man to enjoy himself, son."

"Harris, you're just jealous. Get over it." The script finished and I sent Roxas an emoticon wink in a private chat message.

In reality, none of us lived in the same city. Everything we did was virtual. Briggs lived somewhere in New Orleans. Harris owned a house in downtown Tampa, a few hours away from me in Orlando. Depending on the tourist traffic time of the year, sometimes the drive to the west coast was only a couple hours, but it seemed as of late the interstate was a nightmare to traverse unless you drove it at two in the morning.

Not exactly sure where Roxas lived, other than he was in the Kissimmee area, about fifteen miles south of me. Roxas also traveled quite a bit back and forth to Europe and Egypt from what I understood. He never talked much about his family overseas, but I wondered if there wasn't an old flame lingering. Because of his extensive traveling, and my reluctance to get attached, we had decided to strictly keep our relationship online. It was safer that way. Especially for my heart.

Roxas and I had been dating online for two years now and had worked together for almost three. The arrangement complemented us. We each had our own real world lives, no complications, no commitments – but online we were quite the item. I looked forward to the day Roxas and I might meet in person, but for now, I enjoyed our cyber life. I could keep my heart out of trouble.

Dakota, my little sister, lived with me while she completed her graduate courses for recording engineering in game design. Only one semester left and she would be done. Dakota was the type of girl who went through guys like Kleenex, gamed hard with my team, and never said no to a great time with anyone.

Sheridan, our older sister, lived in Clearwater. Our father had moved in with her soon after our mom passed away. She could still out-game any of us, but nowadays she was much more into running the business side of the company. Together, we loved our work, our family and friends, our fans, and our capitalistic venture based on an old horror obsession.

Even though we were all born in Kerry, Ireland - we moved to Florida when when Sheridan was fourteen, I was twelve, and Dakota was ten. It was odd how each of us talked after moving to the United States. Dakota had acclimated her speech to the Americas more than Sheridan and I had. Sheridan kept most her Irish influence and accent since our father and mother always spoke Gaelic in the house and to us. After mom passed away, eight years ago, daddy moved in with Sheridan and her accent grew heavier being around him all the time.

Working online seemed to be a good arrangement for everyone. If we'd had to commute to a regular office and work side-by-side each day, it would be a fair assumption we would end up clobbering one another. Online we killed everyone in the game each day, and no one thought twice about it. Plus, virtual commuting gave us an extra two hours a day productivity time and nobody gave a rat's ass if I wore a scrunchie in my hair, poured Bailey's in my coffee, or worked in my pajamas.

Chapter Three

"Okay, gents, it's half day Friday. Let's get back to today's tasks." I clapped my hands together to get everyone on the same page. "Before we get underway with the prelims on the next boot sequence, I wanted to cover a quick review of where the gamers have been concentrating in the sims this past month. I've seen a huge uptake in activity across all the simulator boards. What about you guys? Are you seeing anything out of the norm?"

"That's for damn sure," Briggs said. "I'm stunned as hell to see what's happening in the New Orleans sim. Seems like the dragon mafia is seriously putting the screws to the other supernaturals in the city. The ghoulies have gone on strike and dead bodies are being stolen out of the morgues. The freakin' deaders are taking over the place. It's chaos, man. Chaos."

"That's odd. We, too, have seen a huge dead uprising out here in the West coastal regions." Harris pulled a coke out of the virtual vending machine in our sim office. The animated script for his avatar opened the can and shotgunned the cola. "The craziest things are the zombies. We've got hordes of deaders. They're attracting zombie hunters from all over the world. Seems like no one is safe from the damn deaders. They eat anything with *BRAIIINS*. I've got sections of downtown LA where a human can't walk across the sim without an annihilation of some sort."

Lady Caz walked over to the sofa in the sim office where a couple of male and female pose ball scripts were embedded in the couch. She sat on the female pose ball and tapped the cushion beside her inviting Roxas to come and sit. "What about you Rox, are you seeing the dead rise across the European sims?"

"Nothing more than usual, but we do have something weird happening with the werewolves and vamps. The packs are still in their ancient war with the vampires, but there's something new. A sect of evil werewolves are trafficking humans to the vamps for their specialty blood orchards."

"Blood orchards?" My eyebrows shot up. "What the feck is a blood orchard?"

Roxas sat beside Lady Caz on the male pose script built into the the virtual office couch, where I watched in my monitor. His animator override HUD – heads up display – crossed his right leg over his left knee as his arm draped across the back of the couch behind Lady Caz playing with her hair. "I guess in some vampire mythologies, they have it set up where human donors can voluntarily eat the same kind of food or drink for three days and it changes the flavor of the blood. So they have blood orchards for specific bloodwines."

"What makes you think it's always voluntary, Rox? Didn't you say that the werewolves were trafficking the humans for the blood orchards? Do you mean like kidnapping avatars and stacking them up for their blood?"

"Yeah – something along those lines. They must have a permission script they agree to before the kidnapping."

"Sounds creepy as hell to me, though." Harris said, "I'll never get why some third party developers design the things they do for their guilds inside the game."

"Weird. Okay, moving on – within the past twelve months, we've seen an almost eight hundred percent increase in usage across all memberships. Heck, Sheridan decided to drop the thirty day free trial a few weeks ago. People are not only signing up right and left, but they're staying, engaging, and purchasing shares of our ichor virtual currency. We make a ton of money off the virtual ichor currency exchange rate when players purchase products for their avatars."

Lady Caz sat back against the couch and reached for Roxas' hand. "Originally, when we created this game, it was based only on vampires and werewolves. But now, the way it has been embraced by people all over the world, folks are signing up with every conceivable and non-conceivable type creature to live out their fantasies in the game."

I remember when you storyboarded the original simulator," Harris said. "It's amazing how it's morphed into an 'anything goes' type of online environment now."

"When people purchase their simulators, we don't have any need to know what they build or do with their guilds unless someone reports them." I took another sip of coffee. "So we allow users to create whatever environment they want and to be whatever they want – it's all profit for us. Usually a person's membership is only active around six months." I leaned down to scratch Beano between the ears as he stretched out his long fawn legs, pushing against the inside of his doggie bed. "At that time, they'll sign on for an annual membership, or drop off. Sheridan and I expected to see a sharp decline over ninety days ago with the heavy influx of new monthly memberships, but it kept rising. Let's just say I'm glad we're still a privately held company. It helps out in our own profit sharing program at bonus time."

Roxas laughed. "Always nice to have a healthy paycheck." His avatar scooted out to the edge of the couch and put his elbow on his knee. "Inside the vampire sim for Europe, it's basically the same old, same old with the pure blood vampires fighting the rogue vampires. The queen is under the impression the Earth is going to implode or something, and there won't be enough humans for the vamps to snack on. Seems like she has been prepping a lot and building a huge dhampir army under her."

"What the heck is a dhampir?"

"Again, in some vampire mythos. A dhampir is the child born between a human and vampire. They are born with instincts to kill the vampires."

"Wow – that's ... interesting." I knitted my eyebrows together. "It floors me to hear about all the virtual worlds people build in their alternate simulated lives. I never would've dreamed about vampire queens, dhampir armies, and blood orchards."

"That's because you're too busy building cybrators for the web."

"Whatever, Harris. The development of my Cybrator paid off my student loans. It was well worth the dev time. Plus the manufacturers want another version. I'm planning to call it the iBrate."

Laughter spewed forth over the headsets.

"Let me tell you what I've been seeing on the more domestic side of the simulators." I walked over to pour a glass of water from the pitcher beside the coffee pot and grab cereal bar from under the cabinet. Then I returned to the computer command center. "I never would've believed it, but the number of people purchasing virtual farms and growing their own food has been huge. I mean, we've sold more virtual third-party commodities with people growing their own food than any weapons yield. We're seeing little outcroppings of communities where folks are growing veggies in vertical gardens, setting up organic hydroponic farms, selling organic raw milk, and even bartering for supplies from other growers."

"Seen anyone creating anything with GMOs?" Harris asked as he played with the bowl of fruit on the teleconference table.

"I don't think the big name food geneticists are going to need our gaming platform to Frankenstein our food. They have real labs to do that."

"Yeah, I heard that their own employees won't eat the food from their own plants," Roxas said. "It's been banned in Europe quite a bit."

Briggs leaned back in his chair, put his black boots on the table, and crossed them at his ankles. "Caz, people are paying us real hard currency money to farm and garden in the virtual sims?"

"Yeah, pretty wild huh? It's not just gardens either. We've got a ton of grass-fed beef cattle ranches, people raising horses, fish hatcheries, all kinds of sustainable living. I even found a guy who made a little farm with those goats that get scared stiff and fall over if you holler at them."

"That's nuts." Briggs' animated override HUD script outstretched his avatar's arms and placed them behind his head as he leaned back in his chair.

"Right? I even saw this one lady making soaps and had a lot of beehives on her simulated property. I suppose they can't do it in their cramped Manhattan apartments, so they come online and live out their dreams," I said.

"That's totally wild," Harris said.

Roxas added another observation. "Oh yeah, almost forgot. There's a new hot spot of interest down in the South American sim. Been seeing a ton of new development. It's become a huge rage called The Super Market."

I polished off the last bite of cereal bar, crunched the wrapper, and threw it in the recycle bin next to the door. "What exactly is The Super Market?"

Briggs and Harris cleared their throats. Beginning to get the feeling I was being set up for something, I braced myself.

"Well, it's this uniquely cool place. My friend Torchy built it."

"You mean Torchy, your dragon companion in the game?" I asked.

"That's right."

"The one who makes the cute little smoke rings around your head?"

"Yeppers – the one and only."

I nodded in a gesture the guys weren't able to see. "That guy's real? I thought that was something silly you made up."

"Nope – he's very real and he's got the gift of design. The Super Market is a hub where all the supernatural and preternatural beings can use their ichor virtual money and purchase anything they need for their avatars."

Roxas' avatar picked at a piece of lint off his jeans.

"It's similar to the online marketplace where humans can buy clothes, hair, and skins for their avatars. But this place is a bit more custom tailored to their *'special needs'* clients. Products specifically made for supernatural avatars."

We all laughed. "I'll have to go and check it out – it sounds like a lot of fun."

"It sounds like a hoot, Caz," Harris said.

"I personally never would have thought about making specialty products for supes. I guess there's a market for everything." I stood up and stretched my legs. "We have the coolest third party developers who play in our game. One thing that's nice is the commission we make off all sales from their virtual products they build and sell. It's almost free money to the company, since they use our platform to develop and distribute these products."

"Indeed. You wouldn't believe the amount of money made off werewolf conditioner and vampire fang whitener alone," Roxas said.

I laughed. "We are – still talking about virtual products, right?"

Chapter Four

I heard the front door snick open and the click, click, click of Dakota's high heels across the travertine tile. Dakota popped her head into the office. "Hey, Chey. I wasn't sure if you'd still be here."

Dressed to the teeth, even on test mornings, Dakota was the type of girl who didn't go to the mailbox unless fully coiffed. Secretly coveting her leather high-heeled boots, I swore the first opportunity I had I was going to steal them.

She draped a full length garment bag onto the coat rack. After dumping the rest of her packages onto the floor, Dakota turned around to face me with a wicked grin.

Unless I was sure to win, I should've never placed that bet with her. To this day, I still think she had it rigged for me to lose just so she could pick out my Halloween costume this year. Her deviant smile revealed this had *bad idea* written all over it.

I raised a curious eyebrow. "Pray tell, Dakota. What have you done?"

I'd forgotten my microphone was still live to the team teleconference.

Briggs cooed in a sexy whisper, "Hey, Kota, baby."

Any minute now, the speakers in my office were going to ooze sounds of sexual healing from Marvin Gaye. When Briggs was in seduction mode, his voice flowed over you like liquid chocolate silk. Made you want to wrap yourself up in his voice and never unravel.

"Hey, Briggsy, baby. What's the craic?"

"Why don't you fly up to New Orleans tonight and I'll show you?" Briggs purred an invitation.

I imagined, through his voice alone, the confidence he must exude to the ladies around him every day. Often made me wonder how Briggs used his charismatic charms to get what and who he wanted.

"Would love to, Briggsy. Lord knows I sure could use the downtime, but I have a date with big sister this afternoon. She's officially taking the rest of the day off." Dakota giggled.

I looked at her with *Oh no you don't* eyes.

Dakota winked at me as we heard something like a pencil snap over the speakers. "Sorry guys, gotta get Cheyenne ready for the uber-scary research project tonight and believe me, there's a lot to do to get her ready."

I glared at her sideways.

"Crashed and burned again, my friend. Crashed and burned," Harris teased Briggs over the head sets.

Someone launched a sound effect over the speakers of an incoming missile explosion. Leave it to the guys to razz one another. I laughed at their childish antics.

"Wow, Chey. Your office is amazing." Dakota was always good at redirecting a conversation. "I've been at the college way too much lately. Looks like the real world fun is in here. It's like freakin' NASA. What is all this stuff? Are those wall monitors? You turned your walls into a computer?"

"Yeah – they're translucent touch monitors. Check 'em out. *DON'T* delete anything. I'm actually testing them out for Corning Glass."

If a person hadn't been in my office in a while, they'd think it looked like some kind of freakish techno-laboratory superimposed on top of a preschool art class. I had retinal eye scanners, tablets, cork boards, dry erase boards, markers, paint smocks for story boards, wooden artist's models, stainless steel counter tops, and modeling clay for poses.

"Yes, well actually, if you inspect closer, these are glass panels with LED monitors inset into them. This way I can move different aspects from one plane to another and get a true 3D rendering out of them. It's a heckuva lot easier to envision the pose ball animations this way than trying to anticipate the avatar's natural body movement with Play Doh."

Viewing the contents of what I might be wearing to Halloween Scream Nights, I rummaged through the bags.

A long, slow whistle from Harris filled the air. "Sounds as if you might need to upgrade your server cabinet to support all that framework. I've got to come over and check it out."

"Actually, Harris, can you come up soon? I need your opinion on a few things. I'm thinking we might need to expand because I'm planning to turn the spare bedroom into a volume stage for the pose ball animations inside the game. I'm not sure we'll have enough server room. We might need more hardware to increase the firepower, for smoother rendering and handling of the camera angles."

"Gimme a sec – lemme check my calendar." Keys clicked on his keyboard clacking away over the headsets. He had to be the fastest typist I knew.

While Harris checked for a possible date and time for us to get together, Dakota sauntered back over to all the packages. "Here's your costume." Her giggle betrayed her as my eyes focused in on the little bag. She dangled it as if it were a pendulum in front of me.

I balked at her announcement. "Dakota, how is that possible? There can't be a costume inside that dinky pouch. You expect me to go out in public wearing nothing but what's in there?"

She nodded with a gleam in her eye. I knew that meant nothing but torment for me. I grabbed at the eensy weensy black bag, but she snatched her arm back just in time for me to miss and hid it behind her back.

"What is it? A roll of toilet paper for a mummy costume?"

"Close, very close!" Dakota danced around with anticipation. Her angelic face excited as Christmas mornings with Mom and Dad. She had such a way of bringing out the silly in all of us. Wolf whistles and hoots accompanied Dakota's excitement.

"Looks like I can come over on Tuesday afternoon. Does that work for you, Cheyenne? I have a pack meeting over the weekend, and we won't be back out of the woods until then. No cell reception, no nothing – totally off the grid."

"You and your scout troops. Those boys are so lucky to land a scoutmaster like you." I looked at my picture of Harris and his scout troop on the wall by the coat rack. He always looked happiest when the kids were around him. Made me wonder if he was ever planning to settle down and have children of his own someday. "What badges do you have planned this weekend? Geo-caching in the Everglades again?"

"Not this time. We're teaching the kids how to set up a basecamp of operations and Morse code. Ya know, just in case of emergencies."

"Oh how cool is that? I've always wanted to learn Morse code."

"You have the attention span of a lightning bolt." I looked at Dakota as if she had lost her mind. "What would possess you to think you'd ever have the discipline to learn another language, let alone a numeric one?"

She stuck her tongue out at me.

Harris mic'd in over the speakers. "Hey, Kota, come on and suit up with us. We're just getting ready to power up to fight against the Battle Kroc. Cheyenne keeps coding the sequence to turn us into Battle Kroc snack packs. It's been hell trying to figure out how to beat this monster."

"I would love to guys, but we *have* to get ready for tonight. I was serious about her taking off the rest of the day."

"Ah, c'mon, what's more important than us?" Harris whined.

Dakota chimed off her list. "All three of us have mani-pedis at one. Then we're off to the salon to transform my hair into The Mistress of The Night and get some cool highlights in Miss Thang's hair."

"Oh cool – Sheridan's gonna be there too?" An afternoon with my sisters would be nice at the salon.

Dakota nodded as she looked through the bags and took out her new pair of silver platform heels.

"Well, guys, she's right. It'll be great to have some girlie time. Not that you guys understand that kind of thing. Plus, I need to prepare the research for one of my scare zones in the next evolution of the game. It's based on people's phobias. I have most of the game design elements completed, but one of them is giving me trouble, so I need more tests to see how people will react to certain stimuli."

"What types of phobias are you considering?" Roxas asked. "I can help you do that. We can see how the 3d holographic rendering suits interact for scare sequences."

"Thanks, Rox. That would be great. So far, I've cataloged the typical fears most people have: ghosts, spiders, rabid dogs, snakes, antique dolls, graveyards, and creepy carnies. Ya know, the usual. I've also been toying with clowns, monsters, vampires, werewolves, ghouls, witches, and even cannibals."

Briggs piped in, "What about dragons?"

"What about them?" I shrugged. "I don't think people are afraid of mythical creatures anymore. That's like asking if we are including unicorns or leprechauns."

"Don't be fooled by the leprechauns, Chey Chey," he snorted. "Those afflicted with Leporiphobia cringe every St. Patrick's Day. Those Leprechauns will get you every time."

I laughed into the headset. "Gah, Briggs, that totally creeps me out when you say it like that. Okay, you've convinced me. I'll reconsider my thinking on mythical creatures."

"Woot – glad you're including werewolves," Harris barked out loud. "Those things creep me out. What about things like being buried alive, drowning, or being kidnapped?"

"Knock on wood." Dakota rapped three times on the wooden joists holding up the granite counter top. "I pray nothing like that ever happens to me or any of us. That shite would totally freak my shit."

"Maybe I should give you back your vampire repellent you gave me this morning, Dakota."

"Oh no, missy – that's for you. Did you guys know that Caz here has four different kinds of spray on her key chain? It's hilarious when we go out, she starts to look under the car at about twenty feet to see if there is anyone hidden under it to slash at her ankles."

Harris joined in the roast. "Oh yeah, there was this one time ..."

"Harris, don't. Don't tell that story."

"But I have to, Caz."

I moaned in defeat.

"Anyway, we were at a bar down in Bradenton, somewhere, a real dive. Anyway – she comes screaming out of the bathroom cause there was a huge-assed spider under the toilet seat. She sprayed it with one of her pepper sprays from her keychain and the damn thing practically attacked her. She really pissed it off good."

"Well, it was better than it biting my ass."

Laughter spewed over the headsets from everyone, including myself.

Harris said, "I never laughed so hard as to see her running out of the bathroom screaming because of a spider."

"I thought the damn thing was gonna fly or something. Those sprays have saved me from several crawlies that live here in Florida. Hell, you never know when an alligator is gonna come up and eat your dog while you're running along the canals. I'm not taking any chances."

"She's got a point about that, guys," Dakota said.

"Look, I learned a long time ago, I think it was after watching my tenth horror movie or something that I'm not ever gonna be the dumb bimbo who deserves a torturous death because she had to enter the screepy abandoned building to save the crying child."

They all laughed at me.

"Back to the topic. Enough about me and my eccentricities. Harris, I've sourced data which supports these types of real fears in humans. Many people are afraid of being buried alive, burning to death, being kidnapped, or something awful happening to a loved one. There are real horrors most people will never even begin to admit to themselves."

"Ah hell no, that shit ain't funny, man," Briggs said. "Ever since I read *IT* by that King dude, I can't even look at a clown. Gives me the fuckin' willies, man."

"I'm hearing that, Briggs," I said. "That's why I decided to face my own fear of Oldhouseophobia and tackle the dreaded haunted house tonight."

"What? That isn't a real phobia." Dakota laughed.

"I'm not sure what the technical term is for the fear of haunted houses, but it's enough to scare the hell out of me. So I'm going to challenge it. It's a billion dollar industry, so I want to see if I can virtually design one into the game."

"Which one are you going into tonight, Caz?" Harris asked.

"Most likely the insane asylum. It's the creepy little children that always get me. Since it's Halloween, it's the right time to do it. Technically, the people working the houses can't touch you, but still, they're pretty damn scary."

"How about you, Roxas? What are you afraid of?" Harris asked.

The room, speakers, and monitors silenced.

He responded quite simply, "Meeting Cheyenne."

Chapter Five

What did Roxas say? Did he say he was afraid to meet me? Maybe I'm not so whacked after all. Could he be going through the same stuff I am?

"Girl, all I can say is you've got more guts than me if you're going in that haunted house alone," Briggs said, breaking the tension. "I'll fight any online baddie any day of the week and kick its ass all over the screen. But to put my ass face-to-face in a freaky haunted house. Nuh uh – count me out. I've seen enough real voodoo around here to know it could be true."

A heavy sigh escaped my lips. "I'll be honest with you guys, I'm not crazy about doing this tonight. Most likely I'm consuming a few drinks this afternoon before I go. Hell, they say that most horror writers are whacked out on junk before they begin to write. Their inhibitions are lowered, and they can allow themselves to let the creep factor seep in and crawl out through their words."

"Don't worry, guys, she'll be with me." Dakota lightened the mood with her irresistible laugh. "I'll protect her from any baddies in the park. Besides, we're going to be inside a public place with security everywhere. What could go wrong?"

"Guess you're right," Briggs agreed. "So what are your costumes? Give me a visual, dahlin'. I want to think about you all night long."

"You're shameless, ya know that?" It seemed as though Dakota loved the attention. "But if you must know, I'm going dressed as Elvira, Mistress of the Night."

Wolf whistles blasted out in the 3D stereo, causing us both to blush.

"*AND* for Miss Lady Cazenove, over here, I've got her suited up in an unusual costume."

Why in the world did I ever make that bet with her in the first place?

"Ya'll better be careful, sounds like the two of you are serious bait for the right fish tonight." Briggs sent out waves of undertone in his voice.

"I'm not worried. Dakota could beat up anyone with her stilettos. I feel sorry for anyone who tries to haul her ass off. Besides, like you said, what could possibly go wrong in a public amusement park?"

"Well, don't be counting on my spikes, big sis. You're gonna have your own set of streetwalkers."

I gawked at her. Laughter from the three stooges poured out of the speakers.

"You have Cheyenne wearing stilettos?" Harris guffawed. "Miss Queen of the running shoe?"

"It may be once a year, Harris, but Miss *Thang* over here cleans up pretty damn good," Dakota defended.

"Hey, I have an idea, H. Why don't you dress up and help me with the research tonight? I've got an extra cola can worth twenty bucks off the ticket admission. It'll take you a couple hours to get here if you leave Tampa before rush hour."

"Negatory on that one, Chey," Harris replied. "You aren't gonna find my happy ass in any haunted house either. I don't care if it's in the name of research or not. I think I'll pass. What about Roxas? He doesn't live too far out of town. Kissimmee, right? You two could meet and get this virtual love affair crossed over into the real world, ya know?"

My eyes bugged out of my head as the temperature in the room skyrocketed into the nineties. Or maybe it was just me.

Briggs acknowledged the bold suggestion with a, "Oooh. No he didn't!"

Dakota's face flushed beet red. It mimicked my anxiety. Mine must have been pure crimson from the sweat pouring off me and down my breasts. I wiped my hands up the back of my neck to remove the perspiration beading out of my hair. No towels around, I wiped it onto my jeans.

Dakota reached out for my hand, but it was too late. The words were out, and no one could deny they had been spoken.

I wanted to change the subject. I wanted to crawl under the counter and hide. I wanted to write QUEST FAILED on the screen and sign off the conference call, but I couldn't do any of those things. We had to wait for Roxas to respond to the question.

The next time I see Harris, I'm gonna go all 1972 Hitchcock Frenzy Necktie Killer on his ass.

"You don't have anything else to do tonight, do ya, Rox?" Harris pushed the paused silence further.

I closed my eyes and dropped my head between my knees. I couldn't believe Harris was doing this to me. Not wanting to put Roxas on the spot, I hedged. "That's okay. I'm gonna be real busy with Sheridan." Afraid he would say no or worse, say *yes*. I sensed my breakfast on the verge of reverse engines.

Dakota handed me a paper bag and mimed breathing into it. I pushed it away.

"I've got lots of research to do on my phobias. No worries." My voice shook with a stuttering of stops and goes. "Y-you know me, all work and no p-play."

"Yeah, makes you an 'ole dried-up hag."

"Shut the hell up, Harris," Dakota snapped.

She might be my bratty little sister, but damned if anyone ever picked on the three of us. They'd never get away with it. The O'Cuinn sisters fought to the death to protect one another. I felt sorry for the saps who would marry us one day.

Beano stood up from his bed and nudged my sweaty palm. I tried to breathe in the confidence Lady Cazenove always exuded. How would she handle this moment? The tension over the headsets seemed as thick as the humidity outside.

Why doesn't he answer the freakin' question?

"Bloody hell ... sorry about that, Cheyenne," Roxas said.

My heart fell into my stomach. Now I knew I was going to get sick.

"My microphone was on mute, and I couldn't get the damn thing to unstick. I've been talking all this time, but you guys couldn't hear me."

I swallowed.

"Okay. Perhaps we could meet at the park. Around ten, maybe?" he asked.

I sat stone cold, unable to move or react to his words.

Dakota picked up my water bottle and urged me to drink. I thought she always looked funny when she bobbed her head and bugged her eyes at me to respond to people when I was at a loss for words. Was it me, or was every person on the conference call line waiting, biting their fingernails, to hear my answer? It was my turn for silence over the headsets, but I didn't have an excuse.

Taking a drink of the water, I swallowed. Then choked out my words, "Sure. Okay, ten then. How 'bout we meet at the ..."

"Do you know where the Canadian Mountie water ride is?"

"Ah huh." Numb, I nodded in time with my answer – brain dead and redundant all at the same time.

"Aces. I'll meet you under the waterfalls. I'll be the one in the vampire costume. Might even bring my katana with me."

Cheers, whoops, hollers, and attaboys flew around us in surround sound.

A single tear trickled down my cheek when the finality of what I had agreed to do set in. I took a deep intake of air, not knowing how long I'd held my breath, and blew it out with puffed cheeks. I decided to sit on the floor and hug Beano, rocking us both back and forth for comfort.

Did I just agree to meet Roxas? At Halloween Scream Night? In stilettos?

"Well, dudes, on that note, I must whisk Caz away for the night." Dakota, with her impeccably timed charm, called in the dogs. "We need to get dressed in our costumes and get Cinderella here ready for the ball."

Harris foleyed kissy noises into his microphone. Briggs didn't help matters much when he started to gangsta rap the old nursery rhyme about kissing in a tree and baby carriages.

"Padme, close conference line."

The call terminated with Briggs at mid-sentence before he used the words marriage, Roxas, and Cheyenne in the same sentence.

I wished I had the same guts of my online avatar. Lady Caz wouldn't have any problems meeting Roxas, but in reality, I was just plain ole

Cheyenne O'Cuinn. Just another computer programming geek who loved to play games and sucked at relationships.

Harris is soooo dead.

Chapter Six

"Hey, Chey. That was rude. Why did you hang up on them?"

"Because I didn't want them to hear over the mic how I am going to kill you, Harris, and Briggs for what you did to me!"

I threw off my headset and chased her through the hallway. Dakota screamed like we did when we were little girls as we ran through the rooms squealing.

We ran around the whole house, dodging corners, and skating on hallway carpets. Enjoying the animated energy in the house, Beano barked like a crazy dog.

"Oh. My. God," we chanted.

Our laughter vibrant and contagious. My body surged with endorphins – it felt fabulous to run, laugh, and jump. My body felt more alive in the past couple minutes than it had in years. My heart ecstatic, I was going to meet Roxas.

"Oh, Chey, can you believe it? He's going to meet you ... *TONIGHT!*" She flopped on the couch. "We'll have to go all out on your makeover. You haven't had the works since ..." She looked at me and winced. "Oh hell, Cheyenne, when have you ever had the works? We gotta to go."

"Go where?"

"Girlfriend, you have a date with my magician beautician, Armand."

I didn't care if she submerged me in mud or what she dressed me up in. At this moment, this very instant, my heart sang with joy and I couldn't wait to meet this man. I felt like Eliza Doolittle in *My Fair Lady*.

A makeover? I was about to be poked, prodded, colored, curled, waxed, clipped and plucked – but pluckophobia be damned tonight. Finally, I was meeting Roxas, and truthfully, I probably needed the makeover.

***

Back from Armand's beauty makeover, I stared back at the reflection of my new haircut, highlights and manicure in my bedroom mirror. I hoped the red puffiness of my eyebrows would go away soon.

"Hey, Chey, what if you already are acquainted with him, ya know like on *You've Got Mail* with Tom Hanks and

Meg Ryan," Dakota mused.

"I never thought about it, truthfully. There isn't anyone else I know with an English accent. Why?"

"Well, Rox doesn't live that far away from here. I know he travels a lot, but didn't you mail that 3D holographic rendering suit to his house in Kissimmee a couple weeks ago? So, for all you know he's the guy at the coffee shop you go to every morning. Or he's the guy who runs the animatronics at Disney's Country Bear Jamboree. Or ... or ..." Her hamster wheel turned faster than her brain computed words. "Or he even could be that guy who makes the 3D chalk drawings at Downtown Disney."

"Or maybe he's that creepy guy who pushes the shopping cart and talks to the swan boats at Lake Lola," I added.

"Right? The crazy guy who yells at you to stop drowning the swans?"

We both laughed until our sides ached. I hadn't laughed this hard in ages.

Note to self – Take more half days off with sisters.

Dakota decided it was time to reveal my costume. She dangled the small bag in front of me again.

"What am I going to wear, a gift card or something?" I moaned at her, truly hoping it was a gift certificate to the costume shop.

Prancing around after her second cider for the afternoon, she said, "See, you're already in character."

"Huh? What are you talking about? Did you get me a costume for a hooker?"

Laughing out loud, Dakota said, "Sweetie, you couldn't be a whore even if you tried!"

I wasn't sure if that was a compliment or not. Dakota unveiled a skimpy, gauzy mummy costume.

"What the hell is that? And where does my body fit into it?" My eyes and hands examined the *thin*, flimsy fabric. Baffled, I looked at her as if she had killed one to many brain cells from her recreational drugs.

"I don't understand. Is this a joke?" I gawked and stammered. "Is this just the accessory? Where's the costume?"

"This *is* the costume, Chey. Look, it's a bodysuit. You can move the gauze straps to cover the areas you want, but it still looks like you're wearing hardly anything at all. Isn't it bad ass? This is exactly what Lady Caz would wear to meet Roxas."

"Unholy hell, Dakota, I wished I was Lady Caz right now. Then I might have the guts to wear this thing."

As I tried on the mummy scraps I complained, "Are you sure you didn't get this from the girls' department as a joke?"

"No silly, it's Lycra. It'll mold to your body. What I haven't showed you is the skirt that goes with it."

I breathed out a sigh of relief.

Oh thank the Goddess ... there's a skirt.

She pulled out the bag with the shoes and surfaced with another small bag. The skirt looked just as miniscule as the body suit.

I looked at her with a *what the hell?* expression, but she just beamed at me, so proud of what she'd accomplished. That's when I knew something was up. "All told, did you and Harris have this arrangement set up?"

She shook her head in a theatrical gesture and brought her hands to her chest in mock surprise. "Not us, we would never do something as devious, deceptive, and perfectly wonderful for the two of you, now would we?"

"Seriously?" I threw the eensy bits of fabric at her and it fell down onto the bed. "Was Briggs in on this plot too? Sheridan? How long have you planned this?"

Beano sauntered over to the scraps of fabric, sniffed, and grabbed them up in his teeth.

"Hey, gimme that." I rescued the mummy costume from the wrath of Boxer. I held the scraps of cloth over my body. "Where are the panties for this thing?" I prayed for boy shorts.

"Oh yeah. Here ya go." She flung something at me that looked like dental floss with a miniature flag. No such luck on the boy shorts. Dakota put out a hand, blocking my retort. "Just do it will ya – you want to make a good impression on Roxas or not?"

"A good impression yeah, but slut wasn't quite the effect I was going after." I stretched the cream-colored panties over my hips and snugged the floss into place. "I'm not too keen on the crawling cord up my heinie, rubbing me raw all night."

"All the more reason to lose them early." She winked at me.

I pulled up the mini skirt while she helped me tack on the gauzy bandages in various places to give the appearance of being wrapped.

"I have to admit, Dakota, this costume is quite cute."

"I liked the way it displayed on the mannequin at the costume shop. As soon as I saw it, I knew it had to be yours."

Dakota's cell phone rang and she grabbed it out of her bra. She'd programmed the "eee-eee-eee" from the *Psycho* shower scene as her ring tone. I looked at her sideways.

"What? Can you think of a better place not to lose it?"

I shook my head as she left the room. I already knew the contents of her underwear drawer. I did not need to learn anything more about the contents of her bra.

Dakota had returned from the kitchen with more bottles of hard cider when Sheridan arrived.

"Sheridan O'Cuinn is at the front door," Padme announced.

"Padme, let her in please."

Padme opened the door and closed it behind Sheridan. We heard Sheridan singsong as she made her way down the hall towards my room.

"Ding dong. Sorry I'm late. The license plates have changed color, so fall has arrived and you know what that means. All the damn snowbirds are here, and now it takes five times as long to get anywhere."

Beano barked as Sheridan's little Pomsky barked back at him. Stormaggedon was dressed in her ballerina outfit. When Sheridan let her out of her bag, and out onto the floor, Stormy looked awfully cute in her tutu.

"Oh, I *LOVE* it. How wicked is that?" Dakota shrilled out a greeting. "OMG, Sher – she is so adorable. Chey, why don't you have a costume for Beano?"

I just looked at her and took another swig.

Beano and Stormy greeted one another in true doggie style. Sniffs for all my friends, and immediately Stormy decided Beano was her jungle gym, and off they went to play.

"C'mon, Sher, we're just getting ready. Let me get you a drink."

When I returned to the bedroom, Sheridan was asking Dakota, "How are you going to be Elvira with no boobs?"

Dakota put down her cider. She pulled out the full-length black gown from its garment bag and revealed a neckline cut to the waist complete with fake, plastic breasts and cleavage. "I wish my real boobs could pull it off in that dress."

We all stood looking at the costume held in front of her. The fake boobies distorted Dakota's figure so much, it seemed as if we were looking into a fun house mirror. She handed me the dress and proceeded to perform a lift and squish to her A cups to try to emulate the fake breasts.

Mashing her fists up under her ribs to create the impression of heaving bosoms, she sighed. "Why can't I have boobs like yours and Sheridan's? Why did I get the short end of the titty stick?"

"Isn't that what Victoria's Secret is? To produce boobs where none have existed before? I think you have pockets sewn into your bras just to hold everything in there to make them look bigger." I teased her and put the dress on the bed and handed Dakota's cider back to her.

"How did you know?" Dakota punted back at me.

Laughing, we stood gawking at each other in front of the mirror. It was a moment where I wished my eyes could take a photograph because a camera would have ruined the moment. It was rare that all three of us got together much anymore. We really needed to spend more sister time with each other.

Sheridan said, "Hey, remember when we used to play dress up in Mom's clothes, turn on her old Elton John records, and dance to *Crocodile Rock*?"

Almost if on cue, we put down our drinks, wrapped our arms across the tops of our shoulders, and walked the monkey walk in our high heels until we fell down and laughed ourselves silly on the bed.

It felt good to laugh again. It had been too long ... for all of us. This was truly a rare moment for us since Mom had died.

"What is your costume, Sheridan?" Dakota jumped up on her knees. "How are you possibly going to outdo yourself from last year?"

"Uh, uh uhn." Sheridan waggled a finger in front of us. "You're not getting my surprise out of me. You'll see tonight once you get into the park. You won't believe your eyes."

I sat there looking at them both, gaining more and more awareness that I was going to meet Roxas soon.

Dakota touched my shoulder. "So are you nervous about tonight, Chey?"

"I think I've puked up everything I've eaten today, I'm so riddled with nerves."

"There's nothing to worry about. You guys have seen pictures of each other. He's a hottie, so there's nothing to worry about."

"Yeah, I know. But he's fallen in love with Lady Caz."

"Uh huh." Dakota, looked at me sideways.

"I'm just nervous he won't have the same affection after meeting the *real* me."

"Seriously? Are you listening to yourself? One – you're the spitting image of your avatar, and B – you don't think he'll adore you?"

I could tell Dakota had already been shooting the Irish whiskey between ciders since her outlining skills were already confused.

"Look, I'll level with you. I suck at relationships. I'm not sure I'm ready for this. I'm the type of woman who gets all sloppy when I let a guy into my life."

Sheridan sat up on the bed. "I remember that last guy you were all up into. What was his name again?"

"That's not important. But you understand. Remember, I stopped working out. All my spare time went into him instead of into myself. My programming time decreased. It just wasn't healthy."

Dakota said, "Yeah, but you gotta admit, all workie and no nookie can't be healthy either, Chey."

"Don't get me wrong. Lord knows, I sure could use a decent shag. There's only so much fantasizing a girl can do alone, but how can I ever tell Roxas how he makes me truly feel?"

"What if he doesn't feel the same way about me?"

Sheridan grabbed my hand. I looked at her with a half smile.

"I don't think I can handle that kind of rejection from him after all this time together online."

Dakota clinked her bottle against Sheridan's. "Look at it this way. If the relationship doesn't work out, you get the satisfaction of firing his ass."

I rolled my eyes at her.

Sheridan flopped back on to the bed. "I completely get what you're saying, Chey. Ever since we started this company, I haven't had a decent date."

Dakota and I both looked at her.

"Well, think about it. Daddy lives with me, and it seems like every guy I know has a full-blown dossier already filled out on me. They're more interested in how much money the company makes than just being with and caring for me."

I reached out to her. "I'm sorry, Sheridan. I didn't know it'd been that hard for you."

"So I totally get that you guard your heart, Chey. 'Cause it feels like I'll never find that one guy who doesn't need my money, has a cool life of his own, and only wants to take care of me and not my bottom line."

Dakota and I looked at each other and grimaced. Here I was moaning about meeting the love of my life, and she has had no life at all.

Sheridan clapped her hands. "Okay, chicas. Thanks for the gal time. I gotta run. Speaking of getting lucky, that Tech One supervisor at Global Studios is oh so fine, and I don't want to be late." She winked at us. "Ya never know."

"Go get 'em Sheridan," I cheered for her. "Maybe we'll all get lucky tonight!"

Dakota put her arm around Sheridan, and we all clinked our bottles together in one last toast. "Here's to true happiness, and may tonight be the luckiest night of our lives."

Luckiest night of our lives, huh? Then why do I have a sick feeling deep in the depths of my stomach?

Sheridan picked up Stormy and gave her explicit instructions how a lady should act around male puppy dogs. She put Stormy down and Stormy curled up inside the doggie bed.

"They'll be fine. If either of them is doing the humping, it's her. Stormy always shows her dominance over him."

Dakota spewed her cider.

"Okay, I'll see you guys at eight in front of Margaritaville."

"How will we know it's you?" I asked her.

"Don't worry, I'll be around."

In unison, both Dakota and I sang the *dun, dun, dunnnnnn* music sound effect.

"Laters." Sheridan waved goodbye as my front door closed.

***

"So ... Dakota ... when is the last time you went into a haunted house alone? Do you know if Sheridan has done it?"

"Alone? Never," she snorted. "Are you out of your feckin' mind? Those things are scary enough with a group of people and knowing the park employees can't touch you. But damn, are you really planning to do this alone?" Her eyes bugged out of her head, alarmed at the idea.

"Yeah, I decided last year I was going to do this and prove to myself I could. How else am I supposed to understand how fear feels if I don't test it out on myself? Need to immerse the senses kinda thing."

Beano and Stormy ran into the bedroom and into my closet. Seconds later, they each had a bedroom slipper and ran out of the room. Stormy had a little more trouble with her slipper, but she was bound and determined. "Hey, what the ... ?" Dakota and I both stood there looking at each other and laughed our heads off.

I looked at the sun setting further into the west. Time was moving faster than I wanted. "Thank the weather gods, it'll only be down to seventy-five degrees tonight or else I would've frozen in this outfit." I looked over at Dakota's dress. "Aren't you going to roast in that gown?"

"Nah, I'm going Polynesian – so I'll be plenty cool."

I cocked an eyebrow at her. My eyes begged for further explanation.

"Ya know, commando, bare-assed naked."

"Seriously? Are you planning on finding a quiet, dark, abandoned hallway or room somewhere, Miss Dakota?"

"Yes, ma'am." Her seductress grin exuded pure sarcastic wickedness. "Not only that, but there's this guy who is going to be a zombie groom in the undead parade. He and I are going to try and hook up later."

"Wait. What about that Ludovic guy? Aren't you meeting him tonight or something?"

"Yeah, sure. He's a great guy. I like him ... a lot, actually. Maybe that's why I need to back away from him. When it gets to the point where I think I'm really falling for a guy, I have to back out. I can't get attached, cause I know I'll fall hard. So, most likely I'm gonna need to cut bait with him soon. It's just that damn cool Romanian accent of his, ya know? Kinda drives me nutty when he says my name."

"Oh, yes. I so understand that. I love the way Roxas sounds when he's all into me."

Dakota smiled and clinked our bottles together again. "I'm pretty sure Ludovic is bringing his brother tonight though. When his bro tags along – they're kinda weird, so I was hoping to ditch them in the middle of the night. I just want to enjoy a solid shag in some dark alley with no strings attached."

"I'll never be able to keep up with you and your fellas."

"Hey c'mon, let's get going."

Dakota interrupted my morbid imaginations of a guy chasing us around wearing a mask and wielding a hockey stick.

"You've got everything already in the truck, right?"

I nodded.

"So let's get rid of that green *I'm gonna puke look* about you, and into this cool costume makeup."

"Okay, I'm getting nervous. You gotta promise me you won't let me chicken out on meeting Roxas."

We crossed our hearts, set into a series of dizzy handshake gestures, hip bumps and ended with a pinkie swear. It seemed like we added something new every year to the secret sister code and always laughed when we got it wrong. Tonight, however, we were on fire, and we got everything right. We were hot, we were young, and we were ready to live – even if I did have to wear butt floss.

Chapter Seven

Halloween Scream Night

City Streets

Dakota and I arrived at City Streets, got our Halloween Scream Night tickets, and heard a wolf man howling invitations to seek out the abominations behind the walls. We looked at one another and grinned with anticipation of wicked enchantments.

A snapshot moment in my life, the evening seemed destined for one of those nights to remember. Dakota seemed eager to get laid, and to meet up with one of her boy toys from the bar where she worked part-time. Me, I knew my life was changing drastically after tonight. It was as if a pivotal moment in our lives unfolded in a churning tempest of time. A portal, a window of opportunity to examine and explore the other side of life. If I didn't take this chance, would regret haunt me the rest of my life?

Standing at the crossroads of going to meet the man of my dreams, the silver lining to my storm cloud, I should've been prepared … but I wasn't. Instead, I couldn't shake the dread building up inside me. I knew it was stupid to feel this way, but I studied fear, and losing Roxas was one of my worst fears. Sometimes these kinds of relationships don't work out in the real world; could my dreams crumble to ash before me? Roxas and I had such an unbelievable relationship online. What happened if there wasn't any sizzle or chemistry between us? Everything could be lost within an instant.

I tried to shrug off the weird ass undertow trying to ruin my night, and chalked it up to cold feet.

Dakota waved at her friends. We stood waiting for them by the kiosk that sells the candied cinnamon almonds, by the stone tower. We walked back towards the Magaritaville restaurant to meet up with Sheridan. It seemed like an opportune time to get a head start on the night's tequila consumption.

Dakota grabbed her peach margarita from the walk-up window cashier after I got mine frozen with a shot of Chambord. We sat down by the copper-patina wall fountain and waited for Sheridan to arrive.

Slurping a sip large enough for a brain freeze, Dakota winced at the icy shock to her frontal lobe. Recovering, she patted the empty space beside her for Ludovic to join her. Dakota's date, Ludovic Zyryanov, came dressed as the Scream guy, not incredibly original in my opinion. His brother Edric, however, had put thought into his costume. He dressed up as Sherlock Holmes complete with the pipe. I was somewhat impressed.

Snogging her good, Ludovic grabbed Dakota around the waist and pulled her in close. Edric looked as uncomfortable as I felt. My eyes searched for a water hose to turn on them. He politely glanced away from his brother and sipped on his drink as well.

After my sister wiped her mouth with the back of her hand, I grabbed her arm, and whispered in her ear. "Hello, are you like gonna get a room with this guy or something?"

She faked laughter. I shook my head at her. I just hoped she didn't do that to Briggs one day.

Edric studied City Streets as if he had never seen anything like it before. His eyes caught mine, and I smiled. "This your first time here?" Bright strobe lights reflected off his face as he nodded. It was cute to watch him be mesmerized by the energy of the night. I remembered my first Halloween event here. Edric's excitement reminded me of how much fun this event truly was to those who didn't know what scares lurked behind the walls.

Global Studios had a nightlife area separate from the amusement parks called City Streets, complete with restaurants, dance stages, designer shopping, and movie theaters. Sheridan, Dakota and I went clubbing, at the parks, quite a bit before I started my master's degree in game design. When school started, that was the end of clubbing to concentrate on my education.

Three bands rocked the stages throughout the City Streets that night and their music echoed off the lake across from the Hard Rock Hotel. Neon strobes cascaded over every surface. Spooky beacons, LED stage lights, special effects laser bursts, fog machines, you name it. Nothing was held back, and the result was simply intoxicating, or that might have been the tequila in my drink having an effect on me.

Every conceivable costume and disturbing combination of frightful ghoulie was out masquerading in the parks. This was the place to be. Some people were dressed in jeans with bloody t-shirts that said, 'I'm Okay' and other party-goers went full-out Hollywood gala style.

"What are you looking for, Cheyenne?"

I turned back and grinned at Dakota. "Oh you know – a tall, handsome guy with coppery hair, a vampire cape, fangs, and a katana." I winked at her and laid down my drink between us.

Situating my hienie on the rock ledge, I tried to scoot closer to the bush beside me in order to provide some discreet cover. I needed to readjust the butt floss, and I didn't want anyone to see what I was doing. The bush beside me growled and attacked me, pushing me forward onto the ground.

The next thing I knew, I was on my back scrambling the crab walk from my Jr. High P.E. class. My costume snagged onto a branch from the bush. In my haste to get away from the man-eating vegetation, I barely noticed when the branches tore several strands of mummy wrappings off me. Sprawled on the ground, in my high heels and Lycra, I sat stunned and completely exposed for the entire world to see. I must've looked like a roll of toilet paper left unraveled all over the bathroom floor, exposing the inner core of the tube. Mortified at thinking Roxas could be watching at this very moment, I hustled to get myself righted.

Dakota, Ludovic, and Edric howled with laughter. I thought for a moment Dakota might pass out since she snorted margarita out her nose, and it seemed to take her breath away. I looked back towards the fountain and saw the bush had already settled itself back into place, patiently waiting for its next victim. I so fell for the man-eating bush gag, and I never even saw the attack coming.

"GAH – bugger off!" I yelled to them. I sat on my ass, waiting for the cacophony to stop and for Dakota to compose herself long enough to help me get up. I tried to stand in my stilettos, but they made me look like a crab with roller blades trying to Zumba. I stuck out my arm to Dakota for assistance.

The bush got up from its perch on the ledge and offered to help me. "Seen any cute little shrubberies around tonight? You might want to take care for any poison ivy or Lily of the Valley. Especially take care around the fly traps."

"Sheridan?" I peered into the bush, never having expected it to communicate, let alone speak with the voice of my older sister.

"Deadly – that is fantastically savage!" Dakota stood and clasped her hands over her mouth.

I gawked at both my sisters. Sheridan was dressed in a black bodysuit covered in branches and leaves. "Unholy hell, Sher, that is some serious bull shite. Look at you – damn that's impressive."

Sheridan grabbed my drink I'd left behind on the ledge and took a sip through a slit on her face cap.

"Here, help me before Roxas shows up. I don't want to look like an eejit messed up like this."

"Aw, but you're such a cute little idiot."

I smirked at her.

"Gotcha, lil' sis. I had to come up with something no one would expect me to wear. So when I saw the backstage crew gearing up the other day, I knew exactly what I wanted to do."

Still not quite sure whether to be blown away or pissed, I tried to re-wrap myself where the gauze had torn off. "Well, you had an impact, that's for sure."

"Come on into the park and check out what I set up to scare people. I have a special bench area where we wired cameras to monitor the action. Global Studios has a few more of us strategically positioned around the park to scare people tonight. It ought to be epic."

"So you'll be scaring people all night in this costume?" Dakota checked out Sheridan's leaves and branches. The entire outfit looked real, but it was fabric.

"Yes. It's called a ghillie suit or something like that. Hunters and military personnel use them for camouflage. I can't wait to study the stream later on and see how people, like you, fall for the gag."

Hmm ... I wonder if she's videotaping us right now.

Chapter Eight

Halloween Scream Night

Global Studios

We advanced our way past the ticket carousels where our costumes were searched for anything dangerous. We went through metal detectors and x-ray machines, which looked like airport scanners to ensure the utmost protection at the event. I set off the alarms due to the brass costume snake jewelry around my upper arms. The castle guard gave me a few extra swipes of his metal detector wand, winked, and cleared me to go. The extra security measures made me feel a whole lot better about people dressed in scary costumes – at least I knew they'd gone through the same security measures I had.

I thought about how anyone could harm or hurt others in a setting like this. How easy it would be for a crazed serial killer to do his or her cherry picking, and the theme park wouldn't have any way to identify the person. Of course, the logical side of me countered, not only are park employees dressed up, so are a ton of undercover security guards and police. I steadied myself and decided from here on out, the evening was going to become magically transcendental.

As we walked past the front entrance locker area, the park transported us into another realm where we couldn't see the ground through obscure fog. Promises of cinnamony goodness beckoned me further into the murkiness as gourmet goodies drifted their invitations to my nose, tempting my palette. I wanted to find where the delicious pastries where offered, but the night sky, high above the zero ground visibility, revealed a dark new moon. No extra light tonight from the moon Goddess, Diana, to keep the creepies away. My stomach rumbled, and I hoped we would pass the store and I could get a cinnamon roll soon. Dakota grabbed onto my arm, and onto Sheridan's branch of an arm as we penetrated the mist over the bridge.

Animated, indigo lights illuminated the foot path under the foggy shadows at my feet. They scurried around like mischievous ferrets, dashing off before my eyes could catch them. The ambiance tricked me into believing more evilness hid in the fog than I wanted to experience.

We heard a blood-curdling scream through the haze and looked up to follow the sound. My throat dropped instantly into my stomach as I saw the roller coaster, complete a loop-the-loop, not a hundred feet above us. The coaster ride lovers were smashed against the backs of their seats in what looked like more G-force than a human body could withstand. The coaster dipped down and away into the dense fog bank hovering above the water. The dewy night muted the steel coaster gliding of the rails. Not being able to see through the mist confused my senses. I suppose that was the effect the park wanted to obtain. And obtain, they did.

The wailing screams of the riders echoed off the lakefront as the trailing car zoomed overhead. Someone's fake, bloody teeth fell from the skycar and plopped into the water a few feet away from us. The tentacles of fog crept over the comforting, soft glow of twinkle lights which were used to help illuminate the walking paths. Their tendrils stole any assistance the lights emitted, and sucked the illumination in as if it were a sponge. In these shoes, I became weary of each and every step I took.

"Holy, fog bank, Batman," Dakota said.

I murmured back her sentiments. "They have truly outdone themselves this year. I've never seen Halloween Scream Nights like this before. Have you?"

A wolf howled in the distance. Eyes wide, Dakota shook her head and held on to my arm a little tighter.

We took in the full essence of the terrifying special effects laid out before us. Phantasmal music thrummed its way into the night through hidden speakers. My head swayed to the dark, haunted cadence. Deep, thunderous melodies surged through my bones, vibrating my teeth with the electric bolts of lightning inside the orchestration.

"Isn't this bad-assed?" Sheridan asked. "I can't get over how they have transformed the park. It's like walking into one of our sims. I hope you're taking notes, Chey."

My sisters and I knew these parks like the backs of our hands since we had season passes every year. The amazing attention to detail in how Global Studios transformed their family friendly atmosphere by day, to such a frightening adventure by night, was simply fascinating.

Here we were, a man-eating bush, Elvira Mistress of the Night, and a fourth century mummified street walker. Only the mighty O'Cuinn sisters would ever try to pull off such a stunt.

I checked my iPod for placement on my shoulder and checked the microphone cord I'd secured under my hair and into my ear. "Yep, I'm taking notes. I never would've imagined that sort of effect with the fog, but it sure worked on me."

As we moved past super hero land, the brume finally began to clear out a bit, and it was easier to see the people around us.

Dakota straightened up, let go of our arms, and looked around. "Have you two seen Ludovic and his brother? I think we lost them back in the fog."

We periscoped around us and tried to find the Scream mask guy and Sherlock Holmes. I thought it was just my nerves, but with each passerby coming out of the fog bank, I examined the same spectral expression upon people's faces. The iPod recorded my observations. There was something about people-watching that was deliciously mesmerizing. Observing others as freaked out as me made me feel human enough to believe I wasn't the only other scaredy-cat on this planet. Here we all were, in a very public and safe place. Everyone paid a premium price to be in this hair-raising nightmare for just one reason – to have the hell scared out of them.

"There they are." Ludovic and Edric were just coming out of the mist. Raising her voice to embarrassing levels, Dakota shouted, "Hey, guys. C'mon, we're over here."

Sheridan stopped us not far from the water barge rides. "Here we are."

I could hear the churning, riptides from where we stood. It creeped me out to think someone could get thrown in there and no one would know it until daylight.

"You guys stand over here and watch for a couple minutes. You won't believe how people react to this."

"I have an inkling," I murmured and continued to look around for a copper-top vampire. But Roxas was no where to be found.

Sheridan reached in for another hug but stopped herself before the branches caught on my gauze once again.

"Wait. Before you go, Sher, I want to get a picture of us. Ludovic can you take pictures?"

Dakota handed Ludovic her phone and I unplugged my iPod for Edric to take pictures for me. After five minutes of various poses and sisterly nonsense, Sheridan resumed her previous scare factor position in her own web of fears.

We waited until an unsuspecting Superman sat down on the bench beside her tree base. It wasn't long until she sneaked an arm in around the back of the guy's shoulders and attacked him. The man was so scared he actually threw punches at the bush. Fortunately, Sheridan was quicker than the Man of Steel, and he ran off toward the dinosaur lost continent.

I ran up to Sheridan as fast as I could in stilettos and helped her up. "Whoa, Sher, are you okay? Is this a covered event on our health insurance?"

She stood up and readjusted a couple of her broken branches. "Maybe I won't try that tactic again and just stick to the slow movement and growling."

"You should've thought about that before now. Be careful tonight, Sher, and don't let the ghoulies bite."

Sheridan laughed. "I'll meet up with you kids later on. I can't wait to meet Roxas."

Dakota elbowed me in the ribs. "I know, right? Mr. Mystery man finally revealed to all of us."

The secret sister hip bump handshake commenced. Tonight was a night of celebration.

I snapped my fingers. "I get it! You put that song on my iPod playlist this morning. How long have you two been planning this?"

They grinned big stupid cheesy teeth at me. Sheridan ignored my question.

"Let's plan on meeting at midnight over by the insane asylum, all right?" Sheridan pointed towards the haunted house. "That's where we're set up to monitor the cameras from all over the park."

"Seriously?" I whined.

"I hate that haunted house. It's the worst. They always have people in cages who come out after you. Couldn't we have monitored the cameras from the Dr. Seuss Kiddie World or something?"

Again with the cheesy grins.

"Okay – we'll be there." I put on my best *go get 'em* face. "Right now I need to find a bathroom."

"Laters." Sheridan waved and settled back down into her attack mode.

I had the coolest sisters on the planet. Weird, and not a lot of common sense, but definitely cool.

Dakota grabbed onto Ludovic, and Edric walked on the other side of his brother. "Yeah, we're gonna go check out the zombie parade. Love those deaders." Dakota winked at me. I knew what she meant to – hook up with the dead groom for a secret shag.

I looked at my watch. "I have about forty-five minutes before meeting Roxas, so I'm gonna walk to the back of the park."

"Hey, sweetie, why don't you go freshen up in the ladies room and buy a bottle of water or something. You look like the reaper has come to take you away." Dakota put her hand on my arm and squeezed. "You need to keep relaxing and breathe. You're having fun. He loves you and you love him. Just remember that."

She hugged me and even with that kind reassurance, there was still this overwhelming feeling growing deeper in the pit of my stomach. My life was seriously about to change and I hoped it was for the better. I prayed that tonight, of all nights, my old recurring dream from childhood about the Red Man didn't come true.

Chapter Nine

Screepy Caverns

Marveling at the lengths the Halloween horror freaks went into detail of their costumes, I was reminded of how people dressed their avatars in ExsanguiNation.

Many people dressed in ragged clothing with dime store makeup to fit in as grisly ghoulies. My attention was drawn to these strange humanoid creatures with glowing eyes. They had white makeup on half of their bodies and black makeup on the other half as if they were adult harlequin dolls. I expected to see other party goers dressed in Venetian masks following these captivatingly quirky characters.

Women dressed in everything, from Renaissance ball gowns, to a ribbon, a feather, and a smile. Belly dancers seduced onlookers, wrapped in both shimmering scarves and live snakes. Eerie calliope music played off-key around me, making me wonder if this was an inauspicious carny dream or something worse. My mind enjoyed the overload of the warped scenery, but my eyes kept telling me to scream and run.

The music made my head swoon. I pushed my way through the wall of gory creatures. Screams pierced through the crowd. Several angels ran past me as they were chased by a band of frolicking demons.

I looked for the bathroom rest area in the dinosaur park. The fog didn't help in finding the bathroom, but the shrill cries of the tropical birds in covert speakers seriously tested the bladder control.

Desperate to freshen up before meeting Rox, I didn't feel my best after the sister tree attack. I walked along a main thoroughfare, over the water bridge into the back half of the park closer to the log flume ride. There was a bathroom rest area with seating which should be protected from any man-eating vegetation. More weird characters passed me – wizards, ogres, fairies, witches, elves, bounty hunters, and other gothic unrecognizable characters. This place was a madhouse.

The raging river deafened the night as the wailing riders screamed into the dark waters and out of sight. The pond was pitch, but Global Studios had done an impressive job of lighting the menacing creatures swimming inside the ride.

Tempted to remove my high heels for a while, I came upon a scare zone featured on the theme park's website. The locomotive disaster scene, complete with a stalled car across the tracks and dead passengers. This particular spooky corridor revealed too many plants for my comfort. Convinced I was on the vegetation menu, I thought about finding an alternate route. However, the allure of the lonely, faraway train whistle drifted on the humid air and beckoned me forward.

The fog thickened, filling my senses with earthy scents of pine, peat, and wet leaves. Scads of dead bodies lay over the ground, falling out of the car, and across the tracks. Victims were draped across the decrepit engine's tangled wreckage of ruined steel. Several bodies weren't moving, while other dismembered parts of those bodies awakened upon my arrival. The steam engine's light faded off and on, creating a darker blanket of blind spots in the absence of light.

Despite the desperate attempt to apply logic, my eyes kept telling my brain a different story. The scare zone played tricks on all my senses. The special effects engaged my brain and the wheels turned once again. Wow, I knew this was a level of intensity needed in the game. Logic obscured the understanding, but the eyes overruled the logic. I reminded myself that these were actors. They would take a break in an hour or so, remove the gory makeup at the end of the night, and sleep in their own warm beds with body parts intact. It was hard to keep my wits about me while immersed in the wrecked carnage of the scene, coupled with the loud sound effects from the train whistle.

Dying, last gasps of breaths from the bodies echoed in the pregnant fog. Just then, a crawling hand reached out and scraped at my ankle. I screamed.

They're not supposed to touch me!

The animated undead came alive and walked toward me accompanied by trees and shrubs. This ghastly crew must've known they had a live one since the conductor ran after me. Aren't deaders supposed to shuffle or something?

The conductor's mouth hung open, frozen into a perpetual scream. It was hard to stomach looking at his face as the blood dripped from his chin. He dragged a coal shovel along the cement, creating sparks to accompany the skin-crawling scraping and grinding sound effects. I kicked off my heels, grabbed them, and ran to get out of the scare zone. My thoughts raced to imagine what that zombie wanted to do with his shovel. After reaching the safe zone, my heart pumped adrenaline throughout my body causing me to shake. My lungs clamored to obtain more oxygen. Dead bodies, detached body parts, and creepy vegetation reset into control z mode to attack the next set of unsuspecting victims.

I looked around for any additional creepies.

Finally, a bathroom!

Margaritas out, hienie floss adjusted, stilettos on, and lipstick reapplied. It was time to take on the world. I had just enough time to go check out a haunted house before I met Roxas. It wouldn't take but ten minutes to get through the haunted house, and I could expend nervous energy before I saw him. Scared out of my ever- lovin', cotton-pickn' mind to go in to the haunted house alone, I was even more scared to meet him.

Laughter and happy sounds of people reverberated everywhere around me. Since I thought of going into the haunted house, that overwhelming sense of caution crept into my mind again. Anxious to behold Roxas, I looked at every guy in a vampire costume and wondered if that could be him. Especially if the man caught my eyes or stared at me longer than comfort allowed.

I needed an immediate distraction or I wasn't going to go through with this. Why was I so afraid to meet this guy? Hadn't he been my fella online for over two years now? Hadn't he been the gentleman I'd shared so many secrets with on those late night gaming sessions?

What in the hell were you thinking, Cheyenne – why are you doing this to yourself?

Forward movement. I took a deep breath and put one foot in front of the other. I didn't want to stand around looking like a doorknob when he showed up. Even if I was a little late, that would be okay. I wanted to make the impression I was cool, calm and not desperate to meet him. No matter how much I was.

Just keep moving.

If I had to sit and wait, I knew I would explode. It was time to do the haunted house, face my fear, and get it over with. High on endorphins, I figured now would be as good a time.

No guts, no glory

Who the hell said that anyway, I wondered.

A crooked wooden sign hanging over the top of a darkened doorway read *Screepy Haunted Caverns*. I crept into the spooky corridor. Aware of the fact I was alone, with no boyfriend to hide behind, this would have been a perfect opportunity to cozy up to Roxas to break the physical ice. My nerves edged at the anticipation of meeting him.

The cavern was black as pitch except for tiny glow lights on the floor to guide us through the creep show maze. The line moved pretty fast through the twisting corridors.

One of things I liked the most about Halloween Scream Nights was how Global Studios could take innocent rides and walkways and turn them into a haunted house. You never knew if the haunted houses would be inside buildings, outside, or in the middle of the bathroom. Their ingenuity always amazed me.

This year they turned the line queue for the water boat ride into a Screepy Caverns haunted house with all its dark twisted passageways. This was perfect. As soon as I got out of here, I'd be able to see Roxas. One safety feature I realized was missing: the red *EXIT* lights along the ceiling.

Hmm ... weren't the rides supposed to let you get out if you wanted?

Walking in from the entrance, I also didn't recall seeing any legalese signs stating cautions. *If you have any heart conditions, are pregnant, or if you are under such-and-such a height you shouldn't participate in this intense event.*

The screams in front of me, echoing off the walls, told a different story.

A woman so frightened at just the howls ahead dashed back out of the line and knocked me over. I fell against the wall, twisting my ankle in these shoes. I asked for help from the couple behind me, but the shrieks in the cave were too loud for them to hear, and they seemed to be wrapped up in their make out session with each other. Dressed up as a mermaid and Triton, the couple behind me continued snogging. From my vantage point, Triton's mighty sword was ready at the helm.

A pregnant lady in front of me dressed in a nun's outfit saw that I had fallen, and she helped me stand. I smiled and thanked her, but she was anxious to get back in line to view the carnage.

The coarse wall from the rock surface had torn into my skin. My hand came away wet with blood when I brushed the dirt and rubble from my arm. It hurt to touch it, so I used my costume to help brush off most of the damage. My ankle throbbed.

I need to get rid of these shoes.

I limped back into the line, keen to observe people acquire their next junkie gore rush.

Questioning what I was doing here gave me pause to consider my sanity ... again. How many other people did this kind of crazy research for the sake of science? I knew there were ghost hunters and paranormal investigators, but it seemed they liked getting the hell scared out of them. Me, I just wanted to code a program. Why didn't I just hire someone to tell me what was scary? I supposed then it wouldn't be complete enough experience for gamers to believe.

I couldn't help but wonder how all this fear would affect the psyche, my psyche. One thing was clear to me, though, when it came to the flight or fight part of the brain, the humanity part of the equation leaves a person for a brief moment for self-preservation. If a person needed or chose flight, they wouldn't care how or who was hurt, as long as they escaped the danger themselves. This was obviously demonstrated when that girl plowed me over.

Shielding my face to brace for a horrific view, I kept telling myself that these were just actors and there was nothing to be frightened of. Scenes played out from *The Island of Dr. Moreau,* and *The Exorcist* which inspired disgusted screams of gory fun as we continued along the corridor of the haunted house.

I followed the line goers through the darkened corridor. I couldn't see anything up ahead. What I hoped I wasn't going to see were disturbing clowns, dolls with glass eyes, or gortraits watching me pass down the long, dark hall. Real things that made up nightmares.

Chapter Ten

s I followed people into a dark room, my hand disappeared from my sight, instantly setting off the red safety flags in my mind.

Unholy hell - I don't like this.

I heard yelps from people, as scraping sounds of movement circled around us.

"The walls are moving," one woman said.

Shouts from another. "No way – I can't find the walls."

"Where did the damn walls go?" a man said through the pitch.

I reached out behind me and the walls had moved.

It bothered me that I didn't have a reference point to protect me any longer as I was pushed into a room. I heard the click of a door lock behind me. Unable to see, I had no idea if anything would be at my feet. I worried about falling again. I might trip on someone or worse yet, get trampled in here.

The wailing began once again in three-dimensional sound as if it were happening all around us. My breathing hitched up a notch just to control the anxiety since I couldn't see anything of logic to help block out what my ears were telling me. Knowing this had to be a part of the act, I took in slow inhales to remain calm praying that this nightmare would be over soon enough. I wondered how much time was left to meet Roxas.

Will I be late? Would he wait for me? Where's the damn exit sign?

It wasn't long until most people turned on their cell-phones or iPods in order to have a flashlight to help peer through the blackness. I, too, pulled out my iPod and held it down by the floor. I flashed the light onto where I thought the wall should be, but either the room was too dark, or my light wasn't strong enough to illuminate the surface. I took several steps back to where I thought I had entered the room, and indeed, the wall was not there.

The room itself was absolutely black, except for the dim haze which hung around the floor. A rush of air filled the floor with a cool, dense fog. This must be what we saw lingering from the group before us. The brume became thick, and my shoes were no longer visible. The chilly, opaque smoke wrapped around my legs almost as if trying to complete my mummy costume.

A brilliant white, intense light erupted at the far end of the room accompanied by a train whistle. Its haunted lullaby became louder and, more penetrating by the second. The floor vibrated as the train approached. The direction of the light coupled with the vibration of the tracks encouraged people to scramble to get away from the imminent death engine barreling towards us. The train flew past us with the sound of the horn passing leaving us with the loud clackity clack of the cars passing by.

This particular room must have been outfitted with a theater surround-sound system strategically placed for visual and audio effects. The sub-woofers in the floor vibrated for a surreal effect. There were whoops and hollers of appreciation from this hungry bunch of scare hunters. They wanted more.

In figuring the haunted allure to this room, it seemed to me it induced a variety of sense deprivation and overstimulation. The human mind had trouble understanding if the train was real or not. Self-preservation would motivate people away from the sound and the vibrations in the floor. Another light approached from the right hand section of the room. The train whistle blew again. This time people moved sooner, but an additional train came barreling at us from the left hand side. The trains were going to collide. We were caught in the middle. Thunderous roars of screeching brakes on metal wheels and tracks sent people screaming and running in all directions. When in reality, there was nothing in the room with us ... or at least that's what I thought.

Hoping this was the end of the show, I waited for the doors to open up into brightly lit hallways and refreshing night air. Anxious to get out, I looked again for safety security lights along the floor or for any signs to exit the building. People seemed to have calmed down when they realized the train wasn't going to leave them dead and reanimating into zombies. Another dense cloud of smoke blew in at our feet once again.

I heard a man call, "Janey, Janey, where are you?"

This gore fest wasn't over yet.

I looked back to where I thought we'd entered the room, but couldn't be sure anymore since the room walls, floor, and ceiling were all painted black. Completely disoriented, any interior or exterior doors were not discernible from the sides. It looked as if there was no way out. People illuminated the floor with their phones to see, but that was about as far as the light went. The fog reached up with its tentacles and engulfed any amount of light from the devices making it nearly impossible to see. It was as if the murkiness was a creature all of its own and sucked the light and security away from us.

A foul odor filled the room. The stench of rotting meat, old hot dumpster, and sweaty gym shoes filled the air. I envisioned people holding their noses and covering their mouths, same as myself. People next to me coughed, laughed, and sounded grossed out by the odors.

A desperate voice rang out among us. "Janey? Has anybody seen a girl in a mermaid costume? Janey?"

I knew then it must've been Triton from the couple behind me.

Another voice answered back, "Man, I can't see shit in here – let alone your girl."

So far in this room we had been bombarded with light, dark, sound, movement, and smell. They couldn't touch us, so what was next? I wanted out of this crazy room.

"Janey?" The man's voice grew increasingly desperate as he called out his girlfriend's name. Since the girl did have a tail on her costume, I was afraid she might have tripped and could have been easily trampled in the chaos. "Help me. Please, has anyone seen Janey?"

I opened my mouth to answer him, when the train horn blasted through the sound system once again causing me to jump in alarm. Several women screamed at the immediate intensity of the horn blast. It was the loudest it'd been and left my ears ringing. Light shattered the area as a silhouetted horror scene illuminated stage left. A man with hands on his hips stood next to another man at the gallows. I couldn't make out any distinct features other than the blackness of contrast. The masked actor awaited his command to pull the rope descending the man to his swinging deathbed.

Crack!

The man shot through the hole in the gallows. People screamed in horror as the victim twitched and writhed. The lights went out leaving us with only our audible senses to experience the man's death. Gurgling, choking sounds hung heavy in the air. Not a person in the crowd made a single noise. That man hung there at the end of his rope, which must have unsuccessfully broken his neck. His body undulated in my mind. His moans portraying his agony until the shaking in his limbs must have finally gone limp, and he swayed on the creaking rope in silence.

Not sure how to react to this, I did nothing but try to find my way to a wall. I had to get out of there. I had heard many hangings didn't result in a successful snap to the vertebrae for immediate death. The vision of a man swinging to his death, choking from the crushing weight from his own body tightening the noose, made me sick to my stomach. To experience the sight and to hear how his life ended was just too close and personal for my taste.

Feeling sick and uncomfortable, I searched in vain for the wall. I didn't care anymore if this was supposed to be just an act. I was chicken shit, and that was all there was to it. I didn't care if I ever wrote the damn program, I just wanted out of this terrible nightmare because it wasn't fun anymore.

"JANEY! Please has anyone seen a girl in a mermaid costume?" The man's voice was frenzied, and it seemed as if he was on the edge of tears now.

Another stage lit up to my right. I looked around us for doors illuminated on the walls. Back lit again to blind us, the lights faded to a mere ten watt light bulb hanging above a guillotine. The same masked headsman lowered a catatonic man into the death apparatus and shackled his arms and legs to hold his body secure. The man was laid into the machine with his eyes facing the jagged blade. The masked man threw a glass of water onto the man's face. Waking up, it looked as though the prisoner realized his dire circumstances, and he screamed for help protesting the injustice of his death sentence.

The blade fell with a blood chilling slice, as the convicted struggled to escape. The prisoner's head was staged to fall into a basket, but instead, the rusty, dull edge of the blade didn't provide a clean slice. The lolling head hung partially attached to the body with blood spraying the audience with each arterial pulse. Shock and disgust caused utter panic and sheer terror in the room. This was too graphic, too close, too personal, and dammit, *they weren't supposed to touch us!*

"Enough with the gore already!" someone yelled.

The lights went out leaving the room in complete obscurity once again. People shouted they wanted out. At least I wasn't the only one who had maxed out my creep card.

I also shouted to express my anger, but my voice croaked under the thickness in my mouth. The heat was stifling. Temperatures in the room must've been soaring into the high nineties. Sweat poured off me. I kept chanting the mantra, "They can't touch you, they can't touch you," but at this point, I didn't believe a damn thing.

The center stage lit up. I realized I was standing directly in front of it. I pushed my way backwards as others around me also moved back in unison to the scene set before us. A man, who appeared to be suffering from rabies faced us. Thick, bloody foam dripped down his chest and body. He held a screaming, struggling woman above his head. She was dressed in a mermaid costume. His eyes glowed the same way as those Harlequin people I saw earlier. These weren't movie special effects anymore.

A whisper behind me. "Janey? Oh my God. No!"

The demon stood before us.

I gasped out loud, "NO!"

Janey called out, "PLEASE, Jonathan, help me!"

In an instant, the demon ripped Janey the mermaid in half and drank the pulsing arterial blood flowing from her body. After the beast depleted Janey of her bodily fluids, he tossed her corpse at our feet. People around me threw up and ran to the back of the room.

Jonathan, the Triton boyfriend, screamed her name. He'd found Janey. Silent, glassed-over eyes reflected from the dim overhead light.

The light bulbs in the room shattered into a thousand sparks and then went nebulous again. Once the lights went out, no one in the crowd made another sound except Janey's boyfriend who gasped in horrifying sobs.

Everyone must've been standing there in shock, just as I was, unsure if what they'd just seen was real or part of the show. I tried to comprehend if it was real. Could this possibly be what Sheridan had alluded to earlier this morning? She said they had special effects no one had ever seen before. No, this was real.

The Red Man from my nightmares. He's real? Out! Out! Out! I have to get out of here!

A shrill shriek injected the air from the back of the room and I heard footsteps running towards me. Something was terribly wrong. I was going to die in this awful pit if I didn't escape it soon.

The putrid emanations which had overcome the room before, were back, and it made me nauseated coupled with the tang of the fresh metallic blood. Screams were everywhere. My feet bumped up against something. I tripped and landed on my hands and knees. I tried to hide and duck to the floor to stay low and not get caught in a stampede.

People shouted into their phones for help. I turned on my iPod to record the noises.

The densely packed fog beamed the light back from my iPod blinding me as if they were headlights in a blizzard. Still on my hands and knees, I turned my face sharp to the right when I heard the cracking sound of bones and the gnawing sounds of torn flesh. The light revealed the tormented, now dead face of Triton fallen before me next to the mermaid.

I tried to scream, but silence only escaped my lips. My body became petrified into non-action silence. My mind parsing through the nonsense, I scuttled backwards until I felt other bodies behind me. They weren't moving either. Drowning, gut wrenching, screams came from all around me, but this time they weren't prerecorded special effects. They were sounds I never wanted to imagine, or ever try to emulate. This was no longer an act. We were no longer in the Screepy Caverns at Global Studios Halloween Scream Nights, a protected theme park loved by millions in Orlando, Florida. No, we were in another dimension where a horrendous beast killed for our blood. Something had gone terribly wrong.

Sounds of crying, begging, pleading, and praying came from all directions. I wasn't sure anymore if what I heard was real or if it was in my head. Something hard slammed into my side and knocked my only source of light away from my hands. I heard a woman maybe five feet away from me begging to be released. The drinking sucking sounds made me wretch up any remaining margaritas in my stomach.

Desperate to stay mute while gagging in my own vomitus scream, I tried not to draw attention to myself. The room grew intensely quiet as the heat and noxious odors sweltered.

I questioned then, even if I were silent as a rose blooming, was it possible the demon could still detect me. Did the Red Man know I was here? Was he here for me?

My hands and legs were soaked in blood from the bodies I had crawled over. I most likely was already bleeding or pissed myself just the same. I continued to crawl over bodies lying in pools of dark coagulating blood with ripped off arms, hands, and legs. I found another light source from someone's mobile. I prayed I could get through to 911. I picked up the light only to find a hand still attached to it.

Chapter Eleven

I never knew what honest-to-God *fear* meant until right now. I fumbled my way through the sickness flowing under my feet. Broken bones, blood smeared extremities, I didn't care anymore. Overwhelmed, hysteria settled in me like a chicken next in line for the butchering table. Not able to focus, I couldn't figure out what to do.

What do I do now? How do I get out of here? Take deep breaths. Calm down. Think dammit! You can get out of this mess. You're gonna give yourself a damn heart attack.

With the hand still clutching the phone in defiance, I yanked the phone out of its death grip, swiped the screen to open the menu page, swallowed hard, and pressed 911. The dismembered hand fell to the floor with a splat onto my foot. Bile crawled up my esophagus. A silent prayer crossed my lips. It was Halloween. Worst night of the year to prank the police department.

Pick up! Pick Up! PICK UP!

When the operator came on the line, I whispered, "Help us. We're at Screepy Caverns haunted house at Global Studios. Something has gone terribly wrong. People have been killed in here."

"Please hold, Ma'am, I'll transfer you to the complaint department. It is a federal crime, punishable by $50,000 penalty to prank call the 911 Emergency Response System."

"No. No! Wait – please don't put me on hold."

Muzak filled my ear.

Are they serious? Did they just put me on hold?

Another voice came over the phone. I talked as fast as I could until I realized it was a recording. "Your call is very important to us. Please hold and the next available assistant will help you. Please do not hang up and call again, this will only delay your wait time. The current wait time is twenty-two minutes."

Get back to the wall. Breathe. Keep the light down. Find the wall. Find the door. Breathe.

Scooting my feet along the ground, I thought I wouldn't fall again if I took smaller steps. I sloshed in a thick puddle of ooze, and my foot shot out from under me. Sharp pain shot up my leg as my sprained ankle snapped sideways. I fell again hitting my head against the hard, wooden wall. The world became fuzzy for a moment.

I found the damn wall! My heart leapt at the chance of hope.

I reached up to follow the wall, and prayed to find a door handle. Managing to stand and limp along it for a few feet, I realized the room had grown unsettling quiet. The hair on the back of my neck clued me to the fact something other than the obvious had gone terribly wrong. I limped another step. It was my last.

My body wrenched violently around and landed face-to-face with the hideous creature I saw on the stage. The cell phone in my hand gave just enough light through the haze for me to see my attacker was a man. How could a mere mortal do this? Could he have been whacked out on bath salts or some other hallucinogenic drug?

He held me against his nakedness, his erection posed for conquest. I'd never seen eyes filled with such intensity, such lust. His face, hair, and skin were caked in blood. He was the Red Man who had haunted my dreams since childhood. It was this creature, covered in blood and ready to consume me.

I tried to escape, get free from his clutch, thrashing against him, but my hands slid off his slimy skin. He growled at me. This was it, I was going to die. My breath wheezed in and out of me.

Get away! Dammit, Cheyenne, you are not going to die like this!

I shoved the phone into my bra. A trick I hoped to thank Dakota for later. My eighth grade PE self-defense lessons flooded back into my mind.

Kick – Knee – Run!

The monster dropped me. I scampered back desperate to find that elusive door.

I banged on the walls and screamed. "Help us! Somebody – let us out. Call the police!"

Where is the feckin' door handle? Why didn't I bring my keys with pepper spray?

The crippling pain in my ankle shot shards of agony hindering my escape. Endorphins flooded me. I buried the anguish deep inside the recesses of my mind to keep going. My ankle was most likely broken, but I didn't dare let it stop me. I had to escape or I was dead.

I checked the phone again for anybody to help me. "Thank you for holding. Your call is very important to the Orlando Police Department. Your wait time is now fifteen minutes."

Fifteen minutes? Dammit People, I'll be dead in one.

I turned searching through the haze. Had anyone else found a way out? I shoved the phone back into my shirt and squatted, praying my attacker's vision was also hindered by the fog. The creature's hideous, maniacal laugh stopped me cold. I didn't flinch nor move another muscle. The laughter, hauntingly familiar, sent a frigid, wet, dead finger up my spine. I held my hands to my mouth to stop the nervous chatter of my teeth.

The creature fell upon me in an instant. He grabbed me by the shreds of my costume and within seconds flung me up to his face once again.

The beast bit into my cheek and chin. He forced his hand around my jaw and smashed my lips with his fingers. The pain sent my head into a tailspin. I kicked, screamed, thrashed, and struggled in vain to get away from his vice-like grip. His hand clamped on my face and sent shattering fractures of pain through my jaw. I knew this was it — flight or fight. Self-preservation time. Since I couldn't find a way out, I had to fight.

A guttural wail escaped my throat. I pulled my hands free and gouged at his eyes with my fingernails, trying desperately to dig into his eye sockets to blind him. The cretin's hands felt as if he wanted to rip my jaw off my face. He shoved his fingers into my mouth for a better hold while demonically laughing at my feeble attempts to harm him. I must've been the silly little goat to the fierce boa constrictor in his mind.

I grabbed his hand at my mouth and shoved his fingers further in. My back molars crunched hard like a nut cracker to bite off his fingers. I ground my jaw back and forth, stripping off flesh between my teeth. His blood gushed into my mouth filling it with hot, coppery spurts. The beast relinquished his hold with a grunt of pain and let go of my face. I fell backwards away from him.

In an instant he grabbed me up by the arms and shook me until I became a rag doll in front of him.

He held me there, panting. Face-to-face. Time stopped. My eyes tried to focus. Light shined up through my gauzy straps. For a split moment of time, milliseconds of reality, his eyes softened. Spider web creases around his eyes made him look almost human. He looked at me with an intense fire in his eyes as they glowed red. He glanced around us and put me gently on the floor.

RUN!

I froze, cemented to the ground. My legs refused to budge. My body failed me. Utterly paralyzed, I couldn't move. Then I realized my back was pressed up against the stage. When his eyes met mine once again, they were wide and conscious. In that moment, I emblazoned his image forever on my soul.

Two words escaped him enveloping me in rotten breath. "Help me."

I wasn't sure if what I saw, and what I heard were the same thing. My head throbbed with the rush of blood pounding in my ears. He crushed me closer to his chest, knocking the wind out of me again. His voice whispered into my ear, "Please, help me."

Are you fecking kidding me?

Anger flooded my brain synapses, and dumped adrenaline into my bloodstream. My heart pumped new vitality throughout my body. I gained clarity and a sense of peace when he released his grip on my arms. I stepped back with caution and grabbed a shoe not far from my hand on the stage.

Breathe, Cheyenne.

I looked at his face once again. My exterior remained calm while the raging torrent inside overtook my entire body. In an instant, I spit into his eyes and swung the shoe at his face. This stunt gave me just enough time to ram my foot into the inside of his knee, bending him over as I slammed my fisted hands down against his shoulder.

Knowing there was nowhere left to go, my verbal assault spewed forth. "Asshat. Ask me for help? What the hell, you whacked out jerk wad!"

He grabbed me by the hair and yanked me back towards him. His hands stretched my neck in an unnatural arc to the left. He pressed against pressure points in my shoulder, and I became an instant rag-doll once again. Knowing he was going to snap my vertebrae like a green bean, I was no longer able to defend myself.

Anger coursed through me. All I could do is watch him in paralytic horror as my heart pounded out of my chest. Black dots clouded my vision. He held my neck on display, his bountiful feast awaiting him. He licked his lips watching the rhythm of my carotid. The stench of his fetid breath, heaved vomit up into my mouth. He tenderly lavished my neck, stroking it, kissing it, and sucked on the throbbing artery pulsing viciously under my skin.

"911 is this an emergency?" The voice from my bra came just in time to hear the devil sink his teeth deep into my neck and suck out my life force.

A million thoughts, memories, and emotions flooded through me in an instant.

Beano. Dakota. Sunburned weekends at the beach. Daddy. The smell of burning orange peels. Sheridan. Why didn't I ever get around to making a will? Cuban sandwiches from Larry's Deli. Roxas. Why didn't I go sit by the waterfalls? Was this how my life ended? Why didn't I pay attention to my dream this morning? Quest Failed.

My eyes saw a flicker of emergency lights or it could have been the white light everyone talked about when they die. Somewhere off in the distance police sirens wailed.

Dreamily the sirens accompanied the screams, and the horrors of my insane dream. I blew dandelion seeds across the lawn and watched Dakota in the tire swing. Mom baking banana bread. Sheridan pouring glasses of lemonade. I fell to the floor and crashed in a heap. Beano running in the water trying to catch the waves. Sobs faded further away. The painful bliss of my recurring nightmare finally ended. After all these years, it was over. The Red Man finally got me.

As I laid there shivering, in the numbing cold, I prayed that with any stroke of fate from the Norns, and I lived through this, I would never, ever be the dumb bimbo who ventured into a haunted house again.

Chapter Twelve

Interlude

The Caedis Vampyre Coven

Orlando, Florida

Lord Stovall, the Nauclerus Vampire of the Caedis Vampyric Coven, called an emergency gathering on the bow of his ship. His dark skin glimmered in the reflection off the lamps hanging from the marina's dock. The night sky offered nothing but blinking stars and the warm whispers of wind through the cat tails over the lake. The coven met in response to reported attacks after the Halloween massacre.

"I've gathered you here tonight because we have reported sightings and bizarre events growing on Twitter and throughout the instant news sources. People are talking about the unexplained attacks on both animals and humans all across the city. Police are baffled. But that isn't a surprise."

Quiet titters of laughter funneled through the group.

"Of course, we know it is most likely from a rogue vampire or another supernatural blood demon which is openly killing," Stovall continued.

"What about the Weres? They've had a lot of Central American packs recently come through here. Made a damn mess of things," a voice cried out from one of the irritated coven members.

"How do we know it wasn't one of them?" came another voice.

"I understand your concerns." Stovall raised his hands to quiet the questions. "However, reports from the area werewolf clans state that all pack members are accounted for and had not been in a known fugue on All Hallows Eve. Since we don't know exactly what type of creature has committed the attacks, all supernatural beings are being tasked to find it and bring it to justice in front of the Queen. We need to move fast. The bitten neonate transformations are waking up and they need to be assimilated or eliminated. We are setting up a team now."

Amicula Darkrose, the coven's leading member of the IHR team was called upon to lead the Interspecies Human Relations unit. Lord Stovall knew she would most likely be the best choice to hunt and find the newly turned vampires from the horror massacre, but he also wished to give her something to do to get her out of his hair. Amicula, the niece of the Vampyre

Queen Civetateo, knew the power she held in her position and wasn't afraid to use it. Stunningly beautiful with a rare, exotic Latino beauty, she also knew no man could ever resist her.

Khaldon Seters, the coven's best technology cleaner, was called upon to flesh out any fledglings still in the hospital. He needed to scrub their dossiers, and coordinate the absterger teams. From Egypt, the direct descendant of Sekhmet, the Egyptian Warrior Goddess, Khaldon stood six feet tall with long black pharaoh hair he held back with a beaded tieback. Dark silken skin combined with a technological mind brilliant enough to make the heads of the geeks at Microsoft swim, made Khaldon a force to be reckoned with.

Lord Stovall walked to the edge of the yacht where Amicula and Khaldon stood, and addressed them both. "We need you to align yourselves earnestly with the sucklings to teach them what they've become. Darkrose, you must enact the EST – Emergency Suckling Termination – procedures of either induction or elimination. Educate the victims about how to embrace the vampire within and execute control of their thirst. For if they do not, we must terminate their threats of exposure. If they are unable to accept the new existence, then coordinate with Khaldon to eradicate the nuisance and put it down."

Amicula acknowledging her assignment and bowed deeply to her Lord.

Stovall turned to Khaldon. "Seters, infiltrate the hospital computer networks and erase any patient records Darkrose identifies. Get a tally as to how many need erasing. We will gather the resources needed for decontamination. Clean up all traces and complete a thorough dossier on each suckling. Family, friends, employment. Cross reference common denominators. Leave no evidence of the patients who must be destroyed. Wipe the minds of the humans who have interacted with these patients. They must be forgotten."

Stovall turned to address the rest of the coven council. "I am working closely with Queen Civetateo to determine if this is a rogue vampire. Where has it gone and why did it attack in a public place? There are unanswered questions about this unauthorized human attack, and we'll need assistance from all area covens to reel in these neonates. At this point, if we don't get these sucklings and their appetites under control, we could easily have a vampire apocalypse on our hands."

Khaldon dutifully bowed his head in obedience to Lord Stovall while he shot a wry smile to Amicula.

Chapter Thirteen

Interlude

Amicula Darkrose

Amicula signed into the ExsanguiNation portal with her avatar and wrote on a piece of virtual parchment paper. Before sealing the parchment with the crimson wax, Amicula re-read her letter to her aunt, the Queen, one last time to ensure she left out no detail.

My Honorable Queen Civetateo,
Lord Stovall called an emergency meeting tonight. I have been assigned head of the Interspecies Human Relations unit. I get to enjoy the critical task of deciding which humans live and which ones die in our choreographed experiment within the theme park.

How deliciously convenient for us.

After Lord Stovall dismissed the coven, he gave me explicit permission to handle the sucklings as I see fit. Seems as though most of the humans should be well utilized, wouldn't you agree?

Our infiltration into their coven is complete. Even if several of the humans do survive, if they are perceived to be acceptable candidates, we'll be sure to keep them for either the blood trials or the blood orchards. Exceptional ones, might be considered for some of our longer term ventures.

Lord Stovall assigned both Khaldon and me to the same task removal unit, so I must demonstrate caution ensure neither of them to learn too much.

Our strategy is in full swing. I will have Ludovic and Edric pick up the survivors and take them to our testing facilities. What a grand opportunity for free meat. Hands down, I would say your idea was truly a chaotic success. Perhaps now, we can push through your next level of testing on the Solunarae blood, to determine how humans can handle it. It ought to be entertaining to see how it affects their unborn fetuses as well.

I will continue to send you communiqué, via this secure channel, keeping you informed of our progress.

In Your Honor,
Darkrose

As Amicula's avatar folded the virtual paper and dribbled hot wax onto the edge to seal it, she recalled the respect Khaldon held for Lord Stovall during the meeting.

Amicula remembered the way Khaldon once respected her. Once held her so long ago. Once loved her. Her thoughts relished the words on her tongue. *One day ... one day soon. Khaldon will revere me in the same manner as he did before. When I am Queen of the Vampyre Nation.*

Amicula hit the send button and her electronic emessage inside the game was delivered.

Chapter Fourteen

Orlando Hospital

"Hold on, I'll get the n-nurse." My father squeezed my hand.

My vision blurred as I tried to focus. My head felt woozy, like a swollen watermelon full of rancid beer.

Did anybody get the license plate number of that Moose? Dear God – am I still alive?

I wrapped my fingers around his hand, and I tried to smile. Who knew the twelve muscles required to smile could hurt that damn much? Everything hurt – from the follicles on my scalp to my toenail polish. I dropped the smile and decided to go for the *drugged-out patient* look instead of the *I'll be okay, Dad* look, 'cause right at that moment, I didn't have enough energy to care.

"Are you th-thirsty? I have some water."

When he mentioned water I realized how much my parched body ached. Even though I knew better, I could've sworn I'd sucked down several sandpaper milk shakes. If extreme thirst were an Olympic event, I must have medaled for sure.

I tried to nod and found any neck movement caused excruciating pain. My father pushed the button on the bed controls to raise the head of the bed. I contorted in to an upright position to reach the water straw, but my muscles cried out in protest.

"Stop. Please stop!"

My ribs continued to crack. Whimpered cries shed silent tears onto my plaid hospital gown. He pushed the call button again for a nurse.

At once, he lowered my bed back to the original position. I wasn't sure which was worse, going up or down. Any movement left me in a haze of pain.

Finally, the torture device they called the hospital bed stopped moving. Daddy supported my neck for me to drink through the straw. My tongue and mouth savored the icy goodness; it must have been days since I had anything to drink.

Swallowing the water, however, was a whole different story. I could've sworn to the Pope himself that my dad gave me a can of liquid Sterno to pour down my throat and lit it on fire. My neck muscles seized when I tried to swallow. Violent coughs brought up globules of blood and other thick nasty stuff out of my mouth. I spit it out and dribbled the mess all over the front of me. Terrified to take another sip, I pushed the cup away from my face even though I desperately wanted the wet relief in my mouth.

I wanted morphine. I wanted to return to the deep, inky blackness of the netherworld where there was no pain. Please send me back to rest in the blissful arms of Morpheus.

"Dakota? Sheridan?" My sisters flooded my mind.

My father looked at his hands folded up in his lap. It hadn't been a dream – what he showed me in the newspaper – it was true. The newspaper head lines – Sheridan and Dakota were missing from the Halloween Scream Nights.

My words croaked out, "Daddy ... I'm sorry ... my dream ... the Red Man ..."

At first, my breathing became so labored the pain was more than I could endure. I couldn't stop the sobbing, or the ache in my chest, knowing my sisters were gone. The hitch in my breathing shot scorching fire pokers throughout my rib cage as I tried to contain my tears. I cried out in mourning for my sisters. My father hugged me as I cried in his arms.

A young, slender nurse with dark raven hair and eyes answered my father's call and came in to check me. "Hello, Cheyenne, my name is Amicula. I'm your night nurse. Are you okay? Are you in much pain?"

My father sat up and we looked at the person intruding on my grief.

Feckin' lovely. A sarcastic nurse. Am I in much pain? My sisters are most likely dead – yes, I'm in pain.

I nodded with imperceptible movement. Knowing I shouldn't take my grieving out on her, I noted the name on her scrubs. When I felt better, I would apologize. I'd never seen a name like that before.

She checked her watch. "Are you ready for another dose of happy juice?"

Happy juice? Did she mean the little morphine button of long forgotten sorrows? Hmm. Maybe, she wasn't that bad after all. I can't stand feeling like this.

I gave her an agreeable thumbs up.

She typed onto her electronic tablet. The machine that went ping over my head let out another chime, and the nurse smiled at my dad. She leaned over toward his face, patted his arm, and whispered, "She needs to sleep. Try not to upset her too much and don't use the bed controls to move her."

My father politely nodded at Amicula. I wondered why I could hear her whispered words to him as clear as if she had whispered them directly to me.

She turned back to face me and said with inarguable certainty, "You are going to be fine, Cheyenne. You have healing to do of course, but you're going to live for a very – long – time. The doctor will be in to see you soon."

Without moving my head, I looked at Amicula, then back at my dad, and then back at her again. Amicula seemed so ... perky.

She smiled a practiced smile and left the room tapping on her tablet. Glad to have her gone, I needed to be alone. I wanted time to understand and process what had happened to me, and to see if I could remember any details about Sheridan and Dakota. Maybe I could give the police information to help in the investigation.

Clearing my throat from thick mucus, I tried to croak out words without much success. Frogs have sounded better. "How long have I been out?"

"It's been a c-couple of days, Cheyenne."

"There hasn't been any news of them?" My eyes pleaded with him.

He shook his head. "No, nothing."

I bit at my lips to try and hold back the sobs.

"J-just relax now, Cheyenne. You heard the nurse. There's nothing you can do at this moment other than get better. So please, try to breathe baby. O-kay?"

I nodded.

Dad's face wasn't as swollen as I remembered. I knew when he was this upset, his stuttering was worse. The doctors said the stutter came from the traumatic shock when Mom died eight years ago. They weren't sure if he'd ever regain control over his voice in stressful situations again.

A few minutes later, my door opened and I heard an unknown male voice. "Good evening, Miss O'Cuinn. My name is Lloyd, and I'll be here at your beck and call tonight. How are you feeling?"

Unsure how to answer, I tried to wade through the fog in my head. I made a *meh* gesture with my hand.

"Perhaps we'll see how you're feeling in the morning. There's no hurry – we're glad to have you back. Baby steps for now, okay?"

I blinked at him and gave him a slight smile. I liked him better than I did Ms. Perky Pants.

Lloyd raised the yellow bag hanging from the side of the bed for me to see. "Looks like you're draining well. You don't seem to be retaining fluids like you were earlier. That's a super sign of recovery."

Catheterized. This lovely little scenario just keeps getting better.

"Let me get this output logged in your records. I saw the surgeon come onto the floor to make his rounds. I'll let him know you're awake. Overall, you're looking much better from when you first got here. You're lucky to be alive you know that?"

I looked at my dad again. He patted my arm. Why were hospital staff members always so chatty?

"If you need or want anything, you press this blue button okay? Can you see this?" He held the clicker over my face for a moment. I blinked twice to acknowledge his instructions.

"Water. Lip balm." Cracks in my lips hurt, and my mouth still felt as if I had consumed the Sahara.

"You're thirsty?"

I blinked at him again and swallowed.

"Let me get another cup of ice chips for you. We've got mouth sponges to help you with your thirst and keep your lips moist. We've had to be real careful with your throat, so don't try to drink too much yet okay?" His voice spoke as if this were an everyday occurrence. I guess for him – it was.

Lloyd stepped toward the door, snapped his fingers up beside his head, and turned towards my Dad. "Oh, before I forget, will you both be staying with us again, Mr. O'Cuinn? I can arrange for another easy chair recliner if you would like?"

Daddy looked across the room towards the windows and then back at Lloyd. "Yes. Thanks. D-do you know how long the cafeteria will be open?"

I tried to see at what he looked at, but couldn't raise my head high enough to see past his shoulder.

"Tonight is Monday night and the nurses' station orders out to the Honey Wing BBQ House. It's kinda tradition each week. Would you like for us to order you guys something from there instead of the hospital food?"

My father was a chicken wing fanatic, but I couldn't figure out why Lloyd kept saying guys. Was there somebody else in the room?

"Brilliant – sounds aces to me," a voice sounded from the back of the room. "What do you think, Kiernan – ready for something other than bland potatoes?"

My breath hitched in my chest.

Oh no! How could he possibly be here? How would he know? I never met up with him at the waterfalls.

"Thank you, Lloyd, that'd be keen. I app-appreciate that. When can Cheyenne have some food?"

Lloyd answered, "Let me check with the doctor and see if we can get her some broth tonight, maybe even a liquid Jell-O. I'll be right back with the menus." He grabbed his tablet and returned to the nurses' station.

I grabbed at my Dad's arm, struggling to look past him. My eyes desperate to focus and see who was behind the voice I knew so well. The voice I fell in love with so long ago. The voice I had spent hundreds of hours over the headset playing as Lady Caz in the ExsanguiNation simulators.

With a stupid grin on his face, Daddy leaned back to give me a better line of sight on my target. Afraid of what I thought I would find, I saw the outline of a man sitting on a couch across the room. What slowly materialized before my eyes was the face of a man I had never seen before in person, but my heart knew I had heard his voice a thousand times.

Chapter Fifteen

Roxas caught my eyes. My throat seized up as I tried to gain control over my emotions. I gasped. This had to be the worst first date ever. I pulled the covers up over my face and peeked through the threadbare fabric.

Roxas stood up and walked towards the bed.

Daddy got up from his chair and squeezed my hand again. "Sweetie, I'll be back in a few minutes."

I poked one eyeball out from the covers. He smiled at me.

His voice recovered more and more. "It's okay sweetie. He's b-been here since that night you blacked out. I used your phone at your house to call him."

Groaning, I tried to take a deep breath. I watched him head down the hallway in the camera monitor. I half-way hoped he'd stand outside the door. I wasn't ready for this. I loved Roxas, but I wasn't sure if I could handle this. With my sisters missing, I just couldn't have this kind of relationship.

I covered my face again with the sheet until I could barely see over the top. A swoosh of air wafted over me when Roxas sat in the chair my father vacated. His eyes were as verdant as I imagined. His hair and beard were a dark copper shade. He wore a close cropped mustache with a neatly trimmed beard accentuating his jawline.

His fingers touched my hair.

I couldn't believe this was happening.

Not only did I survive a horrific ordeal, but I had to meet Roxas under these conditions. Uncontrollable tears spilled out of the corners of my eyes. I wanted nothing more than to bury my face into his shoulders and, pretend this never happened. Control Z. Do over. But that wouldn't be the greatest of impressions. He was here for a reason. Where was Lady Caz when I needed her?

My shoulders bobbed up and down as I continued to sob.

"It's okay. Everything's going to be simply smashing." His voice melted over me as if were velvety, white chocolate. I wanted to bathe in his accent.

My throat thick, I swallowed hard not able to say anything.

"C'mon now, m'lady. I promise I won't bite."

I peeked over the sheet with both eyes, as he leaned in closer to me.

A faint, clean scent of spice filled my senses.

"I don't want you to worry about ExsanguiNation either. I've been maintaining the servers and Briggs has been handling the admin side of things. We've left messages for Harris, but remember he was out on bivouac with his scout troop in the Everglades and away from cellular coverage. I'm sure as soon as he gets the messages, he'll be here in no time flat."

I tried to smile, so thankful he and Briggs were managing everything.

He smiled at me. "It's been business as usual. No one knows you're in the hospital. It hasn't been announced that Sheridan and Dakota are missing. At least we haven't seen anything come across the forums, nor has there been any mention in the news. Beano is doing great. I like him – he's a funny chap. We also have Sheridan's Pomsky – Stormaggedon, right? Your father let me into your home so I could take care of them for you. I hope that's all right. Promise we weren't snooping in your underwear drawer."

He squeezed my hand. "We've been calling the little Pomsky, Stormy. She lives up to her name. She genuinely thinks she's a full size Husky, doesn't she?"

Somehow, hearing about the dogs helped me feel better. I nodded behind the covers.

"I've never seen anything like it. She beats up Beano all the time – and he lets her. They're staying at my best mate's place having a ball with a couple of other pups."

How thoughtful for him to take care of our dogs. In front of the veil I constructed, posed the man of my dreams. I'd shared most of my intimate life with Roxas for the past two years. I allowed the sheet to fall, and I gestured to him I wanted to write a note. Roxas grabbed a pen and paper from the rolling cart and handed it to me.

I wrote [/Hug Roxas] on the paper as if I'd typed it into our chat program and turned the note around for him to read. Without hesitation, he wrapped his arms around me. My heart fluttered a million miles an hour. It seemed as though nothing could ever harm me while I was in the arms of this man. For a few stolen moments, my life felt complete.

I swallowed hard again as I tried to clear my throat. "You look like your avatar."

"As do you, or from what I can see of you. Right now I think you resemble your mummy costume Dakota described to me." His smile was warm, and genuine as it reached his eyes.

I looked down at my hands and thought about Sheridan and Dakota. Here, I was meeting the love of my life, and I couldn't even enjoy it knowing that I'd survived and they were still out there somewhere under God only knows what conditions.

Roxas put his hand under my chin and I gazed into his radiant green eyes. "It's all right – we'll find them. I promise."

He hugged me again. My breath hitched in my chest as the uncontrollable pain overwhelmed me. My sobs catapulted me into another coughing fit with more globules of blood spewing forth from the injuries in my throat. Roxas handed me a spit cup.

Unholy hell, what a lovely way to meet someone. If I live through this, I'll never live this down.

"Are you in a lot of pain, can I get you anything?" His voice spoke with the kindness of a lover.

I shook my head *no* as best I could.

He headed into the bathroom and returned a few moments later.

"Sorry, I stood you up," I choked out.

Roxas chuckled and carefully dabbed at my mouth with a warm, wet towel.

"Can't say it was the first time. Truthfully though, the park was such crackers by that point, we might not have seen one another regardless."

He washed my face, my mouth, all while never taking his eyes off me. I wanted nothing more than to hide and go away until I was healthy again. The other side of me wanted to throw my arms around him again and pretend this horrible nightmare never occurred. I couldn't believe he was here in the hospital with me. Even if I looked like the Battle Kroc's leftover snack pak, he was still here.

I tried to sit up in my bed. "No, no. It's okay – don't try to move. You need to recover. Just relax, m'lady."

M'lady.

Even for as grotesque as I must appear, he still called me that. I reached for his fingers and looked into his eyes. "What happened?"

"Before I go into all that, I believe there's a little unfinished business between us." Without another word, he bent over and kissed me. I blinked at him. My mouth was terribly dry and I couldn't move. I squeezed his hand as more silent tears escaped my eyes. He reached up to my cheeks and wiped them away.

"There, it's official. We've just had our first date."

If there was any place on my throat where there weren't bandages, then he might have seen the heat blush creep up my face.

An abrupt knock sounded on the door and a man in a white coat walked into the room. My father entered behind him with Amicula. The room seemed smaller with so many people.

The energy shift left me frigid. The doctor with graying hair stepped forward. "You're one lucky young lady, Cheyenne. My name is Dr. Laren. I've handled your surgeries and wanted to come and check on you. You are healing up quite nicely, but overall you've lost a lot of blood. You've had a few transfusions, and we'll continue to administer them until your iron levels are back where they should be. We hope to get you up and doing physical therapy soon. Has anyone reviewed your injuries with you yet?"

I shook my head.

Roxas stood up and walked over behind the bed. "She just woke up a little while ago."

"Do you feel well enough for us to review this now?" the doctor continued. "You're looking much better today. Your color has returned to your skin. If you're up to it, we can get you something to eat tonight. Maybe even a sponge bath for tomorrow. Would you like that?"

I grinned in embarrassment.

Dr. Laren sat in the chair and looked me square in the eyes. "Okay kiddo – you've got quite a laundry list, but you are healthy so we're anticipating a strong recovery. You ready for this?"

Roxas reached over and wrapped his hand around mine. I nodded.

"All right. Your right ankle is broken, you've got a few torn muscles, ligaments, and tendons. They're going to take some time to repair. You're going to be immobile for a few days, so we can't get rid of your catheter. You have suffered deep gouges on your jaw and cheek. There seems to be ..." Dr. Laren broke off and glanced around.

My father nodded at him.

"There seems to be bite marks on your cheek and at the corner of your mouth," he continued. "We had to do some reconstruction surgery on your lower lip."

I took a deep breath and winced at the pain in my ribs. My right hand involuntarily touched my throat to feel thick bandaging, and that's when I noticed the splints on my other hand. My mouth seemed as if it were as large as the Egyptian pyramids pointing off my face.

"Needless to say, you're covered in abrasions, lacerations, and contusions. Does it hurt when you take a breath?"

I nodded.

"That's because you have several broken ribs. Micro-fractures we call them. They will heal in time, but until they do, I'm afraid the best we can do to is keep you wrapped up and hold your chest in tight. Of course, we will continue to monitor your threshold levels for your pain medication."

I looked at him hoping he was done.

"You've broken several metacarpal bones in your left hand, which look like defensive injuries." Dr. Laren laughed to himself. "Hate to see the one who attacked you."

My father cleared his throat again, and I was convinced I heard a growl from somewhere in the room.

Dr. Laren sat a little further out on the edge of the chair. "We're scheduling reconstructive cosmetic surgery for you to minimize any scarring after we get you a bit more stabilized."

I looked up at my Dad, and he smiled at me. Roxas put his hand on my shoulder.

"The good news is, your MRI doesn't show any signs of head trauma. With your physical therapy, you'll be back walking on that leg within several months."

Months? I can't wait that long to help my sisters!

Dr. Laren smiled at me. "I'll be straight with you, Cheyenne. You've got a strong support system here with your family. Be sure to keep them at your beck and call." He turned to my Dad and Roxas. "Now you two, don't be bringing her anything she can't eat. No sneaking in cheeseburgers or chocolates. She needs to heal, and bringing her goodies won't help."

Both of them looked down at their shoes.

My family.

Tears pooled in my eyes and overflowed onto my bandages.

"It looks as though you've been stabbed in the neck. You were incredibly lucky that this injury didn't damage your vocal cords. You might not have ever spoken again. We believe, in the throng of people trying to escape, you must've been stepped on by someone's high heel a couple of times, or you might've fallen onto some sort of stage prop. Fortunately, 911 got there in time to help you."

Got there in time? You mean put me on hold for pranking the police department. There will be a complaint about that after I'm out of here.

I looked at my father. "Did they catch the Red Man?"

"The Red Man?" Dr. Laren frowned.

"We'll talk about that after the doctor leaves." My father patted me on the shoulder. "Dr. Laren, other than the torn muscles, are there any internal injuries?"

"Not that we've seen on her." He looked down at me. "There were no signs of internal organ damage either, but if she's in this much pain tomorrow, we'll run an ultrasound to double check. I'm going to take a look and listen to your heart and lungs now. Are you comfortable enough? How is your pain management?"

"Hurts a lot. Can you give me stuff that doesn't make me sleepy?"

"Yes, we can – but we have to be careful to not let you have too much. We don't want to send you to rehab after being in the ICU." He laughed.

Nobody else did.

Dr. Laren cleared his throat. "Ah, yes. All right now, let's take a looksee at your vitals."

He expressed my heart was pumping just fine, and my lungs sounded clear. He told me to be sure to call the nurse if I needed anything, but to use the call button and try not to talk too much.

His information came at me just a little too fast for me to process it.

He continued to poke and prod as if I were my mother's sewing tomato-pin-cushion. My skin itched when he pulled on the tape for the bandages.

Another man walked in.

It was a freaking metro station in my room.

I realized he had a pitcher of water, ice, and a couple of cups.

"You go easy on the water," the doctor cautioned. "I'd rather you suck on ice chips at first. It's been several days since you've had anything down your throat. But despite your laundry list, you're doing exceptionally well. I think we'll move you out of ICU sometime tonight or first thing in the morning."

Amicula walked over to my IV machine. "I've adjusted the morphine drip to help counter the pain so you can swallow a little easier tonight, and hopefully not put you to sleep."

I glanced at Roxas and my father. I wanted everyone to leave except them so I could rest. I was done learning about me. I needed to know what happened to Dakota and Sheridan.

Chapter Sixteen

They moved me out of the ICU, and into a new room around midnight. After I finally got back to sleep, I was awakened to another hole poked into me. The dim overhead lights at least didn't barrage my eyes, but nonetheless, I hated being woken up every two hours.

"Good morning, Miss O'Cuinn."

A way too cheery Romanian-sounding voice greeted me - or was it Russian? I couldn't tell.

"My name is Cedric. I need to check on your blood shunt this morning and flush it out. We need to check your iron and hemoglobin count every couple of hours to see how the transfusion is holding up."

I glanced over at him with heavy eyes, and then at the clock – 6:58 AM.

"How are you feeling today?"

I cleared my throat. "Better, I think. Can I sit up today?"

"Let me get your nurse and see what we can do for you. Are you still in quite a bit of pain?"

I nodded.

"You've got muscles which were ripped off your bones. Sitting you up might require additional pain medication if you're not ready."

Boy, I can see why they keep this guy in the lab. Not much of a bedside manner.

Cedric's face seemed warm and friendly enough, almost angelic, but hauntingly familiar. For some reason, it no longer bothered me how he dug into my arm as I watched the blood pool into the test tube. Thoughts of yumminess flashed across my brain. I shook it off to not enough sleep and a perpetual morphine induced haze.

"After I get your shunt cleaned out, I'll need to get a couple more vials, and we'll be done here ... for now."

Why does he remind me of Sherlock Holmes?

Cedric filled the last two vials he'd placed on the bed and uncuffed my arm. "All right, missy. That is it for me for now. I will be back to check in on you in two hours and see how your iron levels are doing. Looks like your company is waking up, too. Would you like for me to open the blinds and let in some sunlight?"

I stared at him longer, trying to figure out where I had seen him before, and then nodded. It was if I had known him from a faraway dream.

Florida sunshine poured in the room and flooded me with warmth and hope for a good day. I closed my eyes, dreaming of another three hours of sleep.

I hope I get pudding today.

Roxas opened the door with a tray of breakfast and came over to my bedside. Cedric grabbed up his little tote of blood and Roxas turned to look at him. They stared at one another for a moment, and then Cedric turned and slid out the door.

I reached out my hand toward Roxas. "Hey."

He smiled back. "Hey, yourself. How are you feeling?"

"Cedric is going to get a nurse to come check me. I want to sit up this morning."

"You're sounding much better today. Are you sure you want to do this?"

I nodded and tried to take in a deep lung full of air.

"Okay, let's see what we can do to make you more comfortable."

Roxas glanced over at my Dad still sleeping in the recliner and raised his hand against the morning glare. "Wow – the sun is bright today." He set the tray on the countertop and walked over to me.

He stroked the hair out of my eyes. "Good morning, m'lady. Ready to run that zombie 5K you've been talking about?" He leaned in and kissed me on the forehead. He pressed his temple to mine and gave me a gentle squeeze to my shoulder.

I loved the tender way his touch tingled on my skin. I grinned at him sideways. I wanted out of this bed, and he knew it. Never one to call in sick myself, I always teased the guys that unless they were bleeding from their eye sockets, they couldn't miss work either.

My father woke up and waved on his way to the bathroom.

"I brought you a cup of Earl Grey, Kiernan," Roxas said.

"Thanks – be right there."

Roxas handed me a cup of water and then sat in the recliner he had positioned next to my bed. I remembered how he held on to my hand for most of the night after moving into this new room. Meeting him under these extraordinary circumstances, I prayed that what we had together was the right stuff that made relationships last a lifetime.

Tentatively, I swallowed a teeny sip and braced for the worst. It still hurt to swallow but nothing like yesterday. I took a deep breath and licked at my cracked lips. I took another tentative sip and savored the welcome coolness down my throat. Daddy stepped out of the bathroom, washed his hands, and pulled up a chair.

"With a touch of honey, right?" Roxas handed him the tea.

Daddy smiled and nodded. I gained my physiology from him. Brain functions and coordination didn't work right until caffeine surged through our veins.

Gawd, what I would do for caffeine right now.

"Who's feeding the chickens and watering my tomatoes on the roof?" I asked, trying to get my mind off of thinking about a nice brewed cup of java. Where was Padme when I needed her?

"You've got chickens and tomatoes? On the roof? Roof of what? Your penthouse?" my father asked.

I nodded noting the deep circles under his eyes.

"Isn't that against some kind of city ordinance?" he pressed.

I shrugged. "Figured if my hen-house was two hundred feet above any neighbor's yard, it would be okay." I heaved a deep breath. It didn't hurt as much to breathe today.

Roxas laughed and said, "Only you, Cheyenne, would build a chicken coop on your rooftop. Kiernan, wait until you see this hutch. It's like the Ritz Carlton of hen houses. She's got an air conditioning unit, flowing water, and natural green grass for them to roam. Never seen anything like it on top of a building."

I smiled at them. "Store bought eggs suck. I give the hens my salad scraps and the organic layer mash."

Roxas shook his head at me. "I checked on them yesterday, but they're probably going to need their feeder refilled today. Those are some egg laying fools. I've been crating them up and putting them in the fridge."

"Thank you." I couldn't believe how kind and considerate of my animals and wellbeing he had become in such a short amount of time.

Roxas excused himself to the bathroom.

"You feeling all right, Daddy?" I asked.

"I need to sleep in a bed for a couple nights, and I'll be okay. Taking care of you - that's the important thing."

The door opened and a huge bouquet of pink and yellow roses, fragrant with bright red lilies floated toward me. Closer and closer - until out popped Harris from behind the blooms. He nodded at my dad. "Mr. O'Cuinn, good to see ya again. Hey, Cheyenne – how ya doin', sweets? Man, you look like road kill."

My father cleared his throat.

"What did I say on our teleconference call? I tried to tell ya. This is what you get for hanging out in haunted houses."

I stuck my tongue out at him. The movement hurt to stretch my mouth and tongue, so I put them back where they belonged and reached for the ice.

"I got here as soon as I could after your dad and Roxas called and left voicemails. I'm terribly sorry, Chey, I didn't get here sooner. We'd all turned off our cell phones while we were out in the woods."

Always a bit nervous, Harris shifted from side to side. I could tell he had been pretty shaken up over not being here for us. Harris set the flowers on my bedside table and bent down to hug me. Before he stood up, he broke out into huge sobs after he looked at the bandages and machines hooked up to me and around the bed. My tears joined his as the ache in my heart over Sheridan and Dakota had every nerve raw and on edge.

"Oh, Cheyenne, I'm so sorry. I should've gone with you guys to Horror Nights. Maybe I could have ..." Harris ran his hand through his thick mess of brown curls and rubbed his neck. "I can't wrap my head around this whole ordeal. You, Dakota, Sher – you're like family to me. You're the sisters I never had. I don't know what I'm gonna do if anything happens ..."

Daddy reached out and put his hand on Harris' shoulder.

"I feel terrible about this, but don't worry – we're gonna get it all under control," Harris continued. He pulled up a chair, turned it around, and straddled it. "I've been in touch with Roxas, and he's been taking care of the servers. Briggs, he's wrapping up a few loose ends in New Orleans. He's trying to see when he can come down."

Roxas stepped out of the bathroom and washed his hands in the sink.

"You've met Roxas?" Daddy gestured to Harris.

Roxas walked over and offered his hand. "Live and in the flesh."

Harris stood and took a deep breath as he stared at Roxas. "No, shit, I didn't know you were here, bro."

They stood looking at one another for a moment. Roxas pulled Harris in for the bro hug. "Dawg, it's great to finally meet you."

Harris thumbed his hand back toward me and lowered his voice. "Ya know, she never shuts up about you."

I cleared my throat again and croaked out, "I didn't lose my hearing."

The door opened again. This time it was a nurse with a rolling cart. The room was getting smaller by the minute. "Good morning, Miss O'Cuinn. Ready for your sponge bath today? We are going to try and wash your hair if you're up to it. It'll help you feel a whole lot better."

I perked up at the notion of getting cleaned up a bit. "Yes, thank you. I would *love* that." I gave the guys a pointed look.

"All right, very well. My name is Ruthie Anne. Let me get set up in here." She waved her hands in the air. "Okay gentlemen, you heard the lady – shoo. She doesn't need your sappy faces hanging around while she gets all cleaned up. You'll have lots of time with her after I'm done. You can go outside on her balcony or wait somewhere else."

I liked her already. She had a no-nonsense, not afraid to push the beefy guys around type of attitude.

"There's a balcony?" Harris looked at the window.

Ruthie Anne laughed at him. "No silly, of course not. This is a hospital, and you need to go outside in the hallway, or sit in the waiting room. Shoo."

"Yeah – let's stand out here and give our Lady Caz some privacy." Roxas winked at me.

Halfway relieved they were gone and yet not removed from my view, I'd become increasingly reluctant for anyone I loved to leave my sight.

My eyes followed them into the hallway. The room door didn't completely close so I could overhear the guys talking while I watched them in the camera monitor toward the nurses' station.

I couldn't wait to get a sponge bath. I longed to soak in a deep, hot, bubbly tub. I smelled terrible, and could hardly stand myself. Everything itched under the bandages.

I ran my tongue gingerly across the front of my teeth and behind my lips. The damage to my mouth was still quite extensive, but I was dying for some mouthwash. "Can I brush my teeth?"

I'm glad there aren't any mirrors in this room.

"Sure enough, I've got a toothbrush right here for you. What flavor toothpaste would you like?"

Outside, the guys continued talking. "How the hell are ya, man? Damn, I had no idea you were so hairy," Roxas said.

"Hell, I had no idea you were so ... old." Roxas smacked Harris on the back. It was as if I were watching old friends reunited after years of separation.

"I've got bubble gum flavor, fresh mint flavor, and I might even have spearmint in here." Ruthie Anne pulled the privacy curtain, but I was able to see through a six inch gap between the wall and curtain. Ruthie Anne hummed to herself as she dug around in her cart of goodies.

Harris leaned up against the wall. "So what's going on with Dakota and Sheridan? What are the police saying? Any updates?"

I watched Daddy lean against the opposite wall in the hallway as he spoke to the guys. "No - the police have nothing. They can't figure out what in the world attacked those people in that haunted house. There aren't any traces of animals that were capable of doing the damage. They checked for cougars, bears, and even snakes and came up with nothing. Cheyenne keeps mumbling about the Red Man when she sleeps. She's had a terrible childhood nightmare that has haunted her all her life. She said her dream finally came true and it was a man who attacked and killed all those people, but the detectives aren't buying it. They said no one man could desecrate human bodies like that without tools of some sort."

Roxas inhaled a deep breath and stretched. "Other than the crime scene, does the park have any video footage of what happened? Any camera phones from survivors?"

"No. Nothing." Daddy shook his head. "It's weird, it's like it didn't exist. All they have are the 911 calls that came in from that room Cheyenne was in." Harris and Roxas looked at each other.

"Do you know when I can get this catheter out of me?" I jerked and winced at the pain when Ruthie Anne tried to move my leg to slip in a clean pad underneath me.

"You seem to still be in a lot of pain, Miss O'Cuinn." Ruthie Anne grimaced. "Mmm ... not sure, sweetie pie, we'll need to ask the doctor on that one. Most likely not until you are walking up and down the hallways for day or so. I'm sure you don't want any accidents with those big, handsome guys all around. Your doctor's orders list PRN - pain killer as needed. We're going to have to move you quite a bit and it has been over eight hours since your last dose. Do you feel as if you might need some happy juice?" Ruthie Anne patted my hand. "If not, we'll just let you get some rest and try again tomorrow."

"Ruthie Anne, you're a kick. I think you're right. I don't want to feel uncomfortable. Thanks for helping me feel human again. I hate the way I smell. This is wonderful of you to help me like this."

"All right then." Ruthie Anne typed into her tablet, and it didn't take long for the morphine vending machine to dispense my relief.

My father spoke again. "I'm really getting worried. Several more people have been treated and released from the hospital just to come up dead or missing a couple days later. The police are baffled."

"What do you mean, coming up missing or dead?" Harris asked.

"It's weird, it's like that movie where the kids who missed the airplane that blew up and then death came after them anyway."

In unison, Harris and Roxas chanted, *"Final Destination."*

Daddy nodded. "Yes, that's the one. I'm considering putting a guard here at Cheyenne's door and then at her house after she gets home. I can't have all my daughters missing."

"No shit, Mr. O'Cuinn?"

"Call me Kiernan, Harris – you aren't in college anymore. But yeah, no shite." Daddy leaned against the wall. "Thank the heavens you guys are here. I don't know what I would've done with the girls' company. I guess it would have had to just shut down. I know they would have gone nutters if that happened. They've busted their humps to turn that into the global business it is today."

Roxas touched his shoulder in reassurance. "Don't worry, Kiernan – we've been handling it. Please don't think another thing about it. What we need to do now is figure out a way to track down what the hell is actually going on. If the detectives are clueless, we can't just give up. If Sheridan and Dakota are truly missing, then we're running out of time."

Ruthie Anne gingerly took hold of my arm. "That's what I'm here for, sweetie. Now raise up your arm real careful like. I don't want to pinch any of your bloodlines."

Whatdya mean the detectives are clueless?

Harris dropped the volume of his voice, but I could still hear him as if he were standing right next to me. It seemed as if the attack had given me bionic hearing or something. I kept waiting for the Foley sound effects from the *Six Million Dollar Man* to come across the room every time my ears homed in on what they said. Their conversation had my stomach in knots.

"We should consider not leaving Cheyenne alone for the time being. Each of us taking shifts with her. She doesn't need to know what's going on."

Roxas nodded in agreement. "Yeah, you're right. We shouldn't take any chances." He crossed his arms over his chest. "There seems to be a bigger event going on, Kiernan. You're wise to stay on top of it like you've been doing."

Ruthie Anne hummed in a kind, grandmotherly way. Her calm sense of self helped me to relax a bit.

A long pause between words had me guessing the guys each were lost in trying to come up with any kind of explanation or lead.

Daddy stretched his arms over his head. "Okay, fellas, I genuinely appreciate your help. Keep your ears open and see if you can't find something on those online channel networks – forums or whatever you call them. Maybe somebody somewhere knows where my girls are. I'm thinking it might be time to go to the public for assistance since we aren't getting any leads from the police. I'm gonna go check on those tomatoes and chickens of Cheyenne's. Can we reconvene this afternoon? I'm already in need of a nap and a shower and I just woke up. Terribly knackered."

"You bet, Mr. O'Cuinn," Harris said.

"Anything you need, just let us know," Roxas said.

"Okay – I think I have your phone numbers in my phone."

"Here, Mr. O'Cuinn – Kiernan, let me program our numbers in for you real quick." Daddy handed his phone to Harris.

I tried to make out what the melody was as Ruthie Anne continued to hum. *Claire de Lune?* Frustrated at not being able to go to the bathroom by myself, or even get up out of the bed, I remained helpless to do anything productive to help find Sheridan and Dakota. Ruthie Anne's peaceful energy eased the tense and painful moments of my sisters disappearance, for just a little while. My eyelids grew heavy once again.

Handing back Daddy's phone, Harris said, "Okay – we're both in there. We'll see you this afternoon."

"Later then."

Daddy opened the door and called through the privacy curtain. "I'm gonna go check on your plants, sweetie. How do I get to the roof?"

I motioned to the nurse to let him in, so I didn't have to raise my voice. He popped his head around the curtain. "Daddy, there's a utility door from the kitchen pantry."

"Okay. I'm gonna see what I can do to salvage your tomatoes and then maybe catch a little shut-eye before going to the police station this afternoon. There's a meeting with the detectives. I hope they have found a lead. Love you, honey."

"I wish I could be there to talk to the detectives."

"I know you do, sweetie. I'll record the conversation and let you listen to it when I get back, okay?"

I nodded and smiled at him. "Hey, if they have ripened, just pick them and stick them in the freezer okay?"

"The detectives? I dunno if they'll appreciate much." Daddy winked at me and gave me a half smile. He turned to walk away.

I grabbed his hand. I said to him in the kindest voice I could muster, "I love you, Daddy."

He squeezed my hand. "Love you too, sweetie."

I squeezed back. He scooted out past the curtain, and out the door. The guys resumed their conversation.

Ruthie Anne tried to run a comb through my hair, but it got caught on a thick tangle over my ear.

Roxas gestured wildly towards Harris' body. "What the hell, Harris? You're a bloody werewolf?" Harris scratched his back. "How the hell did you room with Cheyenne in college for three years and she didn't know?"

What did he say? Werewolf? What? Didn't know what?

"I kept it hidden just like you, Vampr." Harris squared off his shoulders a bit and said, "What about you, Rox? Is that why you haven't bothered to meet her before now – 'cause she'd be a nice tasty snack?"

I watched in confusion, trying to understand the energy exchange between them, their words muffled by Ruthie Anne's humming and brushing. They stood looking at one another. If I didn't know any better, I would have guessed it was a posturing standoff between them.

Roxas finally broke the tension. "Listen. Let's just relax. We're still the same guys we were ten minutes ago, ten days ago, and even several years ago. We can work through this. There's no reason for us to raise species hackles just because that's what we've always done. We can use this to our advantage."

Harris leaned on the hand railing and relaxed his shoulders. "Yeah, all right. I suppose. Just wasn't freakin' expecting this, dude. I about went through her bed to get at you a few minutes ago."

"You?" Roxas laughed and then said, "I smelled you coming through the door a mile away." They both laughed. "I can still kick your ass, even if it isn't in the sim."

"At least now we have serious fighting power to get to the bottom of what the hell happened. If the humans don't have any leads, then we need to move underground to find out what the hell is going on."

"Why have several of these victims gone missing after being released from the hospital?" Roxas rubbed at his chin. "Why were Dakota and Sheridan taken? Seems a little too contrived for all three sisters to have random happenings. I think they were targeted."

Vampires? Humans? What the hell? These are some gooOOOod drugs!

Harris pulled out a piece of chewing gum. "Who or what wanted all three of them either dead or gone?" Harris offered Roxas a piece. "Want some? It makes your breath minty fresh and your teeth pearly white."

Roxas looked back at the door again and then back to Harris. Lowering his voice, he said, "No thanks – it sticks to my teeth. One thing I do know is that she's been bitten. I'm pretty sure those people were attacked by a rogue vampire. We've heard reports through the coven that a specialized team has been set up to hunt down any vampire neonates. But here's the deal. We haven't heard of any rogues attacking humans in decades. Why now? Why the O'Cuinn sisters?"

"It could be a werewolf." Harris added. "We've had new packs recently come up out of Central America – Belize area – they ain't too friendly."

"Bollocks. Could you find out from your pack master if they've had any trouble? Whatever it is, it's a supernatural or preternatural that has the ability to make deep puncture marks and rip human bodies apart. It's got to be exceptionally strong and hungry."

Harris hiked his foot onto the handrail and stretched. "Hmm ... we did have some werebears here lately, but that isn't likely. They're primarily herbivores."

Coven? Werebears?

I strained my ears to listen in closer, but sleep wasn't far off.

"Can you follow up on those leads? Anything is better than nothing right now."

"Yeah – I'll go straight there now – I need to check in with the pack anyway." Harris continued to rub at his calf. "Maybe they've heard news through the supe vine. We should crawl the forums in ExsanguiNation to see what the chatter is online. Oftentimes what's happening in the game, is truly happening in our reality."

Roxas nodded, "Yeah – I hate giving those weekly updates to Cheyenne in our meetings. It's real stuff going on, but the humans simply don't see it."

"Oh, shit!"

"What, Harris?"

"Remember what you said the other day about the werewolves abducting avatars for the vampire blood orchards?"

Roxas ran his hand down his face and held onto his chin.

Harris walked over closer to Roxas. "Dude, is that shit for real?"

I watched as Roxas paused for a moment. "Wait. Are you saying what I think you're saying?"

The guys stared at each other for a long while.

Roxas finally answered his question, "Yes, there is that possibility. As well as the fact that if Cheyenne received any of the blood from the rogue vampire, she could easily become ..."

Water rushed past my ears. "How are you feeling now, Cheyenne? Is that happy juice kicking in for you? I know you're gonna feel so much better after getting your hair washed, darling."

Ruthie Anne must have given me an extra strong dosage of pain killer because I had a Dorothy moment. I could've sworn I overheard the words vampire, werewolf, pack master, werebear, coven, and abductees in the same conversation between Roxas and Harris.

Morpheus knocked on my door again and held out a rose for me. Those cast iron skillets replaced my eyelids again. His arms beckoned me to fall asleep safe and sound in his protection.

Silly me, the guys must have been talking ... about ... the ... game.

Chapter Seventeen

"I simply can't explain it. I've never seen someone recover from injuries such as yours in a week, Cheyenne." Dr. Laren removed the last of my bandages. "I want to keep you one more night for observation. The hospital wants to document this extraordinary healing. I'm calling in a specialist to review your case to take a look at your skin. We need to make sure there is no underlying infection or an abnormal genetic mutation."

My eyes bugged as he scratched at his head.

"Joking. You aren't a mutant. You must have one hell of an immune system. There is hardly a scar on your face or neck. The MRI on your ankle looks as if it broke years ago, not last week."

"Oh, Doc, please ... I want to go home. I've got to find a way to help my sisters. Besides, I won't be alone. I'll have my father and Roxas with me. I need fresh air."

There's no way I was going to tell Dr. Laren how my crazy Red Man dreams have been escalating. He'd never let me out if I told him I cried rivers of blood now. He might even want to lock me up in the loony bin for a night or two, or forever.

"You can sit out on the balcony and get all the fresh air and sunlight you need, missy."

"Look, I promise to be careful and not run any tough mudder competitions this week. In two days, I'll be back for my checkup. Please don't keep me another night. I'm feeling magnificent. In fact, I feel stronger now than I have in years."

Dr. Laren glanced at me and then back at his tablet. "Let me review your labs again. It's medically unreal how this has occurred. I must take every precaution to ensure we didn't miss anything." He turned and left the room, still mumbling under his breath.

Roxas sat on the edge of the bed twirling my crutches. He looked up at me. "Well, m'lady – I'd be surprised if he lets you out today. It's crackers for you to have healed this fast. If I were him, I'd be triple checking your labs and calling in specialists myself."

I shrugged my shoulders.

"What do you want to do first when you get home? Rest in your own bed, go dancing, go for a sailboat ride?"

"Oh, hell no. Beano and I need to take a drive out to the coast and walk on the beach to clear out this fuzzy medicine in my head. I can't think straight. I know the answer to who or what took Sheridan and Dakota has got be on those camera feeds. They didn't just magically disappear out of the park. Cross referencing where they were at the time of my attack should help narrow the possibilities. Something, somewhere has to be documented with that many people dead," my voice lowered. "... and missing. I'll go to the police station first and talk to the detectives on the case, see if there is anything else I can do to help them. I'll even try hypnosis."

"It's going to be all right. Here, I brought you something to help you feel better. This'll make you smile." Roxas pulled out his mobile phone and opened up the picture gallery. "Check out this picture of Beano and Miss Priss."

With the bandages off my face, smiling felt good to stretch the muscles around my mouth and cheeks. "Oooh, that's adorable. I love the way she snuggles under his chin that way. Is that your friend Torchy?" I put my head on Roxas' shoulder.

"Yep. That's him."

"Are those his dogs? Black labs?"

"Yes, they are. Meet Ash and Soot – they're litter mates. Torchy's had them since six weeks old. Great dogs."

"Looks like Beano and Stormy are enjoying the company."

"All the more family to love, I say."

"Thanks, I needed that."

Roxas squeezed my shoulder and snuggled me in closer. "Listen, Cheyenne. As much as I want to, I can't stay long today. Do you want me to arrange to have another look out for you here in the room? The fact that several of the people released from the hospital have come up missing or dead – truly worries me. I don't want to leave you alone." He put the crutches on the side of the bed. "I need to follow up on the server crash from last night. We had one go down after midnight, and another one this morning."

"That's weird. Do you think we're being hacked?"

"I don't know until I get into the logs."

"Let me know if we need to upgrade our security protocols."

"The downed server caused a monumental lag on the vampire sim. Pissed off a few guilds. I need to check on their redundancy back up and make sure we aren't losing any of their virtual inventories. Briggs said a bunch of support tickets came in overnight. Harris and I are going to configure another server in the cabinet. You all right to hang out here for a while by yourself?"

"Of course. My dad will be here soon. By the way it sounds, I'm gonna be here another day or night. Dr. Laren seems hell-bent on finding a reason to keep me here."

"Better to be safe than ..."

"Yeah, yeah. Whatever."

Roxas grinned. "I brought you a surprise."

"You did? A cheeseburger?"

"Nope. Your laptop."

"You're a saint." I hugged him around the neck. "I can patch into the database with my remote access from here."

"Just so you know. The wifi is banjaxed everywhere in the hospital, so I brought you my network card. You'll have a stronger signal strength with this wireless hot spot."

"Thank you for thinking of me. I've been totally bonkers without anything to do except scour the news headlines. Thank heavens it isn't an election year." I leaned in to plant a kiss on his cheek.

Roxas turned his face and reached up for my chin. My heart raced. For the first time, my healed lips enjoyed his tender soft, warm fullness of his mouth on mine. Delicious.

"*A hem...*" My father stood in the doorway. "Looks like you're feeling much better today, Cheyenne."

I pulled back from Roxas and blushed. "Hi, Daddy. How are you doing today? You still look terrible. Haven't you slept?" I scooted off the side of the bed, grabbed him by the arm, and urged him toward the recliner.

"I've been sleeping more than I should," he said as he sat down. "Not sure why I'm so darn knackered. Just can't seem to keep any of my strength. Been taking my iron pills too. Maybe I'll just rest here for a few minutes."

"When's the last time you had your blood pressure checked?"

"Just yesterday at the drug store. Said my heart was fit as a fiddle." He pounded on his chest.

Roxas offered him a cup of water. "We're all under a lot of strain right now. I'm sure once you get home and settled with a guard at the house, he'll rest better." He turned to me and planted a smooch on my head. "Right then, I need to go. See you later tonight? I'll even bring you mint chip ice cream. The kind without the green food coloring."

"Nice!"

"What can I bring you, Kiernan? A blood transfusion?"

"Rightly so. I'll take two if you please."

We laughed, but his joke wasn't that far off the mark. A few years ago, he had to be hospitalized from severe fatigue. He claimed my mother was coming to visit him every other night. During that time, his blood iron count had dropped to dangerous levels. That's when we had to get him on anti-depressants to help deal with Mom's death.

"Sounds aces. See you tonight." Roxas wrapped his arm around my waist and pulled me in tight to his chest. I couldn't quite put my finger on what made him smell so delicious. I wanted to devour him. He kissed me again as I breathed in the spicy scent and watched him walk out the door of my hospital prison cell. Trapped like a bird in a cage. Free to move, but not able to leave.

Daddy was already snoring on the chair, and I grabbed a blanket to cover him. His face gaunt with fatigue as if he hadn't slept in days. I needed to check and see what vitamins he'd been taking, if any.

Normally, Sheridan, Dakota, and I took shifts watching over him ever since we lost Mom. With me having to recover and no one else to help take care of him, I'm surprised he's lasted this long.

***

Dr. Laren came into the room a few hours later. "All right, Cheyenne. I'm gonna go ahead and start your discharge paperwork. It might take several hours, but everything is in order. I'll have physical therapy come in and set up your appointments. I want to see you at the end of the week. I'm also bringing in a photographer. We're going to record your progress and compare it to the night you arrived."

My face held more delight than a child eating off her first pair of chocolate Easter bunny ears. I hugged him. "Thank you for everything you've done to fix me. I can't explain why I healed so fast either. I guess I have strong genes."

Dr. Laren glanced at over my Dad. "You need to get him home and into his own bed for a while. Take good care of him ... and yourself."

"I will."

I texted Roxas to let him know that I had been released. Dad and I left the hospital, with me wearing my little bootie cast. We loaded my gifts, cards, and flowers into the back seat, started the car and cranked on the AC. For November, the heat in Orlando was still scorching. It should have started to cool off a bit by now.

"Hey, Cheyenne. I hate to ask, but do you feel well enough to drive? I'm not real sure I can stay awake to the end of the block."

I stared at him, bit at my lower lip, and furrowed my brow. "C'mon Daddy, let's get you home and get a bowl of Mom's chicken soup in you. I've got a batch in the freezer I made a few weeks ago."

Driving home, I thought about everything that had happened in the past week. Last Friday I was getting ready to have the most exciting night of my life, and this Friday, I was leaving the hospital after the worst night of my life. It was time to get things straightened out and learn the truth about what happened to all of us and why.

Chapter Eighteen

I drove home without a hitch in my bootie cast. Never thinking my parking space would be a welcome sight, I pulled in and nudged my dad awake. "C'mon big fella – let's get you upstairs."

We hobbled to the elevator and took the fifteen story ride up to my penthouse. I pressed my thumb against the scanner panel and heard the gentle snick of the lock tumblers opening the door.

Even though I knew no one was home, I still called out to Beano, "Momma's home." As soon as I got him back, life would be close to what it was before the attack. After getting my dad settled I went outside to check on my tomatoes and chickens. They had done a terrific job of keeping everything watered. The chickens didn't have a care in the world. Critters fed and watered, I collected their eggs and thought about dinner.

My mind raced with ideas about what to do or what to eat. I couldn't decide if I wanted to go for a swim, cook squash, go rock climbing, take a nap, bake cookies, or run a marathon. My body wasn't cooperating with my head. I was ravished and ready to fall asleep at the same time. I checked the fridge for something to eat, but the only things in it were spoiled hummus and wilted celery. Checking the freezer, I pulled out a vacuum sealed bag of my mom's chicken soup and left it on the counter to thaw. I needed to go to the grocery store, or we were destined to study take-out menus for the rest of the night.

I went back into the living room to find my father snoozing on the loveseat. "Daddy, I'm going to the grocery store," I whispered in his ear. "I'll be back in a few minutes." I patted him on the shoulder and pulled Mom's quilt over his lap.

"I need to tell you something," he mumbled without opening his eyes. "Can't remember ... your mother ..."

I straightened up. He frequently mentioned Mom in his sleep. Every now and then he would wake up cognizant insisting she was visiting him. The doctors told us to humor him and help him feel more comfortable.

"That's okay, Daddy. You can tell me later. I'll be back soon."

"*Hrmpffh* ... tired ... sleep ..." He moaned a few more inaudible Gaelic words and fell back into his snoring cadence.

I made a mental note to get him multivitamins.

Grabbing my keys, sunglasses, and my purse – I headed out to the grocery store. With my favorite staples in the cart – peanut butter, yogurt, almond milk, and a rotisserie chicken – I considered a bottle of tomato juice on an end cap. Not something I would normally purchase, but for some reason it looked good. I craved something, but I just couldn't figure out what.

I turned down the sweets and crackers aisle, to find what I craved. I instinctively reached down to grab a bag of spicy hot Cheetos for Dakota and loaded them into the cart.

Then it hit me.

I burst out into chest heaving sobs right in the middle of the cookie aisle. I leaned down on a shelf, put my head in my hands and just bawled.

How am I ever gonna get through this? I can't lose my sisters like this!

"Are you all right, ma'am?" Someone handed me a tissue.

I looked up. He couldn't have been more than sixteen. Sweet, young, and genuinely caring. I shook my head.

"Oh my God, lady, your eyes ... they're bleeding. Did you fall on something? Are you okay?"

He held out a hand for me. I grabbed it, stood up, and wiped my eyes with the tissue. I blinked at seeing the bright red blood on it.

"Ah ... it's okay. I ... I just had out-patient surgery. I'm sorry, I was just leaving." I quickly checked for a name on his blue shirt as I continued to wipe my eyes.

He handed me his tissue pack. "Are you sure you're okay?" He gave me a sympathetic smile.

"Yep! Sorry again, Mario. Thank you for the tissues." I walked away, slid the sunglasses down over my eyes, and pulled my hair out of the ponytail holder, letting the curly mane fall to cover my face. I pushed the buggy toward the checkout while wiping my cheeks.

After loading my groceries into the trunk, I turned on the car and sat in the air conditioned driver's seat. I checked the rear view mirror for any more blood.

Unholy hell, my tears are blood? This is just like in my dreams. This is seriously not right. I need to check in with Dr. Laren.

Suddenly a wave of exhaustion washed over me, and it was all I could do to keep my eyes open. I didn't want to sleep in the parking lot – I needed to get home. *Now.* Perhaps I should have stayed in the hospital for another day. Maybe Dr. Laren was wrong about me being healed after all.

I hope I can make it home.

***

The dreams continued to haunt me every time I slept. Again, I saw the mask of the face in the shadows of my mind. That elusive corner the light barely touched to cast the shadow. Darker than the blackest night, the movement in the pitch continued to stalk me – always waiting. The visage of the killer in that haunted house, the one who pursued me kept coming back to take what was rightfully his. Finally, a beacon of light and his face formed in front of my eyes.

Bewitching, the Red Man covered in life-giving blood, emblazoned on my visual cortex time and time again. Never smiling, always looking lost, scared even, and then begging me for help.

Each night as I slept I became compelled to keep moving forward – to find my prey just as he did. I would awaken with bloody scratches on my arms, my faced bloodied from the tears, exhausted and often still sleeping in my clothes. I knew my dreaming had escalated to handle the post-traumatic stress from the attack, but things seemed to be getting out of hand. It became apparent how I could no longer understand the difference between my dreams and real consciousness. Then who was I to determine which one was real in the first place? The only thing I knew was the hunger. The dreams were most vivid when my blood sugar dropped below the danger zone, and I was ready to pass out.

The next night I found an easy target, a young couple making out down by the boat dock at Fairview Lake. Tall industrial fences bordered the old, abandoned Gulf Breeze restaurant to keep out the riff-raff, but it was well-known as a hot make-out place for adventurous teens on the weekends. Okay – so I once was one of those wild, adventurous teens, I knew it would be easy pickings.

Thoughts of cover up flashed through my mind. Maybe I could dump their bodies over by the cove marina. Would that be an easy disposal out into the lake? I didn't care. I needed to eat. To drink. Starved from the inside out, an unknown heritage powered me on, and ordered me to feed it.

The teenagers' hearts thrummed, pounding to the sexual acrobatics in the backseat. I focused in on them. Light flickered from a nearby electric pole, illuminating their naked bodies in the backseat of the car. Half of the light had been shot away leaving a tangled, dangling mess of luminescence.

The incense of sex drifted over the night's sea breeze. Driven by my unknown needs and the scent of their sex, I became desperate to drown in their life-giving blood. It beckoned me closer. I knew, at that moment, above all else, I needed to consume those kids just as the Red Man devoured the mermaid.

In a heart wrenching attack, I watched as the slow motion movie unfolded before my eyes as I killed and consumed the two lovers and secretly desired more. With my stomach distended, I sat on the bank watching the bloody waves break at my feet, unable to understand my actions. Why would I dream the need to consume their blood in order to survive? I wiped my mouth with the back of my hand and licked my fingers.

That weird feeling came over me again. I didn't have any way to explain it other than to call it the *overwhelmings*. It was as if my mind clouded over and I would pass out. Morpheus invited me into his arms once again.

I woke up to the splash of the lake water on my face and the sound of the fog horn. Spitting out the lake water, I pushed up onto my elbow, my clothes and hair soaked and matted in brackish, bloody goo. I dragged my wet self up to the shoreline and looked around. Seeing the lifeless bodies in the car, I knew what had happened — again.

The overhead lamp flickered with a faint red hue. I looked down at myself and realized why I must've been in the water. I stared at the crimson stains on my shirt, my hands, my everything. I tried to wash the kids' pedigree off me, but it stained under my fingernails and around my cuticles. Irrationality set in. I wondered when I could feed again. An evil grin sliced across my face while my heart fell into further recesses removing all emotion from my killings. More – I needed MORE.

I stood up and carried lover boy over to his car and set him by the rear tire. I realized it was Mario, the young man who had helped me inside the grocery store.

What have I done? Why would he be in my dream?

Straggling around to the driver's door, I opened it and popped the latch on the truck. After loading Romeo-no-more into the trunk, I grabbed Miss Chickadee, who couldn't have weighed 100 pounds drained, and I threw her into the trunk with him. As I stood looking at their vacant expressions, I wondered when this nightmare was going to end. Normally by this time, the freakish dream would have ended right after the exsanguination, but this time it didn't seem to be fading away.

I looked at the bodies of the kids sprawled below me with their throats torn out of their necks. I felt no pity – only wished they had more blood to offer me. Humans, somebody's daughter and son – no longer. I had drained them faster than a rain gutter during a hurricane and wanted more.

What the hell is wrong with me? I just ate these kids! Why do I consistently dream I have become a blood-thirsty monster?

Knowing I should be waking up, I instinctively reached out behind the small of my back to pet Beano and reassure myself that all was still right in the world. Only this time, he wasn't there.

Something grabbed my outstretched arm and calmly said, "We need to talk."

Instantly I spun around, a low hiss caught in my throat as I crouched defensively. Amicula stood poised with an arched eyebrow high into her forehead.

"Are you done with the hijinks?" she asked.

Confused, I simply stared at her.

What in the hell is she doing in my dream?

"What's going on?" I murmured, more to myself.

"It's quite simple actually. This is not a dream. Nor have any of the other killings you have been leaving around for us to clean up."

"Killings? You mean there are more of … of those?" I pointed to the dead kids lying in the trunk.

"Here's the Cliff Notes version, Cheyenne." Amicula let out an exasperated sigh. "You, my dear, have been bitten by a vampire. Your natural hunting instincts have kicked into overdrive."

I took a moment to consider her words, but they didn't make any sense. I stammered, "Hunting? Vampire? Instincts?"

Amicula simply nodded.

"Wait. Weren't you my night nurse?"

"Boy, you're a quick one tonight!"

"Listen, just give me a little more morphine, and I'll get over this stupidity soon enough."

Chey, you need to wake the hell up!

Amicula took a couple steps closer to me and I retreated.

"Yeah sorry, guess I can't do that anymore since you're not in the hospital."

"What?" I shook my head trying to make sense of this craziness.

"It was my job to make sure you were fed the blood diet while you were in the hospital. However, when that idiot doctor discharged you early, we didn't have time to reach out to you properly. We've had to track you down for the past couple of days. You've left quite a trail behind you."

"What blood diet?" I looked at Amicula as if she'd lost her mind. Those teens must have been high on bath salts or something in order for me to cook up this delusional concoction. "Couple of days? No – you've got it all wrong. I just went out to go get my dad some vitamins." My nightmares had never been this long or unbelievable.

"We've been watching you to understand how you might handle your first days on your own." Noting her impatience with me, I watched as Amicula shifted her weight to her other foot. She continued in rather a bored tone, "You're failing miserably."

Rubbing my temples, I tried to shake myself awake. I didn't know what to say to this absurd nonsense, but somewhere in the back of my mind a true note rang out.

"You've had your fun. Your feedings will become fully conscious soon. I can already see how you're questioning what's going on."

My hands itched from the sand. I wiped them on the back of my jeans to get the muck off me.

"Sweet as this little scene is, Cheyenne, I need you to come with me, or the coven will have no choice but to exterminate you."

I took a step toward the bank and away from Amicula, even though I was a bit shaky on my legs.

"Where do you think you're going?" Amicula asked.

"I ... I have to get back to my father. He's expecting me."

"You left your house over forty-eight hours ago, Cheyenne. Your father is in trustworthy hands. No harm will come to him if you come with me."

Amicula clicked a button on her shirt. I heard a man's voice speak to her through her dark blue blouse.

"Go ahead."

"I have her," Amicula said. "She just fed and is conscious. Where do you suggest I take her?"

"Bring her to the marina. I will have assistance for you at the lower entrance," the voice replied.

"I need you to send the abstergers out for clean up," Amicula continued. "It's quite an untidy little mess she's created, again."

I gawked at her.

What the hell does she mean, again?

"They've already been mobilized. Bring her to the Resurrection."

Chapter Nineteen

The Resurrection

We arrived at a yacht named the *Resurrection* not far from the docks where I had murdered and consumed those kids. When we arrived, my clothes were stripped off me. I expected the worst. To be tied, bound and gagged. Holed up in a cargo bay with rats. Instead, what I found was a Jacuzzi tub bubble bath awaiting me. I was asked to clean up before meeting a Lord Stovall.

Pretty confused, I finally opened my mouth to gain clarification on all the details Amicula had explained on the ride over. Despite the odd circumstances, the luxurious bath was welcomed. "Okay, so let me get this straight. I was attacked by a rogue, unregistered vampire at Halloween Scream Nights. I spent one week in the hospital while you fed me a blood diet of more vampire blood. I healed as fast as I did because of the amount of vampire DNA I ingested during my attack. Plus to top it off, you've been watching me murder and eat people to make sure I could take care of myself?" I pursed my lips. "So, bottom line is, I either choose to stay a vampire or I am to be exterminated?"

"Well, yes. That about sums it up, Cheyenne. Great to see you've been paying attention. Here's a scrubby to get under your fingernails. Oh, and you have a glob of yuck up by your ear. Be sure to get that when you wash your hair." She handed me a wash cloth.

"How do you expect me to make this kind of decision without understanding the full ramifications?" I looked at her as any sane person would look at Cthulu. "All I want to do is go home. I still don't believe this is even happening. I am most likely dreaming this madness and should wake up any moment with Beano at my back, or I'm in the hospital having a lousy reaction to the morphine."

Amicula looked around the room. "This doesn't look like the hospital to me. Cheyenne, you drove yourself home, remember?"

"Look, I appreciate cleaning me up, but I don't have time for this. I need to get home to my father and to find my sisters. They're missing from that night I was attacked."

"Yes. We are well aware your sisters are missing." Amicula made a *sit* gesture with her hand. "Scouts are in place to help you find them. I assure you, however, as tragic to your humanity as this change is, you are very much Vampyre now. You must make this decision if you want to help your sisters. Otherwise you'll be dead. And, last time I checked, being dead isn't exactly helpful to others."

"How long am I going to be held here?" I settled into the soapy water and used the soft cloth against my skin. "My father is sick, and I need to take care of him."

"Don't worry about your dad. He's being taken care of right now."

"Is he all right?" I sat up abruptly, splashing water onto the tile floor. "If any of you have hurt him, I'll –"

"Relax, wait a minute, don't eat the last chip in the bag. He's fine." Amicula held up her hands. "We needed him to be safe while we talked you through this business. So rest assured – he's doing quite well. Do you want to see?"

I sneered at her but nodded.

Amicula pulled out her smart phone and streamed a live shot of him sleeping in Dakota's bed. "See, check the date and time. He's been given sedative doses to help him not remember. Soon this will be settled. You'll be assigned a pedagogue and be home to cook his supper. Albeit, a couple days later, but he won't miss a thing. He might feel a bit confused when you get home."

I bit my lower lip.

Amicula sat at the vanity and brushed her silken, black hair. "You see, Cheyenne, now that you know the Vampyric people exist, you need to know how to handle the lifestyle change and learn to control yourself. Right now you are endangering yourself as well as the rest of us by feeding and hunting on humans the way you are. There is a much safer way to obtain the sustenance you crave. If you continue, it's a simple matter of time before you're found out by the authorities. If that happened, then there would be no choice but to eliminate you. Such a waste, don't you think?"

I swallowed trying to contain the bile in my throat. I sat blinking at her again. It seemed as if all I did lately was sit and blink at people. My mind weighed her argument, and I tried to understand the situation.

"So, technically, if you want to live and find your sisters, this *is* the better way."

My choices sound like a death sentence no matter which direction I choose." Anger grew deep inside my gut, twisting me in more knots than a sailor's rigging. "Why did this happen to me? I don't understand. Aren't vampires supposed to be dead? Dr. Laren said I was alive and well. My heart is beating. I can feel my pulse right now under my thumb." I lifted my arms up out of the water, my right index and middle fingers on my left wrist. "I'm breathing. How in the world can I be a walking corpse?"

Amicula stopped brushing her hair and refocused her eyes to my reflection in the tub. "This is the most common question I get. It was Hollywood who told you that vampires are the undead. It is true, however, but that undead business does not occur until the vampire experiences the undeniable death. The true death. If you're lucky, that won't happen until much later in life."

"You're saying I am some kind of living vampire?"

Amicula nodded. "Of course, we're all viable until we meet the undeniable death. But until then, you can consume normal human food and drink. However, you must feed the vampire DNA coursing through your veins, or you'll go rabid insane. You'll find a balance in your system in a few weeks. Human food might not be the most appetizing right now, but soon you'll start to appreciate and experience flavors as you've never known them before. You'll be amazed at the delicacies of the foods you've been eating and never knew how fantastic they were."

"Is that what happened to the rogue vampire who attacked me?" I sank back under the suds. "He tried to go without human blood?"

"Mmm, most likely. He probably had an attack of conscience and decided to go vegan. Now you've seen first-hand what that can do to you. Your body must consume human blood. Cow blood, or any other form is acceptable, but your cellular structure isn't bovine. Cow blood won't support your human cells. You must have the human cellular structure to support your vampyric host DNA."

I nodded. "So, no mountain lions or antelope will do it, huh? Bears, maybe?"

Amicula actually smiled a genuine smile in her reflection. "You were one of the lucky ones in that attack, Cheyenne. We had to dispose of quite a few people who were injured by the rogue vampire. They either couldn't accept the possibility of what had happened to them, or they didn't get enough of the DNA to change them. A couple of the victims even begged us to kill them because they felt they were an abomination before Christ and would never be able to return to their lives."

"What happened to them?"

"We obliged with their wishes of course."

My jaw dropped. "Of course."

"You, however, despite the natural tendencies for hunting humans already, are managing quite well. And there is this business of your missing sisters, isn't there?"

"What do you know about Sheridan and Dakota?" I shot straight up out of the water. "Where are they? Are they all right? Have they been turned into vampires, too?"

Amicula lowered her palms again, motioning me to sit down and relax. "We'll help you find them. No, we are not aware of any further changelings. You were the last one to leave the hospital."

I grabbed the shampoo bottle and sat back down in the water.

"Truthfully, Cheyenne, no one expected you to leave because of your extensive injuries. But somehow you managed to get quite a lot of vampire DNA blood in your system. I must ask you about that sometime."

Memories flooded back to me like a melting glacier. "You were my nurse. You know where I live. What else do you know about me? Is my life no longer private? Am I in your vampire database now?"

"First. Tonight. You need to meet Lord Stovall and understand the covenants of the local clan." Amicula stood from the vanity and opened a cabinet. She pulled out what looked like a brandy decanter and a couple of glasses. "If you decide to remain vampyre, then you will be assigned a pedagogue to help you in your first few weeks of acclimation. All of your questions will be answered. I promise."

Amicula opened the second cabinet door and removed what looked like a bottle of dark juice. The crack of the seal sent instant pleasure to my nose.

"Is that what I think it is?" I asked as I moved in the water toward the massive tub's edge.

Amicula turned to face me.

"Mm – hmm." She poured the blood into the cognac and offered me the glass. "Would you enjoy a taste?"

My mouth instantly salivated and my hands shook. Meth addicts had stronger control over their bodies than I did at that moment. She held the glass close to my face. I grabbed it with wet, soapy hands and raised it up to my mouth. I hesitated.

"It's okay. Your body will digest the cognac as long as the blood is included." She gestured for me to drink.

Still not entirely sure I bought this whole idea, I watched Amicula drink the same concoction she had made for me.

I downed it. I smacked my lips savoring the extraordinary heat and intricate flavors of the cognac melding in my mouth. The wood casks, caramel exploded across my taste buds. Delicious. The brandy warmed all the way down and didn't make me sick to my stomach. I held out my glass in request for a refill. Amicula smiled and obliged.

After four more shots of my new favoritest drink, I considered my options while questions poured into my brain. Shampooed, conditioned – I stood up again and rinsed off the bubbles. Amicula handed me a warmed towel as I stepped out onto a plush white rug over the Crema Marfil tile. I stole a couple seconds to take in the beauty of the boat. I'd never been inside a yacht before, let alone in a tub on one. The sleek, streamlined design of the ship's features screamed old money. Everything beautiful in its own right. I asked the first question weighing on my mind.

"I thought vampires were all powerful, all mighty except in sunlight. If I'm truly a vampire, then how come I can go outside and not become a pile of ashes?"

Amicula chuckled. "Really now, you do watch way too many movies. That is so cliché and so *Interview with a Vampire*. Depending on your maker's dynamics, you may be better suited with more solar resistance than others. We do manage to keep a few sunscreen companies well-funded, however. I suppose that's why we purchased them. Oftentimes, newborn vampires require quite a bit of sunblock intervention. Obviously the rogue who attacked you must have quite an affinity for sunlight because you aren't sensitive to it."

"I'm still not entirely convinced this isn't a nightmarish dream." I thought about this for a minute. The rogue vampire who attacked me. Why me? The scaredy-cat, afraid of haunted houses, turned vampire?

A knock sounded at the door. A man's voice said, "Dinner will be served in thirty minutes."

"Thank you. We'll be ready," Amicula chimed back.

I wondered if I was the dinner. I towel-dried my hair. "You're telling me I need to meet this Lord Stovall. Is he like a vampire King or something?"

Amicula laughed out loud. "Oh dear gracious, no. Far from it. But he is required to follow in the reign of the Vampyre, under Queen Civetateo. Just so you know. We call ourselves vampires, but our family name is spelled a little differently. So when you are referring to us as an entity, we are Vampyre, with a y in the spelling. The same goes for vampyric. Not sure why. The Queen's English, I believe."

I nodded, trying to take it all in.

Amicula opened a door from the bathroom into an en suite. She disappeared and left me to wait for a minute in front of the ornate vanity. I noticed the skin around my mouth and neck. It looked as if I had never been attacked. Not a flaw on me. Even that silly red mole up in my hairline was gone. I tentatively smiled at myself trying to unravel the insanity of the situation.

She sauntered back through the door, put the cognac away and closed the cabinets. "By the way," she asked with a knowing gleam, "Have you had any weird dreams lately?"

"That's an understatement. You know I have. You woke me up from those nightmares yourself while in the hospital. I lied to the hospital shrink about the dreams just so I could get out of there."

"I thought so."

As I relaxed in the subdued deliciousness from my drinks, the 'reality' of my situation sunk in.

"I've laid out clothes for you in the next room for you to wear this evening."

"Thanks." I sipped my bloodcognac.

"Amicula, are there others like me? Who survived that room?"

"Many were killed that night outright from the amount of blood he needed to consume. In essence, his cells were starving from the abstinence. Some, like you, were bitten with a large enough amount of DNA transfer. We've had to track all of you down to either complete the change or call out the abstergers."

"You mean there were more humans than just me who were bitten and survived?"

"About five or so have cropped up now."

"Is that why victims were coming up missing after they were released from the hospital?"

"Unfortunately, yes."

"So it wasn't that they were in danger, or a serial killer was after them?"

Amicula nodded. "We hope there aren't many more to crop up. We've had reports around Tallahassee and as far as Jackson, Mississippi but the clans have been successful at capturing the sucklings."

"Sucklings? Is that what you call us?" I crinkled up my eyes in question. "Exterminated - because they didn't want to become a blood sucking monster?"

"We didn't ever get the chance to ask them." Amicula picked up the brush and began to pull it through my red curls. I looked puzzled at her reflection. "You see when a vampire is born, they usually cannot maintain any control over their feeding habits and are often in a fugue such as you were when I found you. After the Halloween attack, the clans banded together to find any sucklings and bring them home for care and education. A couple of the newbies lashed out at us while being captured. If the Vampyric Lady or Lord did not see that the candidate would be an appropriate fit to the clan, then he or she was slated for elimination, or simply removed from the gene pool right then and there." After a delay, she quietly added, "Oftentimes a suckling could not survive the changes in their bodies or minds." A sad expression washed over her. "They can't deal with it. Whether they wish to die or not, all too often, it is by their own hand which forces the decision."

She stared at my hair with a faraway expression in her eyes, still as a stone, hairbrush in mid-stroke. Not quite sure how to respond, I reached for a robe draped over a chair.

Amicula animated back to life. "What have you decided?"

"Is there a checklist to fill out to see if I qualify? I don't want to die, but I'm not sure about this whole vampire thing either. I don't get it. I feel fantastic, but I'm dead. How am I going to be able to see my family and friends, my dog? Am I going to want to eat them? What about my job?"

With what seemed like sincerity in her voice, Amicula plastered on that practiced hospital smile I knew all too well. "You already have better faculties about you than ninety-five percent of the ones who were bitten. I don't anticipate any problems with your new lifestyle. Your assigned caretaker will help you adjust to this new life. Not an awful lot will need to change, especially since one of your dynamics allows you to be in the sunlight. More than anything, you'll need to learn how to manage your appetite and fly low under the radar. Vampyre have been doing this since the dawn of mankind. *The Vampyric Canons* actually state that mankind were placed here for the Vampyric race to feed upon. But somehow Lilith and Adam couldn't figure out how to make it work, and Cain took over. But that is entirely an altogether different story."

I thought about her words.

Whoa - humans were placed on the Earth to feed Vampyres? I can't think about this right now.

I shook my head and dropped the towel. My reflection in the gilded mirror revealed no scars anywhere on my body. I was stunning. My eyes drifted to Amicula's reflection. "Why can I see us in the mirror? What happens with my life now? Do I have to live in a towering castle, wear tight leather pants, and chase werewolves or something?"

Amicula fell over the bench in a coughing fit of laughter. "Now that's one I haven't been asked before. Absolutely hilarious. You're certainly one to keep around just for entertainment, if no other reason."

"Glad to keep you in stitches. So your job in this coven is the local vampire welcome wagon lady. Instead of delivering flowers and cookies, you deliver sucklings to your Lord?"

Amicula stopped laughing as her eyes flashed fire at me. "Tsk ... tsk ... there's no need for snarky unkindness. I appreciate your frustration. All your questions will be answered by *The Vampyric Canons.*"

Not satisfied by her answer I opened my mouth to protest. She held her hand up to quiet me. That sickening sweet smile returned. "Just so we have complete transparency between us, Cheyenne. It was my decision to allow your life to be spared."

I swallowed hard and looked toward the floor. I sat on the vanity seat not sure of anything anymore. Had I just insulted the woman who saved my life?

Lovely.

Chapter Twenty

The clothes Amicula had left for me on the bed couldn't have fit better if they had been custom tailored. Obviously wanting to have fun at my expense, she'd given me a pair of black leather pants and a halter top. All I needed was a katana and a long black leather coat and I'd be that chick in my favorite books. The silk lining allowed the leather to glide on and not cling to my skin. In Florida, it's was too hot to wear anything like this. Just now thinking about it, I realized I hadn't been either hot or cold since I woke up in the hospital.

Someone knocked on the door. I heaved a deep breath and opened it. A tall man with raven black hair as straight as a pharaoh's stood in front of me. His eyes emanated a verdant glow. He looked at me as if he'd seen a ghost. Tall, dark, and pharaoh opened his mouth and then closed it. He stared at me. I looked at him, turned my head behind me, and glanced around the room. Was there another person who had caught his attention?

Finally, he cleared his throat. "Good evening. My name is Khaldon Seters."

Even though I was wearing high heels, he towered over me.

Why did every woman I know insist on making me wear heels?

I stared up at him. "I'm not on the menu tonight, am I?"

"Not that I'm aware." His face softened. "However, things do tend to change at a moment's notice around here."

Butterfly nerves fluttered through my insides. I had a sudden urge to run to the bathroom.

"Please, Miss O'Cuinn, follow me. Dinner is ready." Khaldon offered his elbow. "We don't want to keep Lord Stovall waiting." His eyes were mesmerizing as if he could see right through me. For all I knew – he could.

Still unsure if I was the guest or the meal to this dinner party, I walked alongside this Egyptian god. My fate was yet to be determined. Perhaps I might become both if I didn't roll the dice in my favor.

Would I be deemed acceptable with this crowd? Would they eliminate me if I piss them off somehow?

The cozy dining hall didn't seem too ominous. No hanging chandeliers, no gargoyles in the corner, or blood fountains hanging off the walls. In fact, it looked nothing like what my simulation developers made their gothic castles out to be. The yacht had a normal nautical flare complete with fishing nets, buoys, and starfish hanging in nets on the wall.

Khaldon guided me to a seat next to the head of the table where a man in khaki cargo shorts was sitting. Amicula sat next to him across from me on the other side. I looked at the guests. Most everyone had on normal Floridian attire. Shorts, polos, even flip flops. I was the only one in high heels and tight leather pants. Several other people, or vampires – hell I couldn't tell – seemed amused at my appearance. I became hyper-aware Amicula might not be one to trust regardless of whether she saved my life or not.

As Khaldon drew out my chair, the male vampires stood. The entire table sat after I was seated. This came across totally surreal. I mean, who did that anymore? I liked it, but had never been in a position to experience it firsthand.

"My dearest, Miss O'Cuinn."

A man whom I guessed was head of this clan turned to me.

"My name is Lord Stovall, and these among you now are my high counselors. No need for names until a decision has been made on your part." Stovall gestured with his hand down the table.

I looked at each person and greeted them with a courtesy nod.

"Please, let us enjoy our meal," he continued. "You are acquainted with Amicula. You've met Khaldon. I take it your treatment since coming aboard has been accommodating?"

"Yes. Thank you for your kindness and generosity."

That sounded lame. I just want to get on with this and get the hell out of here.

"You have been an odd case for us, Miss O'Cuinn. Amicula has been in charge of the Interspecies Human Relations unit. That's why she was at the hospital as your nurse. She needed to watch over you while you made your transition."

I nodded and tried to smile at her, secretly wanting to strangle her with these leather pants.

"Khaldon is currently a member of the abstergers team, but his specialty is in computer technology. I understand you're a computer software programmer, correct?"

I nodded and looked at Khaldon.

"You two should get along handsomely." Khaldon gave a sheepish shrug.

That's like saying just because we work on computers, we must know everything Google and be lifelong best friends.

"Thank you, Lord Stovall." I nodded at Amicula. "I am very gracious for your hospitality and ... um ... clothing."

Khaldon tried to hide a smile under his hand. Amicula sat back with her arm draped across the back of chair next to her.

"If I may, Lord Stovall, I have made my decision. I have two sisters who are missing since the night I was attacked. I want to live, regardless of what new capacity, in order to find them."

"Excellent! Now we won't need to eat you." Stovall's voice boomed as tensions seemingly lifted in the room.

That could have been my own nervous perceptions. My eyes felt as large as silver dollars at his last statement. I looked at Khaldon. He shook his head at me and grinned. I shrugged my shoulders and returned his smile.

Stovall clapped his hands. "Let the meal begin."

I heaved a huge sigh of relief. Large trays filled with cheese, fruit, and vegetables were set in the middle of the table. Steamed baskets of crawfish and fried catfish were placed in front of each of us. Our glasses filled with iced tea, water, or wine. No blood anywhere that I could see.

"What's the matter, Cheyenne, are you not hungry?" Lord Stovall spoke with a piece of French bread half in his mouth. "You looked confused, my dear."

I looked at Khaldon and then at Amicula and then finally back to him. I leaned over closer, hoping only he could hear me. "Well, to be honest, I kind of expected – more blood."

"I told you she was blunt." Light chuckles and small titters of laughter were almost drowned out by my 'friend' Amicula's hearty laugh. "She's pure Hollywood cliché, let me tell you."

"You see, my dear, we do crave and require a certain amount of human blood every day. A diet of only one course is unhealthy over a long period of time, no matter what species you are." Stovall picked up his tea. The ice sparkled in the glass. "And to be honest, it is dreadfully boring to have only one food source. We need nutrients from all the food groups as they are now known, for our bodies to thrive and not simply exist."

I looked at Khaldon for a hint of truth from Stovall's words. He picked up a grape and popped it into his mouth. He bit, chewed, swallowed, and smiled. I grinned at his warm-hearted humor.

"In fact, one of the most common myths about vampires comes directly from a diet consisting solely of human blood," Stovall continued.

Khaldon added to the conversation. "We learned our susceptibility to any direct sunlight occurred when our ancestors succumbed only to the blood cravings. Our varied diet allows a moderate amount of exposure to ultraviolet rays. If we are malnourished, we can be reduced to almost mortal qualities with too much solar exposure. We live but do not necessarily thrive as well as we do at night. That being said, normally there is a blood chalice at each setting. A dessert, if you will. Everything in moderation."

Servers appeared carrying an ornate chalice for each person seated at the table.

A younger man filled the cups from a great amphora. My mouth sucked in the saliva which had pooled in between my cheeks and gum. Here was the blood I had been waiting for.

After each chalice had been filled, Lord Stovall stood, followed by everyone else. He turned toward me. "We have to observe certain formalities. Cheyenne O'Cuinn, you who have become Vampyre, must now make a choice to live or perish. Do you wish to live, learn, love, and embrace your immortality? Or do you wish to be set free from the confines of this existence?"

Immortality? I hadn't even thought about that.

My sisters were still alive – I could feel it in my guts. If it meant staying alive forever, I needed to do everything I could to save them. I squared my shoulders and stood taller in my heels. "Yes, I accept this new life and will embrace my immortality."

Lord Stovall drank deep from his chalice. Then he handed it to me and invited me to drink. I looked at Khaldon and Amicula. Khaldon encouraged me to accept. I took a deep breath and closed my eyes. With a swallow, I bound my agreement with immortality. I licked my lips. The most delicious crimson silk coated the inside of my throat plunging it deep into the depths of my soul.

More, I want more.

The blood tasted like pomegranates. It was the most remarkable flavor I'd ever experienced. I drank deep, gulping swallows. Not very ladylike I was sure. I heard laughter from all around me. Satiated, I brought the chalice away from my lips. Everyone at the table cheered. We enjoyed the rest of the meal full of succulent crab, lobster, shell fish, and fruit. I ate and drank as if I never would enjoy such a meal again.

Thank the gods and goddesses they didn't make me sacrifice a virgin or something.

As we stood up to leave the table, Lord Stovall turned to me. "I've decided that Khaldon here will be your pedagogue."

Amicula gasped in shock.

Stovall raised his hand to quiet her objection. "Normally, I assign a same sex tutor of sorts, but yours is quite a unique situation, Miss O'Cuinn, which may require an additional skill set, so to speak."

"I would be most honored, My Lord." Khaldon bowed and then stood taller than I had seen yet.

I nodded at the two men who just determined my fate, still not sure what all this pedagogue business was about. I just hoped it had something to do with more comfortable clothes.

Stovall walked us upstairs out of the galley and onto the bow of the boat. A brilliant sunset with red blazing hues crossed the sky into orange melding into a deep indigo. The sun would be below the horizon soon. We sat on chaise lounges. Stovall lit up a cigar and offered me one. I declined but instead picked up a chocolate truffle offered to me from a crystal tray. An explosion of amaretto, almonds, caramel, and blood oranges danced in my mouth. Never had chocolate ever tasted so divine.

"Pretty good, huh?" Khaldon laughed at me.

Grabbing another chocolate before the tray went away I moaned in delight answering his question.

"Your sisters." Puffs of smoke circled Stovall's face and head. "What do we know of them?"

"That's just it, we don't." I licked my fingers. "The police are stumped.

Clueless. They weren't in the same place where I was attacked in the theme park. As far as I know all three of us were in separate locations."

"That's odd. It's as if each of you were set up," Khaldon said. "Do you know of any reason why you would be targeted?"

"No. Not at all." Shaking my head, I asked, "Have you had any reports on humans being taken anywhere by these rogue vampires? How many of them are out there?"

"We have not," Stovall softly spoke. "Truthfully, we do not have many rogues in this area. They tend to live out west. Most rogues do not bother a soul and simply want to live their lives in peace - away from any current political climes. There have been whole families who wish to be left alone." He leaned forward and placed his elbows on his knees. "However, our dear Queen Civetateo," Stovall pointed to Amicula who was gazing into the water, "Amicula's Auntie, does not concur. She wishes each and every vampire be accounted for and under her rule."

"Where is this Queen?" My eyes darted over to Amicula. I whispered to Lord Stovall. "Does she live on the same planet as us?"

"That's rich. Now we're vampires in space." Amicula laughed at loud. "What movie is that from, Cheyenne?"

Obviously, there was no such thing as a private conversation around vampires. She seemed to have the same sense of hearing that I possessed.

"1985 *Lifeforce*." I held my head up high. "Vampires in space arrive in London and infect the planet. It starred Patrick Stewart."

"Seriously. I was joking." She chuckled again, but this time a little more guarded, while others looked at her.

"Look it's okay if you want to make fun of me, dress me up in *UnderWorld* clothes, whatever. I'm thankful you chose to save my life, but truthfully right now I don't give a rat's ass how much entertainment value I am." I stood up and faced Amicula, mimicking her practiced smile. "I need to locate my sisters and take care of my family. That is all I care about."

"Here's what we'll do for you, Cheyenne." Stovall stood up and looked pointedly at Amicula and then back at me. "We will make every concerted effort to determine if your sisters are with vampires. If they are not, we will help you flush out the human scum to rescue them. We cannot pretend they are still alive. You must be ready to face whatever predator may be holding them. If I were you, I would ask Mr. Seters here about learning a few of the finer vampiric arts to help you understand your new dynamics."

I gave Stovall a puzzled look, but he responded, "There is much for you to learn, Miss O'Cuinn. Please keep in mind – we are also your new family."

Set in my place, I listened.

"I've made the right decision. Khaldon here will assist you on your journey and hopefully can help you uncover your sisters' whereabouts. There's a big storm coming up out of the Gulf tonight. Looks to be a doozie."

Our time on the boat drew to a close when Stovall put on a windbreaker and boat shoes.

I gave a head bow to him and reached out to his arm, "I didn't mean any disrespect. Thank you for your kindness and hospitality. Am I free to go now? I'm anxious to get home to my father."

"I've seen to his safety. But yes, you should go now. We'll be in touch when we learn more about what is going on in the area. Communications will be issued to learn if other clans have unregistered activities."

I smiled at him. My heart full of joy, I stepped toward him and wrapped my arms around his neck and planted a kiss on his cheek. "Thank you for not killing me. I don't understand why all this happened, but you've helped me feel closer to finding my sisters than anyone has."

"Not to worry, Khaldon here will take you home." Stovall seemed taken aback and waved his hand. "He needs to know where you live so he can keep a close watch out. Good night, Miss O'Cuinn. Take care of yourself. I'll be in touch."

***

It wasn't until Khaldon had us parked at my penthouse that I allowed my guard to stand down, and took in another deep breath. I sat in the passenger seat and didn't move. How was I going to face my dad?

Khaldon broke the silence first. "I'm not going to lie to you. It'll take a while before all this sinks in, Cheyenne."

I just stared at him.

"You okay?"

I shook my head. "I don't want to lose control and attack my dad or something."

"All right. C'mon, let's get you settled. Your father will be fine. You consumed a considerable amount of bloodwine at the dinner. You should be well satiated for a few days."

"How often do I need to consume? I don't want to kill any more kids like that." I popped open the car door handle. Anxious to get out of these pants and heels, I wanted to throw on shorts and a hoodie. "I'm conflicted. I feel terrible for killing those kids, but in other ways, it doesn't bother me as much as it should. The human side to me is experiencing serious difficulties and disgust with this. The vampire side is completely indifferent to it. I'm not entirely sure what to do right now. Are you supposed to stay with me until I can be trusted?"

"No. Not necessarily. But I can if you want." Khaldon put a hand on my shoulder. "I'm sure you have a ton of questions. I can help smooth some of those over if you like. But as far as the feedings go, no vampire is perfect. Many prefer live feedings over the bloodwines. I'll show you how to find solace in dealing with your human emotions, and a better way to obtain your live blood, so you don't have to kill anyone. Believe it or not, there is a whole human underground network which has devoted their lives to vampires. The movies aren't always wrong." He winked at me.

My key snicked in the deadbolt and prompted me to scan my thumb print into the digital reader. The internal lock tumbled away as the door opened. I turned my head and looked at Khaldon. "How did you guys get into my apartment without me? The locks are programmed for four digital prints. None of you had access."

"I believe Amicula took an impression of your thumb print while you were in fugue. We needed to make sure everything was all right at your house."

I made a mental note to change security to a retinal scanner.

I opened the door. "Daddy? Daddy, are you here?" I dropped my keys onto the foyer table and walked through the house from room to room. I came back and saw Khaldon looking at my commissioned Steve Hanks painting. He put several bottles of bloodwine on the table.

"Maybe he's in the shower?"

I walked into the living room and found a note on the coffee table. It read:

Cheyenne,

Harris took me back to my house in Clearwater. I hope you're okay. Please call me when you get home. Thank you for letting me sleep. The shrimp spaghetti was delicious.

Love- Dad

A voice greeted me as Padme's hologram walked around the corner from the kitchen. Khaldon stepped backwards.

"Good evening, Cheyenne."

"Amazing! Did you – is this your program?" Khaldon stared at Padme and walked towards her.

"Yep – that's one of my first prototypes," I nodded. "Padme, please welcome Mr. Khaldon Seters."

"Good evening, Mr. Seters, it is very nice to meet you. Can I offer you a refreshment?"

"Please, call me Khaldon, and no thank you." He stared at her and poked his finger through the holographic image.

"Careful, she might bite."

Khaldon quickly retreated his hand as I laughed at him. Handing him the note, I asked, "Someone cooked for my father and he thinks it was me?"

"Yes, to him you weren't really gone. His memories think you've been safe and sound here at the house. He believes you went out for a walk with Beano on the beach."

"How is that possible?" I checked inside my office. Nothing seemed missing.

Khaldon followed me in and fingered the fabric of the blue 3D holo-rendering suit hanging up on the coat rack. He stretched it out to look at it and then gestured to me to explain.

"Oh, that. I design online role-playing games. That's a motion capture body suit."

He nodded and released the fabric and followed me out of the room. "How we manipulated your father is one of those topics we'll need to discuss. It's called mind messaging. You use it when necessary to help erase, absolve, or manipulate the humans around you in case something odd happens."

Puzzled, I looked at him.

He continued to look around my house. "Have you ever driven to work and wondered how in the world you got there?"

"Yeah, I did that several times going to class in the morning. It wasn't until after first period chemistry that I even recalled getting to school in the first place."

"Exactly. We can do the same thing when needed. It's a simple suggestion for memory alteration. Things will be a little fuzzy for him, but as soon as he hears from you, everything will be right as rain."

"Padme, please dial my father's phone."

"Cheyenne, would you like to call his cellular or land line?"

"Try both."

Sure enough, after the second ring Daddy answered the phone. He was home in Clearwater and thanked me again for a lovely dinner. He said he was going to go back to sleep.

Dammit – I never got those multi-vitamins to him.

He proceeded to tell me that the vitamins had helped. I walked into the kitchen and checked the fridge. My groceries had also been put away. I told him I would see him in the next couple of days but to call me if he heard anything about Dakota or Sheridan.

"Padme, end transmission."

"You see, everything is as it was. Your dad is all right." Khaldon walked around Padme's holographic image still mesmerized. "Damn, Chey – this is unreal."

"Okay – so everything's right in the world. I still feel violated that all this has happened, and y'all trampled over my life to cover it up. I need to contact a few people and let them know I'm all right. I'm just really weirded out right now. I need some time to get myself together."

"No worries. Look, I'm only a few minutes away in Kissimmee." Khaldon had picked up on my hint. "Call me if you need anything." He reached into his wallet and handed me a green card with just a phone number on it. He thumbed his fist toward my kitchen. "You want me to put those bottles in the fridge for you or do you want them at room temperature?"

"Dunno." I turned the card over in my hand. "I hadn't thought about it. I haven't had it cold."

"It's great over ice and with a little lemon-lime spritzer on the hot days." The silly grin returned.

"Gourmet bloodwine huh? I guess one day I'll ask how that is made." My mouth betrayed my thirst while my stomach roiled in flip flops. "I think I have an idea, but right now I just want to go to bed and not think about it."

"Fair enough. You've got my card. I'll see you tomorrow regardless so we can go over *The Vampyric Canons*. Get some rest." Khaldon smiled at me.

It was an awkward moment. Was I supposed to shake his hand, give him a hug, or something?

"Yeah, okay." I decided motion was the best thing. Thunder pounded the pavement as we exited the building. He left in a gentlemanly fashion and didn't make me feel uncomfortable in any way.

"Looks like the rain gods are going to deluge us tonight. Drive safe."

Khaldon looked back at me and waved.

Did I really just tell a vampire to drive safe?

I lay in my bed wrapped up in my Hello Kitty blanket and thought about what I needed to do next in my life. Harris and the guys were taking care of ExsanguiNation, so that left me free to find out more about what happened that night I was attacked.

Coming to grips with my new life would take time. More than anything I wanted to know what rogue vampire could have done this to me and why. In fact, the more I thought about how he bit me, drained me, poisoned me, and left me for dead with the rest of the casualties, it downright pissed me off.

Thankful to be alive, in whatever capacity, I vowed to find this rogue vampire and kill him at whatever cost to my soul.

Chapter Twenty One

The Penthouse

Even though I was exhausted, I couldn't sleep. I didn't feel safe knowing Amicula had been in my house.

"Padme, please change the front door security fingerprint verification to left hand ring finger."

"Scanning – please wait – uploading the change sequence," Padme responded.

"Okay."

"Cheyenne, please initiate the manual override protocols."

I typed into my master alarm console and reset all entry codes. I felt better knowing no one else could get into the house now without the additional security codes in place.

I grabbed my laptop and checked my email, and chat mailbox inside the game platform. I looked for any word from Roxas since he'd left the hospital room on the day I went into fugue. I still can't understand how I blacked out for so long and not even know it.

I dialed his number again, but with no luck. He didn't answer his mobile, the office line, nor was he logged into the ExsanguiNation portal. I couldn't find him anywhere. I left him a message on our intranet, hoping nothing had happened to scare him off. I understood a lot was going on in my life. I couldn't halfway blame him for not wanting to get any further involved.

"You have a phone call from an unknown origin," Padme announced.

I wondered if Roxas had to go home to Egypt or something. Without so much as a "Hello" from the other end, I said, "Thank goodness. I've been so worried about you. Where have you been?"

"I appreciate the sentiment, but have you found your sisters yet?" A vaguely familiar voice returned over the line.

"What? Do you know where they are?" I reached for the bedside table to steady myself. "Who is this?"

"I know a great many things about you, Miss Cheyenne O'Cuinn." The voice chided me from the other end of the line. "I'm Dakota's boyfriend, Ludovic. Remember me? I sat next to you while we watched *When a Stranger Calls* on movie night with you and your sisters just two weeks ago."

"Ludovic, are you okay?" My throat squeezed tight. Still not comprehending, I choked out the only words my brain could produce. "Where is Dakota? Have you seen Sheridan?"

"Don't worry about me, my pet. Your precious sisters are well taken care of. But if you ever want to see them alive once again, you need to follow my explicit instructions."

Lightning struck outside with pounding thunder seconds after it.

"Wh-What?" I tried to wrap my mind around his words. "What have you done with them?"

"Isn't it obvious?"

"No. Nothing has been obvious to me lately." Blackness tunneled in across my vision. I choked as if there weren't enough oxygen in the room. "Where are you, and why are you doing this to us?"

"If you want to find your precious Sheridan and Dakota, you need to login to ExsanguiNation. Go find the haunted barn by the cornfield. Do you understand, my pet?"

"What does the game have to do with this?" I ran my hand through my hair frantically pulling it out of my face.

"Everything! You have one hour to find it and follow the instructions. If you don't find it, then you'll receive body parts from Fed Ex to your condo."

Afraid of what he might say next, I gulped. He knew where I lived. Vampire or not, I wasn't safe anymore. Maybe I never had been.

"Okay, okay I'll be there. Where is the haunted barn? I've never programmed a barn in the game."

"Of course you haven't, idiot, I did."

"What the hell are you talking about?"

"Tut tut tut, that's no way to talk to a fellow vampire now is it?"

My eyes grew wide in horrific understanding.

"Cheyenne, GC 89 – we're alive!" Dakota screamed into the phone.

Bile crawled up out of my stomach and creeped into my throat as my hands covered my face.

"Please, hold." The phone filled with oldies Muzak.

As fast as Dakota's voice emerged, it was gone again.

Oh My God – they're alive! Did I hear her right? GC 89? What does that mean?

I jumped out of bed and paced back and forth in the room. The hold music turned off, and Ludovic came back to the line.

"Please let me talk to her. Please don't hurt them." I cried into the phone, "I'll do whatever you want. What do you want, money? Just give me till tomorrow afternoon and I'll get it."

"Thank you for holding, Miss O'Cuinn. I don't need your money. I want you in exchange for your sisters. Be at the red, haunted barn in one hour or you'll live with their deaths on your bloody hands the rest of your pathetic existence."

My mind raced for comprehension. It had been a little over a week since the attack and Ludovic was just now contacting me. How does he know I'm home? Are there any cameras in my house?

I'm bugged!

"Padme, awake!" My computers instantly came online. Logged in into the portal, I typed 'red haunted barn' into the search field of the game. No results returned. Shit. Shit. Shit.

"Padme, mute!" I thought for a moment, "Padme, are there any external cameras added to the system? Any hidden communication or transmission devices?"

"Scanning. Negative. I detect zero unauthorized sensors."

"Padme, unmute."

"Ludovic, how did you know I was home?"

"Wouldn't you love to find out, my pet?" His voice slimed over me.

"There aren't any haunted barns coming up in the search engine parameters."

"Have you checked for any external worlds that aren't on your simulators?"

"What? You hacked into my game? You fecking ... hacker ... you."

"Tsk tsk tsk. Such foul language from a lady. Keep it up and you'll lose another ten minutes."

"What do you mean lose another ten minutes? You said I had an hour."

"You've taken enough of my time today. To answer your question however, good news travels fast through the vampvine. Oh, and one more thing. Don't bother calling your dear father or the cops. If you're not careful, even more loved ones will be joining your sisters. Goodbye, Cheyenne."

The phone went dead.

"Wait! What? Hello, hello? Ludovic!"

Dammit!

"Padme, run a reverse lookup on that number and dial it back."

"Locating."

Lightning crashed again as sheets of rain pummeled the windows. The palm fronds on the trees outside looked as if the wind were at least a hurricane Cat 3. The power inside the house flickered on and off.

"Unverifiable."

Dammit to hell!

I grabbed my cell phone off the charger and called Harris. He was the only person I could trust.

Damn voicemail!

"Harris, call me back as soon as you can. I've been contacted about Kota and Sher. Please call me as soon as you get this!"

I paced back and forth a few moments.

Breathe. Use logic to figure this out. You can do this.

Okay, so what did I know?

Ludovic knew I was home.

I'm not bugged.

He knew my house line.

Dakota and Sheridan are alive.

Dakota yelled out GC 89.

Ludovic hacked into my game.

I grabbed a picture frame of my mother and hugged it to my chest.

THINK!

Who can help me track this guy? I need another hacker.

I swallowed hard and pulled Khaldon's card out of my pocket.

I sure hope he plays video games.

Khaldon answered on the third ring. "Cheyenne, is everything okay?"

"How did you know it was me?"

"I don't give out this number to just anyone."

"No, everything is not okay. I just got a call from Dakota's boyfriend." Khaldon's calm voice pushed me over the edge. "He's the one who kidnapped them. He's holding them hostage."

"Okay. Hold tight. What can I do to help?" His voice was smooth and collected.

"He wants me to play, inside my game, to find a haunted barn where I will find further instructions. I was hoping you could track server side to determine his location. I have less than an hour to find it, or he said he would start sending body parts in the mail."

"I'll be right there. The storm has erupted into a torrential flood of biblical proportions. I'll get there as fast as I can. I might need an ark to get there."

"Hurry. Please!"

"In two shakes of an umbrella."

I hung up on him and went back to my command center. Determined to find this psychopath I checked again to look for Roxas online. Neither he nor Briggs was logged on.

Dammit to feckin' hell! Where is everyone tonight?

I tried the search function again in the game, this time from the navigation bar in the advance tools section. I turned off the debugging features to fade through any online chatter and looked for anything termed haunted. Haunted house, haunted mansion, haunted tree, haunted shack, but nothing with barn. Then I tried just barn and all its synonyms. Shelter, shed, stall, stable. Over a thousand entries for the words. I even got a result for the screaming shack. Someone must have built a wizarding university sim.

A few minutes later, a knock pounded at the door. I flew through the house, praying it was Khaldon. I checked through the peep hole and let him in.

"Thanks for coming so fast." I closed the door behind him. "He said he's vampire. His name is Ludovic. My sister Dakota was dating him. He's been here to my house. He's watched movies with all of us. I'm sure they thought nothing about being at the park with him. They wouldn't have suspected he was a Nosferatu, let alone a kidnapper."

Khaldon left his umbrella in the hallway stand. He shrugged out of his overcoat and hung it up in the foyer closet.

"Okay, take a breath, Cheyenne. Relax. Remain calm." He placed his hands on both my shoulders forcing me to look him straight in the eyes. "We'll get to the bottom of this. Did he say anything else? Did you hear anything in the background such as water, sirens, or anything?"

I snapped my fingers. "Yes, I heard Dakota shout out to me. She said that they're alive and a number. GC89."

"GC89? What does that mean?"

I shook my head. "Knowing her, she's trying to tell me something about where they are."

Khaldon looked at the painting again. "This is nice. Where on earth is this?"

I blinked at him a couple of times.

"That's it, Khaldon. A clue." I clapped my hands. "She's telling me where on earth they are. Dakota is referencing one of our geo-caches!"

"Geo-cache? You mean like treasure hunting?"

"We use to make them all the time. Now most of them are virtual."

Khaldon squinted. "So where is GC 89?"

I shook my head. "I dunno. I never recorded them the way Dakota did. I wonder if she has a notebook or log file where they're listed."

"Come on, we can talk about this in a minute. Let's get me logged on. What game are we playing?"

I showed him my office. "Our company gaming portal – ExsanguiNation."

"You gals run that company? Are you serious? I love that game."

"Excellent. Glad you are familiar with it." I smiled at him despite the circumstances. "That saves us a lot of time."

"Do you have anything stronger we can mix with that bloodwine?"

"I've got tequila and Crown, I think. Why?"

"Hold on tight. I think you're gonna need the extra shot of inspiration tonight.

Chapter Twenty Two

Khaldon suggested shots of Crown with the bloodwine. I grabbed the bottle and two glasses.

"You wouldn't by chance have any O Positive stashed away?"

I looked at him. "Nope – fresh out. It's not like I've been to the local farmer's market and picked up a couple pints lately."

"So, ExsanguiNation is your brain child? I love that RPG. I play it all the time. It's so much fun to watch humans trying to be vamps and werewolves. Gives new meaning to playing with your food. Give me a minute to boot up and we'll hop in."

"Playing with your food? Gah – Khaldon that's gross."

"Perhaps, but I was born this way, so to me it's all the same."

I handed him a glass of the good stuff and poured a double for myself.

I questioned giving him root access to our MySQL database, but there wasn't enough time to set up specified file permissions. I could always change the passwords later.

"Okay, Khaldon, try scanning the externals or see if you can identify anything that looks out of the ordinary. We don't allow any subscriber's peripherals to run on the simulators, so that is most likely what he's doing." I ran back to my seat to resume the searches.

Khaldon turned to look to me, "What's your Avatar's name so I can friend her?"

I typed in the public chat window. [My Avi's name is Lady Cazenove]

"Okay – got her – sending over the friend request now. You want to meet at a central place in the sim?"

"Yep – I got ya, but let's search separate sections inside the simulator databases. Hopefully we'll cover more ground."

"Sounds like a plan. Just relax, we'll find it. Could Dakota's reference to GC89 be relevant inside the game?"

"I'm not too familiar with her own personal sim environments, but that is definitely a great place to consider if we don't find this haunted barn." I looked at the atomic clock on the wall. "We have only twenty-five minutes left."

I logged into the game portal with my other consoles under different avatar accounts, each searching a different set of keyword values. I continued to run searches for the haunted barn, GC 89, and any parallels that might help make an association. "If you need to export the data finds, we'll use a pivot table to filter out any extraneous data."

Desperate, I continued to search, broadening the parameters to include synonyms of the words red, haunted, and barn. I tried synonyms of both the verb and the adjective meanings. Words such as obsessed, frequent, besieged. Nothing but gibberish came up in the results.

"Khaldon, are you seeing anything relevant in the peripherals?"

"From what I'm looking at over here, there aren't any barns, especially nothing haunted. I have found some haunted cornfields though. I wonder if this guy is using an external hard drive to run this file."

I peeked at him over my monitor. "Ludovic would've had to have access into the mainframe. But how would that be possible? Our servers are on 256 bit encryptions. We have the same security as NASA. There's no way it could be hacked. Unless ..."

"Okay got it, there's a barn here in the haunted cornfield. The script is running under a cloak. It looks as if the barn is by an ancient, abandoned silver mine in South America. You ready for the virtual transport to my location?"

"Yes, send it." The first real lead, my fingers felt frozen to the keyboard.

"Unless what?" Khaldon steered me back to my think out loud moment.

"Unless Dakota was showing off one night and gave Ludovic access from her console."

"Oh bloody hell. That would be serious bad!"

"Yeah, seriously, not good." I chugged my Crown and blood. My mind raced to compartmentalize this epiphany. It was as if my brain was set on defrag and just opened up an immense amount of space inside my biological hard drive.

"I swear, if I get her out of this mess, I'm immediately changing her password!"

I clicked on the invite sent from Khaldon to the simulated environment where the barn was located. My monitor screen instantly went black to the space realms during the transport. My avatar, Lady Cazenove, virtually teleported onto another area on an external simulator. It was one I had never seen before and realized Khaldon was right. We must be playing on Ludovic's hard drive. Lady Caz landed with a thud on the external simulator.

"Khaldon, are you coming with me?"

"In a minute. I'm trying to work out a reverse IP on this external. If we can locate it, then we can find your sister's geo location. Then we can go kill the bastard in real life, real time."

"That sounds way too easy."

"Ever watch that TV show *World's Dumbest Crooks?*"

"Okay – you've got a point. I'm spawning at your location."

Inside the game simulator, Lady Caz walked along the dark woods. The ground seemed mushy, and it felt like her feet dragged through boggy mud.

"What's the deal with the lag here? I can barely move. I don't see anyone else here on the map with us to cause such a slow down. We shouldn't have anything on this sim to slow us down," Khaldon asked.

"No, I don't see anyone else either. I checked the simulated environments overhead and underground before I walked to this point, and it was clear of obstacles. Ludovic must have written a script to slow us down intentionally. Let's try turning off our automation overrides and see if that makes any difference."

We both shut off our animator overrides -AOs, the scripts that allowed us to walk with a normal gate within the game. Without AO's, we called it the duck walk. We waddled toward the barn at a frustrating snail pace.

I checked the clock. We had only ten minutes to get in and get the information. We finally reached the barn door. As soon as Lady Caz's hand touched the handle, a horrific scream blasted out over the speakers. Not just any scream, but Dakota's crying scream. Uncontrollable tears ran down my face as my hands shook from the shock.

Khaldon jumped up from his chair and came over to see what was on my monitor. We watched as my avatar rolled the hanging barn door off to the side. Lady Caz grabbed the lantern hanging on a rusty nail and lit it. Punching a hole in the utter blackness, I gasped at the sight revealed by the light. No amount of horror, scary movies, or haunted house research could have prepared me for I saw behind that door.

"Unholy hell ... NO!" I stood up and held onto my face. "Khaldon!"

He grabbed my shoulders behind me.

Inside the barn were rows upon rows of women, tied up and shackled into body harnesses. They were imprisoned on their bellies hooked up to milking machines, their breasts pumping milk into stainless steel container vats. Many of them were prone inside hammocks with their swollen pregnant bellies ready to bust.

I couldn't talk. I stood there with my hands over my ears mimicking *The Scream* by Edvard Munch. I could only stare at the horror of what I saw in my monitor.

"What kind of sick bastard is this guy?" Khaldon squeezed my shoulder.

I moved my avatar forward, looking at all of the women trying to see if any of them were Dakota or Sheridan. There was a yellow lamp light at the far end of the barn. I continued to walk Lady Caz past rows after rows of these helpless women. Another scream set my hair standing on edge. Sheridan's crying, begging voice erupted out of the speakers. I outwardly cried, my hands shaking so that I couldn't control the keyboard to move my avatar.

Khaldon sat down in my seat and pushed the arrow keys walking Lady Caz forward for me. We came up to a support beam holding up the roof of the barn. Attached to it was a piece of a parchment nailed to it. It read:

If you want to see the O'Cuinn sisters
before you meet at the pearly gates,
then it's time to Exsanguinate.

Khaldon moved my avatar around to see if there were any other clues in this barn. We tried speaking to the women. They all seemed catatonic. None of them responded. Their names on the clipboards had been fuzzed out. It was if the script scrubbed out their names on purpose, making the visual animation blurry. The constant sloshing chug of the milking machines pierced through the silence. A light came on about twenty feet from where Lady Caz stood in the barn.

Khaldon looked up at me. "Do you want me to move Lady Caz over to the light to get a closer look?"

I took a deep breath, holding my arms around my waist now, and nodded. He cautiously moved my avatar forward to the other side of the stall where the light illuminated the pitch night.

Nailed to another beam, we found a graphic picture. A real picture of Sheridan inside one of these cocoon contraptions.

"Oh my God! No!"

Naked, she looked unconscious, but she had an IV tube in her arm. Utterly defenseless. A hooded man stood between her legs, erect and holding her hips. I cried out at the sight of my sister's torture and rape. My hands flew to the monitor to try to block out the mental image. I just couldn't bear to believe this HELL was her current reality.

"There's another note. Want me to read it?"

I nodded and pulled up another chair. "Quick, hit print screen."

Meet my breeders. Aren't they lovely? Dakota is next in line to become a mommy if you don't find her in time. We all know what comes of a human mother and vampire father now don't we?

Khaldon let out a slow whistle.

I looked at him. "What? Khaldon, what happens between a human and a vampire?"

His eyes grew wide as he rubbed the back of his neck, but didn't answer when he looked at me. His pained, silent expression clued me to believe whatever it was – it couldn't be a good thing. I remembered Roxas explaining something ...

He continued to read:

From here on out, you will play the game my way, on my terms, and when I tell you. You will be tested and challenged both physically and mentally. If you fail, as I have expressed before, body parts will show up on your doorstep. Don't try any reverse IP lookups. I'm mobile using a proxy server. You won't find me.

Khaldon blew out a heavy sigh. "Bloody hell. I hate this douche."

And of course we don't want to involve the police now do we? Just think of the damaging publicity your game will get on how you secretly breed women to sell babies to bleed every day to satisfy the never ending-hunger of vampires. The headlines would be fantastic – Cheyenne O'Cuinn, head programmer uses monthly revenue from the game ExsanguiNation to sadistically breed and traffic babies for vampire blood orchards.

Of course, the public version would be along the lines of sex trafficking young girls. But you get the picture.

Be in the game at three a.m. We have a few riddles to answer. Be there or delivery trucks will bring one of your sisters in little bitty pieces by noon.

Oh and one more thing, if you try to involve the police or that idiot Stovall, you'll soon find other loved ones missing as well – if not already.

The parchment disintegrated in Lady Cazenove's hands and vanished. The whole building dissolved around her as if it had never existed. Everything gone, the women, the sound of the milking machines, the barn, that horrific image of Sheridan being raped. Gone. I had no proof to take to anyone except the print screen. Lady Caz now stood in the middle of a lonely, dark cornfield surrounding by nothing but the haunted melodies of the wind rushing through the dead corn stalks.

After viewing the incomprehensible horror in the haunted barn, seeing those women savagely hung from life support harnesses with their swollen, pregnant bellies – I just didn't know what to say. Was this the fate of my sisters?

Bright red, bloody tears oozed from my eyes. In a few hours, I would be challenged to solve puzzles and play Ludovic's stupid games. They were going to be tortured even more than what they had already been through if I failed them.

Khaldon stood up and pulled a few Kleenex out of the box and gently wiped at my tears. He put his arms around me. His face seemed just as shocked and stunned as mine to gawk at the horror we just witnessed. He leaned against the counter and pulled me closer into his chest. I finally lost it. I was flat out scared of everything that had happened to me and my family. I succumbed to the grievous pain over the past week. I ached at my sisters' misery. I mourned my own mortality. I sank to my knees and he followed. He held me, rocking me back and forth on the floor.

Moments seemed like eons, and all I could do was pathetically weep. I begged the Goddess for answers that weren't coming.

"Why did this have to happen to me? What did we do to deserve such ridiculous crap served up to all of us?" I sniffed and wiped at my face. "Maybe ... we've been cursed for setting fire on top of 'Ole Man Flannery's headstone? It was only a simple séance to tell him that the new owners of his ranch were real jerks, and he needed to come back and haunt them."

As slow as the decent was into my own self-pity and grief, I ascended out of it in a flash when I realized the immediate danger of Ludovic's last words: Roxas.

In an instant I was on my feet, pounding at the keyboard. Recalling his words. "Khaldon, Ludovic said he would be hurting more people I loved if I didn't comply. How do I know he hasn't already started?"

I was at this jerkoff's mercy, and he knew it. Trying to catch my breath, to calm myself down with my father's breathing techniques, I found it hard as anxiety spooled around my rib cage tighter than a corset on a beer wench. I tried again in vain to find Roxas online. Panic overpowered me steamrolling me into submission.

Khaldon stood up off his knees and sat back down in front of his computer. My fingers smoked the keyboard searching for any possible place Roxas might be logged on. "Roxas never signed off without saying goodnight to me, Khaldon. Never. He wouldn't have left me. He would have called, texted, Skyped, or something."

Khaldon looked at me and bit his lower lip.

"My chat logs recorded our last conversation the night before the attack. Everything else is server side." I checked my messages once again for every conceivable place Roxas communicated. "The last entry was the afternoon I left the hospital. I can't find another data log from that point."

"Who is this Roxas person? Your brother?" Khaldon asked.

"Umm. No. He's ... well. He's my boyfriend, albeit online virtual boyfriend, but we met in the hospital after my attack. He's never been unreliable. If anything, Roxas is my cornerstone programmer for the game. He's been my rock for over two years now. He wouldn't abandon me during this."

Khaldon poured me another drink.

"Come on, come on." I continued to hammer at the keys. "Where are you, Roxas?" Typing desperately into the chat window, I looked to see how long his avatar had been idle. His avatar inside the game had sat idle and away from the keyboard since the day I got released from the hospital. I stepped away from the keyboard and held my hands on the side of my head. "Khaldon, I believe they have Roxas too."

Chapter Twenty Three

Part Two

Dakota O'Cuinn

Breeding Facility #42

Ludovic hung up the phone and gloated. "Other than your little outburst, Dakota, that went over rather well if I do say so myself." His eyebrow arched so high into his forehead it disappeared into his hairline.

I wanted to pluck it off his face. I wasn't sure if he expected me to react, so I just gave him with my best *go-fuck-yourself* glare.

Ludovic turned and looked out the window. Moonlight streamed in on the concrete floor. He opened the wooden window sash and allowed in the night's humid air. The rain had abated a bit. He placed his elbows on the sill. "So, Dakota, do you think your sister took the bait?"

His brother, Edric, stood behind me, breathing heavily against the back of my neck with his hideous breath. "Do you believe our trap is complete enough to get your sister here?"

His hot breath tingled the tiny hairs inside my inner ear canal. I pulled away from him as best I could, being shackled to the chair.

Afraid to answer him, and afraid to not answer him, I closed my eyes wishing for invisibility. I didn't want that man ever touching me again. My body ached after the last time he used me for his personal punching bag. I was afraid the violence would escalate if I aroused him in any way.

Edric showed me pictures of Sheridan on his digital camera. He pointed to his erection every time he forced me to look at the hooded figure naked between her bound legs. His capabilities scared the holy hell out of me. I didn't know why Ludovic had done this to us.

Our mother once told us hell existed. I couldn't have been but eight years old when she told us a story of an evil queen. Now I wished I had paid more attention.

Oh God, how I wish I could see her again.

Silently I prayed Cheyenne would find us, but I knew that Ludovic and Edric would capture her and do the same to her as they were doing to

Sheridan. I didn't want that either. Why they weren't doing it to me already, I had no idea. But wanted to avoid it at all cost.

Low, painful-sounding moans came from a corner of the room, but I couldn't turn my head around far enough to see what it was. Edric spun my chair around, walked over to turn on the light, and I gasped out in horror. Trying to stifle a scream, I saw a woman hanging in a hammock with her pregnant belly hanging below her and her head elevated. She was harnessed and shackled to the posts, unable to move. She had tubes, an IV, and monitor straps taped over her chest and belly. She didn't look alive, but I watched the pinging of heart beats across the machines. I guessed one was for the baby's heartbeat as well. Both heartbeats escalated as the unconscious woman moaned louder. She was giving birth!

"Ludovic, hand me the chart on number thirty-three over here," Edric called out over his shoulder. "She's looking like she's ready to pop any time now. Her blood pressure is spiking, and her cervix is effaced. It won't be long for this one. You might want to go ahead and call the Priestess and let her know we'll have another one soon."

Ludovic left the window and whispered in my ear, "You might be wondering why we haven't found you your own little cozy cubby, huh?"

I looked at him, afraid to answer.

"I want you for myself. Soon you will be *my* eternal mate. I have plans for that bitch Priestess who shows up here every other week to take the squalling babies." He gave my shoulders a squeeze as I stared at him in morose terror. "With me by your side, you can challenge the Priestess and we shall rule together."

Rule together? Eternal mate?

He laughed at me and flashed that wicked smile again revealing his sharp canine teeth.

"What the hell? Get me outta here, you gawd damned freak!" I thrashed against the chains to get out of my chair. Edric shoved a ball gag in my mouth to muffle my screams.

The ball gag made it difficult to breath. I had no choice but to settle down. Ludovic walked away in a peacock strut as he picked up the medical chart tablet held in a rack along the wall. I grimaced looking at the rack – it must have held fifty or more.

How many women are in this place? Is this happening to Sheridan?

I watched in sheer panic as the woman's abdomen spasmed and contorted. She couldn't have possibly been conscious because she didn't scream even though the fetus writhed and contorted her belly. She looked as if the *Alien* was getting ready to burst through her stomach at any minute.

Bone-breaking sounds echoed off the concrete, and Edric donned a pair of blue surgical gloves.

"Want to get a better view, my pet?"

I shook my head, but it was too late. He had that wicked gleam in his eyes already. Ludovic popped the brakes on my chair.

"You should see the climax of our operation here since you are going to become the new mistress of our army." He rolled me over to the woman giving birth.

Edric walked over to me and backhanded my cheek. His smack knocked my head to the side, causing me to see stars. I tasted blood. "There's more of that if you scream. You understand? I don't want you disturbing the patients."

I nodded as best I could, still dizzy from the blow.

Ludovic removed the gag from my mouth, and I gasped for air. The woman moaned louder as her body wrenched up in convulsions. Her harness kept her movements to a minimum, but the contorting fetus inside her shifted again.

Not sure if I could speak, I asked one word with trepidation. "Army?" I ducked my head down into my shoulders waiting for another blow, but one didn't come.

Instead, Ludovic stood proud. "Yes, the world's finest dhampir army bred with ancient heritage pure-blood lines." I looked at him as if he had smoked one too many bowls. Edric's punch must have left me fuzzier than I thought.

"Dhampir?"

"Ah, yes my love. You haven't quite yet enjoyed the fruit of our knowledge, have you? What a beautiful poetic way for you to experience the birth of your empire." Ludovic pushed my chair closer. Much too close for my comfort, but I didn't have a choice.

The woman arched her back, and a scream came from her that brought tears to my eyes. A head crowned between her legs, and Edric stood ready with a birthing table and various implements. The table with all the bloody tools looked more as if he were going to eat the child as opposed to clean it and care for it.

Edric turned his attention to us for a moment. "Ludovic, what'll it be this time? Boy or girl?"

Ludovic turned my chair around to get in my face. "Hmm. Let's see what my eternal mate thinks it will be." I looked into his eyes — really looked into his eyes, and felt nothing but fear. He was on board with this mess, but he certainly wasn't in control of it.

"What is the sex of the baby, my love?"

My stomach roiled queasy with rot. My breath caught in my throat as my eyes glossed over with a film. I tried to shake it off, but he held my gaze and asked me again.

"Boy or girl?"

I felt a pull on my consciousness. Afraid I would black out, I whispered, "Boy." Ludovic released his gaze from me as my head fell limp against my chest.

Slapped back to consciousness, I heard the familiar sound of a baby's cry. I opened my eyes to see a baby nursing from his mother. Not from her breast; it sucked blood from the inside of her thigh – from her femoral artery.

A wave of aversion came over me looking at the monstrosity in front of me.

"Well, well, well Ludovic, looks like your gal pal there just might have the gift." Edric finger quoted around the words the gift. "Or maybe it's just dumb luck, but it's going to be a gwrywaidd dhampir for sure."

I continued to stare at the devil child in front of me and dared to venture forth with another query.

"What is a dhampir?" I asked again.

Ludovic, excited by my inquisition, seemed happy to oblige my question. Not realizing one of them had untied my hands, Ludovic handed me the bundle of baby with blood smeared on his rosy cheeks. "A dhampir is the union of a male vampire and a human mother. We get the best of both worlds. The dhampir has half the vampiric traits and yet born to destroy any vampire it is programmed to kill. This makes them a valuable asset to the Queen's army."

Ludovic watched me with what looked like blissful admiration. "Dakota, I would like to introduce you to our newest male scion."

"Scion? Isn't that the name of a car?"

Edric sewed up the woman and gave her a shot of something in her IV. Not sure if she was still alive, I looked to find her heart still beating in the monitor. Thankful she wasn't conscious, I wondered if she would ever know that she had given birth to the monster I held in my arms.

"Ludovic, that makes four for her. She's gonna have to go to the mending wing for a couple months before we can knock her up again."

"I don't understand. You keep them pregnant all the time?"

"Siring a dhampir only takes three months." Ludovic squatted next to me and tickled the baby's toes. "One month per normal human trimester. Dhampirs grow extremely fast until they reach seven years when they are grown."

My heart dropped. This whole place sickened me. One way or another, I knew I needed to get out of here and help the rest of the women held captive by these lunatics.

"What are you doing here? What is this place?"

"This place is called breeding facility number forty two. We have about 130 top breeders at this facility. But this is nothing. Where I was trained in Romania, we had over four hundred women."

Edric broke in. "The stupid, human authorities think young girls traveling in Europe are kidnapped and sold into sex slavery. Yes, some are. But mostly, the girls are sold to the Vampyric race through online bids from the game portal on ExsanguiNation."

I gasped at thinking our game could be the venue for such horrific trafficking of women.

Ludovic pulled up a chair beside me. "ExsanguiNation is a haven – the perfect playground for supernaturals. Whatever they want, they can get through the game. If they know who to ask. It's the perfect set up – the perfect lie. Authorities will always think it's just a game. They'll never suspect how real monetary gains come from the online selling of human hosts, their body parts, and their blood to the highest bidders."

I looked at this seemingly harmless baby in my arms with his glowing red eyes and sweet chubby cheeks. He cooed up at me. I felt a strange pull in my heart when I touched his silky, porcelain skin. The baby smiled at me. Feeling something as simple as a smile fall across my face, it gave me a chance to forget this terrible place of torment for just a brief moment.

"OUCH!"

Ludovic howled in laughter as I held up my finger dripping in blood. I held the baby in my other arm with blood on his teeth, making sucking movements with his mouth. My eyes grew in alarm as the innocence of this babe, gave way to the horror of what it truly was.

"The Priestess has arrived," Edric announced.

Before me stood a hypnotic woman dressed as pure evil, decorated in lust and greed.

Chapter Twenty Four

Dakota O'Cuinn

Breeding Facility #42

Ablinding light forced me to shield my eyes behind the child while juggling the infant away from any fleshy body parts it could bite. Pure evil incarnate stood before us. The Priestess commanded the sheer air within the room and dominated the breaths she took from me.

"Bring me the suckling," she commanded. Her voice demanded attention.

Ludovic looked up from his position of respect and did as directed. As he took the baby from my arms, instantly and for the first time in my life, I held empathy for mothers who had their babies taken away at birth. I wondered if the child would ever know his mother. Will the mother survive this hellhole long enough to ever know if she had a son? Or several sons?

"What will you do with him?"

The Priestess sing-songed at me. "Ah, Dakota, my sweet. I have been waiting decades for you and your sisters to arrive. Soon my Dhampiric soldiers will be completed with the Irish triad bloodline." Her voice dripped as if vile poison oozed off each syllable.

"When was she inseminated?" The Priestess looked at a chart on the wall and pointed at me. "I gave specific semen to impregnate her and Sheridan both. You better not have wasted it!"

"What the hell are you talking about? What insemination?" This lady was crazy. "What triad? What in God's name are you? And just what the fuck is all this bullshit?"

The Priestess' eyes shut as she smirked at me. She flicked her spiked pinkie finger at my mouth and sealed my lips as though they were sewn together with invisible thread. Panic surged through me as I found it difficult to breathe again. I bellowed muffled screams as streams of briny tears fell and stung the invisible needle holes where my mouth had been sewn shut.

What the hell?

I glared at her, but was afraid that she might blind me too. The Priestess walked away.

"Ah yes, my dearest Priestess." Ludovic bowed in her honor. "I wanted to surprise you with redheaded triplets — to have all three sisters bear you a dhampir general at the same time. Until I have them all, I chose not to inseminate the second sister since we are so close to obtaining the third."

An outrage of toxic energy flew from the Priestess and shocked the room with throbbing, painful blasts. The oxygen left the room. Her fiery fury caused the suckling to wail.

I crouched in my bonds as I watched Ludovic and Edric scramble to remove the sharp implements off the birthing table. A fierce, banshee-like scream communicated the Priestess' vexation.

She slammed her fist onto the table, shattering it with one blow. Shards of wood and metal peppered the fumbling duo with table shrapnel.

"This will be your heads if you continue to make any decisions without my permission. The Queen will have as she wishes, not what you choreograph." The Priestess turned toward me as she continued to rant at the men. The child's screams emulated the Priestess' anger. "I want her inseminated tonight. I will not wait until you obtain the final sister. Am I clear?" The baby continued to scream with moxie. His little hands outstretched to grasp any form of safety. His face reddened to the color of beets as his wails echoed and bounced off the concrete cinder block walls.

In unison, both Ludovic and Edric said, "Crystalline, my Priestess."

Then Edric turned and punched Ludovic square in the jaw. "I knew I shouldn't have listened to you. Idiot!" Sensing the Priestess' approval, he did it again until Ludovic fell to the floor clutching his jaw.

An overwhelming scent of lavender filled the air, calming the energy and quieting the room. It seemed where fury emanated from the Priestess just moments prior, it now had been replaced with grandmotherly kindness.

I felt the needle pin pricks gone from my face and I could open my mouth. The Priestess held up a hand of advice I supposed to warn me to tread with caution.

I touched at my lips. "What do you want from me? From my sisters? What are you going to do to the baby?"

Rocking the infant gently, the Priestess fed him from her breast. I noticed it wasn't milk she delivered to him. He was attached to the inside of her cleavage suckling away at her artery. "I believe I'll answer your third question first. This child, being born dhampir gwrywaidd will be groomed and taught the finest art of slaying none other than impure, rogue vampire scum."

"Vampires? Is that what you are? Queen of the night? Nosferatu? I *vant to suck yer blood* kind of vampire? Are you fucking serious?"

The Priestess raised a curious eyebrow. "Precisely, my dear one. We've hunted lineages the world over to find the truest, most pure-blood of our ancestry. And you, Cheyenne, and Sheridan are the purest I've found. Together with each of you, my dhampiric army will guarantee me the global domination I deserve in the vampyric realm."

I swallowed hard.

The Priestess continued, "Once I have a son from each of you, the trinity will be complete. The prophecy upheld, and my plan will be in place." She held the child sound asleep in her energy.

"Are you telling me that you are planning to use me and my sisters to make – those?"

"My, my, Dakota you learn fast don't you?"

I tried to get out of the chair again, I had to escape this insanity.

"Relax, my dear. You are here to sire my generals. These other women are creating minions for your sons to command and control. Your sons will take over this rogue-infested planet and bring order to the race. You should be honored to be held in such high esteem. Hold your head in the honored greatness you and your sisters warrant and join us willingly. Your every whim will be addressed."

The Priestess walked around the back of my chair. She rolled me to where my nose came within a hair's whisper of touching the belly of the woman who had just given birth. "For if you don't, this will become your fate." The woman's bowels let loose, splashing my legs with fecal bloody mess.

I turned my head and stole a look at her. Her smile could etch steel.

"Take your honored position of prestige in my lineage, and you will be rewarded beyond your wildest imagination." The Priestess' head turned to favor the men in the room. "Be done with it! Edric, continue with the protocol we discussed earlier."

"Yes, my Priestess."

Before I could blink, Edric had more strapped restraints around my arms and pressed my chest. The Priestess and the baby were gone.

"No! No! Please, let me go!"

Edric wheeled me into a room with four poles and a medical table. I thrashed up and down in the chair until Edric slammed his fist into my temple again. Everything went black as my vision blurred and swirls of colorful pain burst behind my left eye. I could've sworn I heard my brain slosh inside my skull.

***

Coming to, I desperately tried to maintain consciousness. My left eyelid must have been swollen shut because I couldn't open it. I felt as if I had been hit upside the head with a crowbar. The pain was so intense vomit erupted and ran down the front of me. With every ounce of energy, I fought the notion that I would either die in this room, or my fate would be the same as Sheridan's if I didn't. Ludovic grabbed my face and tried to calm me.

"Dakota, listen to me. We don't have much time. Edric will be back any minute."

I tried to focus on Ludovic as he wiped my mouth clean with a towel.

"Please. Help me." My words were barely audible to my own ears as my vision faded once again.

"Stay with me, okay? This is what's going to happen, but I need you to play along. I'm going to get you out of here, but I need you to stop fighting. He's going to seriously harm you if you keep fighting him. I've seen him do it. It's what gets him off."

I nodded. Tears filled the corners of my eyes. "How could you do this?" I tried to calm my voice, but my words shook with sobs. "Why would you do this to me? I thought we had more than this. You said. You said you loved me."

"Shh. I know. He'll be back any second."

"Please, I'm begging you. Don't do this to me. I'll do anything. I'll be your eternal mate, whatever. Just don't impregnate me like that. Ludovic, please don't do that to me!"

Edric walked in through the door. I braced my leg to kick him. He lunged at me and grabbed my ankle. He squeezed my shin until I heard my ankle crack.

"Ahhhhg!" Raw, hot razorblades ran up my nerves and into my low back. No matter how I moved, the pain down my leg was excruciating to the point of absolute paralysis. My foot sprawled in a grotesque backward heap.

At that moment I knew there wasn't any more reasoning. They weren't going to listen to any amount of pleading. Weakened as I was, Edric shot a syringe of yellow goo into my arm with no resistance.

Ludovic shoved Edric away from me. "What the hell, Edric? Why did you shoot her full of that?"

Edric shrugged as if it were an everyday event. "Dakota here is prepped to become a part of the Solunarae blood testing. I needed to bathe her muscles in relaxant, or she could have fugued on us."

Ludovic shut his eyes and took several long, deep breaths. When he opened his eyes, he looked down at me.

"Why?" I tried to shake my head. "Why?" The muscles in my body were seizing.

Helpless to move or defend myself, all I could do was wait in terror as to what they were going to do to me next. I prayed Cheyenne would understand my message for the geo-cache and, find us. Would she get it?

"We should put her in the same ward with her sister Sheridan," Edric mused. "How fun it will be to have all three redheads swinging in their hammocks, in a row."

I heard every foul scheming word fall out of Edric's mouth. I swore to the Mother Goddess that if I ever got the chance I would run a hot poker through his eye and feed him to zombies if I didn't eat him myself first.

"Shut the hell up, Edric. I've had enough of your shite tonight. I'll set them in the same bay. Soon we will have Cheyenne in our possession and we can deliver the Priestess what she wants."

I watched through blurred eyes as an evil shroud consumed Edric. A black aura hovered over him. Ludovic held his face over mine for a moment, perhaps to check if I was conscious. I couldn't move my lips, my face absolutely frozen from the injection.

He bit his lips.

"Edric, don't perform the insemination until I get back. Do you understand? I'll handle it myself. Just prep her for surgery. We'll Cryo a bunch of her ova tonight just to be safe if for any reason she can't carry. The follicle stimulating hormone injection should have her releasing several of them."

Edric opened his mouth, but Ludovic exploded. "I said, *DON'T touch her.*" There were a few additional words in Romanian that I couldn't understand. Whatever they were, Edric backed off from his brother and nodded in acknowledgment.

Ludovic turned to look at my face again. His forehead furrowed in what looked like grave concern.

Grateful for his help this time, no matter how slight it might have been, I watched as he shook his head. "I'm sorry, Dakota."

I pleaded with my eyes for him not to leave me with his brother, but my body held me prisoner, incapable of talking or moving. He stole one more glance and kissed my lips. He sighed hard as tears ran down my cheeks and into my ears. He turned and walked away.

Please don't go. Please don't abandon me!

I had heard the soft swoosh of the door close behind Ludovic. Edric was already posed against me. I could feel his excitement pushing through his pants. My face and body frozen, I had no weapons but my eyes, as I glared at him.

I swear to the heavens above, if I ever get out of this place, I will kill you!

Chapter Twenty Five

Cheyenne O'Cuinn

The Penthouse

Khaldon, I haven't heard from him for over fifty hours. There should be emails, instant messages, texts, voice mails – but there isn't a single one." My voice grew more hysterical with each word.

"Calm down, take a deep breath. It'll make you feel better."

I tried to calm down, but it was impossible knowing Roxas was nowhere to be found. My thoughts spanned to every detail of Ludovic's message about taking the rest of my loved ones. Who could that mean?

"We have to go, Khaldon!"

"Go where?"

"We have to go to Roxas' house. I need to see if he's safe."

"Okay, let me get this straight." He looked at me if I had eaten a stupid pill or something. "You want to go find a guy's house to check on him because you think this Ludovic character has kidnapped him?"

"I know it sounds crazy, but yes. After what we just saw in that haunted barn, do you think he's joking about anything? What would you do if the woman you loved all of a sudden fell off the face of the planet?"

Khaldon frowned. "I'm gonna call Stovall and put in an inquiry on this. Do you know anything else about him?"

"He has a Romanian type accent. Hell, if he's vampire – he could be Romanian, right? Or is that considered preternatural profiling?"

"That's a strong possibility, yes. Profiling, I hadn't thought about it that way, but that's the Hollywood stereotype. We have three times as many vampires in Asia as we do in Europe."

I blinked. "Yeah, okay – I'll leave that story for another time. Ludovic works at a bar on City Streets, but I don't know which one. There's at least twenty bars there. He has a brother. What was his name? Eric? Cedric? No. Edric! Yes, he has a brother named Edric. Unholy hell!"

"What?"

"In the hospital. That guy who kept taking my blood. It was Edric. I couldn't make the connection then, because of the morphine, but he was Sherlock Holmes."

"Sherlock Holmes?"

"Never mind. The point is – they knew I was in the hospital. His brother probably told Ludovic I had checked out."

Khaldon called Stovall on his cell and relayed the information. "Stovall says he's never heard of any vampires registered by those names. Doesn't mean they aren't using pseudonyms. He's cautious about who to trust in this situation because if it was an internal tip off, then he could easily cause more issues. He's going to make in-person inquiries and get back to us."

He snapped his fingers as if a thought just occurred to him. "Can we pull up your servers and filter out Roxas' IP address? Maybe check his login status?"

"We certainly can." Clicking away at the keyboard, I filtered out Roxas' internet protocol address. "Here - it says he's been idle since the day I left the hospital. We have to go. We need to go now and get back before Ludovic contacts me again."

Even though it was still raining buckets outside, I hurried to the foyer. Khaldon grabbed his umbrella while I reached for our raincoats.

"What's the address of this guy anyway?" he asked.

"It's here in my wallet. I sent him one of my 3D rendering suits a few weeks ago."

Khaldon stiffened his back and opened up the umbrella over us as we stepped out into the unforgiving rain.

After we got into the car, he turned to me. "Listen. Whatever we find out tonight, I'm here to help you. I am your friend, all right?"

I nodded. I hoped I could trust him. I wanted to ... I *needed* to.

I wiped a tear away from my cheek. "Gah! This is driving me crazy. Why do my eyes bleed? This is so messy and inconvenient."

"Now that your body supports vampyric DNA, there are some human fluids not used anymore. Tears are one of those fluids. In time, you will have fewer tears as your inner vampire takes over the human emotions."

"Lovely."

I wonder if I'll still have my monthly periods too, but I'm sure as hell not going to ask him about that!

The rain pummeled the night. The wiper blades were hypnotic as they swished the water away from the windshield. We drove to Roxas' address via the GPS in the dashboard. I was surprised to learn just how close he was to me. I looked over at Khaldon. He looked a little green, and bit his lower lip.

"What's the matter? Are you okay?" I asked.

"Are you sure you want to do this? What if he's in there? Have you considered what in the world you are gonna say to him?

"I know, I know. But I don't have a choice. We can say you're a part of the detective team helping me look for my sisters."

He narrowed his eyes.

I sighed and finished. "Yeah ... lame. No use in lamenting on something that might not happen anyway. C'mon let's go."

We got out of his car and ran to the building's entranceway. He ran his hand through his hair. I tried to stay optimistic and think how I wouldn't kill Roxas in the first minute if I found him home.

Finally the doors opened. I bolted through them.

"Which way?" Khaldon asked.

"Not sure, I always choose the wrong way." The hallway didn't give any numeric direction to the units, so I choose a path. Looking for his unit number, I learned I needed to turn around. "Crap."

Walking back towards his apartment I heard a familiar sound. The closer to his door I walked, the louder I heard classical music. I recognized it and froze.

We stood outside the door. Khaldon pushed his hair away from his face and rubbed his neck. "That's the online music Rox and I listen to when we we're in the dungeon." Realizing what I said to Khaldon was wildly inappropriate for the moment, I swallowed hard and turned around.

The door hung slightly ajar. My knock pushed it forward without resistance. No answer. I knocked again. "Roxas, are you here?" Still no answer, only the classical music.

We stepped into the room and Khaldon closed the door behind us. I stood there inside his domain and covered my mouth with my hands.

On almost every surface of the room were images of Lady Cazenove and Roxas Morgwain.

I gasped at the life-sized canvas oil painting elegantly mounted over the fireplace. "Khaldon, this is from the night Roxas and I were engaged inside the game. We're standing on a bridge I built near our virtual home."

"It's stunning." Khaldon looked around the condo and then whistled. "This guy has the blazin' hots for you."

"You mean the human me before I became vampire. I guarantee you now that I walk with the living dead, he isn't gonna be all that into me."

I suddenly realized how my immortality would outlive him, and every other mortal person I loved. Logically I knew this would happen, but until now the emotional impact had not set in. My heart ached at the losses before I ever experienced their realities.

I crossed over to his fireplace mantel to admire a bronze statue. "Looks like Roxas had this commissioned from our last anniversary. He took me dancing on the Titanic." My eyes glassed over as I held the sculpture in my arms as if it were a newborn child.

Khaldon looked at me and put his hand on my shoulder. "You okay?" He lifted my chin. I must have been feeling rather addle-minded at the moment. I could have sworn he sounded like Roxas just then.

Keep it together Chey. Don't lose it here and now.

I nodded my head and explained to Khaldon what I was holding.

He smiled and nodded back.

We searched the apartment and found no one home. I walked through the house looking around getting to intimately know the man I had been virtually in love with for so long.

"I dunno. Seems kinda creepy stalkerish to me." Khaldon shrugged and continued to look around. He picked up a picture of Lady Caz and Roxas riding horses.

"It's not. It's how we've had a relationship for the past two years. This is how we dated. Don't you have pictures of your girlfriend?"

"Yeah, I see your point." He placed the frame back on the table exactly where it had sat.

"These are just pictures of our avatars, instead of us. It's the only way we've known each other until I met him in the hospital the other day."

Khaldon fingered a knife blade mounted on the wall. "Well, it doesn't seem like anybody's home. Let's see what he keeps in the fridge?"

I didn't say anything, but kept studying the shrine this man held for me, or rather, for my avatar. Roxas obviously felt the same love for me that I did for him. I found his home office and went inside. He had an ancient weapons collection adorning the walls that could have put any museum on its knees. My fingers lightly stroked the edge of a pair of battle-axes hung in a crossed pattern. The intricate carvings on the wood revealed an ancient medieval dragon fight.

"Hey, Khaldon come in here. Take a look at these. They're..."

Khaldon walked in with a bottle of bloodwine. "Ah, my favorite." He took a long hard chug on the bloodwine as my mouth fell to the floor.

"What the hell is that?" I demanded. "What are you drinking?" I grabbed the bottle away from him, spilling the wine over his chin and onto his shirt.

"Crap, Cheyenne, this was one of my favorite shirts." He gestured to his chest as he tried to wipe the blood off with his sleeve. Using the back of his hand to wipe at his chin, he stopped in mid-swipe to read my face.

"Did you ... just now, get this out of Roxas' refrigerator?" My thoughts processed faster than a multi-core processor. I held the bottle out for him to look at. "Why would Roxas have a cold bottle of bloodwine in his refrigerator? Or any bottle of bloodwine for that matter?" Khaldon pursed his lips. I didn't let him answer. "Don't only vampires know about this stuff? Isn't it specially ordered from those vineyards Stovall talked about?"

"You mean the blood orchards?" Khaldon's eyes grew wide.

"Whatever the hell you call them. Yes, those." I sat the bottle on the office table next to the computer and sat in Roxas' office chair behind his computer. "I don't understand. How could I have missed this? Roxas either is or associates with vampires?" I said aloud to myself. "How is this possible? Why would he not have told me?"

Khaldon glanced up me with that confused look on his face again. "Maybe he is vampire and knew you were a human. Maybe that's why he couldn't meet you in real life."

My eyes lit up. "Khaldon, I could kiss you." I jumped up and took a sip of the wine. "That makes perfect sense. Of course – so it wasn't me all this time. Oh, thank the Goddess. It was his issue of us not meeting for so long. We have to find him. He has to know what has happened to me."

In my jubilation I accidentally bumped the mouse next to the keyboard on his computer when I put the bottle back down. I saw an opened email on the monitor as the screen woke up from its hibernation. I leaned down to read it.

Khaldon quickly jumped over in front of the monitor. "We shouldn't be reading the guy's stuff, now should we?"

I raised an eyebrow. "You didn't seem to have any trouble making yourself at home by raiding his fridge now did you?"

Khaldon grimaced. "You have a point."

"Maybe it's a clue as to where he is." I turned back to the email and read a note from what looked like a friend.

See you at three, lover. I'll be at our corner booth at Club Mordez-Moi!
We'll discuss what to do with the sisters then.
Forever Yours ~Darkrose

My face went numb. I dropped the little bronze statue I had been holding and it made a loud thunk onto the floor, right beside my heart. Khaldon had moved behind me and I supposed had read the email over my shoulder. He cleared his throat and reached out to touch my shoulder. I turned around in the chair and looked up at him – madness hazed my vision.

Khaldon forced me to look into his eyes again. This time, his waves of interference forced me to relax. "Breathe, Cheyenne. Things aren't always as they seem." His voice soothed me as my heart felt like it shattered into a million pieces.

The air grew heavy and I recognized the change in energy between us. Khaldon was in control, suppressing my emotions. Blood pooled in my eyes. Tears expressed from utter joy just moments earlier, had in an infinitesimal moment turned to frigid tears of hated betrayal.

I sucked in my lower lip, trying to maintain any modicum of self-control. "Have I been so blind?" I whispered through clenched teeth. "Is Roxas involved with my sisters kidnapping? No wonder he had to be gone so much while I was in the hospital. Look at this email. It says – sisters." I looked away from Khaldon's gaze as he relinquished whatever force field he had over me. "Did you read that? It's from some chick named Darkrose. Roxas and I made a promise to each other not to date anyone else."

I stood and squared my shoulders toward Khaldon. "So where is this Club Mordez-Moi? What the hell does that mean anyway? I need to confront this sonofabitch."

"Whoa now, filly, hold on a minute. Club Mordez-Moi means quite literally, Club Bite Me. It's a pretty nasty vampire hangout. Not a place for noobie vampires."

I could have staked him with my eyes.

"Look, we have less than a couple hours to get you back and ready to receive that call from Ludovic. Are you gonna compromise getting instructions of how to find your sisters by going after this guy?"

"What choice is there? It's the only lead, unless I try to come back here again later in the morning. I have no idea how long Ludovic is gonna make me play inside the game."

"I'm not keen on this, Chey. It's not a good idea. Bite Me isn't exactly a place that serves high tea and chocolates." Khaldon reached around the back of his head and pulled the silken knot out of his hair. It fell all around his shoulders. "What happens if you find him there? What are you gonna do? Shoot him in the corner all gangsta style?" Khaldon held out his hands to form mock guns shooting from the hips. "You can't possibly understand what kind of hell you might be getting yourself into."

I swallowed hard, trying to take in his logic. My mind tried to counter with objections, but his argument was sound. I sat back down in the chair and hit the print screen key.

"Why don't we do this – I take you back to your apartment and you wait for Ludovic. I'll go to Mordez Moi and stake it out. I'll see what I can uncover for you. I'll casually run into Amicula and see what's hanging."

"What?" I turned to face him. "Amicula? Darkrose is Amicula?"

"Yes, her formal name is Amicula Darkrose. She has gone by that name since, I dunno, forever."

I stood there blinking at him.

My Roxas is dating Amicula?!

"Things are not always how they seem. Look, it's almost one-thirty, so we'll have just enough time to get you back home and me in position at the club. It's the best plan and you know it. You can't afford to miss Ludovic."

I opened my mouth in protest, but I stopped myself. He was right. That kind of gamble wasn't worth hurting Dakota and Sheridan. "Okay, but for the record – I don't like it. I want to know for sure if Roxas is a vampire or not. If he or Amicula are behind my sister's kidnapping, I'll kill them both. I swear it."

Khaldon crouched down on one knee in front of me and reached out with his golden skinned hand. He held his mouth in a half smile, as he held my chin up to his face once again. "Look, you won't have to kill Roxas."

I returned his gaze questioning his statement. He took a deep breath and changed the tempo and pitch of his voice. In a clear distinct British dialect Khaldon said, "You're gonna think this is crackers, m'lady, but I've been here all along."

If my heart weren't already dead, it would have been from his words.

Scooting my chair backwards out of his hand, I gaped at him. For the second time that night, I stood frozen, rooted in my socks, unable to comprehend the enormity of the bomb just dropped on me. I shook my head to try and clear the ridiculous hallucinations. My mind galloped with a thousand thoughts at once, none of them making an ounce of rational thought – except one.

With my heart on fire from the betrayal, the hatred, and the fear that I would never see my sisters again – furious anguish dashed my hands around Khaldon's throat choking the ever-living life out of him.

Chapter Twenty Six

Roxas Morgwain's House

"What the hell have you done with him? I'm going to kill you ... you sick, sadistic bastard! I should've known it all along. Where is he? I swear to the Mother Holy Goddess Herself if you have harmed him in any way, I will personally kill you!"

Both of us breathed hard, Khaldon held my arms as I attacked his face time and time again. I relentlessly kicked trying to hurt him in any way I could. His eyes wild at my explosion.

Khaldon threw me up against the wall and shouted in my face, "Just bloody hell calm down will ya! You've got to believe me – I am Roxas!" His green eyes squinted in anguish. Those gorgeous malachite eyes welled up with emotion. Something so familiar about those eyes ...

"Like hell you are. I can't trust anyone and now this?" I thrashed out at him again. "I can't feckin believe it. I gave you the security pass codes to access the databases. How very clever of you. You must have accessed our chat logs. How could you possibly tell me anything to prove to me who you are?"

I looked at the front door. He followed my eyes as I bolted toward it. Faster than me, he slammed the door shut after I just got it opened.

"Wait! Cheyenne, just listen to me."

I stood there with my hands on hips looking around for anything wooden or silver to stake this a-hole with.

"M'lady, I ... I love you ... I mean Lady Caz... and I'm just as shocked about this as you are. I couldn't ever trust myself enough to meet you because I am Vampyre. I was born this way. I knew I would never be able to meet my Lady. But fate tipped the scales in our favor. I was assigned to Lord Stovall's task force after the attack, but I didn't know you were involved until after your father called me.

"When I saw you on the boat, I knew it was only going to be a matter of time before I had to reveal myself to you. Didn't you see the shocked look on my face when I picked you up at the door to take you to dinner?"

Khaldon continued to barrage me with a thousand questions that I didn't listen to, even though admittedly he was beginning to make sense. I had a thousand scenarios of images, chats, visuals and pose balls floating through my relationship with Roxas.

"I don't believe this." I slammed my fist hard against his jaw and wrenched open the door once again.

"Blimey, Chey, I know this is hard to understand, but there's a reason you haven't heard from Roxas. It's because I was called by Stovall to watch over you for the past two days." I stopped two steps outside the door and looked into his eyes.

"Why don't you look like Roxas then? The Roxas I know has dark copper hair and a beard." I pointed to the picture on the wall. "He looks like that. That is who came to see me in the hospital."

Tears welled up in my eyes just thinking this creep had taken over Roxas' life and was now trying to impersonate him. I turned to leave and felt that energy shift around me once again. In my frenzied manner, I looked back and watched how the man who stood two feet in front of me morphed into another human being.

Instinctively I stepped toward him, but stopped knowing this was just some kind of vampire illusionist trick I hadn't learned. I couldn't take my eyes off the exact replica of the man I met in the hospital a week ago.

"Cheyenne, you asked me what size I wore so you could send me that 3D holographic rendering suit. Do you remember? We were talking over Skype. I told you 34 waist and I was 5'10". I also suggested you to send it to my post office box if it helped you feel better about the anonymity thing right? Remember?"

I looked at him and everything around me.

"I helped you pick out the name for Beano. We talked over your cell phone when you were at the breeder's house. You aren't going to find that information anywhere, in any database. Remember how you wanted the female, but her underbite was too big?"

"This is your place?" Remarkably, this man knew specifics that no one else could possibly know and hadn't been recorded on any harddrive.

He nodded and held is hands out to me.

"Why do you live this double life?" I walked back in to his house and looked at him closer.

"My true name is Khaldon Seters." His shoulders dropped. " I have kept my anonymity for hundreds of years, because my lineage is at war with dragons. I am a direct descendant from Sekhmet, the Egyptian Warrior Goddess. To keep things amicable now, I go by Roxas Morgwain."

I closed the door behind me and sat on the leather sofa.

"M'lady I can't express to you how I have wanted to tell you. I knew one day it would come out, but I didn't expect you to be so protective of me ... of Roxas. I shouldn't have brought you here." Khaldon kneeled in front of me. "I was so afraid of hurting you, possibly even killing you since you were human. I never wanted to take that chance."

"Then why did you agree to meet me at the theme park?" Tears broke over the brink, a single drop cascaded down my cheek as I watched his frustration. The more I listened, the more I realized he was right.

Undeniably, Khaldon Seters was Roxas Morgwain. I turned to look at him for the first time in a completely different light.

"I didn't really have a choice now did I? Everybody set us up. If I had backed out, it would have crushed you. I had to take the chance and find a way to make it work." He stood up and grabbed the bottle of bloodwine I had set on the table. "Bollocks, look at the mess this has become."

He left the room for a moment as I contemplated what to do next. Not sure if I had been zapped with some kind of vampire hypnotic voodoo or this was the real deal, I threw my head back against the couch in exasperation. A few minutes later, he came out of his bedroom with a clean shirt on looking like Khaldon once again. I stood up to stand face to face with him. He handed me a tissue, my face bloodied and smeared.

We just stood there looking at each other. Really looking at each other for the first time – completely revealed as our true selves. No avatars, no secrets – just vampire to vampire – man to woman.

Knowing and remembering all of the late night conversations until five in the morning I'd had with this guy, he knew me better than I knew myself. I remembered all of the hidden shared dreams and emotions we revealed from deep buried depths. Those truth-or-dare erotic phone calls in the middle of the night, drunk off my ass. So many things about our relationship clicked. Why we hadn't met. Why we decided early on never to video chat or send pictures of each other. Why we both worked professionally under pseudonyms to protect our identities. Why we both promised to not search for each other on the Internet. It was *all* making sense. He was a vampire. Tumblers fell into place on the rock hard, rebar-cemented safe guarding my heart.

Was the conversation between him and Harris at the hospital real? It wasn't about the game?

Khaldon reached out for me. My eyes blurred as emotion overcame the reality of the situation. He caressed my cheek as another tear slid down his thumb. Finally I had the nerve to stare into those brilliant green eyes once again. I saw the truth. He had been the man of my dreams for over two years and he knew things about me that I wasn't even willing to admit to myself.

I reached up and held my hand to his face, feeling the warmth of his skin next to mine. Was I dreaming? Had the shock of the kidnapper's call been so much for me that this was my defense mechanism?

He pulled me close and hard as if our bodies would never have another moment to touch and he kissed me with all the life left in him. As if this would be the very first and last kiss he would ever have, his hands folded into my hair and held my jaw close to his face, unrelenting, as he kissed me with a fury of a thousand soldiers returned home from war. I gave way and struggled to get as close to him as possible. My breasts inflamed with the touch of his chest and the anticipation of his mouth biting at me.

"Roxas, is this for real?" I questioned his eyes as I tore myself away from his mouth for just a moment. He stopped and slid his strong arms down to hold my hands. "I really have no idea what this is, or why the Norns have given us this second chance, but together I know what we have. What we have experienced in the past, and how much I knew Roxas was in love with Lady. We will find our way with these two real humanoid vampire bodies, just as we fell in love with one another as avatars online."

Khaldon's eyes were now the ones flowing with tears of joy and I cradled him in my arms. I never knew a man to weep before, but I sure felt the power behind it. His ability to show emotion in that way sealed any doubts I had anywhere. I knew this man loved me ... and everything about me. My avatar, my person, my vampire! No one knew more about me than this creature I was holding in my arms.

"I can't tell you how I have prayed to the gods to allow me to have you." His eyes glowed crimson under the green.

I began to feel my inner core heat up in a way I hadn't experienced before. A primal surge swelled inside me. The relief became a voracious hunger and I wanted him. I wanted to drink him, to consume him, to have him inside me – flowing through me. I wanted to be filled to the brim with ecstasy as we feasted on the pleasures of the flesh. Desire pushed me forward as he kissed me holding me so tight in his hands. I reached to touch at his chest, maybe dare to unbutton his shirt.

My cell phone went off. I didn't want to look at the damn thing, I only wanted to ravage this man. The caller ID showed it was from Ludovic.

Shite!

"Khaldon, it's Ludovic – Dakota's boyfriend – he's calling back." I showed him the phone.

"Can you put it on speaker?"

I nodded and swiped open the phone. "Hello?"

"So I see you aren't at home. You have been naughty, Cheyenne. Who are you with, my dear?"

"I just went out for some fresh air. I needed to focus and to think. To get ready for your game. I went to get some bloodwine, that's all."

Ludovic was silent over the line.

"Are you still there, Ludovic?" I swallowed hard and looked at Khaldon. "Do you need me to go home now?"

"I think I'm going to give you a pop quiz, since you left the house. Are you ready for your first clue, Cheyenne?"

"I want to talk to my sisters first." An evil, sadistic sounding laugh came across the receiver as I tried in vain to keep my composure.

"Now, now, my pet, you aren't the one making the rules here. If you win the puzzle clue, then I will give you one minute to talk with one sister. However, if you get the question wrong, you will receive a surprise present in the mail."

I bit my lip till it bled to keep myself from any further outbursts.

"You do understand that no cops and no outsiders can help you now, or you will pay the consequences, right?"

"Yes – I understand." I looked at Khaldon.

"Good, because you wouldn't want anything to happen to your precious siblings, now would you? Oh and what about Harris, Briggs, or even that chump Roxas. They can't help you now."

Khaldon clenched his fists.

"So here's your first riddle to solve."

Scrambling for a piece of paper, I scribbled a pen to get the ink flowing. Khaldon stood at his computer ready to type the question into the search engine. Afraid Ludovic would hear him typing, I put my finger to my lips in a gesture to be quiet. He nodded acknowledgment. It was like our avatars giving silent signals when we played inside ExsanguiNation. We could almost read each other's mind. Still reeling from the shock that I stood in Khaldon/Roxas' living room, I looked at him wondering what the hell I was going to call him now.

"What do you get when you cross a yeti with a vampire?"

I was quickly brought back to my current reality. "What? What do get when you cross a yeti and a vampire?" Stunned that my sister's fate rested on a schoolyard joke for third graders, I threw the pen down onto the table. "Is that what you said?"

"You have thirty seconds to give me your answer – I've set the timer." Ludovic hummed the theme song to Jeopardy gleefully onto the phone.

"Shite, Shite, Shite!" I muttered under my breath and prayed for the Goddess to send me clarity. I took in a deep clearing breath of oxygen and concentrated on the obvious. "What do get when you cross a vampire with a yeti?"

"Fifteen seconds left." Ludovic's humming got louder as he started the final chorus. Khaldon had typed the question into the Google search engine as quietly as possible and turned his laptop screen to me. I widen my eyes and looked at him. Khaldon shrugged.

Tentatively, I said, "Frost Bite?"

"Ding, ding ding, what do we have for her, Bob? A lovely set of cutlery and a year's subscription to *You're Still Screwed*," Ludovic answered in a ridiculous game show host voice.

"I answered your question. Now let me talk to them." My skin crawled when I heard him cackle in such a maniacal tone.

"Tut, tut, tut my little impatient one – not so fast. I didn't say *when* you could talk with them."

"You lousy, cheating sonofabitch, you let me talk to them right now. I answered your stupid question. You put one of them on the phone, or I'm going to call the police and have your ass nailed to the wall with a power hammer!" Shocked at my outburst, I immediately knew I had made a mistake. My chest heaved as I realized that he could still harm them no matter what I said.

"Oooooh, Bob – what's that? The penalty round? I'm afraid you're all the way back to zero, Cheyenne, and we'll just have to send you Dakota's consolation prize instead."

What have I done?

"But wait! There's more! You also qualify to receive a vacation for one in Nowhere Hole, Arizona. In August. Shall we have your mail forwarded?"

"NO!" I cried out. "I'm sorry, I didn't mean, I'll do anything you want me to, just please don't hurt them!" My fingers nervously shoved hair out of my face. My stomach curdled from the stress coursing through my body.

"Be sure to watch for the Fed Ex guy tomorrow morning. And don't be late for our six a.m. appointment in just a few short hours. My, my, you must be exhausted. Better get some sleep – 'cause you're gonna need it," Ludovic cooed into the line as it went dead.

"NOOOOO! Stop!" I screamed back at him.

"Bollocks! I almost had him. He's using a mobile IP that's refreshing every time the server calls the location from the broad bands. I'm not able to pinpoint his location."

"What we do now?" My eyes pleaded for this nightmare to end. Khaldon glanced at his watch. "What time does Fed Ex usually deliver?"

"I don't know – usually around eleven in the morning, I guess. I honestly don't pay that much attention to it," I said, flatly defeated.

"I have just enough time to go meet that tart at Mordez-Moi and try to find out what the hell she's going on about."

I turned and looked at him. He swallowed and grabbed me by the arms to face him.

He took a deep breath. "In full disclosure – Amicula and I at one time dated. But that was several mortal lifetimes before you."

I looked at him and willed his brain to collapse into his skull. I was so done and over this day.

He backpedaled from my expression. "It was centuries before you ever came into my life. We've barely been acquaintances since that time. I hated the fact I was assigned to her team under Stovall. Amicula is playing us both for the game and I'm going to find out what's what."

"You need to go." Against my better judgment, I trusted him. "Amicula might be the missing link we need in order to help find them."

***

We drove back to my penthouse, and I found a surprise waiting at the front desk wrapped in a red bow. Beano was in his crate with Stormy. As soon as he saw me, Beano barked and rocked the hallway. Stormaggedon barked in her loudest big girl voice to tell me how excited she was to see me too.

Bennie the night watchman explained. "A very thick Scottish accented chap dropped Beano and Stormy off. Good thing I know these pups, or I wouldn't have let them stay. Couldn't understand a word he said."

"That would be Torchy," Khaldon explained.

"Nice to see you again, Mr. Seters." Bennie shook Khaldon's hand after I made formal introductions. "I sure am glad you were able to help Miss Cheyenne when she was in the hospital."

Khaldon reached out to take my hand. "My pleasure, Bennie. It's good to know she has people watching out for her here."

We continued up to my penthouse, and I softly closed the door behind us.

He lifted my chin to make me look into his eyes. "I knew you didn't want to be alone right now, so I asked Torchy to bring them by for you."

I hugged him around the neck.

"I'm sorry, m'lady. I didn't want us to happen like this. Truthfully, I wasn't sure how I was going to tell you. I kinda hoped maybe you might fall in love with Khaldon, ya know, and forget that Roxas ever existed."

Words escaped me. I rubbed my hands over his cheeks and kissed his mouth.

He clasped his hands over mine as we touched foreheads. "Get some rest, love. You must be absolutely knackered."

I loved listening to his British accent. I could listen to him all day. Hearing it close up in my ears though somehow managed to have an unanticipated effect on me. Albeit, delightfully surprising.

His breath tickled my neck in his whisper. "Let me go so I can get back to you as soon as I can. I should only be gone an hour or so." He kissed me once again. Lightly his tongue brushed my lips. Khaldon pulled away and I immediately ached for him. Before the elevator door closed he held his arm blocking the sensor. His smile reached all the way up into his eyes. "Oh how the Norns have twisted a mean fate upon us, my love. I bid thee adieu till it be morrow."

With that – the door closed and he was gone.

Chapter Twenty Seven

Khaldon Seters

Club Mordez-Moi!

K haldon opened the door to meet Amicula at Club Mordez-Moi! with trepidation. She would be there and he hoped to locate her before she spotted him. Slim chance though. This bar seethed with vampires, human servants, and wannabes. Most likely her hawk eyes would recognize him immediately. Across the bar Khaldon spotted her with the chair positioned to observe the door. Amicula held up a glass in a toast. Grumbling words harsh enough to carve his path, people cringed away as Khaldon made toward her.

Several hands reached out to Khaldon to lure him into a conversation, but he declined as he narrowed his approach. Khaldon had earned his reputation as an easy-going guy who normally was quite congenial. However, this night was different. He needed to find out what Amicula knew about Cheyenne's sisters and passed the outstretched hands with no apologies. Could he woo Amicula into thinking he still carried a torch for her, or even a small burning ember?

Amicula Darkrose sat casually in her well-worn metallic chair. Two drinks on the table and an untouched basket of spicy bat wings completed the scene. Amicula, never one to disappoint a crowd, dressed in an off-the-shoulder, form-fitting dress which left nothing to the imagination. Khaldon knew right off this meeting wasn't about the cleanup or the missing O'Cuinn sisters. This was a seduction ploy. Perhaps he had a better shot at getting information than he had thought. He needed to play it cool, play it right.

It amazed him how she couldn't get over him, even after so many centuries. Sure they had an enjoyable couple of decades together, but that was it. Her constant bloody thirst for whores bored him to death. He wanted to learn technology and move towards a different direction in life, evolve, while she had grandiose visions of conquering the world. Why she couldn't let go of their drunken trysts of the past he would never understand.

A stunningly beautiful woman, Amicula always packaged herself as if she were freshly pressed from a fashion magazine. Khaldon remembered how her voluptuous beauty escaped no one, including himself, but that vision came with a price he wasn't willing to pay – again.

Don't do it. She's just a mesmerizing snake full of poisonous charms. Don't trust a word that comes from her succulent mouth.

Khaldon knew Amicula's darker side – intimately. Past experiences of misdeeds replayed in his mind as silent movie credits rolled past his eyes. Seduction wasn't her only goal for the evening. It was her cover.

"Good evening, my dear. You're looking ravishing, as usual. What in the world did you want to discuss tonight that we couldn't talk about at the coven meeting tomorrow?"

"Why, Khaldon, I want nothing more than an evening of your time." Amicula extended her hand to him. "Well, to be honest, I want more than just an evening, but that would just be a yummy appetizeaser now wouldn't it." Her eyes danced over his face and sent waves of vampiric pheromone through the air.

Khaldon gingerly took her hand and kissed the inside of her wrist, never taking his eyes off her. He sat across the table leaning in to make an impression of crossing personal space between them. He waited to hear the screech of wooden chairs move around them to turn and look at where the alluring aroma originated. Amicula gestured to the champagne she had in a glass waiting his arrival.

"You know I'm a reformed man." Khaldon chuckled. "I'm afraid my answer will be the same tonight as it was the last time we had this conversation." His smile oozed charm while his words told truths.

"Oh, really now. I do love a delicious challenge. They're such wicked fun, don't you think?"

"So, why have you called me out here in the middle of the night to talk about sisters?" Khaldon cleared his throat, trying to figure out the ruse. "I didn't know you had any sisters."

"Oh Khaldon, you always were the card." Amicula laughed. "I don't wish to talk about my sisters or my cousins. I want to discuss with you something especially vital. Something my Auntie has entrusted me with and I would very much like your help in completing."

"But ..." Khaldon began, only to be cut off.

Amicula shushed him with her finger across his mouth. "My Auntie has requested my return to South America several times, and I keep telling her I will be along soon." She drew her long fingernail down over his lips.

He looked at her out of the corner of his eye as he waved down a barkeep.

"You see, Khaldon, Auntie wants me to bring you back to help sire and train an elite fighting force to ensure protection for all Vampyre."

"I'm sorry, I don't quite grasp the reference to the sisters if you want me to go to South America with you." Khaldon scrunched up his eyebrows in question and non-understanding. "What do you mean to sire a new fighting force?"

"The O'Cuinn sisters, silly. Soon we'll have all three of them, and we'll be able to use their ancient lineage to help birth the generals for the new army. The Queen has chosen you to do her bidding, and I need your help in seeing it through to completion."

"Blimey, what in the world are you talking about?" Khaldon sat back against his seat, putting distance between them. Running his hands through his black hair, he stared holes through her eyes trying to figure out what in the bloody hell she was going on about.

Sire an army? Have all three sisters?

"Don't you see, Khaldon? I risk angering my Auntie, the Queen, every time I deny her. Do you have any idea of how dangerous that is? I cannot deny her any longer. When we arrive before her, she will permit us powers unlike we have ever known. Together you and I could be stronger than our individual dynamics."

Confused, Khaldon slowly nodded and pressed for more information. He needed to learn more without making it look as if he thought she was bat-shit crazy. "Yes, but what do the O'Cuinn sisters have to do with your new army? I still don't follow. Are you referring to Cheyenne? Do you know where her sisters are being held captive?"

"I don't want to bore you with the petty details." The barkeep brought a ruddy ginger ale for Khaldon and set it down in front of him. Amicula ran her stiletto up and down Khaldon's trouser leg. She flirted a smile. "Just know that the Queen's plan is in full force and we are ready to begin. I wanted to formally extend my invitation to you tonight."

"If you remember your history, Ami, I'm the direct descendant from a queen many times the power and cruelty of yours." Khaldon eyed her. He shotgunned the ginger ale and slammed the glass back down on the table. "I know full well what she has, and does not have, to back up her edicts and how far she can push and pull her subjects."

Amicula sat up a bit in her seat, whisked her hair out of her face, and repainted on her smile.

"Even though I am most flattered about your offer, I'm afraid I must decline." Khaldon grabbed his cell phone and his keys out of his pocket in a gesture of exit. "I came here to talk about Cheyenne's sisters. Not your personal interests, even if those interests have me in mind."

"Could you excuse me, Khal for one teensy weensy minute, I have to use the ladies' room." Amicula took another sip from her champagne and dabbed at the corner of her mouth with her napkin.

Khaldon felt the metaphorical ice forming on her words. He stood as she left the table and picked up the other glass of champagne considering a drink. "No," he said to Amicula's empty chair, "I don't think I'll drink anything poured before I got here."

He turned in his seat to scan the bar, contemplating leaving before she returned. He drummed his fingers to the music.

What the hell is she talking about? A new elite military to protect Vampyre. Protect Vampyre from what? I hate this woman, always so damn cryptic.

"So glad to see you're still here." Amicula's sudden return surprised him as she slid a hand across his back. "I agree with you, so for now we will discuss business. Enjoy a drink with me. Relax."

"I don't think so, Ami. I'm not drinking anymore, you know that."

"Oh I forgot, how silly of me. I did order you another ruddy ginger if that's all right?" She removed her arm and slid back into the chair beside him.

After the new drinks arrived, Khaldon sipped with some hesitation.

Amicula began the conversation about her email, by discussing how many additional sucklings had been found and slated for removal since Cheyenne.

Half way through the glass, Khaldon loosened up his shirt collar and ran his hand back through his hair again. The beginnings of a slight slur formed in Khaldon's voice. "They aren't any more sucklings. Cheyenne was the last one. Have you learned something of Cheyenne's sisters or found their whereabouts?" Khaldon poured a glass of water from a pitcher left at the table. "Damn, it feels as if the temperature went up in here by fifty degrees."

"Oh, Khaldon, you silly goose." A slight smile parted Amicula's lips. "The O'Cuinn sisters who went missing on the night of the attacks, they are the central part of the plan for the Queen. All we need to do now is collect Cheyenne, then we can get on with the program. She is, however, a little more complicated now that she has turned vampire."

"I ... I'm not following." Khaldon held tight to the edge of the table and took in a look around him. His eyes landed on his glass. "Bloody hell, Ami, what did you put in that drink?"

"Really now, Khaldon, that isn't polite. You know jolly well that Mordez Moi only serves top shelf blood to the likes of you and me."

Khaldon tried to push away the glass but his hand was barely able to move it.

Amicula's smirk found its way clear into her eyebrow. She leaned in to plant a kiss on his cheek and then whispered into his ear. "I love it when you call me Ami. But the issue at hand is what I had the server slip into your drink."

"What?" Khaldon exclaimed as he attempted to spring from the table. The sudden motion only served to throw him off balance and almost to the floor. He grabbed onto her shoulder to steady himself. "Whaat di yoo put inmy drink todo thish?" He sat himself hard back onto the chair he just vacated.

"Oh, nothing you haven't experienced before. You see my love, I have fantastical plans for you and me. I want our little tête-à-tête tonight to end in a manner that pleases us both. But since I knew you most likely weren't going to cooperate, I changed the game. I knew Stovall assigning you to Cheyenne was going to cause a few minor inconveniences. My Auntie always gets what she wants. I suppose since you won't remember it by the morning anyway, I can tell you all the nitty-gritty details on the ride to my condo. I'm rather looking forward to tonight. It will be a most pleasant experience, for me."

"Whatter you taalkin aboot, Amickula?" Khaldon struggled against his words. "Why do this?"

"Fret not, my sweet." Amicula stood up and put a shoulder under his arm to lift him up out of his chair. "All will be revealed in the morning. Let me help you to my car." She broadcast to the watching neighboring table. "Boy, you are a big guy." With a smile, she whispered to the nearest group of young vampires, "He never can mix blood with his ginger. Happens at least a couple times a year." She winked at them. The younger vamps nodded in understanding.

The barkeep accepted more than a couple hundred dollar bills from Amicula as she slid them across the bar. She grabbed the barkeep's hand and squeezed until his hand turned red. His face, arm, and hand froze in alarm.

"We were never here tonight. Right, my good man?"

The barkeep nodded one time to acknowledge her and her warning.

She winked at him. "Perhaps I can rely on you again in the future?"

He nodded once again. "Any time, my good lady. Any time."

"Amikoola" was all Khaldon managed to say as she arranged him into the backseat of her waiting car.

Amicula barked off a command to her driver. "My condo at the beach, and come back for his car when you drop us off."

Chapter Twenty Eight

Cheyenne O'Cuinn

The Penthouse

"I got here as soon as I checked my voicemail, Chey. You've been contacted about Sheridan and Dakota? Are they okay?" Harris scrambled through the door. He grabbed a towel from the coat closet to dry his head. "Damn, that storm's intense."

"Did you park at the next lot over and walk into the parking garage?"

"Yeah. Why all the covertness?"

"I'm worried that you'll be seen. C'mon inside." I hugged him around the neck.

"Thank God they're okay, Chey."

Don't cry. Your tears will be bloody... don't do it!

"I'm in Dakota's room. I can't take any chances of Ludovic knowing I am getting any help. I don't want you to get hurt."

"Ludovic – that guy Dakota was seeing? He's the asshole that took her and Sheridan?"

I nodded as we walked into Dakota's bedroom. "What the hell, Chey? Don't give up on her yet. Why are you already packing her stuff into boxes?"

Harris leaned and glanced around the room.

Sniff, sniff.

"I'm not packing up her stuff. I got a call from Ludovic tonight and I heard Dakota yell out GC89. So I'm trying to find anything in her room with the alphanumeric code on it. I have no idea what it means, and I haven't seen anything in here that references it." I pulled out a huge box of crap from under her bed and threw it up on top of the covers. "Maybe I'll find something in here."

Sniff, sniff.

"All right. We'll at least we know they're alive. What is that smell, Cheyenne?"

"Wish you could have been here sooner. What smell. I don't smell anything other than you. You smell like a wet dog."

He looked at the bottoms of his shoes. "Cheyenne, something smells wrong in here."

I bit my upper lip. He stopped in mid-sentence.

Sniff, sniff.

"It's like..." Harris leaned in towards me and with his right hand tentatively pulled up a lock of my hair as he took another whiff. "Holy mother of a monkey on a stick!" He dropped his hand and took several steps back.

"Harris? What's the deal?" I raised my hands in a palms up WTF expression.

Cocking his head and scrunching up his eyebrows, Harris blurted out, "What's the deal? Oh for fuck's sake, Cheyenne. You've become a vampire. It was a damn vampire that bit you, wasn't it?" His voice shook on the verge of panic as he took a few additional steps towards the front door.

"Wait. Don't leave. What do you mean, vampire?" I stood in the doorway to block his exit.

What the hell? How could he possibly know this?

"You know damn good and well what I mean by vampire. This place reeks of vamper. I smelled it immediately when I walked in but thought you were burning that dragon's blood incense you're crazy about."

I swallowed hard and turned around to walk back towards the living room, leaving Harris to stand alone.

He followed directly after me and got up in my face. "I'll be damned. Roxas was right. He suspected that you had been bitten by a vampire. But we weren't one hundred percent sure yet."

"What are you talking about? You're friggin nuts."

"Am I? That scent intensified when you put that box on the bed. And then in your hair, that's when I realized the vamper smell wasn't on you. By Crom, it *IS* you!" Harris howled with laughter at the intensity of the moment as we walked back into the living room. He grabbed my arms and turned me on my heels.

Holding me at arm's length by my shoulders he said, "'Fess up, Chey. You can't hide this from me."

I thrust my fists on my hips. "By *Crom*, Harris, your inner nerd is showing again. Wait? Just how the hell do you know what a vampire smells like?"

"Well, technically, you and I are supposed to be mortal enemies. But that went out of fashion a couple centuries ago." Harris let go and plopped into the recliner planting his feet on the ottoman. "I'm a werewolf, Chey, but I'm not supposed to talk about it."

"So that conversation at the hospital with Roxas was real? Do you match your avatar inside the game? Unholy hell, Harris. We ... shared a house for three years in college. How could I not know?"

"We keep it hidden, just like you're gonna have to keep your secret now, too."

"Well, I'll be damned." I sat down across from him staring as if I'd never seen the man before.

"Most folks say you're already damned. I don't know though if that's true or not. You're only the third vampire I've met."

"Fourth. Roxas is a vampire too. He'll be pissed when he finds out I told you."

"Nope, third. Already knew about him when we met at your room. Pissed, nah. He's crazy nutso about you."

"Yeah, I'm pretty crazy nutso about him too." Recollection of that day in the hospital flooded through my mind. "I vaguely seem to remember you guys talking about vampires and werewolves, but the nurse had just given me another dose of morphine. I thought you were talking about the game, so I didn't think anymore of it, until a few hours ago."

"He's a great guy, even if he is a vamper. Not that I don't trust him, we've been pals ever since you brought him on board with the team."

"Listen. There's a twist to this whole Roxas/vampire thing," I hedged.

Harris looked at me with a 'fess up look on his face.

"Yeah. Okay, so this is gonna sound weird, but Roxas isn't really Roxas."

Harris looked sideways at me.

"I know, just hear me out. His real name is Khaldon, and he's been a vampire for like thousands of years or something."

"What? Are you shittin' me, Caz?"

"No, I'm not. Tonight I practically killed the guy because I thought Ludovic had done something to Roxas since I hadn't heard from him since getting out of the hospital. Roxas said he was going to put in a new server in the cabinet with you."

"Oh yeah – I couldn't get away from my client. I had to cancel. You mean you hadn't heard from him since Friday?"

"No, I hadn't. So Khaldon and I went over to the address Roxas gave me for the 3D holo suit. I found this email, there was bloodwine in his fridge, and nothing was making sense."

"Whoa, whoa, whoa. Roxas is this dude named Khaldon? How did you hook up with him?"

"It's a long story, but basically I had to meet the local vampire Lord, and Khaldon was assigned to watch over me. When Ludovic contacted me, I couldn't get hold of you, Briggs, or Roxas, so I called Khaldon 'cause he's a hacker too."

"Take a breath, Chey. Slow down. Then what?"

"After Ludovic threatened that he was going to hurt others that I loved if I told anyone he had contacted me, I realized I hadn't heard from Roxas. That's when I kinda went mental."

Harris looked at me as if that wasn't any new real news to him.

I punched him in the arm. "So I had Khaldon take me over to Roxas' house. Khaldon found a bottle of bloodwine in the fridge, and we found this email on his computer ..."

"Wait. You went into Roxas' house, nosed around in his fridge and computer files? Not cool, Chey – so not cool."

"No. Well. It didn't happen quite like that. Let me make you some breakfast, and I'll start from the top."

"Tell you what, I'm going to take Beano for a walk before he lets loose another noxious green gas cloud. I'm sure Stormaggedon could use a little time outside too. There's a covered walkway between the buildings. I'll have a chat with them. When I get back, we'll talk through this. Have you contacted your dad to tell him?"

"No, I haven't called him yet. It's 2:15 in the morning. You're going to talk to the dogs? Can you do that since you're a werewolf?" I looked at Harris, confused.

"I'm shitin' ya, Chey. Order a pizza and let's open a bottle of wine. I have a feeling we've got a long night ahead of us."

"Thanks, Harris. I mean it."

"We'll see if you still think so when I give Beano my fleas."

Harris stepped out the door with the dogs. I picked up the phone to order a meat supreme pizza. Do they deliver this late at night? If not, Harris would have to settle for a pound of bacon from the freezer. Now his carnivorous eating habits and monthly cyber-hypochondriac nonsense, all made sense.

Chapter Twenty Nine

Harris returned with the pups about the time the bacon finished thawing in the microwave. "No dice on the pizza – they stopped delivering at two a.m. and don't begin delivering until eleven, so I'm making you an omelet."

"Yeah, I was afraid of that. I sure do miss that twenty-four hour pizza joint by where we used to live."

"I can't say as if I miss that place – seemed like it was never quiet enough for me. Did you canines have a nice walk?"

"We did actually. I found out that you haven't been brushing your teeth twice a day like you're supposed to," Harris quipped.

"What? How? Are you kidding me? Beano told you I haven't been brushing twice a day?" My left fist clenched on my hip while my right waved my spatula around.

"Nah, but I figured since you weren't eating as much, you probably weren't, and now that you have all those extra canines you most likely will avoid your dental care. Proper hygiene is a must for vampires."

"You haven't changed a bit, have you? You are still as neurotic as the day I met you in lab. I bet you count how many loads of laundry detergent you get out of a container too."

"Every time." He winked at me.

"Come on, let's eat. What do you want to drink? I have juice if you want. I want to eat and get back into the office. Ludovic is supposed to contact me at three a.m." I gestured towards the kitchen, and we got out plates and glasses. He opened the fridge and seemed startled to see bottles of bloodwine.

"So you gotta tell me. How did you turn into a vampire, then find out Roxas was a vampire, and you hadn't told me?"

"Where the heck have you been since I've been out of the hospital?" I retold last night's events in detail and even though Harris laughed at me through most of it, in the end he was glad I didn't have to kill Roxas.

"So you think Ludovic is watching you?"

"Or having me watched."

"Somehow he knew I wasn't home, and he called me while I was at Roxas' house. Padme ran an unauthorized protocol on the house and couldn't locate anything internally. So, yeah, I think he's either got lookouts, or a camera on the penthouse somehow. That's why I've got everything closed up. It was safer to bring you in through the maintenance entry."

"Makes sense. Hopefully it worked."

"Otherwise, he's threatened he's going to cut off more body parts and send them to me."

"More body parts? What the hell, Chey?"

"Because I wasn't in my apartment, he gave me a pop quiz. Even though I got his stupid question right, he wouldn't let me talk to Dakota – so I went off on the bastard. He threatened I would be receiving a Fed Ex package today."

Harris gulped. "Listen, Chey, I want to run a tracer on his IP address. How much time does he spend with you on the phone? Does he give you a time limit before he hangs up?"

"Roxas tried doing that earlier, but he said every time the server called his connection, the line would jump to another IP."

Harris' face grew red. He opened up his shirt collar a bit more. "You got a fan?"

"In the other room. You okay?"

"I'll help you track down this asshole, Chey. It really pisses me off to hear this has happened."

"Uhh ... let me go get that fan now before you blow yer gasket." I had never really seen Harris upset before, and now that I knew he was a werewolf, I thought it was all a little bit creepier. I wasn't sure I was ready to see him wolf out.

We moved into the office and he whistled. "Damn, Chey, you have seriously been building haven't you."

"I wish I could share the beta results on the prototype suits, but until I get my sisters back, I can't even think about work."

We got seated and logged into the portal. I was anxious to see if any messages had been sent while I was out.

"Harris, do you think that maybe GC89 is referencing a geo-cache? Do you have any of Dakota's old geo-cache archives?"

"I think so. You're right, Cheyenne. That's how she catalogs them. I totally didn't make that connection. Dammit! I have several of her books and they all begin with GC and then the number. Why didn't I catch that?"

"Where are those books now, Harris?"

"Hmm. Not sure. I remember scanning a few of those into the database when I needed inspiration to set my own caches. I have a couple of boxes she gave me under my bed at the house. When I leave here today, I'll go get them."

"Okay good. I'm gonna tear apart her room some more and see if there is anything specific about that one location."

"Have you thought about checking Dakota's intranet account? She creates geo-caches all the time. Have you tried that?"

"That's a fantastic idea. I'll log in and check."

I opened up the portal on two machines and neither account had any messages, except ones for Dakota. It was full of messages from Briggs. "Oh crap," I muttered.

"What? Did he contact you?"

"No, but Briggs is goin' nuckin' futs looking for Dakota. I think we need to contact him and get his ass down here."

"How about after we get through whatever is gonna happen here in a few minutes, I call him up and talk to him."

"Are you sure that's something you want to do? I appreciate the gesture and all, but ..."

He gave me the hand. I knew there was no point in arguing anymore. Years of living with him had taught me when he was done.

I just grinned at him. "Thanks, I really appreciate the help. I feel so weird, so lost, like everything has changed since Halloween night."

"Well, think about it, little sis. You died, became a vampire, your sisters have been kidnapped by another vampire, you find out Roxas is a vampire and is this Khaldon dude. The only thing that hasn't changed is Beano."

I smiled at him.

"Oh, and don't forget, I just found out you're supposed to be my mortal enemy as well." Harris smiled and punched me in the arm. "If there's gonna be any fighting it'll be me and you against the baddies. However, trying to convince my pack to fight among vampires – well that might be a different story."

I grimaced at both our realities.

A ping popped up on my computer screen and a text message rolled across the monitor. I motioned to Harris to begin the trace and to monitor the databases. We needed to determine where this transmission originated.

[Fang Boy] Who do you know who has a birthday this month?

I thought about this for a minute. Who has a birthday in November?

My father's birthday is in November.

I froze with terror. Ice water cascaded through my veins.

Afraid to answer the question, I chose a generic route.

[Lady Cazenove] I know several people whose birthdays are in November.

[Fang Boy] Perhaps so – but which one is related to you?

I didn't respond to the instant message but hollered at Harris instead, "You gettin' anything on this creep?"

[Fang Boy] Unscramble These Words to Learn Your Next Clue

"Chey, he's using an anonymonizer IP off of a proxy server. Damn, I hate this guy. Looks like this address is coming in from Germany. Is that where you think they are?"

"I don't know. We weren't able to get a firm location last time. We might have to wait to see if he uses the same IP address again.

[Fang Boy] odnw noe Ethre nda cninsouot og.

[Fang Boy] When you figure it out, call me on Dakota's phone.

[Fang Boy] Do you understand?

[Lady Cazenove] Yes. How long do I have?

[Fang Boy] The sooner, the better. They don't get to eat or drink until you answer me. Don't keep them waiting!

[Fang Boy] Be online at 8 a.m. sharp for your next clue!

"I hate this fecker!" I screamed.

I typed into the chat window, but the message indicated the user chat had gone offline and the message did not go through. "Shite – I hate word scrambles – I totally suck at them!"

Chapter Thirty

Amicula Darkrose and Khaldon Seters

Cocoa Beach Condo

"Airplanes," Khaldon slurred. "I hear airplanes. Are we going somewhere?"

"Shit!" Amicula snapped. "He must be gaining a tolerance to this stuff." Carefully, she used a hospital syringe to squirt more Solunarae blood into his mouth. Smiling, she watched his eyes drift closed again as his arms continued to reflexively strain against the bonds. "Relax, my love, we'll be at my house soon enough and the gentle sound of waves will calm you."

Amicula's driver looked back at her in the rear view mirror.

"Damian, I'm going to need your help when we get to my house. I need him inside quickly before he wakes up."

"Yes ma'am. I've never seen Mr. Seters look like this before. Is he doing all right?"

"He's fine, a little inebriated, but fine. Just be a good boy and drive the damn car, would you? I'll take very good care of him."

Minutes later they arrived at her condo in Cocoa Beach. Amicula helped Khaldon stumble into her bedroom and onto her bed. "Here we go, Khaldon. It's showtime! Time to perform for me once again."

"Wha, whats going on Ami? Why is everything so fuzzy?" Khaldon followed this with incomprehensible noises.

Amicula concluded these must be the slurred versions from his now extinct native dialect. Whatever that had been. She tugged at his shoes and threw them across the room. "Such a special treat – don't you feel fabulous? Who would have thought it? Solunarae blood is like crack to vampires. No wonder the Weres can't handle it. I've kept the lunar blood dosage small enough to keep you groggy but not enough to send you on a full blood rampage." She admired her handiwork as Khaldon lay against her pillows in a blissful stupor. "We wouldn't want that now? Would we, dear?"

"Why, Ami, I told you ..." Khaldon drifted into incoherence again.

Amicula unzipped the side of her dress, letting it drop to the floor revealing her exquisite nakedness and moist eagerness. "Khaldon, lover, I am going to take your clothes off now, and you are going to have a good time whether you remember it or not." She unbuttoned his shirt and unbuckled his belt. She folded his shirt and pants and set them neatly on the dressing chair in the corner. "We must not wrinkle your fine shirt now, you still have to look presentable in the morning."

"Cheyenne, I'm sorry. I'll help you do what ever you need me to," Khaldon slurred.

"Well, now, Khaldon, that certainly is a mood breaker, isn't it?" Amicula hissed through her teeth. She pulled out the vial of blood from her purse once again. "Well, a bit more won't hurt you. Just enough to make you forget about that stupid O'Cuinn bitch."

After Amicula poured the remaining blood from the vial into Khaldon's mouth, she tied his wrists to the top of her poster bed with silver-lined fabric. Not enough to burn him, but just enough to weaken him.

Before completing the final knots at his ankles, Amicula sighed, "Oh my! Would you look at that! Mmmm – I remember that fondly." Humming softly, she deftly removed his tented briefs, and completed securing him to the bed frame. "There – that should do you nicely."

Lightly stroking her finger up and down his shaft, she easily brought him to full hardness.

Amicula grinned mischievously. "Well ya know, Khaldon, I was going to use this cock pump on you." She gestured to a case near the bed as if he were able to understand her. "However, I don't see any reason why I shouldn't have some fun tonight. I have missed you dearly after all."

Slowly she kneeled on the bed, again stroking Khaldon. "I just hope I'll be able to tell when you are ready to give me your little legacies. I don't want to waste anything so precious."

Lifting her left leg, she straddled Khaldon's knees. Taking him into her mouth, she fully lubricated him with her saliva.

Khaldon moaned in his stupor.

"Oh I have missed this, Khaldon. I know you have too. Soon you and I will be together again – just you wait." Taking him in her hands she slithered up his body. "Mmmmm," Amicula moaned softly as she lowered herself onto him. "This, Khaldon, this is what I've missed." Settling herself all the way down, she began the seductive bump and grind.

"I wish you would be able to remember our fun in the morning. I guarantee you, one day soon, *I WILL* have you back begging me to fulfill all your fantasies."

It wasn't long before Amicula milked Khaldon for all he was worth several times, literally, and contained the precious life-giving semen in test tubes. Her mission was complete. For now.

***

"Wha? Where am I?" Khaldon's eyes opened in confusion. He tried to sit up in the bed but immediately dropped back onto the pillows. Rolling his head to the side he opened his eyes once again. "Amicula's? How the hell did I get out here?"

One arm still tied to the bed post, he sat up and untied himself. Khaldon spotted his clothes in the corner and noted the time – eight a.m. He looked around and shouted for Amicula, but no one answered his call. As he stood, he realized how sore his testicles felt. "What the hell? No feckin' way!"

Khaldon held onto his head while looking in the mirror, struggling to remember the truth of the situation. He grabbed his briefs. "Gawd dammit to hell, Amicula! How did you do this to me?" Finishing the last button on his shirt he walked into the living room and saw a note on the table. It read:

> *Khaldon,*
> *Thank you, lover. I had a very good time ... in fact, several good times.*
> *You should be proud of yourself. You performed superbly, as always,*
> *and this time you supplied me with four more vials of your legacy.*
> *These will make Auntie Queenie very happy, for now.*
>
> *Your car is out front with the keys in it.*
> *It's full of fuel and ready for you to go home.*
> *Always Yours ~Amicula*

Khaldon crushed the note in his hands and shoved it in his pants pocket. She was nowhere in sight, her car gone. He reflected on her words. *This time? Four more vials?*

He knew he'd never freely given her any of his swimmers – she'd gone too far.

Her aunt has driven her bat shit loony.

He stood in front of the bay window overlooking the Atlantic and hung his head, trying to make any feckin' sense of the situation. "What did she do to me? What the hell is she going to do with those vials?"

Khaldon stared at the oil painting over the fireplace mantle. Amicula had it commissioned from their days of debauchery. He remembered posing for the painter, Diego Velázquez in 1647, the same year Diego painted *Venus at Her Mirror.*

Khaldon tore the painting off the wall. He slashed Amicula's face with crystal vase he destroyed from the mantle. He then swung the painting into her bay window, shattering the glass into a thousand pieces. The frame and painting tumbled down onto the rocky beach consumed by the saltwater waves destroying it and any memory of them forever.

***

On the drive back to Kissimmee, Khaldon dialed a phone call to the coven. "Johan, can you tell me what you know about last night? Why am I at Amicula's house in Cocoa Beach?"

"Not much, Khaldon, all I know is that Damien drove you and

Amicula to her beach house. He came back and got Roland, and they took your car out there. Hulderich took Damian's place as her driver because he can take the sun."

"Where is Hulderich now?"

Soft tapping on a keyboard in the background. "He's on his way back to the clan."

"Where's Amicula now?"

More keys clicked. "Huldrich called in and said he dropped her off at the airport near her place. Said she told him she was going to visit her aunt for a few days."

"Thanks, Johan. I appreciate your help."

"You know, Khaldon, I'm not supposed to give this kind information out, but you helped me out with my sister and that online picture."

"Thanks, man. Yeah, I know. I owe you one now."

"No worries, Khal – for you, anything."

As Khaldon drove back into the city, he wondered if he could ever look at Cheyenne with honor again. What would she think about this? Would she understand? She trusted him to go and find out information about her sisters – not to get drugged, hijacked, and raped.

He moaned. "How in the world will I ever be able to explain this?"

Chapter Thirty One

Cheyenne O'Cuinn

The Penthouse

"Was that supposed to be a joke?" Harris asked.

"Huh? What? I don't get it?"

"You suck at word scrambles. Get it? You suck? You're a vampire, Hello?"

"Okay, Mr. Wise Nerd, help me figure out what these words say."

"Seriously? He won't let them eat or drink until I can solve this? That sadistic evil son-ova-be'atch! Harris, I'm afraid he is threatening about my dad. I need to check in on him." I sat in my computer chair in a huff and grabbed my phone to dial my father's number. I looked over the instant messages again.

"I don't want to make life any more difficult for Dakota and Sheridan. There's no telling what lies Ludovic is feeding them. Do you have that anagram descrambler program yet? I don't like this. Daddy isn't answering."

"It's three in the morning, so he's probably asleep, don't ya think?"

"Voicemail. Dammit to hell. Padme, can you dial my father's house line?"

"Certainly. Please hold while I ring him," Padme responded.

"Hmm, let's take a look." Harris navigated his keyboard with short cuts that sent my head reeling. "It might take a few minutes, but we can get thousands of variations on these words to help decipher. It shouldn't take too long. In fact, the program has an algorithm to detect what words might best fit on either side of it. Sort of like a shingle analysis search engines use on web pages."

C'mon Daddy, please pick up the phone.

"Cheyenne, I have received a voicemail machine. Would you care to leave a message?"

"Can you try his live-in nurse? She's suppose to answer 24/7."

"I think I have it deciphered. It's not a difficult scramble ... but, Chey, this isn't good." Harris turned to look at me. "Did you get ahold of your dad yet?"

"No – not yet. I'm trying for the live-in nurse who is supposed to be there with him. What are you seeing, H?"

"Cheyenne, I am being prompted to leave a voicemail for the nurse," Padme said.

"All right, we'll call back in a minute. Go ahead and terminate the call, Padme."

Harris turned his monitor toward me, his face ashen.

I looked at his screen and read the unscrambled words.

Three O'Cuinns Down One to Go

"Daddy? No, please, please no!" I fell to my knees in front of his computer. "I ... I just spoke to him earlier this evening!" Guilt and those horrible overwhelmings cascaded all over me again.

Harris came over and placed his arms around me. "Chey..."

I held him out at arm's length with snot, blood, and mascara running down my face. "Did it say anything else?"

He handed me a tissue from the box of Kleenex I kept on the table. I blew my nose and tried to clean up my face, but the horrendous pressure of my father becoming Ludovic's victim was more than my brain could wrap around.

"Chey, you go ahead and contact him on Dakota's phone and I'll call Briggs."

"Should we wait for Khaldon, Roxas ... oh hell, whatever his damn name is? He should be back anytime."

"Look, Cheyenne, you read what he wrote. They could be starving or dying from dehydration. You need to call him now!"

I nodded and sniffed. I called Dakota's phone and left the message as instructed. I drove to my father's house, praying against all odds that he was truly home and that this joke was on me. But something told me that wasn't the case at all.

Chapter Thirty Two

By the time I got back to Orlando, Harris had left to go hunt for Dakota's geo-cache notebooks. That maniac Ludovic had both my sisters, and now my father had disappeared right under my nose. I clutched the note that had been left in my father's apartment for me. It mimicked the word scramble Harris and I solved.

Three O'Cuinns Down and One To Go!

I would never forget those visions of my father's caretaker dead on the floor drained of all her blood. Why did they have to kill her too? What was the point of all this insanity?

I am responsible for her death! I should've never let Daddy out of my sight!

Flat out exhausted, I waited for the time Ludovic said he was going to contact me at eight a.m. I checked the time, it was 7:45 a.m. I stumbled into my office to check my computer. Nothing. My phone chimed it had received a text message. Sure that it was Roxas, I swiped open the lock screen.

"Hope I didn't wake you, my pet. I'm not ready for your next clue. But here is that message from your sister I promised you." Bile clung inside my throat as I read Ludovic's text.

There was an Mp3 attachment to the message. I wasn't sure if I opened it that the message would contain a virus, but I couldn't wait. My finger shook as it hovered over the attachment file.

I clicked it.

I watched as the file downloaded and opened up in a media player on my phone. Instantly I heard Sheridan's screaming. Her pleading begging sobs for them to stop hurting her echoed out the speaker. I heard a thud and a clanging of metal and she grew quiet.

Instant tears rolled off my face. I collapsed on the couch. I hated this awful, sadistic man with every fiber of my being.

Why would he do this to us? I'm so sorry ... I promise I will find you!

***

Fed Ex was due to deliver in a few hours and I needed to get some sleep. I couldn't think straight any longer. Worried, furious, and even more distraught about what the delivery package would yield, my body was completely numb. I saw a notepad on the coffee table.

Chey – Ran back to my house to get the geo-cache notebooks from Dakota. I'll call you immediately if I find anything that references GC89. I called an emergency pack meeting to get some help. Briggs is driving in tonight. I'll be back soon.
Hang in there. Love ya – H

Beano and Stormy jumped on the couch and licked my face. It seemed when everything else in life was shite, my pets were always there for me. They loved me no matter how shitty a sister or daughter I was.

I spoke out loud to the pups, "Where the heck is Roxas - Khaldon? I need to figure out what I'm gonna call him."

I was beginning to feel like the freaky stalker chick from *Fatal Attraction*. Anxiety settled in the pit of my stomach worried he might be in my next list of clues and or disappearances.

Harris is right. I just needed to hang in there.

I puffed out a few breaths and petted the pups for a few minutes. I decided on a shower and to try and get a little bit of rest. The package would be here in a few hours, regardless if I slept or not. Hopefully Roxas and Harris would get back before it arrived.

Cranking the shower water all the way to hot, trying to scald off the day's events, I languished in the steam. Finally, the woman in me gave way, and I decided to shave my legs only to discover there was no need. Guess that's another thing vampires don't need to do. I pulled up the teak bench and sat under the steamy mist and gave up. I tried in desperation to make sense of it all.

How in the hell did this happen? Why are we being targeted? My entire family is being controlled by this puppet master freak? What in the hell for if he doesn't want any money?

With every inch on my skin exfoliated, I fell into bed. In a flash, Beano jumped on the bed and Stormy tucked herself under the covers. He circled around three times and planted himself into the small of my back - just as he had done since the day I brought him home. Now he was a sixty-five pound puppy asleep and snoring. I always felt safer when Beano slept beside me. Nothing bad could happen with my big protector in the bed with me. If he felt calm enough to sleep, then I knew it would be safe for awhile.

I vowed tomorrow to find where Dakota kept those records of the geo-caches. They had to be close.

Where is GC89? Where are you my sisters? I'll find you, Daddy!

***

The pounding on the front door and the incessant ringing of the doorbell slammed me out from the depths of sleep. My ceiling clock blinked at me – 11:11 a.m.

Oh shite – Fed Ex.

I grabbed an overnight shirt and a pair of boxers – my red hair flying wildly across my face as I stumbled toward the door with Beano on my heels. Barely able to focus, I gave Beano the hand command to not move unless I gave him a signal to attack. Tentatively, I opened the door, pulled my hair back behind my ears and saw the familiar blue and orange uniform. I saw a drop-dead gorgeous delivery guy who was so amazingly good-looking he had to be gay.

In his hands, he held a very small box. I didn't even know they could deliver such a small box. I gave the guy a puzzled look. He mocked my expression with a look that said, 'I have graced your presence with my six-pack-abs, but you don't have the right plumbing, so never mind.'

He held the package out to me. Truthfully, I didn't even want to touch it. I had no idea what could be in it. Would it be my next clue, or perhaps a bullet he had used to kill one of them? I just couldn't bear thinking of what could be in such a small package. What was I expecting? Something big enough to hold her head?

"Sign here, lady," Mr. Model Man said and handed me the electronic tablet.

I stared at the little white box. "Can you put it on the table please?"

He rolled his eyes at me. "Sure. You don't have any mean dogs in here, do ya?"

Beano growled at him from behind my legs. Stormy pranced up and began to bark. Super-hot delivery guy dropped the box on the foyer table and ran out the front door. Stormy continued her barrage at the poor guy.

"Good boy! Keeping Momma safe, that's your job isn't it ... yes, it is. You're a good girl too Stormy." I scratched them both behind the ears as we watched the guy run back to the elevator.

Beano's nose twitched as he sauntered over to the package on the foyer table. This prompted my intuition to dive into my sense of smell. The odor of decomposed flesh curdled my stomach. It roiled to associate the rotten smell with my sister.

"I can do this. I can put on my big girl panties, and I can do this." Holding the box to my face, I looked closer to see if I could find anything about it which would help clue me into its origins. I shook the box and something solid moved inside it. "Oh, Beano, I have a bad feeling about this."

Pulling the sealed tab along the edge of the box, I prayed it didn't have a live snake or some kind of spider in it. I just simply couldn't handle it if that were the case. Big girl panties or not, I didn't do critters with more than four legs.

Instead, what I did see dropped me to my knees in less than a heartbeat. Inside was a small box that an engagement ring would normally be in. Inside the box, resting on a cushion of black velvet was Dakota's pinky toe. It still wore the Hello Kitty toe ring I had given her for her last birthday.

I had no words – only more tears as I recognized Dakota's signature toenail polish.

Beano licked my salty face, consoling me. I reached out and hugged him to help endure the guilt over the damage I'd done to my sister.

Chapter Thirty Three

I awoke cradling the black velvet jewelry box to my chest and the incessant ringing on the door bell again. I don't know how long I lay on the cold tile. I got up and tried to straighten out my appearance, even though a quick glance in the mirrors proved my face looked like a pink Stay Puft marshmallow man.

Beano sniffed the air at the same time I noticed an odd tinge to its flavor. Floral and sweet.

"Okay, I'm coming – lay off the damn bell, will ya?" I shouted. "Beano sit. Stay." Again, I gave him the hand command to not move unless I gave him a signal to attack.

Opening the door revealed a huge bouquet of birds-of-paradise and lilies in the arms of a not-so-cute delivery guy.

"Are you Cheyenne O'Cuinn?"

I nodded.

"These are for you."

At least this guy has manners.

He had a nice smile, and he actually greeted the dogs. "Hey there, good boy. Is it all right to pet him and give him a treat?"

He's a dog person – he's got to be okay. I nodded at him.

He continued to pet Beano as he handed me the flowers. The vase was so huge it took both my hands to hold it. I propped it up on my hip in order to sign his delivery pad.

"Here ya go, ma'am. Can you sign here, please?"

I reached up to take the pen from his hand and with a lightning stroke he managed to clamp a silver handcuff onto my wrist. I was caught by surprise as my skin burned from the precious metal.

I looked down at Beano, and he staggered, almost stumbling backwards with white foam falling from his mouth. My skin smoldered, and it stung like boiling ice.

"What the hell?" I cried out.

"Shut up, bitch!" Mr. Not so Nice Delivery Guy pushed me inside and shut the door.

I swung the glass vase into the side of his head. Shattered shards of glass crashed and fell all over the floor. Slipping in the water, he stumbled backwards grabbing at the silver handcuff for balance, pulling my arm down with him. He tried to secure my other wrist into the cuff as he sloshed around in the water and glass.

So over the games, the clues, the grief, the everything, I simply uncorked on this asshole. I swung him around, throwing him into the wall where my commissioned Steve Hanks painting hung. His head exploded the frame.

Beano, wobbling, was at my side and dove atop the guy. Stormy barked as if her little life depended on it. Beano bit and attacked the man's face several times. Mr. Flower Delivery Guy punched Beano's chest and my poor puppy went flying into the next room. I heard a yelp and then there was silence. His paws were bloodied from the broken glass. Stormy pattered around Beano as she licked his head.

I turned back to the jerk. "Oh no you didn't, you mother fucker! Nobody hurts my dog and gets away with it!"

I grabbed a larger piece of glass from the broken shards as he stood. He stepped hard into me. As we crashed into one another, one of his long arms clipped me on the chin. Stars blasted behind my eyelids. His momentum sent him past me, giving me the opportunity to slash his face with the glass in my hand, gouging a deep gash in his cheek and over his ear. He screamed like a trapped insane asylum victim.

At this point I was so angry I didn't care anymore. I grabbed the closest thing I could find to kill this guy and ripped it to shreds. Unfortunately, that was my grandmother's rocking chair. I pulled out the heavy wooden dowel from the backing and attempted to beat the guy senseless with it. He sat there cradling his head after I pummeled him time and time again. *What is this guy made of? He should be limp by now.*

"And this is for my sister Sheridan. And this is for killing my dog!" I kicked at his ribs, relishing in the crunch of his bones as my toes crumbled with brute force against him.

He lay motionless and unresponsive. I stomped on his head one last time and said, "... and this is for destroying my Steve Hanks painting!"

Nothing. He didn't move. "Asshat!"

I limped on broken toes to gather the velvet box I had dropped in the doorway, grabbed it, and hobbled to Beano. I kneeled in my own bloody mess from the shards of glass and grabbed Beano up into my chest. I needed to know if he was okay or if I needed to call a 911 Vet. He was breathing. I could hear his heart beating – rhythmic and steady. But he was knocked out cold. I rocked him back and forth, consoling both of us. So completely overcome with grief and despair, I sat there, getting angrier.

I am not going to take any more losses, dammit!

A deep gasp escaped me as a blow to my head sent my teeth rattling inside my mouth. I fell sideways as the delivery guy wound up his electronic tablet for another blow. I picked up the wooden dowel from the rocker and braced myself. The idiot ran into me. I let us fall backwards, allowing his momentum to carry him right onto me, skewering him like a Sunday BBQ shish kebob.

The wooden dowel tore through the back of his spine. I laughed as his breath wheezed in and out of him. "Oh, you are so in deep gris gris right now, boy." My eyes grew wide as my despair turned into lunacy.

I turned the wooden dowel, twisting his insides as he howled out in pain. "How does that feel, you gobshite son-of-a-bitch?"

He screamed, and suddenly my inner vampire became famished.

"I'm gonna suck yer head like a mudbug, jerkwad. Nobody tries to cuff silver on me and hurts my dog!"

I sat down with my meat on a stick and thought about this scenario for a moment. I had my own human body on a stick. Caught between whether I should deep fry him or drink him with a straw, I wondered how I should enjoy my little delicacy. I've had deep fried Twinkies on a stick, a Snickers on a stick, and even a fried pickle on a stick, but this was my very first human on a stick. I wondered how I could sell human bodies on a stick at state fairs all across the country. Do vampires go to state fairs?

Who cares?

I shrugged, and I sank my teeth into his neck, drinking deep as he continued to struggle and scream for his life. His howling tickled my lips, and I sucked harder. The sweet, very different, tang from his blood flowed into my belly, and filled me with more adrenaline, more power, and something else, almost euphoric. My body awakened with every swig from his artery. He was all but shriveled up to a prune when Khaldon ran through my front door and gasped.

"Cheyenne! What happened here? Are you all right? What are you doing?"

With a mouth full of blood, I shrugged. "What?"

A little bit of blood dribbled down my chin. Momma always said, 'ladies don't talk with their mouths full.' I swallowed and wiped my face with the back of my hand. "He tried to kill me! Can you get these damn things off of me? Bitch, this shit hurts." I showed him the smoldering silver handcuffs etching deeper and deeper into my skin as they dangled off my wrist. My head felt heavy as I started to list sideways.

"Bloody hell, Chey!" Khaldon threw off his sunglasses and patted the delivery guy down for keys.

"Be careful. He might have a needle on him. He did something to Beano."

Khaldon ripped off the guy's front pants pockets in a single pull and found the key ring. Within seconds, the destructive metal clanged to the floor.

Throwing the depleted corpse off of me, Khaldon helped me up and hugged me tight. I was over crying. I didn't want him to see how weak I was, how defeated I felt.

"Are you okay? You haven't told me, are you all right?" His voice was kind, and calm, but I was still angry as to why he did not contact me or come back last night.

"I'm fine." I let out a loud belch. It echoed off the tiles. "Well that wasn't very ladylike now was it?" I dropped out of his grasp. "I'm a big girl. I can take care of myself."

"That's not what I said, or implied, Cheyenne."

My name, why did he have to say my name? God I loved how his English accent said, 'Cheyenne.'

I walked away, picked up Beano, and limped over to the couch in the living room. Folded like a blanket in my arms, he gave no resistance – simply passed out and lifeless.

"You're bleeding." Khaldon noticed my bloody footprints tracing my steps. "Let me get some towels and stuff. You don't want glass to embed in your skin. Believe me, it itches like hell later on." Khaldon walked through my house as if he knew exactly where everything was. It kind of freaked me out.

He returned with my red towels and a warm washcloth.

Good choice.

He plucked out the few shards of glass embedded in my feet and some larger pieces from my arm and knees.

It felt good to be touched. To have someone caring for me. I absorbed Khaldon's kindness and talked to Beano. I looked for Stormy. She was huddled under my mom's quilt and shaking. I pulled her next to me while I tried to rouse Beano back to consciousness. My heart leapt when I finally heard him whimper a little.

I cooed to him as he licked my nose. "It's okay, buddy. The bad guy is all gone. Mommy kilt him for you – oh, yes she did. Nobody messes with my Beano Puppy ... nobody." He licked my cheek again, laid his head in my hand and closed his eyes. Stormy licked at his nose and laid her little body beside him.

"Remind me never to bloody well piss Beano off in the future, all right? Those are some ferocious dog bites on that guy's face." Khaldon cleaned my wounds with the washcloth.

The movement tickled and I squirmed under his touch. My eyes drooped.

"What the hell happened in here? Who is that guy?" he asked again.

"Ludovic! Ludovic, that prick." I pointed to the little black box lying on the floor next to the skewered flower guy. My voice sliced through the momentary calm as memories flashed into my head. "He cut off Dakota's toe and sent it to me." My voice tremored. "The gobshite bastard."

"Then whoever this guy was, he tried to take me with him. I crashed the flower vase into his head after he cuffed me." I felt my face flush. I was overcome with heat. "Now I have a hurt puppy, a broken painting, and a dead guy on my floor. And where the hell have you been?"

"Never mind that." Khaldon looked at me. "What I want to know is who the bloody hell is sending you flowers?"

Chapter Thirty Four

K haldon held me close. He smelled freshly showered. "Do you realize you just killed a man who tried to capture you?"

"Where have you been? Why are you making me become a crazy *Fatal Attraction* bitch? I've never had to ask you where you've been." My voice tenuous, I pitched up a couple of decibels. "You've always shown up on time when we gamed in the simulators. You've never been late to a date."

"I know, I know ... I'm sorry about that. That is what I came here to discuss with you. I think we have a bigger problem than we thought."

It was hard even trying to stay mad at him with his arms wrapped around me. He rocked me back and forth in a calming motion. It was as if we were in the surf at the beach with his gentle swaying. I was still so tired, I almost fell asleep.

I belched. "Oh, excuse me. That surely wasn't very ladylike either." I think that guy might have been a bit intoxicated, because I feel funny. D'yaknowhatimeanlike?"

"What do you mean by funny? Funny like ha ha or funny like – you thinkn' it might be the Montezuma's Revenge coming upon you now?" Khaldon, still holding me, took a cautious step backwards.

"More like I'm fawin' aboot, phised as a fart, ya know? I'm pretty sure this fella here was full of the falling down juice. I'm hammered." My body felt like Jell-O as I sank into the couch.

"Ah – I see now, you had a bloody elevenses then have you? Come on now, let's get you a bit more comfortable." And with that Khaldon picked up the blanket from the back of the couch and covered both of the pups and me. I wrapped my arms around his neck feeling the muscles under his shirt as he tucked us in.

I could get used to this.

He stood and propped his hands on his hips staring down at me. I tugged at his pant leg to indicate I wanted him to down here and have a snogfest, but he wasn't havin' anything of it. "You sound just like Torchy when you're drunk."

I scrunched my face, not understanding. "Torchy? Your friend who took care of the puppies, or your dragon inside the game?" The firewater in flower delivery guy's blood hit me like a lead brick. "Did you say I sound like a dragon?"

"Well, Chey, kinda yeah – I suppose. Torchy is from Scotland, though, and your heritage is Irish."

"Are you calling me a skenker? How dare you call me a Scot?"

"No, m'lady, of course not, but I don't believe Torch will be all that happy with you if you refer to him as skenker. All right?"

"Whoever this Torchy fella is – whateveryoucallhim - I need to meet him." My words began to slur with every passing syllable. I was fading fast.

"Torchy is my best chap. You'll meet him soon." He continued to look down on me and pulled his mouth over to one side. "I think the best thing you need is to get some rest. You really need a shower."

I shot him a dirty look, but I knew he was right. There was just no way in hell I was going to be able to take a shower and support myself.

I'm not getting naked with him in the vicinity no matter how much I want to.

He sat on the couch beside me. The cuts in my feet healed as I watched. His hands caressed my feet as he pulled them onto the couch atop of him. Khaldon rubbed my feet, and I didn't even have to ask.

Oh glory Mother of the Goddess – I have a guy who likes to give foot rubs?

"Check!" I said in a singing voice.

"Check?"

"I probably will regret telling you this when I can think straight. But every time you say or do something that really softens my core, I give you a check mark. I have to tell ya, you're filling up my card."

His strong hands kneaded deep into the healing flesh of my foot. It felt heavenly.

"So ... Ima trying to get this ... you have a pet dragon? How come you never mentioned him before?"

My eyelids were heavier than my Aunt Margie's combat boots.

"You know the dragon I carry around my shoulders?" he said.

"Oh yeah - I remember now. The cute little red one who blows smoke rings out his nostrils. He's sooo cute." Clarity was the farthest thing from my mind. "And how is he your best friend? Do you speak dragon?"

"No, Chey. You're really mallard. Torch lives here in Orlando. In fact, he's in the same condo complex as me, a couple of buildings over."

I nodded. "So when *do* I get to meet the elusive dragon?"

"Perhaps after you sleep, cause you really need the rest. That dhampir's blood has you in a bad way."

Beano close to my side, actually got up and lay back down on Khaldon's foot. "You've been accepted." I smiled. "You still haven't told me where ... you've ... been."

Chapter Thirty Five

Khaldon Seters

The Penthouse

Khaldon sat on the couch, rubbing Cheyenne's feet. Even though she was sound asleep and even snoring a bit, he didn't seem to mind. Any amount of time with her was better than what he went through the previous night.

How in the hell am I ever going to be able to tell her about Amicula? I love Cheyenne – she is the most amazing woman I have ever known and now that she is vampire, I believe my life won't be complete until I make her my own. Look at her – she's beautiful, and these feet – they're so damn cute.

Khaldon looked up around the house and saw his avatar Roxas reflected in much of her home, similar to what he'd done with her avatar. She had a breathtaking watercolor painting she'd commissioned of their avatars kissing in front of a waterfall. It was her favorite picture. Now it lay lopsided in broken shards against the wall. Hopefully the impact hadn't damaged the canvas, but it would have to be re-framed.

Khaldon gently pushed Cheyenne's legs off of him and tucked them back under the blanket when he stood up. He admired her for a moment and hoped she could get a little rest sleeping off this drunk.

He picked up the painting to examine it for damage. Beano looked up at him curiously. "Well, Beano, I don't see any holes in the canvas. I think we can get this fixed up at the Super Market. Now what do you think we should do with this flower delivery guy?"

Beano growled and licked at his cut paw. Stormy peeked her nose out from under the blanket

Khaldon called Lord Stovall to arrange for the abstergers to come get the delivery guy. He swiped off his phone and set it on the table. There was glass everywhere. He didn't want to wake up Cheyenne, but it wasn't safe for Beano and Stormy to keep walking around.

In the kitchen, Khaldon found a broom and dustpan and began to sweep the tile floor. He noticed a small etched figurine. It was their dragon heart he had given her the night they partnered in the game.

Boy, I sure am glad the guy didn't hit this.

Khaldon looked over at Cheyenne. She took his breath away. A smile danced across his face as he continued to get the mess cleaned up.

After wrapping the body into what looked to be an expensive area rug, Khaldon stashed it in her spare bedroom closet. He looked around to see what else he could do to clean up and decided to work on Beano.

He carried Beano into the utility room and ran warm water in the pet bath. Carefully removing any embedded pieces of glass, he cleaned Beano's paws and applied doggie Neosporin to them. "Okay now, don't be licking this stuff off your feet." He gave him a good scratching all the way down his back and checked his legs for cuts as well. "Ya know, Beano, since we're here ..." Khaldon pulled out the shower handle and rinsed him down while Beano happily wiggled around. Khaldon dried off his new friend and rewarded him with a biscuit. Khaldon picked him up and placed him gently on the floor.

Beano trotted off and Khaldon followed him into Cheyenne's office. Beano curled up in his doggie bed as Stormy crawled in beside him.

On her desk was an out basket with lots of letters addressed to Roxas, but never sent. This put Khaldon into a precarious situation. He wasn't snooping, but they were very visible and they were addressed to him. "What would you do, Beano?" Beano looked up at him and wagged his nub of a tail.

"What do you mean, what would Beano do? Who the hell are you? Why is there another vampire in this house?" Harris stood in a defensive posture at the threshold of Cheyenne's office.

Khaldon sniffed at the air. His fangs almost fell out of his mouth, but he gained enough composure to not attack him. "Don't get yer pants into a pandemonium. Perhaps I should inquire the same, wolf." Khaldon gave him a wink.

"Rox? Are you Roxas?" Harris' face lit up with recognition.

The posture standoff was over just as fast as it had begun. "Damn dude, she wasn't kidding, you don't look anything like Rox. This is gonna take some gettin' use to."

"This is the real me. So hopefully I can stay this way for awhile."

Harris walked in and plopped into Cheyenne's chair. "It's good she's asleep – she's been a basket case, dude."

"I can't imagine the pressure she's under. But I've put in a call to the local Lord and hopefully we'll get some answers," Khaldon said.

"What happened to Beano?" Harris asked.

"What happened was when I walked in here about thirty minutes ago, Cheyenne was snacking on a flower delivery guy. Come to find out, he's a dhampir. He had silver cuffs on her and I guess was trying to capture her. But she and Beano totally whipped his ass! I would've loved to have seen it."

Harris nodded. "No shit! So that must be his truck parked downstairs. Where's the body?"

"I've got him rolled up in a carpet until the abstergers can get here. We need to identify this guy, and I don't have any scanning equipment on me. She drained him like a bathtub. To top it all off – the guy was totally intoxicated. That's why she's passed out on the couch."

"No shit?" Harris repeated.

"Yeah."

"Hey, Briggs is on his way down. He's driving in from New Orleans."

"Seriously? That's righteous. We got the Fed Ex package in the mail. Cheyenne is convinced it's Dakota's little toe."

Harris' eyes bulged. "That Mother Pus Bucket really did it. Dammit! You heard they have Kiernan now too, right?"

"BLOODY HELL! Are you serious?"

"Yeah, that was the clue he sent to her last night. They nabbed Kiernan and drained his live-in nurse. Cheyenne sent me a text after she got back from his house early this morning."

"No shite!" Khaldon said.

"Yeah. And then on top of it, Ludovic told her she *had* to be online at eight a.m. for her next clue," Harris continued. "She said the jerkwad had sent her a message that he wasn't ready for her. Instead he sent her an Mp3 of Sheridan screaming. He's jackin' with her mind and her sleep I think. Making her real tired so she'll start making mistakes, know what I mean?"

"It's just one thing after another." Khaldon sat on another office chair and let a long sigh.

Harris swiped the computer monitor to bring up the gaming portal, hoping there might be some tidbit Ludovic had left for them to discover. Anything to help them get one step closer to rescuing his adopted family. "What exactly did Cheyenne do to make him so angry? I mean, I know she's got a snark to her, but she would fight to the death to protect her sisters."

Beano nudged at Khaldon's hand. Khaldon scratched behind his ears and opened the jar of treats from the desk. He handed Beano a biscuit and another one for Stormy.

Propped up on his elbows, Khaldon leaned on the desk. "Ludovic promised if she got her pop quiz correct, he would let her talk to one of them for a minute. She got the clue right, but he reneged and told her, 'I didn't say *when* you could talk to one of them.'"

Harris nodded and also let out a long sigh. "Chey and I went through Dakota's room last night. Cheyenne told me about the GC 89. We figured out it must be a clue to a geo-cache that Dakota had made up, but we couldn't find any of her logs here. I drove to my house this morning to get the box with her notebooks she had lent to me. But I can't find any reference that goes that high."

Harris grabbed a couple of dog biscuits for himself, as he broke one in half and crunched on it. "Hmmm. Really is new and improved bacon flavor."

Khaldon looked at him.

"Blimey, dude?" Khaldon walked toward the living room shaking his head. "I can't believe he really cut off Dakota's toe. That psychotic pervert is so dead when I get hold of him."

"Well, I think you're gonna have to stand in line," Harris said between bites.

"I should've been here for Cheyenne last night."

"Yeah – you should have. By the way, just where the hell were you anyways?"

Chapter Thirty Six

Cheyenne O'Cuinn

The Penthouse

"**H**ey there, sunshine. Welcome back." Khaldon stroked my hair. I'd been moved to my bedroom, and Beano was nested in behind me.

"How are you feeling?" Khaldon's eyes looked deep into mine.

I wanted to sit there and gaze at him, but I had to pee something fierce. I rubbed the sleep out of my eyes and sat up. "Not bad, considering. I've got a killer headache. Maybe a shower will clear it up." I had the mother of all hangovers and my mouth tasted like the bottom of my boot.

"Sounds like a good time." A smile spread across Khaldon's face. "You might want to get a move on. We're supposed to meet Briggs at the Super Market in an hour."

***

Roxas, Harris, and I walked out to the garage.

Harris gawked at my car. "What the hell, Chey? Is this the Limited Edition roadster you were hinting at? When did you get this?"

I pushed the keyfob, and the familiar alarm beeped when the doors unlocked.

"How do you have this car?" Harris kept on. "This vehicle hasn't even been released. It's still in the prototype stages, and YOU have one?" He looked at me out of the corner of his eye.

"It's nice to have friends in the industry." I nonchalantly shrugged. "Perks, my friend. Perks." I shined my teeth at him.

"Well strike a light, m'lady, this is spiffing. I just might have to get me one of these babies. Can I drive?" Khaldon asked.

"Drive? Oh no. That is one of the items in the contingency, no other drivers. No can do, sorry." Both of them looked like I had just stolen their lollipops. Harris was my best bud for years now and Khaldon, well, I wasn't sure what he was to me, but Roxas ... he was ... is my everything.

"Let's just pick up Briggs and talk about this later," I murmured.

Fortunately I-4 wasn't jammed-packed with traffic, just the normal bumper-to-bumper at 75 mph. It took only about twenty minutes to get out to near the airport where this Super Market was located. We parked next to an old, abandoned building.

"Guys. What is this place? Are you sure we're meeting Briggs here?"

Harris got out of the car and ran his fingers along the paint job. "You see Chey, humans hardly even recognize this place. Inside it's really a massive structure. To them it just looks like an old warehouse building out in the middle of nowhere." Harris explained. "Basically the witches have been able to manage several glamours around the property. They can keep the unwanted away and it keeps the area safe for supers."

"Supers? Witches?"

"Right, as in supernatural creatures. Ya know, preternaturals, things that go BOO in the night. We need a place to go shopping, just like humans do." Harris elbowed me in the rib cage.

"So that place you were telling me about in the teleconference meeting was real?"

Khaldon placed his arm around my shoulder and squeezed me into his side. "Come now, m'lady, let me show you the most amazing attraction you will ever see in Orlando."

"So we're meeting Briggs here? Do you guys know what he looks like?" I asked.

Harris jumped over a cart railing practicing his parkour. "Rox, you said you knew him, right?"

"Yeah, we met. Damn it's probably been twenty-five years now or longer. Believe me – you can't miss Briggs, and he'll know who we are as soon as he sees us."

"What's that supposed to mean Rox?" Harris asked.

And about that time, one of the largest, darkest, and sexiest black men I had ever seen in my life, stepped into view from behind a Land Rover. We each stopped and just stared at the mountain walking towards us.

"Chey Chey!" The man roared.

A big stupid smile crossed my face. I stood shocked to see the man behind the silken, chocolatey voice who I'd only known as Briggs. This was really good – meeting everyone and getting together, despite the circumstances.

"Briggs - Oh my stars – is that you?"

"In the flesh, dahlin' – in the flesh!" Briggs grabbed me up and spun me around. I thought for sure he would crack me in half. He was bigger than Khaldon, and I wasn't sure how that was possible. I hugged him back, and felt an immediate sense of relief that I had these three very capable guys to help me find my family.

Briggs set me down, and Khaldon stuck out his hand. "Damn, Briggs, it's been a long time."

"Rox, my man! Wasn't your hair red? And who is this?" Briggs turned to Harris. "Wait, let me guess. Well I know the girls don't have a brother, so you must be Harris. Right? Damn you about as white as they come."

Harris laughed and stuck out his hand. "The one and only!"

"Hey, let's go grab something to eat and catch Briggs up on everything. I want to go over what we've uncovered in the past few hours and just kinda start from the beginning." They all nodded at me.

I stood in awe of the programming magnitude in front of me. These guys were on my team.

"But wait? Is this the right place for Briggs? Will he be safe in here?" I turned to Roxas.

"Uh ... I wouldn't worry about that, Chey," Harris answered the questions instead.

"Wait? What? Are you trying to tell me that Briggs is a werewolf too?"

"What? Oh *hellll* no – I ain't no daawg." Briggs puffed up his chest in a mock sign of aggression. "No offense, Harris, my man."

"None taken," he responded. "Cheyenne, take a deep breath and tell me what you smell and feel."

"I feel power, and a lot of it – and I smell smoke, sulphur, the ocean, some other things I can't tell yet."

Briggs picked me up by my armpits and brought me up to his eye level. He clicked his eyes vertically instead of the normal horizontal up and down. It sent extraterrestrial shivers through my chakras to think he was some kind of alien from the black lagoon.

"Baby doll, what you see here is one fine, black ass dragon. I am a Gargouille – a water dragon."

"No shite! A dragon! Why is it that everyone on this team is a supernatural being, and none of us girls knew it?"

He put me down and laughed. "Most likely because we all work so remotely. Hell, Rox and I go way back to Compuserve days, and we just got to know one another over the years. I didn't know about Harris until we met tonight. You can't ever shake that smell from a werewolf."

"Hey – I resemble that remark." Harris laughed. "I need a good scrubbing and dip, but I don't smell that bad, do I?"

We all just looked at him.

"C'mon – let's eat – I'm starving." Briggs slapped Harris on the back as we walked towards the old door that looked as if it would fall off its hinges if we touched it.

As Briggs and Harris took the lead, I assessed what definitely had Dakota's interest. He was one fine, man.

Khaldon cleared his throat and wrapped his arm around my waist and pulled me in tight. His bright eyes met mine. They dug daggers into me. "See something you like, m'Lady?"

I kissed him on the tip of his nose. "As a matter of fact, I do."

Chapter Thirty Seven

The Super Market

How does one describe The Super Market? It was unlike anything I'd ever seen or heard of in my entire life. The place was architecturally magnificent. I felt as if I were walking into the Taj Mahal, it was so grand. The floors were marble and walls must've been lined in granite. I could hear running water in the far-off distance, like a waterfall of sorts. The energy of the place was that of a spa. The Super Market was divided into huge sections which catered to every need of the entire Supernatural community. We walked up to the reception desk where an alluring green woman greeted us with a cyan smile. I couldn't help but look at her mouth when she talked. I had never seen blue teeth before.

A melodious voice sang out, "Welcome to the Super Market. My name is Z'anima." She looked right at me but didn't bother to address the guys. "You haven't been here before, have you?"

I looked around at each of them. "What? Is it that obvious I'm a noob?"

"No, not at all, my dear." Z'anima's smile sent waves of ease crashing through me. I immediately felt better. She continued, "Would you like me to explain the services we have to offer?"

Not sure what this amazing creature was or how to respond, I simply nodded my head.

People walked in and passed us through the massive foyer as she slithered out from the counter to the marquee. That's when the oddity of the situation began to make sense. Behind the counter displayed the most massive salt water aquarium I had ever seen in my life. It was as if whales could have fit inside it – the tank was so large. The tank teemed with every imaginable sea creature and a few I didn't know existed.

Z'anima glided her way over to the marquee. She didn't have any feet. A wet tentacle extended to the map. I swallowed hard, trying to keep myself composed, unable to figure out this supernatural being.

She suctioned a cup to the map at where we were standing. "Here at The Super Market we offer all types of amenities and services which are specifically tailored to the unique needs of each and every one of us. Inside you will find our specialty grocery and clothing stores, but we also offer a fine selection of restaurants, blood bars, live feeding arenas, and human sustenance volunteers."

Stomachs rumbled all around, including my own.

Z'anima continued, "We also have an award-winning Wiccan apothecary, a well-stocked lending library – membership, of course, is always complimentary – a bookstore, and several multi-national and species specific spas."

My eyes lit up. "Spas?"

"I highly recommend the spas. They have every health and beauty amenity available including sunscreen treatments, teeth whitening, debarnacalizers, scale shed and shines, breath freshening, tongue scrapings, wing massages – with or without the happy ending."

I looked over at Briggs. He seemed very interested in the offerings.

Z'anima continued to list the myriad services I never knew could possibly exist. "Teeth and claw sharpening, horn scraping, soot flush, and we even have a wide assortment of deodorizing insecticide dips."

Z'anima stared pointedly at Harris who was beginning to look a little self-conscious as he scratched behind his ear. She wiped a tentacled arm below her nose, but her smile erased all insinuations. "We also have professional services in the forms of walk-in health clinics, dentists, beauty parlors, custom tailors, insurance and travel agencies, along with tax accountants, and munitions specialists. It is easy to get lost in here and enjoy a mini-vacation from the confines of humanity. What are you interested in tonight?"

Brigg's nodded. "We're interested in finding a quiet place to grab a bite to eat, pick up some supplies, and then find a place to freshen up."

Z'anima pulled out an electronic tablet. "Would you like for me to make a reservation at your spa for after you eat?"

Both Briggs and Harris nodded enthusiastically and booked their appointments.

Khaldon removed his arm from my shoulder and reached down to hold my hand. "Great – Cheyenne, that'll give me time to show you where to get the best bloodwines and get a case for you to have at home. We can pick you up a full copy of *The Vampyric Canons*."

"It's not often we get such an eclectic mix of patrons in one group. Did you want to dine together, or find your food and then meet up a little later?" Z'anima asked.

We looked at one another, and for the first time I stopped to consider our troop. Here I stood with a werewolf, vampire, and dragon in front of a green octopus lady.

Khaldon stepped forward. "I think we'd like to dine together. Can you recommend a restaurant to suit multi-naturals, or are they all segregated?"

"Absolutely," Z'anima said as she laid a slimy suction cup on Khaldon's arm. This informal gesture triggered an insane sensation of wanting to cut off her arm and make sushi out of her.

Z'anima smiled at me. It could take awhile to get used to looking at blue teeth. "We have many fine restaurants to accommodate all of you – let me suggest The Rusty Anchor. It serves up a mean rack of ribs and some the best bloodwines available from The Broken Fang. How does that sound?"

I couldn't tell whose stomach growled louder, Harris' or Briggs'.

"Sounds damn good to me – let's eat," Harris said.

"Might I suggest a wonderful dessert for the lady after your dinner and spa treatment?" Her farthest outreached suction cup landed next to a place called The Tasty Pastry. The sight of the name made my mouth water. I could smell the cinnamony, buttery, glazed sugar from here. All thoughts of serving her up Kobe style instantly disappeared from my thoughts.

A loud whoosh of air and sea spray cascaded over the entrance way. I watched as dolphins and seahorses raced along the tank's edge.

The green lady laughed. "Silly boys – don't mind them, they're itching to get into the open sea tonight for the Atlantis Race trials."

"I love those games." Briggs nodded and smiled at me. "Hopefully this mess will be cleared soon. Maybe we can take everyone to the Olympic Games."

"My favorite event is the long dive," Harris chimed in.

Our hostess smiled. "Again my name is Z'anima, and if you need anything, please find a server walking through the departments, and they will help you find whatever it is you are seeking."

We all thanked her for her attentive assessments and walked into the bustling hall. Never in my life had I dreamed of humanoids, kelpies, ghosts, banshees, tigers, and a variety of creatures I couldn't begin to identify sitting and talking to one another in a cafe' espresso shop.

We followed the signs to The Rusty Anchor. I turned to Khaldon. "So ... Rox, err, Khaldon ... what was that all about?"

"She's a kraken." Khaldon gestured as we walked farther into the Super Market past the oceanic tank. "Normally, you don't see them out of the water much. Usually there is a merman at the information center, several times however, I have seen a mermaid there as well."

"A merman? A kraken? You mean as in big, angry, octopus-like, sea monster who bites ships in half and drags them to their watery graves kinda kraken? And merfolk who save the lives of sailors from those doomed ships?"

"The distinctive invertebrate herself. Kraken possess an innate sense of personality and oftentimes pick up on sonar-like waves from your mind and are able to ascertain your name, needs, and your most primal desires. They work alongside the Sirens quite often." He mussed up my hair and closed my open mouth. "It's not polite to gawk and stare, Cheyenne. Try not to look so shocked. Did you think vampires, werewolves, and dragons were the only kinds of supers on the planet?"

"No, but I ... I don't know. I had no clue. Honestly hadn't thought about it. There's just so much going on here. I really don't know what to think. I'm still trying to wrap my mind around the fact that mermaids are real." I stammered back at him.

Briggs snorted at me.

Just then a voice rang out across the vestibule. "Hey, Rox – wait up."

"Hey, Torchy, you silly bloke – where've you been? Shagging the ladies I presume?" Khaldon introduced a strawberry blond man who was heavy on the Scottish.

"Aye! How ye dae'in? Ah've no seen ya for yonks. Wher've ye been?" Torchy inquired.

I wasn't quite sure what he said, but by Khaldon's reply, I guessed it to be 'a haven't seen you in a while' kind of thing.

"You can call me Khaldon, they all know who I am now. Torch, I'd like you to meet my Lady Cazenove – Cheyenne O'Cuinn. Cheyenne, this here is my best bloke, Torchy. He's the one who has been taking care of Beano and Stormaggedon while you were in the hospital and such."

Instantly I liked this man. He had taken very good care of our dogs.

"An O'Cuinn you say? Can ye tell me, from where on the Emerald ye are from?" Torchy looked at me as if I was supposed to know how to answer him.

"He wants to know where in Ireland are you from." Khaldon explained, quickly saving me from utter embarrassment.

"Oh yes, of course." I blushed at not being able to understand his thick accent. "My sisters and I left Ireland when we were younger. I believe we're from Kerry. My parents never spoke too much about Ireland. I'm not sure why, truthfully."

"Torch here is a Celtic dragon, technically Welsh, but he is from Scotland so he is twice as confusing. He and I have been hanging for well, let's just say a very long time."

Briggs shot a look at Torchy and then back at Khaldon. His eyes squinted closed just a bit and then he stretched out his arm for a welcome fist bump. "Nice Bro – always great to meet another dragon."

Torchy smiled and gave Briggs a dragonly fist tap of acceptance. "Ye looking for some grub? Ah could eat a scabby horse a'tween two pishy mattresses."

I looked at Khaldon for a translation. "Yes, all right. Let's move along – I could really go for some chips myself – I'm famished." He slapped Torchy across the back. "Hey, Torch, you might want to go easy on the Scottish, or no one here is going to understand a bloody word you say."

"Aye, you've got a point, mate. Fair enough. I'm starved – let's eat." Torchy noogied me on top of my head as if he'd known me for years.

"C'mon, Chey, you'll feel better after we get some clean blood in you. We have a lot to catch Briggs up on and Torchy needs to come in on this party as well. Once we get everyone settled, and up to speed we'll get you home." Khaldon put his hand in the small of my back to guide me down the torch-lit hallway.

Home. I thought of what home used to be and how much my life had changed in such a short period of time. Just a couple weeks ago, home meant, my office, my computers, Dakota swinging in borrowing some money, going to the bars, and me playing inside my virtual game with this man standing next to me. Everything had changed.

The loss of my sisters gnawed at the fringes of my thoughts and deep into the pit of my stomach. How were we going to save them? Did we still have time? Any minute Ludovic could renege and do something horrific to them. Was that really Dakota's toe? Had other women been kidnapped as well?

We only had until morning and then Ludovic was poised to contact me again. Maybe now I had a fighting chance with Puff, Shaft, Scrappy Doo, and Dracula on my side.

Chapter Thirty Eight

The Rusty Anchor

I n no time at all we were seated, beverages poured, and the boys were up to their eyeballs in BBQ sauce. Who knew dragons and werewolves could eat so much? I was actually beginning to wonder who was gonna pay for this feast. Torchy and Briggs both decided on a dark ale called Moose Drool, and Harris decided to indulge in a beer called Blue Moon. Khaldon had the waiter serve us up a bottle of Apple bloodwine, which had a wonderful aftertaste of warmed cinnamon. I wondered if he knew I was craving it from when we were out in the vestibule.

Briggs stopped chewing a few times when Khaldon and I explained what we had found at the haunted barn and then when I explained about Dakota's toe.

"That's okay – she doesn't need all ten toes – I still love her and want to get her the hell out of there." Briggs shrugged. "I don't care where in the world she's at. I'm not leaving until we bring everyone home."

"Hey, Briggs, has Dakota ever mentioned anything to you about GC 89?"

He shook his head.

"The first night Ludovic contacted me, I heard Dakota scream GC 89 over the phone, and we've been trying to figure out what it means. We think it's a reference to a geo cache. We've gone through everything. Her room, her ExsanguiNation account. Hell, I even turned her car inside out, and I can't find a trace of it anywhere. I was really hoping you could help with this piece of her puzzle."

Harris stopped chewing and put down his fork. "I went through the boxes I had at the house, Chey. I brought them with me, but I didn't find anything that went that high in numbers. The last entry I found was GC 82."

"What? Really?"

"But while you were passed out this afternoon, I found a GC to-do list inside her account. I was going to see if there was anything under that file name while we were here tonight."

"Chey Chey – you were passed out? A little too much nipping on the bloodwine I take it?" Briggs elbowed me.

"Not quite, Briggs. Wait until I tell you the story of how Lady Caz here bagged her first dhampir. She was attacked early this morning and she turned him into her own Battle Kroc snak-pak." Harris seemed to be bragging about my weird victory.

"No shit, Caz?"

"Yeah, Briggs, no shite."

"Someone came after you? What the hell is going on? Is this from the same ass hat who has Dakota, Sheridan, and now your dad?" Briggs asked.

I nodded. "We've got a lot to catch you up on." I grabbed his shoulder and squeezed. "I'm so glad you're here."

"Look, Cheyenne, I found some of Dakota's geo-cache to-do lists." Harris picked up his tablet phone and logged into the gaming portal.

"What are you doing? We don't have a mobile version of the game."

"Oh yes we do. You aren't the only one who can code and develop. I've been working with Briggs to show you the mock-ups on the dev server of what the mobile versions could look like."

I smiled at him. I wanted to be terrifically excited that our game had mobile and tablet versions for the next rollout, but the news of that victory was overshadowed by the current events. After I had gotten my family back, I would remember to handsomely reward them both for such a tremendous achievement.

It wasn't long until my fettuccine Alfredo with sundried tomato-crusted scallops arrived.

"Eat and I'll log in and see what I can reference." Harris pointed to my plate with his phone.

Khaldon threw down a plate of lasagna and garlic bread in nothing flat and hailed a waiter.

"Dude, aren't you supposed to be allergic to garlic or something?" Briggs asked.

"Not any more than people are allergic to peanuts. We all have our quirks."

Khaldon drained the rest of his third glass of bloodwine and heaved a heavy sigh. "Listen, I have some bad news, and it pertains to last night and why I wasn't back like I said."

I didn't want to ask him and even though we were technically dating and exclusive, I also didn't feel I had a right to pry, but now that he had opened the proverbial can of worms, I didn't hold back any longer.

Torchy hailed another server. "Another round o' firewater if ye please."

"So what happened? You said you were gonna be back – did she not show up or something?" I tried to hold down the snideness in my voice. I didn't want to seem too creepy a girlfriend already. "Thank the heavens Harris was close by or he would've had to drive up from Tampa to help me."

"Thanks, Harris. I sincerely appreciate you showing up. You've always been a good chap to her." Khaldon's face scrunched up in pain as if he were trying to squelch down an awful headache. His eyes narrowed and then began to shift from side to side.

"I can tell you're upset, but we're all here – your friends. Tell us what happened that has you so shaken." I ran my knuckle down the side of his face and then grabbed his shoulder. His eyes softened, but he remained silent.

Torchy was a little less subtle and kind from my point of view, but they'd been best pals for ages. "Just bloody well spit it out – what's troublin' ye?"

"Going to see Amicula was a lot worse than I had intended it to be. There is another whole thing going on bigger than your sisters, Chey."

"Get the fuck out o' here, that Amicula nutter again? She's a pure mad mental," Torchy said.

"You know her, too?" I asked.

"Aye, and I ain't saying as I like the queer-hawk," he replied.

"Rox – who's this Amicula chick and what does she have to do with the kidnapping?" Briggs asked then chugged down a bit more beer.

"What do you mean, worse than Dakota and Sheridan being taken by that crackpot, Ludovic?" I set down my glass and tried to compose myself, but all of this was just too much. "How could there be more problems over and above me finding my family?"

Harris put down his phone to listen.

Khaldon continued, "You see, it's even worse than I understood at first. I knew there had been an attack on the theme park. Several vampires were found guilty of using the Solunarae lunar blood and that's what caused the attacks. I found out Amicula is the one giving out the Solunarae lunar blood and caused much of the chaos. The whole attack on the park that night was a huge ruse to kidnap you and your sisters. Cheyenne, you were attacked by one of the vampires Amicula infected with the lunar blood instead. You were only supposed to be kidnapped not attacked. Now she's trying to entrap you by having you find Dakota and Sheridan. She wants you too, Chey."

I rubbed my temples, trying to understand what he was saying to me. "What is Solunarae lunar blood, and why does it make vampires go crazy?"

"You see, Chey." Harris took another swig of beer and set his glass down hard on the table. "The lunar blood gives supernaturals like me, werewolves, the ability to change our form. We carry the Solunarae gene, and we can usually control the blood and call upon its properties when we most need it. The lunar part of their blood is deadly to vamps, though. They go into a fugue, and if too much is ingested, it can bring out the blood demon inside us all."

"A fugue? You mean like a black out? You wouldn't have any recollection of what had happened?' I asked. I took another sip of my wine.

Khaldon motioned to the waiter to bring another bottle. It was going to be a long night.

"You mean this Solunarae blood is like meth or crack to you guys?"

Torchy chimed in, "Aye, it's been said ye get a few shots of the

Solunarae blood in ye and ye're good as zombified. Sometimes ye be singing to the porcelain goddess for days until it purges from ye backwards and forwards. I've even heard of some who have died of it."

"So let me get this straight," I began sounding incredulous. "Amicula asked you to the bar last night to tell you how she drugged several vampires to attack the park to cause a riot so Dakota, Sheridan, and I could be kidnapped? Is that what you are saying?" I was having a difficult time accepting this. "But I thought Amicula was my friend. She said it was by her decision alone that I am still alive."

Khaldon ran his hand through his tousled black mane and ended up massaging the back of his neck. "That's why I couldn't figure out what her note meant about the sisters and that's why I had to meet her. You need to remember she doesn't know anything about you and me, Chey." He took my hand. "Amicula has no idea you and I have been dating online for over two years. I had to wait and hear her out to try and find anything I could on where they might be so we could locate them."

"Did you get the bitch to spill her guts?" Briggs asked.

I blinked up at him. "Khaldon, you mean, I could have been kidnapped as well that night? Is that what you're saying?"

"Wait - why do you call him Khaldon?" Briggs asked me.

Khaldon replied, "That's my real name. I've been going by Roxas Morgwain for several centuries now."

Briggs nodded, took another swig of his beer, and leaned back in his chair.

"Anyway, I believe that was the plan," Khaldon continued. "You see, Amicula is called a gatherer. She has been finding descendants from pure ancestral races to help find qualified breeders to build Queen Civetateo's dhampir army. They've been planning this for decades and it is soon to come to fruition."

"Are you saying that Dakota and Sheridan are being used to breed these ... whatever you call them ... dhampirs?" Briggs asked.

"I'm afraid so," Khaldon replied.

"But I don't understand why you didn't come back until after noon."

"At the bar, Amicula told me of the Queen's grand plans, and how I should be honored to be the prized Father of her army. I needed to listen to her, but I couldn't accept what she was offering me. So I refused. I told her she was a right Charlie and crazy as a nutter. I thought the jig was up when she offered me her drink, but I knew better than to drink anything already poured. I wanted to get more information on the sisters as her email had implied so I waited until she got back from the loo.

"She asked the bartender to pour us another round and he did. That's where it all starts to go dark on me. All I know is this morning I woke up at her house in Cocoa Beach with silver bindings around one of my arms, but I could tell where she had chained me down to the bed. I honestly don't know what happened. She must have slipped me the Solunarae blood because I cannot remember a damn thing from last night."

"Was there anything else you can remember from the night, Khaldon?" I asked.

"So spill it, what else did she say?" Briggs looked directly at him.

"She said the Queen is planning on annihilating all rogue vampires. Completely eradicating them from stealing the human food supply. Innocent rogue vampires are slated to be eliminated if they are not of pure blood descent."

"Wait a minute," I said. "I totally am not getting this. Are you saying this Queenie is planning on some sort of vampire apocalypse?"

"Yes, and if that is the case, then the rogues will fight back. They'll begin to turn every human they can find to build their own armies to fight against her and the dhampirs. No matter what, the humans lose in this scenario. That's where you and your sisters come in. I believe the Queen wants all three of you to be a part of her breeding program to create some kind of super dhampir."

"But why? We aren't from pure blood vampire lineages. We're humans."

"I'm not sure, Cheyenne. None of this makes any sense."

The neurons in my brain scrambled. I remembered the horrific pictures of those women strapped up in the milking machines of the haunted barn. My glass of bloodwine slipped through my fingers. The crystal crashed and shattered against the marble floor. Crimson stained the linen table cloth as images of my possible future abduction and rogue vampires attacking humans flooded my brain.

Chapter Thirty Nine

"I think I know where they are!" Harris stood up while swiping madly at his phone.

"What? Where? Did you find something about GC 89?"

"Yeah, but I don't know how helpful it is. The only thing she has listed under the Geo-Cache 89 is an old abandoned warehouse by a lake. It doesn't give any reference to anything else."

"What was the item for the geo-cache?" I asked. "Maybe that will give us an additional clue."

"It looks like the person is supposed to take a picture of himself in front of the fishing nets on the docks and then load the photo onto the website."

"I don't ever remember doing anything like that. I have no idea where that is."

"Yeah, that's the problem. It's under her to-do list. Looks like she hasn't done it yet."

"Dammit. There could be hundreds of places like that by the water. But it sounds like they aren't too far away." I bit my lip, frustrated.

It was getting late, and the check arrived. I reached for the check and four hands struck past mine to claim it. I looked at all of them and was so thankful to have such wonderfully weird friends. I stood up to go to the ladies' room and only then realized how much I had to drink.

Upon my return, the guys stood up. "Hey, looks like I'm gonna be staying in Orlando a few days, so I need to grab a few things here at the market," Harris said.

"Yeah, man. I need a few things too. Harris, you wanna come crash with me at the condo?" Briggs asked.

"Thanks. I appreciate that. I think Cheyenne and Rox could use some quiet time." Harris winked at me.

"All right then. Torch, you wanna come with me over to the munitions department. Let's take a look at what they have for inventory? Briggs, Harris – you guys want to meet me over there after your appointments?" Khaldon asked.

Weapons inventory? I sure wasn't expecting to find anything like that here. Maybe an army surplus store or something. But I guess they really wouldn't have anything to kill a vampire, now would they. Hell, I don't even know what people use to kill them anyway. I made a mental note to ask Khaldon what type of weapons and ammo we were gonna need to rescue however many more women there might be.

I followed Harris and Briggs over to the spa area where they had a huge menu listing items for all kinds of supernatural creatures. For vampires they had teeth brightening, whitening, and filing. They even offered services for crown bridges to add additional teeth structure in your mouth.

I bet that is costly orthodontia work.

Harris decided to have the full spa treatment, clean up, dip, bath, haircut, and de-fleaing. I looked over at the tremendous array of beauty products just for werewolves. I picked up a fragrant apple de-tangler and glanced at an enzyme bloodstain remover for a werewolf's hair. They also displayed a boat load of conditioner and all kinds of brushes, combs and shedding combs. I'd never really thought about how were-creatures would always want to look and smell their best, even if Harris was unaware of his own odor.

I walked towards a department sign that read 'Vampyre Health and Beauty' and was amazed at all the hygiene for the mouth. I guess it made sense, though. With drinking so much red blood, my teeth were bound to become stained. I grabbed a bottle of what looked like teeth whitening mouthwash. There were Waterpiks to remove chunks from between your teeth and at least twenty different kinds of toothpastes for every mouth malady. Who would have thought vampires would have a need for a sensitive toothpaste and one to help with bleeding gums? I never in a million years would have stopped to consider why vampires needed denture adhesive. I'd had problems choosing toothpaste when I was human, how was I going to figure it out now?

As much as I wanted to explore this amazing shopping experience, I really didn't have time for this. I could spend days in this place, but right now I needed to get back home and figure out our next steps, before Ludovic contacted me in the morning.

***

We gathered up my bags of groceries and books from the Super Market. The guys seemed fairly refreshed from their spa appointments, and they loaded boxes of munitions into the back of Briggs' Land Rover.

Khaldon opened my driver side door to the roadster ushering me in. He offered me a kiss on the cheek as he shut my door, then hovered with his arms on the window. I returned the kiss and tried to give him my best "I'm fine" smile. I don't think I was very convincing.

I had a lot to think about, and frankly I wasn't quite sure where to start. The last thing I wanted to be was Ludovic's puppet on a string. I needed to find a way to turn this around and start playing the game by my rules. I felt helpless sitting around waiting for him to call the shots. It was one thing to be prepared for when we uncovered their location. It was another wondering if he was just yanking my chain and had already hurt them.

"You're awfully quiet. Everything all right?" Khaldon startled me out of my thought parade.

I seemed to get stuck in an endless line of questioning which usually brought me back to my original question. Never really solving anything just made me feel even dorkier for analyzing how I felt about it.

Khaldon stepped away from the window and walked around the front of the car.

Briggs, Harris, and Torchy drove up behind the roadster and blocked me in. "Hey, you two love birds, race you back to Chey's place," Briggs hollered.

Khaldon shielded his eyes from the headlights. "That's okay – think we're gonna have to meet you there." And with that I revved the engine, and Briggs took the clue.

I wasn't about to turn down a road rally and blow off the chance to release pent up steam.

I gave Khaldon a sideways grin as he got into the car. "You might want to buckle up," I said as the tires screamed cheetah wheelies before he even had the door closed.

Khaldon looked at me with a 'Do I really want to be in a moving vehicle with you' kind of face. Briggs peeled out of the parking lot towards the interstate. I took the roadster through to the other side of the parking lot. Briggs might race cars, but he was on my home turf, and I navigated the orange groves in my sleep. My route might take a little longer, but I was able to go faster than the speed limits. Not that Briggs followed speed limits, mind you.

Khaldon seemed more afraid of my driving and for his life at this point, as he reached up to hold onto the 'Oh shit!' bar as I hurtled the car over several speed bumps.

Holding on to the steering wheel with one hand, I faked holding an intercom in my right hand and said, "Ladies and gentlemen, please return your seats to their upright position, stow any carry-ons under your seat, and extinguish all smoking materials at this time. We have air!"

As we peeled past the orange juice plant where the burning rinds perfumed the air, Khaldon rested his other hand on my shoulder in an obvious sign of nervous caution. I noticed his knuckles were turning a bit whiter than normal as his hand almost broke off the bar above the window.

Driving fast always made me want to crank up the stereo. I needed something like "Highway to the Dangerzone" or "Born to Be Wild" when I raced.

Khaldon slapped my hand away from the stereo. "Umm ... could you just concentrate on the road? I'll get the music, okay?"

The *DOVE* syndicated radio station love songs for suicidal lovers came out of the speakers. "Nope, definitely not. Gimme me speed, baby,"

I said, as I gripped on to the steering at the ten and two o'clock positions. Winding through the grove's dirt roads, I prayed there wouldn't be a farmer out on his tractor at this time of night.

Khaldon found an adult pop-rock station, and I belted out to "Dirty Diana".

"Seems to be a correlation between how loud the music is and how fast you drive."

I took a forty-five degree turn through the field and almost plowed down a fence post.

Most likely trying to get me to slow down before he needed to change his shorts, Khaldon rubbed my neck. "Looks like you need to blow off a little steam, so how can I make this all go away for you?"

I heard the sincerity in his voice, but I wasn't sure how to answer him. The way things had been going, I was on a collision course with death and had no idea how to get off this evil carnie ride.

"Khaldon, I think we both need some alone time. We need to sort through a few things." I caught his nod in my peripheral vision. "But we really don't have that kind of luxury right now. How can I even think about being happy and making love with you while my family could be getting tortured this very minute? For all I know, they could already be dead."

I downshifted into third as Khaldon broke off one side of the 'Oh shit' bar and squeezed my leg with his other hand. I veered left, barely missing the road closed sign. I wasn't even sure if I wanted him to agree with me. I revved back up to speed and headed out on an old gravel road. The roadster shifted in 4th and up into 5th as we flew past the orange trees. I thought about his words. Maybe he was right. Maybe I did need to blow off a little steam. How long had it been since I'd had a good bronco buckin' in the haystack?

Don't answer that!

I decided I didn't want to think how long it had been since getting laid and broke into another chorus of, "Dirty Diana..na ..na."

With a note of resignation in his voice he said, "You're right, Cheyenne. We have plenty of time to figure us out. We need to concentrate on finding your family."

We were right, and that was exactly what I wanted to hear, but the last thing I needed was for him was to be thinking about Amicula and her little stunts.

If he can't remember what happened last night, what else did she do with him? Is he telling me everything?

He was a man, and dammit if he didn't have needs too. Was I truly that stupid? Was I really giving him the brush-off?

I'm so confused.

"Feck it!" I decided it was time to lose the race. My right foot let off the accelerator.

I grinned at him. "Do you wanna blow off some steam, or do you want me to win the race?"

He looked at me for a moment and then planted a slow, sweet kiss on my cheek. That was all the answer I needed.

The door handle above the window completely broke off in his hand with a clang, accompanied by a sheepish, questioning grimace. "I guess I'll need to get that fixed."

I smiled, relaxing my face. I loved this man. What the hell was I waiting for? Instantly, color flooded back into his face and his grip on my leg relaxed. I slammed on the brakes, shifted down into second, and pulled the car off into the orange grove where there was an opening in the fence line. I drove about a half mile in between the trees and shut down the engine. I was ready.

I grabbed a blanket out from behind the seat and met his gaze. Without another word, Khaldon jumped out of the car and in a flash, had me out of the car and in his arms.

He kissed me with quiet whispers. His mouth still tasted of the cinnamon tangy bloodwine we had drunk at dinner. I reached my arms up around his shoulders and felt for the steely frame under his silken skin. Never in all my dreams had I envisioned him this vivid, this complete. I nestled my head into his shoulder as he kissed me deeply and thoroughly. This time there was no holding back, no niggling of guilty feelings. Here was the man of my dreams who had been in my dreams for so long, literally. His hair was soft as it tangled in my fingertips. He had hair I could kill for. Long, black, thick. I couldn't wait to see it falling around his shoulders.

Our song came on the radio as if by magic. *"In Your Eyes"* by Peter Gabriel. I had visions of an actor holding up his boom box serenading me outside my bedroom window. But instead Khaldon began to dance us in the headlights. It was wonderful to get lost in his breath, to get lost in his kisses, to simply just get lost hoping he would find me.

Chapter Forty

O f course just when I thought Khaldon and I might have a moment alone, my cell phone chirped at me. I really tried to ignore it. I kept on kissing him, knowing it was most likely the guys looking for us. But then, it came across as Dakota's text message ringtone. Whenever Elton John's "The Bitch is Back" came across my phone, I knew it was Dakota.

I pulled away, mid-lipped from Khaldon, and grabbed my purse in the car. The text display read:

Where can you find a dragon, a virgin, a pineapple, and a dinosaur? Use the Force to find your way.

"It's definitely from her phone, but I don't think the message is from her." Khaldon was instantly at my side. He was the one who, as Roxas, had helped me pick out the ringtone for Dakota and knew this had to be from her. "Just another way for Ludovic to mess with your mind."

"Use the Force? What is he some kind of Star Wars nut? Is he gonna send a Sith after me now?" I cursed at the campiness of his riddle. "Seriously, does he think I'm stupid or something? Anyone who lives in Orlando knows exactly what he's talking about."

Khaldon looked at me with a raised eyebrow. He was trying to understand the riddle. "A dragon and a virgin. Well we really don't have any castles around here except for Cinderella's Castle at Disney. But I don't recall seeing a pineapple or a dinosaur in the mist around the moat."

"You're close," I said. "It's Downtown Disney. They have a dragon made of Legos floating in the water, a huge Virgin records store. The Pineapple is a Cuban Café, and then there is the T-Rex Dinosaur Café. It's all right there."

"He must have something waiting for you then. He couldn't have them in such a public place. Let me read the text again."

I held the phone up for Khaldon.

"Use the Force to find your way. What do you suppose that means?"

I slapped at my arm where a mosquito tried to spear me with its bloodthirsty straw. "Why in the hell do mosquitoes drink from vampires? I thought for sure I would be rid of these damn things once and for all! Anyway, I don't know about the Force part, but I know someone who will."

I had Harris on speed dial, and within seconds I could hear them singing to "Friends in Low Places" when he answered.

"Cheyenne, when you get the guys, tell them to meet us at my place. I want to pick up a few things before we go."

I nodded at Khaldon while I spoke to Harris.

"Hey, Chey, where are you guys? We beat you back to the house."

"Harris, listen. Meet us over at Khaldon's place. I think we have a lead on where Dakota and Sheridan are being kept."

"No shit! Okay – we'll be there in just a few minutes," Harris replied.

"I'm gonna forward you a text I just got from Dakota's phone. See if you guys can figure it out, but I'm pretty sure it's Downtown Disney. It's just the Force part I can't figure out. I'm hoping you guys can Star Wars the logic out of it and we can come up with an answer by the time we get to Khaldon's. I'll explain more then."

"Okay – you got it. Send it over, and we'll meet you there."

"Oh, Harris – wait."

"Yeah?"

"Can you walk the pups for me, or bring them with you? Either way, they need to go out I'm sure."

"No problem – will do."

"Thanks, see you soon." And with that I shut the phone and we hopped back into the car. I smacked another vampire mosquito as it bit into my cheek. It actually hurt. "Ouch! Damn mosquitoes."

"It won't be long and they'll stop biting you. Right now, they aren't sure what you are, so you are inviting. Soon your smell will change, and then they'll just buzz on by."

"My smell will change? Okay, that one will have to wait for another day. Right now I need to concentrate on this Force thing. Why do you want us to go to your house first?"

"I just don't think you should go into a potential situation unarmed. I have katanas, a cross bow, and several pistols. I haven't had the need to kill any of my own kind for a long time. I also haven't used these weapons in years except on a firing range, but I keep them clean and in good shape." Khaldon rubbed the back of his neck. "I think it's a good idea to arm ourselves, to be prepared, but you have to remember something – we immortals live in a regulated society among humans now. We can't just go walking around with these kinds of weapons in public places and not get arrested. Downtown Disney is a family vacation spot. Granted, there won't be many people there at three in the morning, but still. We must heed caution."

"Okay, I get it. You've got a point, but still the next clue leads there, and I don't want to be caught off guard. You're right. I do need something to defend myself with. Do you have any ultraviolet light bullets?"

Khaldon snorted a hearty laugh at me. "Cheyenne, I think you watch way too many vampire werewolf movies. There is no such thing. Well, at least I don't think there is. Anyway, why would I have UV bullets? I seldom need to kill a fellow vampire."

I felt kinda stupid for asking, but I just had to. It was worth a shot anyways. How was I supposed to know those things weren't real? Hell, vampires and werewolves weren't real a couple weeks ago.

"Ludovic doesn't know I have any of you helping me. I'm sure he is expecting me to be alone when I arrive."

"We need to figure out a plan to keep us out of sight, but keep you protected at the same time," Khaldon said.

It wasn't long until we arrived at his condo. The guys had decided to bring the pups with them. "C'mere, baby. Gimme some sugars." Beano and Stormy followed us in as if they'd been there a hundred times before. Stormy ran up to Torchy, and he scooped her up into his arms.

"Here, they can play out back. It's fenced." Khaldon slid open his lanai door and the dogs ran outside.

Walking through Khaldon's home, I took a moment to look at his place again in a different light. There was a different feel about it this time. I looked around again at the shrine he had created to our relationship. It was amazing. *He* was amazing.

"Damn, somebody's got a hard-on for the Lady Caz!" Briggs let out a long whistle as he walked into the condo.

"Welcome to my humble abode, Briggs. And yes, you could say that." I blushed.

Khaldon moved with an elegant grace, pushing buttons to reveal hidden closets and desk drawers. Gathering the troops and getting armed made this situation feel kinda badass. Breathing in an anxious breath, he took a single second to kiss me on the forehead before he picked up a deadly looking weapon. He set the spiked bowling ball hanging from a chain down on the table and handed me a baseball bat.

"What am I going to do with this?"

"I'm not sure at the moment, but it's wood, and it might come in handy."

Briggs threw a huge bag onto the sofa and opened it, revealing guns, knives, clips of ammunition, and even a handheld crossbow. Harris and I peered at his arsenal.

"Why do you have this kind of stuff, Briggs," I asked.

"It's nice to have connections," he grinned.

"Remind me never to cross you or your connections." Khaldon laughed at him.

Briggs continued to unpack his bag and explain what each weapon was and what kind of bullet it took.

I saw blue glowing light bullets. Picking them up and pointing the clip toward Khaldon I said, "But I thought, these weren't real. Only used in movies?"

"They're real. Especially when you need to kill vampires. I also have a few clips loaded with silver bullets and some filled with colloidal silver." I saw both Harris and Khaldon take a couple steps backward.

"It's all right guys. I'm on your side, remember?" Briggs teased.

"Why would you have these kinds of weapons, Briggs?" I asked again.

"Well it's like this, Chey Chey. When you live in a big city for as long as I have, you tend to make connections. Sometimes those relationships go sour, and the need to collect on those connections becomes a necessary evil."

I looked over at Khaldon and Harris and they eased back up towards the table where the weapons were laid out.

Briggs continued, "So I had a few of these made up when some scum bag didn't fulfill his end of the bargain. Well. Let's just say I put a cap in their ass and made 'em an offer they can't refuse. "

Between the arsenal Khaldon had and the bag of goodies Briggs supplied, I thought for sure we had enough stuff to open our own Army Navy Surplus store. "I'm glad you guys are on my side."

Chapter Forty One

Part Three

Ludovic Zyryanov

Breeding Facility #42

"We have another couple bodies to incinerate," Edric radioed over the walkie headset.

Ludovic stretched his legs in his chair as he watched Dakota in her coma. He brushed the red locks from her face and kissed the sleeping beauty before leaving the room.

How the hell did I get messed up in this crap?

Ludovic walked down the flights of stairs to the main floor of the breeding facility. Rows upon rows of women strung up in hammock nets hummed in tune with the electronic equipment maintaining their life essence. Everywhere, tubes going in, tubes going out. Babies growing. Women in labor. Normally, Edric had calculated the timed births down to a science, but occasionally his calculations were off on the dosages. That's when the breeders woke up and realized where they were. Echoes of the terrified screams always haunted Ludovic. Thousands of babies had been born at this selective breeding den in Orlando. It was convenient to the airports and easy for The Priestess to take the children via private transport to South America to begin their specialized training under the Queen's guard.

Ludovic rounded the corner. "Jeez, Edric – what are you doing to these test subjects? Why have so many of them died?"

Edric shrugged. "We won't have any more die on us. The Priestess is shifting test subjects. Those two over there need to go in the incinerator."

Ludovic wheeled the toe-tagged victims over to the hot box. Toe tag number 736 was a budding girl, couldn't have been older than nineteen. Opening the scorching furnace revealed fiery hot steel where they destroyed any physical evidence of the body's existence. Ludovic shook his head as he loaded the second corpse – toe tag 198 – into the fire and cranked it up high. Every time he threw another female into the furnace, he wondered – who were these women? Would their families ever know the truth about their disappearance?

I'm sick of this shite. I'm tired of being The Priestess' patsy.

Ludovic walked back over to Edric and found his Dakota being rolled out of the elevator and wheeled over to a table in front of him.

"Edric. What are you doing with Dakota?"

"The Priestess said to stop using the polluted human test subjects." Edric grinned at his brother. "We are going to use the Abarhtac lineage sisters to assess the Solunarae blood. The Priestess feels if we start with a pure lineage, then their bloodstream should be able to handle the changes."

Ludovic stopped Edric from rolling the gurney. "You're not going to do anything like this to their father, are you?"

"No, she was adamant about that. We've been given clear instructions not to harm him in any way, or the Queen will have our heads! He's resting peacefully. Not particularly happy about where he is, but at least he's safe from any other threats."

"There's just no need to stress him any more than he already is. If anything happens to him, we might as well meet our undeniable deaths right now. We have to keep him safe."

"Well, he's safer here with us with those rogues on the loose in the area. If they get hold of him, there's no telling what the Queen will do."

Ludovic pulled Dakota's gurney away from his brother. "Please, Edric, reconsider this. Have you thought through the consequences? We don't know if the Solunarae blood will kill them, too. And if it does, then we will have lost a tremendously valuable resource."

I can't lose Dakota. I've got to get her out of here, somehow.

"The Priestess wants us to remove oocytes from each sister. We'll extract the eggs needed to impregnate the prepared hosts for in-vitro fertilization. We'll cryopreserve the embryos until more hosts are ready, including the sisters, and that can take up to two to four weeks depending on their cycles. The Priestess also said they were moving in a few hundred more hosts, from other facilities, to become impregnated with the sisters' oocytes."

Ludovic's mouth grew as arid as a desert. "What exactly are you doing with Dakota now?"

"I'm prepping her for surgery, of course. We need to take out her first batch of eggs for insemination with the sperm specimens The Priestess brought us yesterday. We'll examine the oocytes in the Solunarae blood bath and see if they are viable. If they are, we'll impregnate Dakota with the embryos and continue feeding her the Solunarae lunar blood."

Not wanting to comply with the Queen's plan for Dakota, Ludovic's eyes widened in disbelief.

"What's your problem? It's what the Queen wants, Ludovic," Edric said. "And of course, when I find the winning formula, I will get credit for discovering how to harvest humans and win back the integrity of our race. I'll be famous."

"Let's try this out on Sheridan first. She's older and healthier than Dakota. She's been doing yoga. No drugs in her system. Dakota might not be such a pure sample. Let's see how her eggs react first."

"I don't care. We just need to get it done." Edric shrugged. "But first, I have been ordered to start the preliminary injection on Dakota to learn how she reacts to the Solunarae blood."

Edric had the syringe prepped before Ludovic could stop him. Edric screwed it into the blood supply line and pressed the plunger. Dakota didn't move. Her body lay still until her eyes shot open in alarm. Her arms and legs thrashed.

"Hold her legs, Ludovic."

"Edric, she's going to hurt herself. We're gonna have to restrain her."

Her violent convulsions caused her body to flail. They held her limbs down as best they could, but her spasms fiercely rocked them off their feet. Her hand shot up and smacked Edric in the face, bloodying his lower lip. As abruptly as the spasms came on, they disappeared. Dakota's heart rate steadied. Her respirations became normal once again. Her blood pressure had stabilized.

"That was weird. Never seen any of them do that before." Edric wiped the blood off his lip. "I'll schedule her for regular doses for a few days until we understand how the tests are running. Let's get the older sister prepped for surgery in the morning. I'm ready for bed."

"Sure, Edric. Let me clean up in here. What kind of Solunarae blood did you try on her?"

Edric smiled wickedly. "Lunar Blood. We will consider the solar blood on Sheridan and study how they differ."

Ludovic nodded while clenching his fists. "Thanks. Good to know. Wouldn't want to get them mixed up on my rounds." Ludovic grabbed the edge of Dakota's gurney and wheeled her back into her patient area.

In the elevator heading back to her room, Ludovic lovingly touched Dakota's skin as he rolled her into the hammock harness. Emotion overflowed down his cheeks as he secured her catheter and other excrement tubing. Ludovic pressed the button to hoist her into the air, suspended above the floor. He checked the netting to make sure nothing was cutting off any circulation, and the air temperature in the room was set to keep her comfortable.

I can't let them kill you, Dakota. I love you too much. How am I going to be able to help you? I'm so sorry I didn't know this was going to happen. My plan was to -

Ludovic's phone rang out in a text message.

[Cheyenne O'Cuinn] Okay – I got it. I'm standing here at Downtown Disney. I've got R2D2, C3PO, and Darth Vader next to me. How much more "Force" do I need to find?

Ludovic thought fast. He texted back to Cheyenne.

[Fang Boy] Change of plans. Meet me at Club Mordez Moi at noon tomorrow. If you don't, Dakota will die. Period. Come alone. If you bring anyone, I will have your father killed immediately.

***

Edric slid aside the curtain of Dakota's room. He had another bag of blood to hang for her IV. "I'm gonna stay and watch her for a while, Ludovic. I've got a steady drip going into her system with the lunar blood, and I just want to make sure she handles the volume well. She's due for another dose here in about a minute."

Ludovic swallowed hard and nodded. "I'll go finish the prep for Sheridan's morning procedure."

"I already have the room done. Prepped it earlier today thinking I needed to deliver that ten pounder via C-section. But the human host crashed, so I just finished cutting out the suckling. It's in the nursery now. I put the host mother next to the incinerator for you." Edric droned on as if it was just another dull day on the job – killing women and birthing babies.

Ludovic left the room for his nine p.m. rounds. He made notes on his tablet for host #492. She was in the early stages of labor. He increased the oxytocin level one push. Sometimes these things took days, sometimes hours, and for the top breeders, it was usually calculated to minutes.

When his phone alerted him that Dakota's life support machines were reporting distress, Ludovic took off running to get to her patient area. Slamming back the curtain he found Edric had left Dakota unattended. Her arms and legs bent in macabre contortionist positions. The spasms were more intense than he had witnessed before in any other test subjects. He saw drops of blood falling onto the floor from her mouth. She was dying!

Ludovic disconnected her feeding and excrement tubes. He immediately lowered her onto a gurney table and removed her from the hammock harness. Dakota's heartbeat escalated to deathly levels. Panting as if she were giving birth, her face contorted in pain, Dakota wailed an unconscious, involuntary cry. He held her at arm's length as he watched her eyes roll backwards into her skull.

She's in pain! I have to do something to stop this!

He pulled her close and whispered, "Dakota, I want to help get you out of here. Edric is killing you." Ludovic sank his teeth into her throat and injected his vampire DNA into her. If anyone was going to kill her, it was going to be him.

He savored the flavor of her blood – deliciously intoxicating. He wanted more. Pulled in by the taste temptation of Solunarae, he released his mouth from the succulent feed. He quickly grabbed a syringe plowing it into his own artery from his arm and sucked out his blood to give to her. Within seconds, he plunged the full syringe deep into Dakota's still beating heart and filled it with his vampire blood.

Her breathing and her heartbeat slowed. Her arms and legs relaxed as her eyes rolled forward once again. It would only be a matter of time before Dakota's body began to support and nurture the vampire DNA. He didn't have long to get them both to safety. He laid her back down onto the table and breathed a sigh of relief that her life was no longer hanging by a thread. Now they were both in serious jeopardy and needed to escape.

When the Priestess found out about this, she would kill him. He needed to get them both out of there tonight. He whispered into her ear once again, "I'll be right back, my pet. I must confiscate some computer files, and we can get you to a safe place." He left her on the table and ran for his office.

Ludovic's phone alerted him once again to Dakota's medical emergency as he heard a scream and a crash from her patient area. He heard the scream again – but this time it was from Edric. Ludovic rounded the door and beheld a bloodcurdling scene – even for a vampire.

He saw Edric, ten feet in the air and plastered against the wall, pinned by a bloodied, winged monster with taloned gripped claws.

Edric screamed at the top of his lungs. "Help me, brother!"

Ludovic couldn't find Dakota anywhere in the room. He threw a fire extinguisher at the demon's head – that only managed to piss it off. The demon turned to face Ludovic as he gasped out in shock, "Dakota?"

With that, she speared her other clawed wing into Edric's groin and savagely gouged her teeth into his throat.

Ludovic watched in horror as she feverishly dug and tore at his neck and ripped his unit off him. She flung his penis and man sack across the room. Her wings pinned his body immobile to the wall, shredding him apart as she sucked deep, heaving pulls of life essence until his mere eight pints were drained.

When Edric was sucked dry, Dakota removed her speared talons from his flesh, and let the body hit the floor. Dakota turned towards Ludovic. She lashed out at him with her tongue and wrapped her long serpentine muscle around his neck. She tightened a hold of him and squeezed. Ludovic on the verge of turning blue, reached for a pen out of his pocket and stabbed her tongue repeatedly with it. Dakota released her neck hold and recoiled. She sent out a sirened scream to make any Banshee duck and hide. She looked up to the overhead glass ceiling.

Ludovic followed her gaze. He choked out the words, "Dakota, wait – I can help you! *Don't* ..."

Dakota jumped and shattered the domed glass ceiling into a shower of deadly slicing projectiles onto Ludovic. He covered his head to protect his eyes and face from the falling danger as he ran out the building to see where she had gone. But she was just that – gone.

Chapter Forty Two

Dakota O'Cuinn

Blood Demoness

FREE!

Dakota huddled behind a ventilator turbine on the massive roof of the breeding facility. She looked at her arms – they had become appendages for wings. Her hands were now claws with talons. Her wing span extended another four feet out beyond her hands. Her brain marveled at the mesh-like appendages where her arms used to be. She couldn't quite grasp where she'd been, or what she'd been doing. She knew she desperately needed to do something, but she couldn't remember what it was. As if thoughts and memories belonged in a different dimension with a different Dakota.

A part of her mind wondered what'd happened to her, to turn her into such a strange and marvelous creature. This new form gave her a sense of empowerment and knowledge she had never known before. One thing she knew was certain, she had a starving thirst. Nothing, not even daylight, could keep her away from satiation.

The moon was heavy into her wax and the night was young. She heard Ludovic scream out her name from the front of the building. As quiet as a bat, she flew into the inky blackness of the night away from that man. Dakota flew to where she knew she could get food.

***

Interlude

It was the perfect evening for Andrea. Finally, Tony had proposed after two long years of dating. The fettuccine Alfredo, his favorite meal, cooked al dente. The wine was a perfect pairing with the tiramisu. Tony got down on his knees in the middle of his parent's restaurant and popped the question.

Promising to remember the moment forever, Andrea blushed as she squealed in delight her answer. She jumped into his arms and the entire family and restaurant stopped what they were doing, stood up and applauded the newly engaged couple. Andrea couldn't have been more excited to come into the Renaldi family. Who would have ever known her life would change so wonderfully when she became a waitress at the restaurant? Tony would be a good provider, a great dad, and forever her friend. She knew now she never had to be afraid of anything hurting her again. She could complete her schooling in dental hygiene, and then they could start a family.

After their meal Tony took Andrea to a romantic ride on the swan boat out on Lake Lola. She basked in the moonlight as Tony paddled them farther out into the lake.

With a thud, Dakota landed on the back of the swan boat. She drove her steely talons through Andrea's skull. In the same movement, Dakota ripped off Tony's head and turned his body upside down to drain him of all his blood. In less than five minutes, Dakota had exsanguinated both of their bodies and had thrown them into the lake along with all their hopes and dreams.

***

Interlude

"I don't think we should be out here – it feels too open, Aiden," Callie said as she squeezed his leg.

"Don't worry about it – she's at work. She never comes out here anyway. I told her I was out with the guys at City Streets. She'll never know. This is what you wanted right?" Aiden slid his hand under Callie's shirt and snapped open the front of her bra.

Callie looked around and didn't see any other swan boats in sight. They were way out in the middle of the lake. "I love how you talk dirty to me, Aiden, don't stop." She slid her hand up his leg and grabbed his excitement.

A gentle breeze blew by and Callie saw little ripples in the water.

Aiden had her skirt pulled up and her panties wrapped around his fingers.

"Oh Aiden… don't stop. Tell me what a dirty slut I am!" she whispered.

He stood her up in front of him and pushed her head down. "Suck me, you dirty whore, or I won't pay you what you're worth. You'll have to fuck that greasy slime ball of a landlord again to pay your rent."

"Yes! Yes!" Callie exclaimed before greedily taking him into her mouth. He stood at full attention as he shoved her waiting mouth onto him.

He rocked her head back and forth as she swallowed him whole time and time again. "Damn, bitch, wish my ole lady fucked me as good as you."

Dakota speared Aiden in the back while landing on the rear of the boat with the faintest of movement. She held Aiden up in her talons as she watched Callie enjoy her dicksicle. Dakota greedily sucked the lifeblood from his neck while Callie slurped his future generations.

The warm, salty goodness flooded Callie's mouth. It wasn't until the wetness continued running down his body that she realized something was off. She opened her eyes and saw glowing, fiery globes for eyes where Aiden's head should have been.

"What's the matter, slut? Don't you want to fuck me no more?" came a demonic voice. Dakota shoved Aiden's head in front of Callie's face. Callie screamed. Dakota threw the head into the water and laughed while grabbing the home wrecker with her claws. She yanked the screaming slut to her mouth. "This'll teach you to break up marriages!" Dakota tore out her throat to stop the incessant screaming and drained Callie's body cavity with a few strong pulls.

***

Dakota sat on the edge of the bloody swan boat and thought about where she was and what she was doing. She thought how Ludovic turned her into this thing, this monster, this powerfully fantastic creature.

There were five more boats out on the water that night and Dakota killed every last passenger in them including a young family with children. She didn't care. They were all there for her taking. Humans were her food – like cattle. No remorse – no worries. Just her sustenance.

Her enlightenment provided understanding – humans were not the superior race on this planet. She was the apex predator.

Nothing could stop her. She was free, she felt power surging through her like never before, and with a full belly she was ready for sleep. But where? She sat on the edge of the boat for hours, drifting on the lake contemplating what to do and where to go. She could feel the sun coming up over the horizon and instinctively she knew she needed rest and protection.

She flew to the highest building with an open vent shaft and crawled in for the day. Little did she know she would have to fight a gargoyle for the same space.

Chapter Forty Three

Cheyenne O'Cuinn

Club Mordez Moi!

For a Friday at noon, Club Mordez Moi was packed, hardly a seat available. The place was alive and on fire. My nerves itched with electricity. The music was loud, but soothing. The steady boom, boom, boom, actually helped to quiet the anxiety roiling inside my guts. The bartender brought me the day's special – a Bloodied Zombie. It was a mixture of white chocolate liqueur, O negative, and distilled raspberries. I waited for zombie eyeballs to float up to the top of the glass, but none did. Maybe that effect was reserved for the Frog's Eye punch the club was famous for.

Khaldon, Briggs, Torchy, and Harris sat at the table behind me, playing poker. They looked innocent enough and did not pay me any attention. As soon as I saw Ludovic's reflection appear in the mirror behind the bar, I became unsettled. My breath hitched in my chest as instant fury blazed through me.

The place was packed, hardly a seat available. I guess he considered it safe because he casually walked up and held onto the back of the stool where I had my purse. I grabbed it as he kneeled on the stool. Turning in my chair, I glared at the ass hat who'd ruined my world, tortured my sisters, and kidnapped my father, I needed every ounce of strength not to rip out his vocal cords through his nostrils.

I hate this guy!

Dakota's perfume lingered on him mixed with a pungent cleaning solvent. I remembered when Dakota brought him over to the house, he always smelled of spearmint. I figured he had chronic rancid breath, but now I knew he was masking the stench of death.

"A muddy squab with a mouse chaser."

The bartender nodded. Ludovic looked at me and around us.

I followed his eyes.

"You alone?" Ludovic turned the back of the seat around and straddled it all macho, western style.

"Umm ... no. There are about 250 freaks in this joint. What kind of drink is that?"

"Pigeon blood power drink with chaser shot of Disney cast member." Ludovic eyed me and looked around us again.

"They keep Disney's employees on tap for just such an occasion then?"

Ludovic laughed at me. Raucous laughter burst out at the table behind us, but the guys made it seem as though Torchy had won the poker hand. Ludovic ignored them.

"So what's the deal? Why the change of heart?" Heated, acrid fumes plumed color up my neck. I took in a deep breath and consciously tried to relax. Playing it calm, I decided on a different approach. "Boy, it's hot in here. This drink is really getting to me." Fanning myself with my napkin, I wanted Ludovic to think I was weak, easy for him to take. To bait him into feeling in control. I opened another button on my blouse.

"We have a slight bit of a problem."

"And you needed me to acknowledge that?"

He pursed his lips and squinted at me.

"What I need to know is where you have taken my father."

"He's safe. Safer than Dakota was, I fear. But if you keep wasting our time."

I held up my hands in mock defeat. "Continue."

"Seems the Queen's plan wasn't working out as she anticipated, so she's decided to conduct her experiments on Dakota and Sheridan instead."

They've killed her.

"Don't worry, they aren't dead, or at least I know Sheridan isn't," he said.

I squirmed in my seat, uncomfortable with how casual he referred to my sister's well-being, or lack thereof. "Go on." I spoke through gritted teeth.

"Queen Civetateo ordered Edric to inject Dakota with the lunar, Solunarae blood to see if she could handle it. If the lunar blood proved to be compatible with her, then her dhampir children would become stronger than the ones born from a regular human."

I furrowed my brows at him.

Ludovic swished back and forth on the seat. "The human test subjects before Dakota were dying off like flies in a hurricane."

I gasped at the intake of breath behind me. Nerves caught the best of me. I rocked my foot up and down on the stool foothold. I prayed Ludovic wasn't paying attention to anything but his drink and my cleavage.

While continuing to fan myself, I turned forward a little more to face him. "I'm not quite sure what this Solunarae blood stuff means. Can you spell it out for me?"

"Well, you and your sister's lineage has a throwback gene. Instead of Dakota turning into a vampire when I changed her, the lunar fugue blood sort of had an opposite effect." Ludovic ran his hand through his hair and rubbed the back of his neck. "Dakota has now become a blood demon, instead of just a vampire."

I heard a glass crash to the ground.

"A what?" Desperate to hold back the ferocity inside me, I took another long swig of my drink and then slammed it down on the bar.

"Bartender! 'Nother round." Briggs barked out, scaring the shite out of me. They couldn't be taking this news any better than I was.

Clueless to the energy shift around him, Ludovic continued unfazed. "A blood demon. Basically, picture a Hollywood vampire that looks like an ugly rat, has wings, taloned claws, and an insatiable blood lust. No conscience. No remorse. They hate everything. They think a human's only purpose is to provide for them."

I stared at him while my hands itched to claw out his eyes. "Are you saying this is what Dakota has become? A blood demon with wings and talons? What do you mean by our lineage?" I finger quoted in the air.

"The Priestess has been searching the world over for the purest of bloodlines which trace back to vampiric ancestral roots. Both your parents are carriers. So, yeah, I'm afraid this is exactly what I meant."

"Ludovic, that's insane. We aren't vampires. We are human. My mother died eight years ago. If she were a vampire, then she would still be alive."

"That's not the issue at hand. Right now I need help in capturing Dakota. She has escaped. I'm thankful she's alive, but something backfired when I gave her the vampiric DNA and how it mixed with the lunar blood. She flew out the glass ceiling of the facility. I have no idea if she's injured or if I can even get her back."

"And, just how are we supposed to catch her if she can fly?"

He held his drink in both hands and wiped the sweat of the glass with his thumbs. He refused to look at me. "The real problem is, how she won't care if she kills, or attacks anyone." He lowered his voice to almost a whisper. "Did you hear about the massacre on the swan boats last night?"

I nodded and stole a glance in the mirror. The guys had become intensely quiet.

"I'm pretty sure that was her. Without the lunar Solunarae blood, she's starving. Regular blood won't satiate her nutritional needs."

I took another drink and recalled the article about the massacre. "And you're sure this blood demon business is Dakota and not somebody else?"

Ludovic turned to face me again. "Listen, you aren't going to buy a word I say, but the truth is, I love your sister. That's why I turned her in order to save her life. Edric kept forcing the lunar blood on her in larger dosages. He was going to kill her if I didn't intervene." His eyes were sincere, almost to the point of tears. "I ... I couldn't stand to lose her."

"Touching, Ludovic. Not buying it for a minute. But here's the deal, ass wipe. You take me to get Sheridan and my father now, and I'll help you catch Dakota before we kill you. That way you know she's safe, Romeo. Or maybe we'll feed you to her."

Ludovic looked at the quad surrounding him.

"No tricks or these guys will eat you. Got it?"

Ludovic looked at Harris. Werewolf poured off him. Khaldon's fangs dripped with bloody saliva. Torchy's eyes glowed orange as Brigg's fiery breath leaked steam from his throat. He was on fire.

"You ... you said you were alone," Ludovic whined.

"No, I didn't. I told you I was here with 250 other freaks. Now let's go!

Chapter Forty Four

Club Mordez-Moi!

Parking Lot

"I don't like it." Khaldon pushed Ludovic into the side of Briggs' Rover. "It could be a trap for Cheyenne."

"I honestly don't know what else to tell you people." Ludovic fisted his hands in front of his chest. "The only thing you're going to find in that building are comatose women."

We stared at him.

He eased his hands to his sides and relaxed his shoulders. "The Priestess is what they call a gatherer. She's been gathering descendants from pure ancestral races all over the world to help find qualified breeders to create Queen Civetateo's dhampir army." He leaned back away from the guys. "She gathered Sheridan and Dakota, and now she's after Cheyenne, too."

"Look – waiting around isn't going to get me any closer to my family. So we need to go in guns, teeth, and swords a-blazing, and we get them out. Okay?" I threw my hands into the air in frustration.

"I've already told you. Only Edric and I maintain that place. There's no need for guns, but bring them if it makes you feel any better. The women are in various stages of pregnancy, and unconsciousness. Your dad is safe in the caretaker's quarters."

"You mother piss asshat! Why the hell did you do take him?" I slammed my fists into his chest. "You could've killed him. I hope you were smart enough to let him take his medication!"

Briggs stepped in close to me.

"I'm sorry. It was a directive from the Queen. We had to get your father to keep him safe. If we hadn't, it would've been our heads."

"Maybe that wouldn't have been such a bad thing," Briggs growled.

The air grew pungent with pheromones of wolf, dragon, and vampire. The mix became an empowering intoxication.

"Keep him safe from what? You're the only danger around here," Khaldon asked.

"It wasn't clear. Something about a rogue vampire on the loose, and it was better to keep him safe."

I came at him again.

He threw up his arms in defense. "That's all they told us, I swear."

"Why should we believe you?" Harris growled under his breath.

"This property has been unmanned because of its location. When the Priestess picks up the babies and takes them to South America, that's the only time the dhampir guards are around."

Could his story was foolish enough to be true.

"Edric, my brother, is dead now because Dakota killed him."

"Don't expect me to feel any kind of sorry for your lousy ass. How can you think anyone would feel for you after what you've done to my family and how many countless others?"

Ludovic looked down at his feet. "If the priestess finds out what happened here, I'll be dead, and we'll never get Dakota back."

"No matter how much I don't want to trust him, Cheyenne, he's got a valid point." Khaldon put his hand on my arm. "If what Ludovic says is true, then he's her creator, and only he can call her. He will always have a bond with Dakota, even if she doesn't want it."

"Prove it." I glared at Ludovic. "I don't believe a word of it until I know he can communicate with her. If he can't prove it, then I say we kill him right now!"

Ludovic backpedaled. "I have never sired before, I'm not sure how to contact her. Besides, if you kill me now, you might as well write the death certificate for your sister and all those other women. I'm the only one who knows how to manage their life support systems now that Edric is dead."

"Mother pus bucket!" Harris exclaimed. "I hate this jerk. If it's true, then we can't risk it, Chey. We can't gamble with Sheridan's life like that."

I rubbed my temples. Under duress, we nodded in unison. His argument made sense.

"Okay, let's go stake it out. Harris, once we arrive, can we count on your pack to help us out?"

"I can sure try, but no guarantees on that one, Chey. Weres and vamps tolerate one another, but..."

"Okay then, maybe explain this rescue mission isn't for me, but to help rescue my family from evil vampires. You think they'll enjoy the idea of getting to off a few of the local vamps? I know one in vamp in particular I'd like to off about right now." I looked at Khaldon.

He quickly glanced at his feet.

"Khaldon, you contact Lord Stovall. If there are a lot of women, we're gonna need medical assistance to help them." Khaldon nodded and reached into the chest pocket for his cell phone.

"Briggs, who can you call in for support? Can you get me ops intel on this building? Scope out the locals who own this joint – find out what's actually inside?"

"I'm on it. You got it, Chey Chey."

Suddenly it was as if they were on fire. All they needed was a little direction. Within an hour, we had a legion of men, werewolves, dragons, and vamps all ready to open up a can of whoop ass on this little building.

***

"This is the Queen's facility Lord Stovall," Ludovic explained.

"Then why wasn't I notified of its presence in my region – and its purpose? This is a blatant violation of The Canons." By the look on Lord Stovall's face, he was not pleased with this situation. "How long has this damn operation been here anyway?"

Ludovic responded with a slight, respectful bow. "We have been here for almost four years, my Lord."

Stovall looked disgusted.

Briggs approached with an update. "Looks like he told the truth. The parcel was leased by an anonymous corporation for a ten-year term, with an option to renew indefinitely, and that was close to four years ago. Plus it was paid in full and with a no-entry clause."

"Why the hell would somebody agree to those terms?" Torchy asked.

"Because ," Ludovic let the word roll off his tongue into three syllables. "The Queen demands her privacy and pays handsomely for it. Everyone has his or her price. Even you, Lord Stovall, have a price." Ludovic had to have known his words could cause a battle of vampiric proportions, but he pressured the situation. "I don't know why you're wasting this much time. I told you what is in there and what has happened to Dakota."

"We have a crack team ready to surround the place and watch from the outside if you are ready to go in. We are," Harris said.

I saw glowing eyes peering at us through the cattails and the high brush area around the building.

We reviewed our strategy around the entrances and the exits. "We'll have the dragons up top, the werewolves on the ground and the vamps going in. Anyone trying to get in or out of this building will be toast," I said. "But one thing we do need to know – what happens if the Queen decides to show up?"

"Then leave that part to me. I'll handle the Queen," Lord Stovall said. "Believe me, you'll know it if you see her. She never travels alone. She always has an entourage with her, especially her right hand, Aisling.

The name caught my attention, and I glanced at him. That was my mother's name. God, how I missed her and thanked the Goddess she was dead. I was glad she didn't live long enough to see the day her daughters had become a vampire, a blood demon, and a dhampir breeder.

Khaldon handed me a gun and holster.

"What am I supposed to do with this? I've never held a gun in my life."

"Pretend we're playing inside the game." Khaldon showed me how to hold the weapon while rolling my shoulders forward to steady the aim. "You simply point the red laser at your target and shoot. More than anything, it's another layer of protection. Until I can get you combat trained, I want you to stay close and be careful. I'm not losing you now, m'lady." His smile was warm and caring. He gave me a forehead hug and pulled me into a kiss. It wasn't even a passionate kiss, but it was one that said, 'I care about you and I don't want you hurt.'

I returned his smile and nodded.

"Sheridan will be over on the right hand side of the facility. Her harness area is 303." Ludovic cleared his throat.

"You mean as in the third floor – room three?" I asked.

He nodded.

"Just how many of these women are in there, Ludovic?" Lord Stovall asked.

Ludovic grimaced. "Well there were a lot more before Edric started experimenting on them with Solunarae blood."

"They really were giving that blood to the humans? And their unborns?" Khaldon questioned.

Ludovic nodded. "I'm trying to tell you – the Queen is building a dhampir army to rid the Vampyric race of rogue vampires and impure bloodlines. She needs the dhampirs to train and hunt them down. She is convinced she's doing the right thing. The Queen doesn't care for vampires who will not enter into a coven and pay for her protection."

"I can identify with that," Briggs said.

"Well I can see her point on some of these items, but you can't make a rogue do anything. Rogues are a pain in my ass, but that is why they are rogues," Stovall countered. "They don't want to follow rules. They're like Ex Pats – they don't want the hassle of the government they can't support. They do tend to kill more and are sloppy about it. That's why we have the cleaner crews."

"What I don't get is why the Queen insists on using humans to reproduce these dhampirs. Isn't that going to create a half blood type of vampire?" I asked.

"That's exactly right, Cheyenne. But here's the deal. Because they have a vampire father and a human mother, the dhampir are able to live twice. She has twice the troops."

I shook my head. "I still don't understand."

"Bollocks! I get it!" Khaldon exclaimed. "She's using dhampirs because when their human bodies die, in a battle or attack, their vampiric DNA will take over. They'll rise again to fight as a vampyre who has died the undeniable death. They don't have the sun's resistance any longer, but at night they will become a deadly force. She's getting twice the army, for half the time. She's creating a super army!"

"Hell, I am in so much trouble for even talking about this. I'm probably a dead vamp anyway. But regardless of what you think about what we do here, I love Dakota. I *need* to help rescue her."

I took in a huge breath and allowed the gravity of the situation to sink in.

Ludovic daringly grabbed my hand. "Last night it was the swan boats.

There's no telling where she'll strike tonight. Please let's just get inside and decide what to do next."

I shook my hand out of his. "Enough already, I'm fed up with the wait. Ludovic, why are you helping us? You know Dakota will never love you."

"I'm a dead man whether I do or don't. Maybe this way, I'll be forgiven."

Chapter Forty Five

Breeding Facility #42

With Harris' pack outside, surrounding the facility entrances, he was free to get inside and locate my father as quickly as possible. With Briggs' team up on the roof, Ludovic unlocked the building and disabled the alarm system. I could see broken glass shards all over the place. When we walked into the building, it looked as though it were a makeshift hospital without the curtains for privacy.

Khaldon whistled. "Bloody hell, man! What in the Queen's name are you doing in here?"

"That's precisely what we *are* doing here, but not for Her Majesty, the Queen of England, but for Her Majesty, Queen Civetateo," Ludovic answered with a solemn voice.

"Okay, Ludovic, show me this computer system, so I can move the medical files to a secure location. We need this info to help try and reunite these people with their families," Khaldon said. "Lord Stovall, where do you want to move these women?"

Stovall stood with his hands on his hips, shaking his head. His face held stern in concentration. "How many women are here right now?"

"I believe around 145 or 146 now," Ludovic said.

Khaldon said, "I'm in. I see 146 active beds. Sheridan is in 303. Looks like Kiernan is down that hall." Khaldon pointed behind him.

"And to the left – three doors down," Ludovic finished his sentence. "The combination to the door lock is 4283."

"I'm on it. I'll have him out of there faster than wolves at a pig roast." Harris ran down the hall.

Torchy sighed. "Holy shite – I can't believe how many women are here. How many have died? How many babies have been born? It's sickening."

I ran to the staircase and jumped two steps at a time, Torchy right on my heels. Of course, room three was all the way at the end of the building instead of at the front. It reminded me of an airport. Always seemed as though the gate you were flying out of was at the farthest end of the terminal.

I peeked into the areas they called rooms. They were just spaces of air lined out in paint on the floor. The room was cold and uninviting. A draped sheet hung around room area three. I looked at Torchy and took a deep breath. Now was not the time to freak out. Not the time to be scared, and definitely, not the time to cry, no matter how much I wanted to. I inched the drape back and stood frozen at the macabre sight of my sister.

"She looks like she is sleeping," Torchy said. He swallowed hard. "She's beautiful, Cheyenne." He hugged my shoulder. "We've found her. She's safe now."

I didn't have the faintest clue how to get her out of this hanging harness. She was suspended from the ceiling in a nylon net apparatus. Electrodes were taped over her body, pulsating different muscles while she lay unconscious. She had tubes everywhere. I couldn't start tearing everything down, it might endanger her even worse. I walked up to her and reached out my shaking hand toward her. I took a deep breath and stepped closer. I whispered into her ear and peered through her oxygen mask to see if she could respond to me.

"Sheridan. Sheridan, sweetie, it's me – Cheyenne." I touched her arm through the webbing. Her skin was cool, not cold, but clearly not warm. "Sher, are you okay? Can you hear me?" I saw her eyelids flutter.

"Keep talking to her, Cheyenne – it looks as if she can hear you. I'm gonna get Ludovic to help us take her out of this. I'll find a table or a wheel chair. Hell, I'll carry her if I have to, but she's coming down out of this now!"

I wasn't surprised at the urgency in his voice. By the look on his face I sincerely believed Torchy was as disturbed by all of this as I believed the rest of us.

I reached in and touched her forehead and brushed my fingers through her hair. She looked like she hadn't had a bath since she arrived. "It's okay now, Sher – we're here. Cheyenne, Roxas, Harris, and Briggs – we're here to rescue you and these other women. You're gonna be okay. Oh thank the Goddess you're okay!" Tears ran down my nose. They dripped onto her arm as my voice cracked under the emotional pressure. I wasn't sure how much longer I could hold it together.

Her eyelids fluttered again. I reached for her. "Squeeze my hand if you can hear me. This isn't a dream." The slightest movement from her fingers told me she could hear me. My voice grew excited. "That's it, Sher – you're safe now." She didn't have the strength to squeeze, but I knew her, and I knew she was using every ounce of power under the sun to tell me she understood.

"Okay good – hang in there. Torchy went to get Ludovic to help you get out of here." Suddenly the machines around Sheridan spiked and alarms rang out. It reminded me of when I awoke in the hospital. Sheridan began to move her hands, and she grimaced. Was she in pain? Tears puddled in the dark wells of her eyes.

I grabbed a Kleenex and wiped the Vaseline goo which had her eyes caked closed. "Shh … relax, Sheridan, everything is okay. We'll have you out of this thing real soon. Take a deep breath and just stay with me. I'm not leaving you – pinky promise sister swear."

Her lips twitched up one corner. She had heard me. The alarms began to abate, she was relaxing. Nothing could betray the mighty sister pinky swear. Nothing.

It was then Ludovic and Torchy returned with a gurney and some tools. They didn't look too inviting, but at this point, I didn't care. I just wanted her down.

As soon as Sheridan heard Ludovic's voice she began to slap again and murmur.

What is she going through? What is she trying to tell me? Most likely she's telling me to run, get away from this monster – but she has no idea what had happened to Dakota and how we need this psychopath to help us.

"Do you know how to take blood pressure?" he asked.

"Aye, I know how," Torchy jumped in.

Ludovic pressed a series of buttons at Sheridan's computer terminal and brought up her record. A humming sound turned on as she was lowered onto the gurney they brought with them. "Careful. Don't start pulling things out of her. There is a sequence to bringing them back. First we have to unhook the excrement tube and catheter tubes. These get changed out daily."

Was he proud of his accomplishments? I looked at him with disgust.

"Once we unhook them, then we can lower her all the way down. Be careful not to snag her IV shunt in the webbing. It's a bitch to get back in." He looked at me sheepishly. I could see the swollen, purple, mottled bruises Sheridan had at her collarbone.

I didn't let go of her hands, and I kept talking to her. "It's okay, Sheridan, we're going to remove the tubes now."

She gave the faintest little nod of acknowledgment.

"Don't go crazy on me – no fast or rushed movement. You're still hooked up to quite a few things."

Finally we got her onto the table, shunts, IVs, and blood lines removed.

"There are clean gowns in that closet. Can you grab her one?" Ludovic asked.

I grabbed the gown. "When can she have water? Her lips are cracked and bleeding."

"We shouldn't try to give her anything until she has regained full consciousness," Torchy said. "What drug is she under? How long will it take to wear off?"

"It depends." Ludovic shrugged. "It's Propofol, the standard anesthesia, just a smaller dose when used for inducing coma. Some women need heavy sedation, where others don't. Since she is coming down off her cycle and would have had another dose in thirty minutes, this was excellent timing. She could be conscious and responsive within an hour."

I looked at Torchy. "Come on – let's get her home."

Chapter Forty Six

" **H**ow is she?" Khaldon met us at the elevator.

"Fine, considering the circumstances." I tried to hold back the emotions harboring in my throat.

"Your father is outside in the truck with Harris, waiting for you. He's okay, Chey. He actually looks well-rested. Harris isn't leaving his side."

Tears of relief ran down my face.

"The cleaner crew and the medical teams are dismantling the harness systems and, helping to stabilize the women. We're taking them to safe-houses where they have equipment, mid-wives, and other available resources to help until we can find out who they are," Khaldon said. "Truthfully, Cheyenne, I'm not comfortable with you and Sheridan going to your place. If the Priestess shows up, that'll be the first place she'll look for you."

"Where else would we go? I guess I can take her to the Super Market."

"They can stay at my place, Khaldon," Torchy offered. "I've got that huge house. In fact, I have room for two more women if you need the extra beds."

"Torch, that's a fantastic idea." Khaldon grabbed his shoulder. "I know they'll be safe with you. If I trust anyone on this planet, it's you."

I smiled at them. I'd had no idea they were as close as brothers.

"Is this okay with you, Cheyenne?" Khaldon asked. "Do you have any problems with this arrangement?"

"Where's your home, Torchy? Is it far?"

"It's just around the corner from Khaldon's place. You can practically talk over two cans and a string between us." Torchy smiled. His eyes were kind. We would be safe with him. I also trusted Khaldon never to do anything to hurt me. *Ever.*

"Okay – fair enough. When do you think you'll be able to come by?" I asked Khaldon.

"We need to get this place cleared out, the women and babies safe, and the equipment removed. This could easily turn into an all-nighter – even with the teams Briggs and Harris brought along. We need to stay on alert and make sure this is an empty tomb before daybreak."

"I understand. I wish I could help, but I'm not leaving my family's side."

"No worries. Not to sound like a chauvinist, I know you're tough, so please don't take this wrong – you've been through a helluvalot. Stay with your family tonight, Chey. Seriously, let us take care of this. You take care of yours, okay?" He looked at me with *please don't be angry* eyes.

I honestly didn't have any strength left to argue. I wanted nothing more than to have Daddy and Sheridan safely tucked away, and to plan our next move. I gave him a sideways smile as he kissed me on my forehead.

"We need to complete the logistics of discreetly purging this facility tonight. There's a lot more women here than we first thought."

Let me know if you need any help from the Super Market. We have a new wing of rooms that are just opening and have not had any guests yet."

"Excellent Idea Torch, we may need it. Let's get this done." Not willingly, I accepted this current plan of action. "Please call me if you need an extra pair of hands, or if we need to make room for those others. But I have to be honest here, I just don't know if I'm capable of handling the mental health of women who've been here for God knows how long. Hell, when they wake up, they may not even remember who they are."

Khaldon bobbed his head at Torch and me to step away from Sheridan's bedside. My eyes never left her. He lowered his voice. "Listen, I didn't want to say this out loud, but I believe you need to know." He ran his hand through his hair and then placed both his hands on my shoulders. Khaldon looked me straight in the eyes. "Sheridan is pregnant."

"What? Oh no! They did it already?" My hands held the side of my face.

Khaldon nodded. "I'm so sorry, Cheyenne. She was impregnated three weeks ago when she arrived here. From her records, it seems they placed two embryos for viability. She could have twins."

"Twins!" My eyes felt as though they bugged out of my head.

"I'm going to kill these feckers!" Torchy's face blazed.

I pulled away from Khaldon and turned back towards Sheridan.

He grabbed my arm and pulled me back closer. "Cheyenne, the one thing about a dhampir pregnancy is we're talking weeks to months ratios. So in essence, she is close to moving into the second trimester with this baby, or babies, we won't have confirmation until we get her in for an ultrasound."

I swallowed hard at his news, not wanting to believe any of it.

Oh Sheridan. I'm so sorry I didn't find you in time. Why did this happen? What are we going to do?

"She's going to need very specific food and nutritional supplements to maintain her and the baby's health," he continued. "Otherwise the dhampir fetus will take everything her human body has to offer."

"Come on, Cheyenne. Meet me at the front entrance. We need to get some good food in her. Ain't no way in bloody hell we're gonna let anything else happen to her. You hear me?" Torchy grabbed my elbow as we walked towards Sheridan's gurney. "I'll go get the truck. We can put you in the back seat with Sheridan. Let her stay flat until she can sit up on her own."

"Yes, all right." I stammered still trying to understand this news and figure out how the hell I was going to tell her.

We jostled Sheridan through the vestibule, as the broken glass crunched beneath the gurney's wheels.

"I'm sure your dad is starving for quality food too. There's no telling what they've been giving him. I'll make dinner when we get to my place. Do we need to stop and pick up the pups?"

Numb from horrific shock, I was grateful Torchy held the level of concern for us that he did. I hardly knew him, and yet he was taking care of us as if we were family. I gave him a wry smile and nodded in agreement. He took off to get the truck.

My heart raced when I saw my father next to Harris. Daddy waved at me. I pushed the gurney forward. Khaldon stopped me. I turned to face him.

"At least we found them, Chey. I know you're still worried about Dakota. Look at it this way. Tonight we not only rescued your sister, but it looks like we rescued a lot of other sisters, mothers, wives, and daughters here as well. You've done good."

Chapter Forty Seven

Torchy Gravenor's Home

Feeling a bit relieved to have Sheridan and my father safe with me again, I watched out the window as a photoshopped Florida sunset graced us with its presence. Torchy's home had a magnificent view of the Big Sand Lake. Just across the way from Khaldon's condo, Torch had a lakeside view with lighted marinas docked at each home. I watched as a little green lizard darted across the lanai patio off the side of the guest room.

Torchy and I sat in his comfortable guest room trying to stave off the tension of when Sheridan would fully awake from the anesthesia. We each held one of her hands and watched *True Blood* on HBO Go using Torchy's laptop. It was curious to see Torchy so attached to my sister. I remembered when Khaldon had explained to me how smitten Torchy was with Sheridan. He loved how smart she was in her interview. After he had seen her photo in *Gamer Magazine*, he wished one day to meet her. Who wouldn't? She was one of the most successful women in the gaming industry having built a global, multi-mass player role playing game. None of us would have ever found one another if it weren't for the overwhelming success of ExsanguiNation.

I heard Sheridan moan as she slowly moved her head.

Standing up, I cradled her cheek in my hand. "Hey there, Sher – how ya doing?"

It was easy to tell she was confused and most likely coming out of a nightmare. "It's okay, Sheridan. I'm here. You're safe."

Torchy sat closer to the bedside, but not too close.

"Wha ... where?" Sheridan whispered in a groggy voice.

"Sheridan. It's me, Cheyenne, your pain in the ass little sister. Remember me?"

A partial smile curved at the side of her mouth. "Yeah." Her tongue snaked out across her lips. They were cracked and dry.

"Do you want some water? I have a glass and a straw here," I asked.

She nodded.

"Okay then, I'll have to set you up just a little. Can you open your eyes?"

She nodded again. She pulled at her eyelids with the muscles in her face, and they tentatively opened. Squinting at the light in the room, Torchy immediately grabbed the remote and turned down the brightness.

"Are you okay?" I asked. "You've been through quite a spell." She nodded again. "My friend here, Torchy, is gonna help me pull you up, all right? We have lots of nice, comfy pillows here for you. They're white – your favorite color."

A wry smiled crossed her face. "Okay here we go. One, two and a three." Torchy and I carefully propped her up on the pillows and stashed more under her arms to help stabilize.

She had her eyes opened, still trying to adjust to her surroundings. She looked up at me, her puffy face made me want to burst out crying, but I held my composure to keep her as calm as possible. "There now, you look like a princess, sitting there with a hundred pillows at your beck and call." Stormy jumped on the bed and cuddled in beside her. She stroked the furry monster.

I grabbed the water cup off the nightstand and held it for her while she sucked it down greedily. After a few moments, I pulled the cup away.

Her mouth grabbed for the straw again. "Mo ... more," she said.

"You need to take it easy, sweetie. You've been in an induced coma, and your body needs to adjust. If you drink too much too fast —" And with that, she promptly threw up on me.

"It's all right. Go easy – just easy little sips now. I'll go get some towels," Torchy said as he got up and left the room.

"He's kinda cute isn't he?" I winked at her.

She nodded again with a stupid grin.

"It's good to see you smile and even better that you're safe here with me." I leaned in for a hug. "Sher – I thought for sure I had lost you."

She hugged me back with what little bit of strength she had.

Torchy returned with towels and something that looked like a vanilla milk-shake. "Aye now, lassie, here ya go." He handed me the towel and we got her sopped up. "I've brought you something here you might not like, but it's got vitamins in it to help you gain some strength back."

"I think it's the same stuff you gave Daddy when he was in the hospital."

She scrunched up her face.

"Yeah – I know, not a Ghirardelli gourmet shake. Let's just stick with water for now, until your tummy settles. You'll be hungry enough soon."

"Daddy? Where? Is he ...?" she stammered.

"He's okay. He's in the next room catching a snoozer." Torchy stood up and opened the adjoining door to the suite. Our father was sleeping on a bed with Beano nestled up against his back. Sheridan winced as she turned her neck and reached for the place where the blood shunt had been located. She nodded and turned back to face us.

Torchy sat back down beside her. "Are you hungry? Are you in any pain?"

Almost on cue, Sheridan's stomach rumbled. She held her arms frozen across her belly, her eyes opened wide. I held the water straw in front of her again, and this time she managed a tiny sip. She looked down at her belly and ran her hands over the top of it.

I could see the hamster wheel of questions running through her mind when she looked up at me. "What ... happened? I don't remember."

I let her take another sip of water.

"There is a lot to explain, how do you feel?"

She looked at me and then again at Torchy.

"It's okay – he's one of the good guys," I explained.

"I hurt. Everything is sore. Like a moose ran over me or something. I'm starving. What happened? Where's Dakota?"

How was I going to explain about her kidnapping, pregnancy, and Dakota? Let alone me – how was I going to explain to her, I was a vampire?

"Dakota is all right. She's not here right now. I hope she'll be back soon."

"Cheyenne, can you help me to the bathroom? I really feel terrible. Can I take a shower or something?"

"Absolutely," Torchy said. "Let me draw you a bath." He jumped up and left the room.

Within moments, we heard the hot water filling the tub. I helped her walk gingerly to the bathroom. Sheridan stopped mid-step with her eyes glued on the mirror. With shaking fingers, she touched the swollen, purple bruises at her collarbone and between her thighs.

I swallowed hard not sure of what to say. Words could not express the pain I held in my heart for her. I wished I could take her place and could have saved her from this awful nightmare. She remained silent and headed for the steamy bath water. When she was ready to talk, she would let me know.

Sheridan continued to cry silent tears as I washed and conditioned her hair.

I finally broke the heavy silence. "I'm going to find you some pain medicine. You need a good night sleep tonight without any worries, okay?"

She nodded.

"There's a lot to tell you, but just for tonight, let's concentrate on you feeling better. Everything is gonna be just fine."

I turned to leave the room. She shot her hand up out of the water, splashing the floor. She grabbed my arm. Her eyes frightened.

"I'm here – I'm not leaving. Do you want me to leave the door open? I'll be right back. I promise."

She slowly released the death grip on my wrist and nodded. I kissed her on top of her head. Suddenly I understood what my father had felt like when he took care of me in the hospital.

***

Following the smells of dinner cooking, I met up with Torchy in the kitchen. "She's pretty shook up, Torch."

"I can't even begin to imagine the horror and violation she must be feeling inside." He chopped an onion into the skillet and seared it in the garlic and butter.

Abruptly, a loud emergency signal blared out of the television.

"We interrupt this regularly scheduled broadcast to announce a mandatory lockdown of Lakeshore Palms Community Golf Course and Driving Range. Anyone around this area is asked to stay in your house. Lock all doors and windows. State police and National Guard are securing the surrounding area. An unknown force is killing people on the golf course. Over ten eyewitness accounts have seen a flying creature terrorizing the golfers and homeowners. Repeat ... this is an emergency broadcast encouraging residents of Lakeshore Palms to stay indoors under mandatory lockdown."

I looked at Torchy and rubbed my forehead. "Well, I think we've found Dakota."

Chapter Forty Eight

I dialed Khaldon's phone.

He picked up on the second ring. "Hey, sweetie. How's everything going? Sheridan and your dad doing all right?"

"We're fine. Daddy is sleeping. Sheridan has come out of the fog, and she's in a bath. We stopped and picked up the dogs, so they're over here. But listen, I know you've got a ton going on right now, but have you seen the news tonight?"

"No. What's going on?"

"It looks as if Dakota is out feeding again. The National Guard has been called out and they're evacuating Lakeshore Palms golf course. A flying creature is attacking the golfers. Is there anything we can do to try and catch her tonight?"

"Bollocks, Chey. This is not good news nor terrific timing. We've got Ludovic helping all the teams properly prepare the women to be moved. Let me pull him aside for a few to try and communicate with Dakota."

"Do you think he can get a message to her to stop killing? She needs to be warned she's in danger. They'll kill her if she stays out in the open."

"We'll do our best, Chey. We simply don't have the resources. Where would we keep her tonight even if we did manage to catch her? I'm not sure you understand the savageness she is capable of."

"Where are Harris and Briggs?"

"They just got back after moving a few of the patients. They're right here with me."

"Good. Can you put me on speaker?"

"Okay, you're on speaker."

I explained the situation again about what Torchy and I just heard on TV.

Harris said, "Chey, if Ludovic can't contact her, Briggs and I will track her tonight to see where she goes."

"Yes. That's exactly what I was hoping. To map out a plan B for her location."

"You've got it, Chey Chey," Briggs said. "Harris you know how to get over to this golf course?"

My voice hitched up a notch. "Briggs, don't fly tonight. The news said the National Guard is out looking for a flying creature."

"Thanks for the heads up. We'll only track and follow."

"We'll call you soon with an update, all right?" Harris said.

"Fair enough. I know you guys will do everything you can. Thank you. Just ... be careful dammit. I'm scared this is going to create a lot of attention and the Queen could show up at any time."

Khaldon agreed. "You've got a valid point, but the best thing we can do tonight, is stick to the plan. To keep suspicions down, Stovall is working with a local Wiccan coven to help set up glamours in the area. With all the cars, trucks and vans in and out of here, there was bound to be a tip off from a private citizen, and that would make the news. We've got the facility half way evacuated. This has turned into a logistical nightmare. Stovall is trying to find enough places to accommodate the women. We are taking you up on that offer Torchy. I got in tough with Z'anima and the Super Market is going to provide hotel room access for most of the patients until we know what to do with them. Stovall isn't sure how to proceed at this point and isn't exactly entertaining the idea of contacting the Queen about all this."

"Will Dakota be alright?"

"She will have to nest down before dawn," Khaldon said. "She'll stay put during the day and we can plan out our mission. We'll meet you back at Torchy's house in the morning."

We hung up, and I felt so empty inside. Maybe it was the looming conversation with Sheridan that had me in knots. I prayed for sleep. So many things needed to happen in the next twenty-four hours.

***

Close after dawn, brilliant streaks of orange rays against pink clouds, cascaded ribbons across the sky. Khaldon had called earlier letting us know they were on their way. He explained how after removing women from the breeding facility and cleaning the bloody remains from Dakota's attacks, he and Lord Stovall were whipped. The abstergers were still sanitizing the minds of the humans who were involved, including the National Guard.

Khaldon sat out on the patio with me. He had fresh kolaches with steaming cups of mocha coffee in the to-go tray.

Peering into the bag of goodies I inhaled the deliciousness of the spicy cheeses. "Mmm ... my favorite. How did you know I love the jalapeno, cheddar ones?" I asked him.

"Seemed to match your personality. One fine, spicy kolache." Khaldon winked at me.

Torchy walked out onto the lanai where I sat watching the sunrise. "How did you sleep, Cheyenne?" he asked.

"It was sporadic but other than the couple of times Sheridan cried out from night terrors, it was fair. I slept much better than I expected for not being in my own room and worrying about everyone."

"Rox, did you by chance bring anything a little milder here for Sheridan?" Torchy asked. "She can't handle any spice right now. Her tummy is a bit queasy, and I don't think she cares much for my saltines."

Smiling at Khaldon, he handed me a coffee and said, "As a matter of fact, I brought vanilla almond milk and some old-fashioned cake donuts. Thought maybe she might like to dip them." Khaldon arranged the goodies on a serving tray.

Before he could hand it to Sheridan, Torchy grabbed a single bud flower vase from the kitchen table and placed it on her tray.

Sheridan walked out onto the lanai and joined us. "Thanks, guys. This looks delicious, I just hope I can keep it down. I don't know why I feel so nauseated and hungry – all at the same time." She ate for a few moments and we sat in silence, just watching her. Stormaggedon pranced out onto the porch with Ash and Soot behind her. Beano trotted along behind them. "Hey, Pookie, come here, sweetie." Sheridan cuddled the little Pomsky in her lap.

"Wow, looks like we have the whole family. And who are you fellas." Ash and Soot wagged their tails as they sniffed the breakfast bags for future promises of crumbs.

"You definitely look and sound like you're feeling a lot better this morning, Sheridan." I handed her some of the almond milk.

Sheridan looked around the room and stared out the screen enclosure at the morning sun. "I do feel better, but I have a lot of questions. Such as – who are you?" Sheridan pointed at Khaldon.

I nudged her side. "Sheridan ... you'll never believe in a hundred years who this is."

"And you're gonna make me try and guess?"

"No, silly. This is Khaldon Seters a.k.a. Roxas Morgwain – in the flesh!" I said.

Sheridan's eyes widened in surprised. "Well, Mr. Morgwain, it is about damn time I get to meet the man I send a lot of money to for developing my software."

He grinned ear to ear. "All I can say, Sheridan, is we're so very happy we got you out of that place." Khaldon came over and sat by me.

I gave him a hug and a kiss on the cheek.

"I see you two didn't waste any time," she said.

"Harris and Briggs just turned down the drive. I'll meet them out front. Do you feel well enough for more company, Miss Sheridan?" Torchy asked.

Sheridan turned to look at me, her eyebrows arched. "Miss Sheridan ... I kinda like that. What are those two clowns here for?"

I grabbed her hand. "Sher, we have a lot of things we need to discuss with you today. Things you've never heard of before. Things that are real, and with real consequences. We need our team, our family, to get through this."

The energy in the room shifted from light and fluffy to dense and heavy. Khaldon looked up at Torchy and gave him a nod. Torchy left to greet the fellas. Ash and Soot were hard on his heels to go to the door. I heard a couple of car doors slam outside as Ash howled out the warning.

Sheridan took a small sip of the almond milk and moaned. "Gawd that's good. Okay bring them on in. Let's get through this together." She looked around. "Is Daddy still sleeping?"

"Yeah – I expect he'll sleep for a while. He hasn't been consistent on his medication, so I'm taking him into the doctor today for a checkup and make sure his blood levels are all right. I'm gonna go peek in on him."

It wasn't but a few more minutes when Torchy returned with Harris and Briggs. Harris ran over to Sheridan and hugged her. "Hey, Sher. How ya doing? It's good to have you back."

She smiled at him. "Thanks for helping. I'm still pretty confused about everything." Sheridan's eyes widened when Briggs came in through the door. "And you must be Briggs."

"At your service, boss. Good to finally meet you. Not necessarily under these circumstances." Briggs bent down to hug Sheridan.

"I'm beginning to think the Christmas party would have been a much better venue," I joked.

We pulled extra chairs onto the porch and got settled.

"So, Sheridan, I'm not real sure how to begin or even where to start. I was hoping perhaps you could tell us what you remember last. Then we can fill in the blanks and probably add in a couple of chapters." I gave her an apologetic smile and sat back down.

She looked around the room at all of us. "Okay, this is weird. I know most of you very well, and yet I feel as if I'm sitting in a room full of strangers."

"Maybe we should put on headsets and talk with our eyes closed," I teased. "Face time is strange when you aren't used to it. But seriously now, what is the last thing you remember Halloween night?"

Sheridan breathed in and exhaled a slow count. "I remember being at the park. I was taking a break from scaring people in that Ghillie suit. I was going to the ladies room ... and then nothing. Next thing I knew, I woke up in the room where I couldn't move. I remember seeing Ludovic and Edric thought I was safe, but then everything went black again. What day is it?"

I squeezed her hand. "It's November 19th. It's been almost three weeks."

Chapter Forty Nine

"Unholy hell, Sher," I began. "I know you're confused, but for me to answer why you've been in an induced coma for almost three weeks – well – I need explain a lot of things first. Things that aren't going to make sense, and most likely you're going to think I'm whacked out on bath salts or something. But I'm not, and these guys aren't. I just need you to suspend current, rational beliefs and reality as you know it."

"Criminy, Cheyenne. It feels like you're gonna tell me the zombie apocalypse has started or something."

"Well, you're close. I don't really know where to start. So I'll start from the beginning." I smiled at her and quirked my eyebrows up. "It all starts with our online game, ExsanguiNation. What would you say if I told you that almost every mythological, supernatural, and preternatural being existed?"

Sheridan stroked Stormy in her lap. "You mean in the game or in our reality?"

"Well, technically both."

She sat in silence and blinked at me.

"Do you remember the morning of Halloween when you called me and I told you how much I didn't want to go into the haunted house?"

She nodded.

"Well, the haunted house I went into changed me forever."

"I'm not following you, Chey." She shook her head and shrugged.

"Okay – yeah – I suck at this. On our game we have mostly vampires and werewolf type avatars, and then there's a lot of people who've created other types of creatures such as dragons, ghoulies, and witches, right?"

She nodded. "What does that have anything to do with today?"

"What if I told you that those kinds of avatars are indeed real creatures, and they have existed alongside humans since – forever. There are vampires, witches, werewolves, and dragons ... even zombies."

Sheridan reached for her milk and took a sip. "So, okay, funny ha ha, what day it is really? You've had your fun. I know, let's play a joke on the boss."

Harris stood up and held his hand out to her. She took it. "Sheridan, we aren't joking." His hand morphed into a large, hairy paw.

She pulled her hand back and gasped. "W-W-What did you give me to make me halucin-n-nate, Chey? That's n-not funny."

"No drugs, this is our new reality. Do you remember how Roxas had so many ideas about how to structure the vampire society simulators? Well, he did such an amazing job – because he is a vampire."

Sheridan looked over at him and swallowed hard.

"Look, I know this is nuts, but I have a lot to tell you. The sooner you start listening to what I'm saying and let go of earlier conventions, the sooner you'll understand."

An hour later I'd unveiled the entire story to Sheridan. Each of us had to prove what type of supernatural being we were before she understood the full impact.

"Two vampires, two dragons, and a werewolf."

"Yes. But seriously, Sheridan, this isn't all of the news we need to share with you. There's a lot more we need to cover before tonight," I said.

"All right, lay it on me." Sheridan sat up in the daybed and stretched out her legs. "I need facts so I can make decisions."

"I knew once you grasped that an alternate reality co-existed beside us, that you'd be able to handle what I'm going to throw at you. I don't know how else to say it, but to say it. Halloween night when I was attacked and was changed into a vampire, you and Dakota were both kidnapped and put into an induced coma by other bad vampires. We rescued you last night, but Dakota escaped from the facility the night before."

"Bad vampires?" Sheridan's eyes widened. "You said Dakota was all right."

"Yes, just like there are horrific humans, there are vicious vampires." I scooted closer to her on the couch. "Dakota is all right. She escaped from the vamps, but what you don't know is why you were there to begin with." I reached for her hand. "It was a breeding facility. They captured you and Dakota, and they were supposed to kidnap me as well to turn all three of us into dhampir breeders."

Sheridan took in several deep breaths and rubbed over the top of her belly.

"Dakota escaped, but not before terrible things happened to her. I've explained that I have been bitten and turned into a vampire. Edric and Ludovic were experimenting on her and turned her into something worse. Ludovic got a sudden case of conscience and attempted to save Dakota's life, but the blood they were giving her didn't bode well with his vampire DNA. Something went bad wrong."

"Wrong? What could be worse than turning into a vampire?" Sheridan exclaimed. "Present company excluded, of course."

"Dakota was given a couple different types of blood." Khaldon jumped in to help me. "We're pretty sure she's become a blood demon."

"What the hell is a blood demon?"

"A blood demon is like a vampire with no conscience, more abilities, more thirst, and one hell of a pissed off attitude. For millenia we have killed these demons as we find them. They lack control or morals and are very difficult to transform."

"Are you saying you're going to kill Dakota?" Sheridan shouted as she tried to stand up from the couch. "You can't do that." The exertion brought a wince of pain to her face.

"Sweetie," I continued, "calm down please, we don't know. We're going to try and get her tonight. Briggs and Harris followed her most of last night, and we have a pretty good idea where she is. She sleeps during the day, but when the sun sets she'll come out to hunt again, and we have to capture her somehow."

Khaldon reached over and gently removed a tear from my cheek.

"We think she may have a chance. She was given the blood to be a demon, but was turned by a vampire to save her life. Once we capture her and see what she is like, then the decision will be made. It'll be out of our hands."

Sheridan closed her eyes and lay back onto the cushions for several minutes before asking her next question. "And all of this happened because of our game?"

"You aren't going to believe this either, but as it turns out, one of the reasons we've been so successful is due to the fact that real supernatural beings play our game. Deals are made, merchandise is transferred, world-wide commerce happens daily in ExsanguinNation. Good and bad."

Sheridan blew out puffed cheeks. "I don't want to ask this next question, but I have to. So if I was in this breeding facility, then I'm not crazy thinking I feel pregnant. I haven't felt normal since I woke up. I keep thinking something is moving inside me, and I've been praying it's gas."

A heavy silence filled the room until I broke it softly. "Sher, you are pregnant. When you were in the coma, those bad people inseminated you."

"But that was what – three weeks you said?" Sheridan screeched as she sat up. "Why do I look so big?"

I looked at her and took a deep breath. I reached out for her hand. "Khaldon, can you help explain this to her a little better?"

Khaldon stood up and looked around the room at everyone and then squatted down to talk to Sheridan eye-to-eye. "I'm afraid you were impregnated with the semen from a vampire."

A single tear escaped Sheridan's eye.

"You are carrying what is known as a dhampir. A dhampir fetus develops much faster than a human. You will deliver within a couple of months, but we're not sure exactly when."

"This can't be real. This can't be. What am I going to do? Is this thing going to kill me like in *Alien*?" Sheridan's voice increased in decibel and pitch with each question.

I squeezed her hand. I hated seeing her face filled with fear. "I'm here, Sher. We'll get through this together. I promise."

Sheridan took her hand away from mine and rubbed at her belly.

Briggs asked in a quiet voice, "Is there still time to … ya know … *not* keep it. Will it cause her more harm than good?"

"No!" Sheridan exploded at Briggs. "I'm not going to do that. Regardless of how this happened, this is still my baby. There's no way in hell I'm going to let anybody hurt him ... her." She looked down at her belly as she sobbed. "Why did this happen to me?"

Briggs stood up and walked toward Sheridan. "I didn't mean any disrespect. I'm sorry."

Sheridan grabbed his hand and looked up at his face. "I understand. I'm not upset at you. It was a logical question." The anguish in her eyes told me that with all my own adversities, mine simply did not compare to what my sister was going through right this minute.

She stood up and let go of Brigg's hand. "Do we know who the father is?"

Oh crap, I hadn't even thought of that!

I looked around the room at the guys. Harris, Khaldon, Torchy, and I stood up.

"I don't know, sweetie. Maybe there's record of it on the logs Ludovic keeps on all the women."

Khaldon looked down at his feet and shuffled his weight from one foot to another. "Umm ... I know this isn't going to make any sense right now because I haven't wrapped my own head around the logistics, but the sperm donor box on the her medical chart, well ... it has my name in it."

I blinked and tried to understand what I thought I just heard.

"No fuckin' way!" Harris exclaimed.

"This is not good." Briggs said.

"Fuck me, I dinnae expect that, mate," Torchy said.

I was frozen and couldn't meet anyone's eyes.

Khaldon stepped closer to my sister. "It's mine, Sheridan. I don't know how, because I'm not a part of this insanity. But my name is on the paternity."

Something inside me died.

Chapter Fifty

I grabbed Beano's leash and headed out the lanai screen door. "C'mon, big fella."

Once out the door, I ran to the boat dock with blood running down my face.

Unholy hell! Khaldon is the father of my sister's baby? My Roxas - Sheridan's baby daddy? I can't feckin' believe this! I love my sister and I love Khaldon, but this ... this is just too much! How in the hell am I going to look at him again? How did this happen? Why did it have to be Khaldon? Is he secretly a part of this hideous plan? Can I really trust this guy?

I picked up a stone from the walkway and threw it into the lake. I heard loud shouts coming from inside Torchy's house. I guess they were as happy about all this as I was.

There has to be an explanation. This is crazy talk. Sheridan doesn't need this. She needs rest. I need to take care of her. So what happens now? Do they have to become a couple in order to raise this child? I can't handle this. Do we raise this baby together? Oh my God, this is seriously whack.

I paced back and forth and threw a few more rocks into the water. My heart ached with each plunk. I heard Sheridan crying for everyone to stop shouting.

Get over it, Cheyenne. You need to take care of her. You can figure this out later, but right now, you need to take care of her and stop this selfish pity party.

I ran back to the house with Beano at my feet. As I opened the door I heard Torchy shouting.

"What the hell, mate? You've got to be stark raving mad to believe that crock. This is seriously banjanxed."

"None of it makes any sense." Khaldon threw his hands up in the air. "I'm not any happier about this than you are. How do you think I feel about it?"

"Just because your name's on the medical record doesn't mean it's true," Briggs said.

"We could do a paternity test," Harris said.

"Stop it! All of you. Just stop it. I want to go home!" Sheridan screamed at everyone.

We turned to look at her. I stole a glance at Khaldon. The corners of

his own eyes were stained with crimson. Torchy's entire body glowed a
fiery heat. Briggs leaned against the wall with his arms crossed, lips tight.
Harris stood closest to Sheridan reaching out to her. He dropped his arm
back down to his side and looked at me.

Think, Cheyenne. What do you need to do? Forward Action.

"It's okay, Sher. Just relax."

Sheridan started to shake.

"Whoa there, c'mon sit down. Everything is gonna be all right. We're
all family here. Regardless of the hows and the whys, let's go home and try
to gather some perspective on this. We'll get to the bottom of this, just not
tonight."

"I still don't think it's a good idea if you go to your ..."

I shot Khaldon an *eat shit and die* look. Irritation crawled under
my skin the more I thought about this new development. The possibility
Sheridan could be pregnant with his twins – this was more than I expected,
or wanted. Khaldon looked away from me.

"I think this is all great and wonderful." Briggs pushed off from
the wall and walked toward Khaldon. "We're going to have a couple of
bambinos running around soon, but right now we need to figure out how
we're going to get Dakota."

Sheridan stood up and walked outside and out onto the boat dock.
Khaldon touched my shoulder as I started to follow her. "Maybe we should
give her a few minutes to digest everything."

Briggs was right. We had time to work through this, and I certainly
didn't need this distraction today.

What would Lady Caz do right now?

I bit my lower lip, and plopped back down into my chair. "What's
the status with the rescue operation? Did the Super Market accommodate
all of the women?" Khaldon, Briggs, and Harris looked at one another and
then either down at their feet or out the window. "What now? I can't take
anymore shockers, guys."

Khaldon took a deep breath and blew it out in a long, slow blow.
Obviously they were hiding something from me. "Where's Ludovic?
Shouldn't he be with you?"

"Ludovic is being watched by my pack," Harris said. "He's not getting
away with anything. In fact, I think he's had a few good bites from them."

"There was an unexpected development last night. It is taking longer
for about seven women to get moved." Khaldon cricked his neck from side
to side. "Chey, they've been there for four years and have given birth to over
a dozen dhampirs. We can't just unplug them. We'll kill the life support
sustaining them."

I sat still, blinking at this news. "I can't imagine the horror these
women have lived through."

Sheridan walked in the door. "What do you mean, they've been
there for four years?" She pressed her hands onto the small of her back and
pushed her hips forward. "Gah, my back is killing me."

"Here, let me rub your back for you." I walked over to Sheridan and helped her lean over the arm of the couch. I tried to give her a wry smile, but I felt like a ninny because it wasn't fooling even me. "Okay, Sheridan, I'm just gonna tell ya. You're not the only woman this has happened to. Last night we discovered 146 other women in various states of pregnancy. Some of them we cannot move because they're dependent on the life support systems because they've been there for four years."

"They could give birth any time now and it's just too delicate to unhook and remove them from the life support," Khaldon said. "Ludovic has to be there to help us. If we don't wait, we'll end up killing both the mothers and babies."

"But why? Won't they eventually come out of the induced coma if you remove the drugs?" Sheridan asked.

"This might be a little tough to handle. Do you want to sit down?" Briggs asked. His burly presence seemed to reassure her, and she nodded. But instead of sitting, she walked to the window and looked out over the water.

"We discovered from the records that these women were among the first to arrive when the facility was set up. They haven't been conscious since before they arrived," Briggs continued. "If we try to remove them from the life support, they might go into premature labor. If they do come out of the coma, can you imagine what is going to happen them? They'll be insanely scared and might flat line anyway. It's a bad situation all the way around."

"Oh my God, that's terrible. I hate them. How could they be so horribly cruel?" I remembered I needed to keep it together for Sheridan. "Okay, so it's risky to move them. What happens if the Priestess comes back and sees her other breeders gone? What's going to happen then? Will she kill those women?"

"Ludovic doesn't seem to think so, but we're planning on having surveillance around the clock." Harris grabbed for his fifth donut. With a full mouth he said, "We know he's anxious to find Dakota. The problem is, Ludovic says it's time for the Priestess to visit. She comes every two weeks to pick up sucklings and fly them back to South America."

"What I want to know is this ..." Torchy gulped down a swig of coffee. "I saw in the computer interface that this facility is numbered. Number 42. Does that mean there are forty-one other places like this around the world doing the same thing? Are there more?"

No one spoke. I processed the hideous image of buildings upon buildings of these helpless souls being destroyed to placate this vampire Queen.

"Dude, I can't even go there right now," Briggs spoke up again. "All I know is we need to get Dakota back tonight, and I don't care what it takes. She can't go on like this. There has to be a way we can curb this blood lust of hers."

Sheridan walked into the bathroom and closed the door behind her without saying a word. Moments later, we heard her retching her breakfast into the toilet. Torchy got up to fetch some clean towels and a glass of cool water for when she came out.

"Khaldon, didn't you tell me there two kinds of Solunarae blood?" I asked.

"Yes, there is a lunar and a solar. Why?"

"Ludovic said she was given the lunar blood right?" He nodded. "What would have happened if he'd given her the solar blood?"

"I honestly don't know what effect the solar blood would have on a human." He shook his head. "The lunar blood had killed so many, I don't know if the solar blood would have done just the same."

"What does the solar Solunarae blood do?" I asked.

"It gives vampires the ability to have a stronger daylight exposure, if their dynamic doesn't allow it. A few times of year when I know I need extended hours in the daylight, I'll arrange to ingest the solar blood. But primarily, I work with my diet and make sure I get plenty of vitamins and enzymes to help absorb all the nutrients I can. It's damn expensive and the Solunarae do not part with it easily. That's one reason so many vampires are destined for the night. If they can't afford it, if they don't have the dynamic from their maker, and if they have a crap diet, then they can't handle the sunlight."

"The Solunarae are a protected race," Briggs spoke up. "I believe everything is brokered through Kalina, descendant of the Goddess Kali and you don't want to mess with her. She's got bad news written all over her."

"Legend has it, it's how the werewolf creatures evolved," Khaldon explained.

"I've never heard that!" Harris snapped his head toward Khaldon.

"Have you ever asked about the Weres origins?" Khaldon asked.

"Not really. I figured it was just the way things were."

"Precisely. Like I said, it's a legend, but oftentimes what is born of legend is truth."

"What would happen now if we gave the solar blood to Dakota? Would it turn her into a daytime blood demon?" I pressed. "Or could it reverse some of the effects it has had on her for a short period of time? Could it weaken her? Would it make her a nicer demon? Is that even a possibility? Reverse the demon with the right blood? The way doctors can regulate conditions with the right type of medication?"

"She's got a point, Rox." Torchy walked back out onto the lanai and grabbed another donut. "What if the reason Dakota is killing so much is not because of being deranged, but because she's hungry? Didn't Ludovic say that's why she's killing? What if the Solunarae blood is the only thing that can satisfy her thirst?"

"Exactly, Torch! What if we lured her back to the facility tonight with the Solunarae blood? Briggs, do you think you could fly in close enough to Dakota to have her follow you?" I asked.

Sheridan emerged from the bathroom pale as a ghost. Torchy helped her to sit back down and gave her the glass of water. She seemed a bit embarrassed. "Okay, I've been listening while tossing my cookies. So let me get this straight. First of all, I'm not having a bad dream and I'm really pregnant." We all nodded at her.

Sheridan continued, "Secondly, all this crap about this blood demon shit is real? And you are seriously considering baiting her with this solar blood stuff?"

It wasn't very often I heard my sister cuss, so I was actually rather taken aback at her candor.

"Yes, Sheridan. I know this is totally whack, but that's the plan so far. Dakota has been the one killing people just to survive. She can't help what they have turned her into any more than I can change who I am now."

Sheridan nodded.

I continued, "She was supposed to be like you are now, but Ludovic was, slash, is, still in love with her and he couldn't handle her becoming comatose, so he turned her into a vampire."

Briggs growled. I turned to look at his face. For a black man, he was redder than a boiled crawfish set out to cool on the Sunday newspaper. "Down boy – we have to keep Ludovic alive, remember? He has the only connection to her right now. Even though I hate to admit it, truthfully, he's the best one qualified to help Sheridan when the twins are born."

"Twins?" Sheridan stood up and ran towards the bathroom once again.

Crap. Way to go, Cheyenne.

I watched her close the door. "Okay, here's what we're gonna do."

Chapter Fifty One

Breeder Facility #42

When we arrived at the facility, we found Ludovic chained to a snarling werewolf. Ludovic stood up and blew out a long breath when we entered the control room. "I'm so glad you're finally here. Mr. Chompers and Mr. Hyde here have barely let me move." He pointed towards the two werewolves assigned to watch him. One human, and one in wolf form.

"You mean Frank and Kyle?" Harris pointed to the guards.

"Thought those names were kinda funny." Kyle laughed.

I noticed how Ludovic's shirt appeared to have several claw marks ripped through it. "Has the Priestess sent any communications?"

"Yes. That's why we sent the message to Harris for you all to get here, quick," Kyle continued. "Didn't think you'd want Mr. Idiot here to be contacting anyone."

Ludovic glared at the guy. "She sent a text wanting to know if there were any sucklings ready to pick up." He pointed toward the computer. "I'm afraid if I don't contact her soon, she's going to get suspicious and come anyway."

"I don't like it," Briggs said. "But he's got a point. If we don't maintain an appearance of normalcy, it could raise a few red flags."

"I agree. If we do nothing, it could cause more harm than good," Sheridan said.

I took a silent vote and looked at everyone. All heads nodded in agreement, including Khaldon.

"All right, Ludovic. Who has your phone so I can text her back and tell her there aren't any babies ready." I took the phone from Kyle. "Tell me exactly what she needs to know."

The text was sent. A few minutes later, we received a standard text reply from the Priestess of *'keep me informed.'*

I responded *'okay'* in a text message back to her. "It looks like the communication worked. Hopefully we were able to postpone her visit."

"Thanks, Frank, Kyle. I appreciate you keeping him under control and contacting us the way you did." Harris relieved his pack mates. "I'll take over for a while."

"No worries, man. Frank got in a few good bites." Kyle grinned. "C'mon, Frank, let's go get some grub."

Frank snarled at Ludovic one more time, and then gave Harris a paw to fist bump before he padded out of the room.

"We should have enough time to attract Dakota here tonight and try to see what changes we can bring on. But there's no guarantee she'll come back here. What are you planning to do?"

"Leave that part to me. For now, we need access to the Solunarae blood," I said.

"I'm afraid that's not a very bright idea. Who are you planning to give it to? You've seen what it has already done to her."

"I am exceptionally clear about what you and your brother have done to my family." I spoke through clenched teeth. "Now where's the blood?"

Sheridan grabbed Ludovic's arm. "Where the hell is the blood? If you don't get it, I'll turn you into a Dakota Scooby snack." There was no question left in my mind about how determined Sheridan was to get her little sister back. For as petite in stature as Sheridan was, she was a force to be reckoned with today.

Ludovic gestured for us to follow him. We arrived at the supply area next to the medical rooms. He stopped in front of several large barrels. One marked S and one marked L. "These are the two barrels. Dakota was being fed with the contents of this lunar barrel."

"Then I take it that the solar Solunarae blood is in the one marked with the S correct? Don't want to make any assumptions." I pointed to the other container. He nodded.

"Okay, Ludovic, here's the plan. We know Dakota is starving. It's obvious she's lacking essential minerals she was getting from the Solunarae blood," Khaldon said. "Have you tuned into her lately – to see if she has moved?"

"She isn't far. I've tried several times to send her direct messages. I'm sure she is getting them. When she realizes the connection is made, she cuts off the stream," Ludovic said.

"What do you mean, direct message? Like an instant message? You have a way of sending her a text?" Sheridan asked.

"That's a good analogy, but it's more in the mind." Khaldon walked over to stand beside Ludovic. "It would be as if you had permanently planted ear buds in your head, and your mom and dad always had access to it. You wouldn't be able to turn it off. Because Ludovic is her creator, he has this connection with her that she can't turn off. But she can ignore it."

"Does it matter how far away from him she is? Can it be broken?" Not knowing anything about this, I wondered why my maker hadn't tried to contact me.

"No, I can sense her," Ludovic said. "Just not exactly where she is. I'm not a GPS sensor. I know she's been holing up in the amphitheater over in the Lake Lola area."

"That makes sense. That area is a natural aviary. At dusk, Beano and

I sit on the rooftop and watch the bats fly out."

Sheridan nodded. "Oh yeah, I remember when we watched that one night. You mean she's sleeping with bats?"

"Yes, that's where we tracked her down last night. Briggs and I followed her all over town. She settled in not far from the penthouse," Harris said.

"Harris and I were surprised to learn she stayed so close. I figured she would've flown the coop," Briggs added.

"Okay, so we need her to come back to this building. Can we tempt her with the blood? Will she be able to smell it if we do a fly by around the area with it?" I asked him.

"What do you mean 'fly around' with it?" Ludovic snarled at me. "You can't fly, even if you are a vampire."

"No, but my big pals Briggs and Torchy sure can." I moved aside and allowed them to step forward. Ludovic's eyes came up to about Briggs' nipples.

"What are you, some kind of dragon who eats knights and rescues princesses?" Ludovic sneered.

"I've been known to eat a few in my time, yes." Briggs flashed his teeth.

Ludovic swallowed. "You're a dragon? I thought they only ran the undergrounds, the Mafia, and hoarded their wealth."

"Most of us do. That's why your arse is in a whole lot of shite if you don't start cooperating," Torchy said.

I'd finally had enough of this jerk's snideness. "By the way, asshole, did you seriously cut off Dakota's toe? And what was up with the flower delivery guy? I didn't appreciate the jerkwad I had to kill because you ordered him to abduct me." Anger got the best of me. When Sheridan gently touched my arm, I calmed down a little. I still wanted to eat his face.

Ludovic squirmed. "The flower delivery idea was Edric's, and no, it wasn't Dakota's toe. It was the little toe off number 337 before I threw her in the incinerator. I grabbed the polish from Dakota's purse and pulled off her toe ring. Voila – instant torture scene." He snapped his fingers and smiled as if he were proud of his intelligence.

"Seriously? You sent me a dead woman's toe to mind fuck me? I swear to the Goddess, Ludovic, I will savor the moment you are killed. You'll join your brother when I feed you to Dakota. I promise you, I will!"

Ludovic turned and looked at all of us.

We all stepped in a little closer to him.

He held up his hands in front of his chest. "All right, let me try to communicate to Dakota to tell her we have the blood she needs."

***

"Do you have any ideas about how Briggs can carry the blood without it splashing and pouring off of him?" I asked Khaldon.

"Good question. We can't just poke little holes in the barrels and let it drip out. This stuff is way too valuable. And if it gets into the wrong hands, well, it could easily kill someone. Especially humans."

"We obviously learned that lesson," I said. "Do you think Edric should have gotten a clue, perhaps, after – what, maybe the third test subject who died instead of the 137th? Was he genuinely that dense? No wonder Dakota did him first. I would've, too."

"Such an unladylike thing to say, m'lady." Khaldon winked at me. "I like it."

I blushed.

"Edric was a scourge, got his jollies off of hurting others, especially women. Probably never got laid unless they were comatose."

Briggs jabbed me with his elbow. "Me, too. I like the way you think, Chey Chey. Maybe I should put you to work here in the Orlando area after this is all said and done. I think you'd be one helluva lady Mafioso."

"I'm not sure what all that entails, Briggs. All I want is to get back to my old life of running simulator game sequences against the virtual Battle Kroc of Doom instead of trying to rescue the world from the likes of this clown." I pointed at Ludovic.

Khaldon held out a hand as if he needed to sneeze. "How about a sponge pad or something else absorbent?"

"Not sure I follow." I shook my head.

Khaldon's face lit up in excitement and he snapped his fingers. "The lure for Torchy to carry. What if we soaked a sponge or some kind of pad with the blood? Would it be enough to get her attention?"

I walked over to the white board and picked up a pen. Structural design wheels turned in my mind while mechanical pulleys melded thoughts and ideas together. The sketches flowed out of my head and through my hand as I drew onto the whiteboard. It wasn't long until I had a saddle contraption to secure a device onto Briggs and a flag of blood soaked pads device for Torchy.

"Wait a minute. Oh *helll*, no. I ain't wearing no saddle. What do you think I look like, something out of the *Dragonriders of Pern*? We aren't fighting a thread here, Cheyenne."

"No, we're trying to lure and catch a blood demon, who can kill you, to follow you, and frankly that hits a little too close to home for me. I want her back, but I don't want you or anyone else dead in trying to do so."

He stood still for a minute, looking at me, and then squinted.

"Do you or Khaldon have any Kevlar vests in those arsenals out in the Land Rover? I need time here at this board to design Briggs some armor."

Briggs opened his mouth to argue with me.

"GO." I pointed out the door.

You would've thought I'd sent the naughty little boys to go bang erasers on the wall outside, but what I was trying to do was keep Briggs protected and save my little sister's ass.

"Harris, can you take Ludovic and round up any leftover nets, hardware, and webbing from the harness systems? Ludovic, we're gonna need tools. Drills, wrenches – do you have a welder?"

He nodded.

"Good, we're gonna need that too. Let's meet back here in fifteen minutes."

"We're on it. C'mon, buddy old pal o' mine." Harris shoved Ludovic out the door with Torchy and Sheridan on his heels.

While everyone was out hunting down supplies, I looked into the barrels of the lunar and solar Solunarae blood. I opened the clamped lid on the lunar and took in a whiff. Its pungent aroma smelled strongly of Harris. I could understand how the legends could be true for the Were creatures' origins with this stuff. I closed that lid and opened the one labeled, solar. Arming my olfactories for another attack, I was surprised to learn it was devoid of odor. I looked down into the crimson liquid and realized there was the absence of smell altogether. How was that possible? I closed the lid and finished drawing out my contraption.

Khaldon and Briggs returned with several tote bags full of guns and crossbows, but nothing to trap a demon. Kill one, yes, but that wasn't the scope of this plan. Briggs did have some of those nifty ultraviolet bullets, but I wasn't planning on using any of those on my sister.

"Okay, fellas, come take a look at this." I motioned them back over to the white board and showed them a rudimentary drawing. "Briggs, I'm pretty sure you have scales, right? Really tough ones, like the armor for your avatar?"

"How did you know?" he asked.

"'Cause it seems we make replicas of our strengths on the game, and you have the baddest game assist armor I've ever seen on an avatar."

He smiled with pride.

"But it also means you have a lot to protect because you're vulnerable. That's why you take so much precaution to protect yourself." He looked at me with downward, squinty eyes as if I had just revealed he slept with a stuffed teddy bear.

"So – I'm thinkin' with the Kevlar vest covering your most vulnerable parts, we can make this work. Whatdya think?"

"Does that mean I have to tell you where I'm vulnerable?" He smiled at me sideways.

"No, silly." I smacked him on the arm. "I'm trying to keep you alive. Dakota might not have any sense about herself. Human or otherwise."

"One thing for sure is Dakota sure as hell isn't going to believe it's you flying around in a dragon suit, "Khaldon said. "In fact, you just might want to keep that little factoid to yourself until later ... much later."

"There's a ton of netting and rigging in this place. I've got Harris, Ludovic, Sheridan, and Torchy rounding up tools and pulling in as much netting as we can recover. We can repurpose it into a snare for when you're back on the ground."

"Khaldon, what about Torchy's dragon form? Does he have any

vulnerabilities?" I asked.

"I'm sure he does, but he can spike out his scales and that keeps him safe from things clawing and stabbing at his more sensitive areas. In fact, he can be downright scary to look at."

"Okay super. 'Cause I figured out a way to have them fly in tandem. Torchy to lure and Briggs to carry."

***

Torchy had found a pile of half-inch-thick mattress pads with blue plastic backing. "Will this work?" he asked. "Maybe we could soak a few of these and use them as the flags. That'll get her attention."

"That'll be perfect, Torch. We can combine several of these. With your tight maneuvers, you'll be able to draw her down to where Briggs will be carrying the blood."

"Dog's Bollocks – I'm liking the sound of that." Khaldon clapped his hands. "What if we secure one of the big water tumblers with blood in it – maybe with a straw?"

"I'm not sure if that's stable enough, we need to find a stronger container. Maybe a plastic tote or something." I looked around at the pile of accumulated possibilities, hoping something would catch my eye. "Maybe we could use ..."

"I've got something better." Sheridan grinned her big cheesy teeth grin at me. She held up an empty beer pony keg. "I found this in the lunch room. Thought maybe we could attach this to the harness and fill it with the blood she needs."

"That's perfect, Sher. A great find." I hugged her shoulder. Everyone was busy brainstorming on what could work with what. In my mind, I was beginning to think our makeshift demon catcher plan just might work. MacGyver's writers would be proud of us.

"Ludovic, what kind of mouth does she have? Can she drink from that pony keg?" Khaldon asked.

Ludovic grimaced and rubbed at his neck. "She has a long tongue. It's pretty creepy. It's strong, and you don't want to get near it. Her mouth is still shaped like a human's, but she has this insanely long tongue. I would say she could lap up the blood from that hole in the keg."

I swallowed hard trying to envision this monster as my sister. I puffed out my lips on an exhale.

Stay focused, Chey.

"Briggs, once you have Dakota on your back, do you have some kind of tractor beam built into you?" I asked.

"What the hell, Chey Chey? You think I'm the Enterprise or something? The closest thing I can do is emit a gluey substance. If she gets her legs wrapped around me, she'll stick until I release her." Briggs roared with a thunderous laugh.

"Sounds kinda kinky to me," Sheridan said. She looked over at

Torchy and asked, "Can you do that?"

Torchy didn't say a word. He simply smiled at her.

Sheridan's cheeks blushed a rosy pink.

"Where do you imagine all the dragon and the fair maiden stories come from?" Briggs' silky seduction voice flowed. "Do you honestly believe they just stood there and took it? I had to glue their asses down."

"Great fellas, another visual. I will forever be warped with visions of Edric getting his jollies off on the defenseless comatose, and now fair maidens seduced because they were caught in a sticky tangle of spider web goo," I said.

"No. No. Not spider webs – Dragon Essence." He held the beat on the "s" in essence while arching his eyebrows up and down in quick succession. It must be the male seduction dance to the female. We think it's cornball. They think it's an amorous tease.

Combining the team's efforts, we had the complete makings for a makeshift dragon Kevlar riding harness, a flying bed pad flag system, and a blood demon snare. It was a ridiculous enough plan, it just might work. Or at least I prayed it would.

Chapter Fifty Two

The sun was due to set that night at 5:55, so we didn't have a lot of time to get Briggs and Torchy outfitted and, to make final adjustments. We moved into the larger loading dock area of the breeding facility where we were able to open up the bay doors similar to an airport hangar. Even though the facility was still under the Wiccan enchantments for privacy, the doors and parking lot faced the lake where the cattails and Bermuda grass stood tall, helping provide additional cover from would be onlookers. It's not every day people saw two towering dragons walking out of a building. From this viewpoint, I could see why Dakota had given us the clue for GC 89 because it was exactly how she had described. Boat loading dock, cattails, and fishing nets.

Even though Briggs and Torchy had told me they were dragons, I of course had not seen them decked out in all their glory. We laid out the rigging for each dragon. Torchy's rigging was going to hold the blood soaked mattress pads, and the rigging for Briggs contained a harness to secure the pony keg of blood. It was time for the fellas to morph into their dragon forms.

Nervously, I stood next to Sheridan and realized she was shaking as much as I was. "Cheyenne, I want you to know no matter what happens tonight, I'm sure in our hearts that we're doing best by Dakota. Thank you so much for saving me and for coordinating this rescue for her."

I looked at her with tears in my eyes and tried to speak, but the emotions welled up deep in my chest, and all I could do was hug her. I finally choked out, "Nothing can ever break the power of the mighty sister pinkie swear!"

"When are we going to tell Daddy about all this?" Sheridan asked.

"I was hoping we could tell him after we were successful in getting Dakota back tonight. Regardless of what happens, we'll need to tell him soon because my little niece or nephew isn't going to wait very long to make their arrival."

Sheridan looked at me with uncertainty all over her face.

I hugged her. "We'll get it figured out, I promise. No matter what."

She gave me a half-way smile and hugged me back.

About that time, the hangar clouded over – it was as if someone had turned on a powerful fog machine. The air was so thick I could hardly see my hand in front of my face. It was then I realized it was coming from two of the largest fog machines ever known. Both Briggs and Torchy had transformed into the most magnificent creatures I'd ever laid eyes upon.

Torchy chose a smaller dragon form than Briggs in order to maneuver in tighter formation around Dakota, but his scales were a brilliant crimson. They shimmered in luminescence as if they were peacock feathers when he breathed. His eyes were frightening to look at. They glowed a fiery orange lava quartz, his pupils vertical slits. He had sharp, angular, interlocking scales on his legs and body. His back was ridged with razor-sharp barbs on protruding spikes which matched his wings. I'd be afraid something could easily impale itself on his defensive armor. At the very end of his tail, he had a vicious blade to easily chop his prey in half.

Briggs was simply ... epic. He was just as beautiful in dragon form as he was in human form. His scales were so glossy black they were almost purple. He unfolded his wings to span over thirty feet revealing a phosphorescence glowing under them. His legs were muscular in order to hold up the long, colossal serpentine body. His eyes shined like azure, opalescent moonstones, which could easily seduce me into a dreamlike state if I stared at them long enough. They were alluring. His eyes beckoned me to gaze deeper into his abyss and get lost. His tail wrapped around his body aligning his scales to form a stair step up onto his back. I wondered how many fair maidens had fallen for those eyes and made that perilous climb.

As I stood there in awe of these two magnificent beasts, I thought about their personalities and how much they either emulated who they were in their human forms or were the antithesis of that embodiment. Sheridan stood rooted to the ground, her eyes wide. Torchy blew steam towards her and pulled his head in towards his chest beckoning her to come closer. I watched as she took one tentative step in his direction. He opened up his wing and called her to him. Within moments, she had reached out to touch his chest. He curled his wing around her and scooped her closer to him.

I checked around us to make sure Ludovic was close by. Harris had found some rope and had made a makeshift body lasso around Ludovic so he couldn't get away. I was going to have to praise him for his ingenuity later. Our captive could have escaped during foggy dragon transitioning.

We found a pile of clothes on the ground under Briggs and put them aside. The same for Torchy. "Ah that makes sense. Now I see why they put up the smoke screen, so they can change in privacy," I said to Khaldon as we strapped the Kevlar to Briggs' underbelly and around the front of his chest.

"Yeah, it's a real hip trick. It also comes in handy whenever you need a diversion," Khaldon said. "How's everything going over there for Torch? Are the straps long enough to hold up those mattress pads?"

"It looks as if we might need to get a come-along to tighten a few of these into place," Harris answered. "But yes, we're looking good over here.

How about you two?"

"We should be good. If Dakota tries to bite him anywhere on the backside, she would most likely lose a tooth against the glass scales." Khaldon answered. "Hopefully her claws won't be able to get through them. The Kevlar will help protect him underneath just in case she tries to attack him from below."

"The Kevlar isn't a hundred percent protection," I said. "But it's better than nothing since we honestly have no idea the extent of what we're up against."

We soaked the bed pads in the lunar blood and then folded them onto Torchy's wings. Then we secured the pony keg mixture of one quarter lunar blood and three quarters solar blood onto Briggs. Since the solar blood didn't have any smell, I thought perhaps if Dakota consumed it, it might weaken her, or at the very least, calm her down. Dakota would either gain more vicious strength from the lunar blood or she might lose some of the strength she gained from drinking the solar blood. We wouldn't know until we tried.

I grabbed my smartphone and snapped a picture of the dragons while Briggs was fussing with a strap under his wing.

A voice filled my head as if another person were inside with me. Shocked at the telepathy, I needed a second to figure out how the voice was in my head. I looked around to see where it was coming from. Then the voice changed its rhythm and pitch. Briggs' chocolatey smoothness flowed into my mind.

"Hey, Chey Chey, that shit better not make it onto Facebook."

I pointed at myself. "Moi?"

Briggs smiled, baring his teeth and winked his opal eye.

"I wouldn't dream of it," I said.

"Wouldn't dream of what, Cheyenne?" Khaldon stood beside me admiring the dragons.

"Briggs – I just found out that he can talk in my head. Look, it's getting close to time. We need to get final checks in and get them up in the air."

"Yeah, that's pretty cool when they talk in your head – and sometimes annoying. Let's ask them to move outside. You're right, it's time for Ludovic to contact Dakota." Khaldon put his hand in the small of my back as we walked out of the open hangar doors.

Harris followed with Ludovic in tow. The dragons walked outside, and they took the opportunity to fully stretch up on their back legs and extend their wings. I couldn't believe how majestic they were.

"Pretty amazing, huh?" Sheridan said as she put her arm inside mine. I was simply mesmerized.

"I feel like the actress from *Jurassic Park,* when they see the living dinosaurs for the first time. Remember? They were speechless trying to take in their massive size and magnificent beauty."

Sheridan nodded at me as we continued to gawk at the dragons standing in front of us.

Khaldon untied Ludovic from Harris. "All right, Lug nut, have you been able to communicate with Dakota?"

Ludovic stretched. "She isn't responding to my requests."

I glared at him.

"She did, however, move her energy when I mentioned you and Sheridan. So she's still cognizant of you both."

I scratched my head. The sun was getting lower in the sky. "Khaldon, I should go with Briggs. I know Dakota will respond better if she sees me holding the blood out to her."

"There's no way in hell you would survive something like that, Cheyenne. She might know who you are, but until she's blood satisfied, you are just another meal. And her human side would hate herself the next day for killing her sister."

I ignored his warnings. "Ludovic, let her know I have the blood she needs. We're sending her an escort to fly her back."

Briggs snorted and sarcastically threw out thoughts in my head. "Oh great, now I'm a freaking escort service. What will it be next? The demon welcome wagon? Meals on Wings?"

Chapter Fifty Three

L udovic, obviously never having sired a vampire before, wasn't particularly adept at summoning Dakota. In fact, he downright sucked at it.

I watched as Khaldon took the time to show him how to connect to Dakota as her maker.

"Ludovic, you're trying too hard. To communicate effectively with her, you have to embrace the connection between the two of you. You have to let it flow out of your heart with the passion of your love for her. Do you need a visual?"

Ludovic nodded.

"Picture in your mind a figure eight with a shining thread of golden energy. Now extend that energy cord down from your heart to your sacral chakra and down through your loins. Send that golden energy cord to Dakota's heart and then down through to her sacral chakra. Wrap the thread back to your heart and complete the circuit of the figure eight."

"I know you don't like this." I patted Briggs on the back. I whispered close to his head. "It's the only way we can communicate with her. I don't like it either." Briggs sent another blast of steam out of his nose, making a temporary fog bank around us.

Ludovic stood with his eyes closed and his hands out in the air as if he was trying to catch the rain.

"Now feel it in your heart and find where Dakota lives within you."

It was intriguing to observe Khaldon talk him through this.

"When you find her, capture the communication down into your rocks and let it flow. Send the golden thread to her with no message. Just create the open portal of communication."

Ludovic opened one eye to look at Khaldon.

"Trust me, okay?" Khaldon said. "Watch me." Khaldon closed his eyes, and it looked as though a peaceful calm came over him.

Who is he contacting? Has he sired anyone? Is he sharing a sex bond link with some other woman? Why hasn't my rogue creator ever tried to contact me? Maybe he doesn't know I exist.

I became aware of heat coursing through my body.

"I've got it! I found her!" Ludovic cried out. "She's accepting the thread. She says she's hungry."

"Good. Relax. Take a deep breath and hold onto her," Khaldon continued to coach. "Acknowledge you understand. Tell her you have the blood she needs. You'll keep her attention."

Am I picking up on Ludovic's signal? Could Ludovic be my attacker?

My pulse hammered through my chest.

Briggs pulled me into his wing. "You all right, Chey Chey?"

I could barely catch my breath. I felt the pull of the golden thread coursing through my body, and it pulled thoughts out of me. As suddenly as it appeared, it was gone.

"I'm all right. Just got a little winded there for a moment."

I stood bolted to the floor as if someone had played a joke on me and super glued my shoes. I couldn't move. My head hammered with the energy jolt. What was that? Why did I feel it when Ludovic sent out the signal? Could this dweeb be the guy who attacked and killed all those people on Halloween night and left me for dead? Was he experimenting with the lunar blood too?

Keep your head on, Cheyenne – you need this guy to get Dakota back. Just play it cool. You can address this later.

"Don't worry, Chey Chey, I'll help you get rid of the little creep after all this is over." Briggs spoke in my mind.

"You can hear my thoughts too?" I mind-messaged back to him. "Isn't that a violation of some kind of preternatural privacy act or something?"

Briggs snorted and puffed out a bit of vapor.

"She's got it!" Ludovic cried out again. "I told her we're bringing the blood to her. She thinks it's a trap."

"Tell Dakota I'm here, and everything is okay." I walked over to him.

"Let me try," he said. "She says to prove it."

"Tell her I pinkie swear promise. Find out where she is, Ludovic. Tell her I'll bring her proof." And with that I climbed aboard Briggs and strapped myself onto his back. Briggs began to beat his wings and created a fog around us.

Khaldon screamed out, "NO! She'll kill you!"

"Ludovic, tell me. Where is my sister?"

"She's just landed at the Cove Florida Lighthouse towards Miami."

Khaldon yelled at me and now at Briggs, "Don't do it! Bring her back!"

Harris and Sheridan were right next to Khaldon, yelling after us, but I couldn't hear what they were saying.

"Come on, Briggs, the only way to bring her back is to go after her!" Briggs soared up and within less than a heartbeat, we were flying through the night sky. I had to close my eyes and keep my head down. I looked behind us, and Torchy was right on our wings.

It was much cooler up in the sky than I'd anticipated. But the heat coming up from Brigg's body, up between my legs, was enough to keep me warm. I checked the blood-filled pads under Torchy's wings and they were secure. Once we got closer, he was going to unroll them off his wings.

"We need to head south. I don't know how long it'll take to arrive, but we'll need to haul ass if we are going to get her back before sunrise."

I heard another voice in my head. "I know exactly where that lighthouse is – follow me."

I watched Torchy take off ahead of Briggs. Obviously, they were communicating because before I knew it, Briggs was heading straight up into the sky after Torchy. I could've sworn the stars were close enough to touch as the dragons performed a backwards loop and switched directions. Thank the heavens I was holding on tight. I tried to adjust my hand for a better hold on the ropes and realized my arms and legs were glued to Briggs.

"Thanks for holding me down on the loops. Wasn't quite expecting that, guys. Is the roller coaster portion of this ride over, fellas?" I could feel Briggs' belly laugh underneath me. The laughter sent vibrations up between my thighs. It felt a little *too* good. "Hey now, enough of that. I'm a taken woman."

Briggs flew us close hovering just over the water off shore. "The way I see it, you're still up for grabs. If your Khaldon boy ever fails you, you just let ole Briggsy know, and I'll take care of him for you."

"C'mon, big fella. Let's go find Dakota!" I patted him on the back.

Horrible visions of blood demon Dakota filled my head. I didn't care if I had to open up a vein, she was still my sister and I was going to bring her home.

***

I called Khaldon on my cell phone, hoping to be able to get reception while moving this fast. People talk from mobiles on planes all the time, so why shouldn't I get dragon reception?

He picked up on the first ring. "Where the hell are you? Why would you do that, Chey? Do you have any idea - "

"Stop," I said. "There's nothing you can do about it now, so this is what I need you to do to get ready for our return."

"You mean *IF* you return, " he snapped at me.

"Fine, we can do this one of two ways. You can either help me, or I can try to do this alone. I won't lose her, Khaldon. If this is the only way to do it, then it's worth the risk to me."

I heard his *hrmped* grunt into the receiver. "Okay fine, but if you don't make it back here..."

"Seriously, Khaldon, unless she runs a wooden stake through my heart, or tears off my head, it's not like she can kill me. You have to let me be a vampire and stop treating me like I'm still a human."

Silence.

"Okay, I've got the extra drums of blood into place and the harness system. How long do you think it's going to take to get your bloody arses back here?" Khaldon asked. "If I know Torchy, he can probably have you both back in about an hour or so if everything goes as planned."

Briggs must have been able to hear the conversation because I could feel his body nodding in agreement. "Yes, Briggs agrees. Please get everyone and everything in order. This is going to go down a lot faster than any of us thought."

"Just one more thing," Khaldon demanded. "Well, maybe two more things. I want you back."

"And the second thing?"

"Don't get too cozy with Briggs vibrating between your legs. How the hell you think he's wooed so many princesses out of their virginity?"

Briggs belly roared and tipped his wings into the water creating a beautiful cascade of waterfalls beside us. A little embarrassed I said, "Well, it's a good thing I'm taken then, because it has been one helluva ride already. I've got to figure out a way to mimic his vibrations for my next cybrator."

I heard Torchy laugh at the joke as he mind-messaged me, "Nice one, Cheyenne."

"I love you, Cheyenne," I heard Khaldon say over the receiver.

"I ... I love you too, Khaldon." It was lucky I was glued to the dragon because I might have fallen off.

Khaldon told me, Cheyenne, that he loved me. Not as our avatars, but for who I am now.

Chapter Fifty Four

"There she is!" I pointed to a winged creature sitting atop the peaked roof of the lighthouse, effortlessly balancing on the vertical pole. The strobe spun on its 360 axis blinding me with each revolution. As soon as I focused, the light rotated again.

We flew down the beach along the shoreline to turn around. The cove, a small rocky inlet, looked as if a red tide had crashed upon its jagged boulders. The beach's formerly pristine ocean waters ran crimson rivulets over the pure white sands. Each wave crashed and puddled around the leftover body parts where seagulls plucked at the human remains.

"Torchy, undrape the mattress pads. Dakota is on the roof of the lighthouse," I messaged him in my mind. I watched as Torchy unfurled the pads from a flapped section under his wings, almost as if they were pockets. Now every time he beat his wings, the coppery blood perfumed the air, beckoning even me to follow him.

Briggs and Torchy sped past the top of the lighthouse and shattered its triangular windows. Dakota screeched at them and took off into the night sky after us. I gasped in horror as I saw what my baby sister had become.

Briggs released the dragon essence as I pulled up on the harness. I needed to turn around to face her. "Torchy, keep flapping, it's working!" Operation Blood Soaked Pads was already a success. The scent of the Solunarae blood drew her in close. I prayed she wouldn't land on me thinking I was the one providing the snack.

Carefully I removed one leg from the stirrup straps and swung my leg out in front of me to face backwards. Suddenly, Dakota shot underneath Briggs and cut him off under his belly causing us to have a mid-air collision. Her clawed wings tried to grab hold of me as she flew over us. I crooked my elbow under the netting harness to prevent her flying off with me. Briggs countered to the port side and helped to pull me out of her grip. He immediately corrected his course and righted us. Dakota's razor sharp wingtip talons ripped open deep gashes in my bicep. My blood had become its own beckoning call to her.

Torchy slowed his pace and flew beneath Briggs to keep Dakota from attacking us from below again. Dakota circled back around. Briggs evasively turned his belly away from her. I lost my grip and slid from his back and held on for dear life. Torchy and his poisoned spikes were mere feet away from me. From my position, I lost track of Dakota, but her screech blasted my ears to the point of silence. I scrambled for the netting as Briggs righted his side up, helping me hang on. Dakota came back at him, as though she were trying to attack him for the blood. He rolled over to starboard this time and, my boot barely had time to wedge itself under the netting. I grabbed onto Briggs' wing, this time he seized me in with his dragon glue.

Torchy maneuvered above Briggs while we flew at ridiculous speeds. I felt as though I was a part of the US Air Force Thunderbirds, but I didn't recall any dragon divisions.

Dakota came up along the back of the two dragons. Briggs released me so I could unscrew the lid to the pony keg.

The deliciously tempting Solunarae blood swirled inside the lid. I dipped my fingers into the round hole and then brought them to my mouth, sucking my fingers clean. I wanted Dakota to see that I would drink it, too. I dipped my hand in again and then let the droplets fly off my fingers and onto her face. "Dakota, it's me, Cheyenne. I have the blood. Stop attacking us!"

She screeched at me again. It was if a banshee and a screech owl joined together to make her song.

"Enough of the damn screaming already. Get down here and drink this blood!" I yelled at her while pointing to the container.

From the corner of my eye, I saw Torchy fly off to the side and then sidled underneath us and starboard. It made me feel better knowing if I fell off of Briggs again that I wouldn't land on Torchy's spikes. I looked at my arm, amazed it was already beginning to recover from Dakota's attack, but it hurt like hell.

I remembered Khaldon saying to Briggs, 'whatever you do, don't let her take the keg away from you. She'll fly away with it, and this might be your only chance.' "Briggs, slow down just a little, so she can land on your back," I hollered through the wind.

Her claws caught the netting secured to his back. He slowed even more, and she was able to pull her legs in under her belly and land gracefully. I scooted back away from the keg. I barely recognized Dakota's face as she appeared emaciated with the skin barely stretched over her skull. If it hadn't been for her red hair, I'm not sure I would have recognize her like this. She looked ancient and exhausted. If I didn't know better, I would've guessed she was a thousand years old. I sat three feet away from the barrel opening and pushed my back up against Briggs' neck. The Solunarae blood cocktail sent splatters flying onto her face as she licked at the droplets with her serpentine tongue.

"Dakota, drink it!" I yelled. "Drink the blood. It's what you need."

Instantly she was over the top of the keg and in my face. Open mouth screeching with fetid breath. Her jaw contained hundreds of fangs. She looked like one of the monster piranhas that live in the depths of an Amazon River. Green wisps of smoke seeped out of her throat as black liquid goo dripped from each jagged tooth edge.

I screamed and pushed at her nose. "Dammit, Dakota, I said drink!" I shoved her face again and guided it toward the keg opening.

Dakota looked into the barrel and then back at me. "Go ahead. Do you think I'd hurt you? I'm your sister, remember?"

Her eyes glared daggers at me.

I raised an imaginary glass as if I were drinking and motioned for her to do the same. I pointed to the hole in the keg. I prayed that somewhere, hidden inside her hideous demon shell, she could understand me. I swallowed hard as my eyes rained crimson tears seeing how horribly my sister had been suffering.

Dakota wrapped her clawed appendages around the keg. Pieces of rotting flesh were impaled upon her talons. She looked up at me and snaked out a long, serpentine tongue.

Did she seriously just stick her tongue out at me?

She slithered her tongue into the opening and sucked through it as if it were a straw.

Unholy hell – she's a giant mosquito!

"Now, Briggs!" I shouted in my mind. "Do it now!" Instantly both our bodies were sucked down onto his scales with dragon essence. I didn't think Dakota noticed she had become ensnared in our little trap as she continued to drain the keg faster than a rugby team.

Her wings and body muscles seemed to relax a bit as she lay quietly on top of Briggs' back. As she sucked up the blood, Dakota looked up at me. Even if it was the briefest of moments, I could've sworn I saw delight reach her eyes when she smiled.

With her tummy distended, Dakota sat up and looked around. "Guys, she's full. She might try to fly off. How far out are we?"

"We're about five miles out." Torchy messaged me. "Can you call Khal and let him know we've got her?"

"Dakota," I yelled to her again. "It's okay. Don't go. Everything is all right. Come back with us. We have the blood you need."

Dakota looked over at Torchy and then looked back at me out of the corner of her eyes. I knew that look. She was getting ready to play a trick on me. Chase me around the house, steal my favorite blouse, or pour cold water over me in the shower. But instead, she opened her wings.

Her wingspan had to be ten feet across. The air caught under her wings and pulled Briggs off course. She struggled to remove her legs from his sides, but she couldn't. She screeched again.

"Dakota, drop your wings – you're going to make us crash!"

She screeched again, only this time in my face. Her glistening, serrated teeth were a mere breath from me as I squished myself as far into Briggs as I could manage. I hid my face as her teeth scraped at my neck.

I hollered at Briggs, "Go faster, and please don't let her fall off!"

CRACK!

Dakota's demon appendages made a horrible cracking and tearing sound as the wind broke them backwards. Her shoulders bled as the bones protruded through the joints in contortionist angles. The muscle surrounding the breaks flapped in the wind mimicking Torchy's bloody bed sheets. Tears ran down my face when I saw the excruciating pain Dakota was in. I could do nothing to help her. She screamed as loudly as a train horn over and over. I heard the faint echoes of breaking windows as we flew by. Perhaps they broke from the soprano screams of her pain.

I pulled out my phone and dialed Khaldon. "We've got her. We're almost there. Please get ready. Her wings are broken." Nothing but static as the wind rushed past my ears. I had no idea if he heard me or not. With the barrage of her moans, I swiped the phone off and said a prayer to our mother to send us angels.

Dakota laid her head down along the dragon's back. I wanted to touch her beautiful red hair, now matted with blood and dirt. I prayed the blood she had drunk would help her mend her torn body quickly after we landed.

I felt the descent in our altitude and looked towards the ground. Torchy was already preparing for his landing. I saw the breeding facility and looked back at Dakota's torn body. I whispered, "I'm so sorry, my sister. This was the only way."

Chapter Fifty Five

Breeding Facility #42

"Hang on, Dakota! We're almost there. We can help you!" We circled lower and lower, spiraling down toward the earth. The wind speed slowed to the point where I could hear the painful sobs coming from her. She looked weakened, and I wanted to hold her so much.

"What makes you think I want any help, dear sister?" a possessed voice spewed forth from Dakota.

"You can talk?"

"Of course, I can talk, but I prefer my other voice, don't you?" she snarled.

"Truthfully, no. Not really." I shook my head at her sarcasm. "The screeching was a bit hard on the ears don't you think?"

"That's because you are a weak, prosaic vampire – a lower demon, at best. I am a blood demon. You'll never understand the power I have over you."

"Yeah, all right. Look, Dakota, I don't give a rat's ass what you think you are, or what kind of baby sister payback you're entitled to, but you've got to stop killing people."

"Why should I care? They exist solely to feed me."

"We have the blood you need. Regular human blood won't satisfy you. You don't have to do this. The military is out looking for you. If they capture you, you're as good as dead."

I thought to Briggs, "Don't let us go – she isn't friendly."

Briggs flew into the open hangar doors and dropped to the ground in a perfect landing.

"Isn't that just lovely, my own flesh and blood turned against me ... and just how do you think I am going to venture anywhere with broken wings, dear sister?" Dakota's demonic voice shuddered through me.

Khaldon and Ludovic rushed up to us.

Dakota hissed at them both, then her tongue struck Ludovic in the face. "That's for kidnapping me you, wormy asshole." She smacked him hard again. "That's for your insane brother." Ludovic fell backwards onto his butt. His hands and feet scurried backwards to get out of her reach as she lashed out again, narrowly missing his foot.

Sheridan ran up behind Khaldon with Torchy. He'd already changed back into human form. "Oh, Dakota! Are you all right? Hang on, we'll get you help."

Dakota turned her head and hissed at Sheridan.

Her eyes grew wide. She stood frozen, staring at the little angel she once held and cherished.

Torchy grabbed her by the elbow and encouraged her to step back as he pointed towards the ceiling.

"Okay, Briggs, let 'em go." Khaldon pushed the control button and dropped the demon snare net down over the top of us. The sheer weight of it hurt my head.

Knowing the plan, we knew Dakota would struggle and entangle herself in the net, but with her broken wings, she didn't move much.

"Hold on and we'll help you mend your wings."

"I hate you, I hate you all – you'll pay for this I promise. If I have to kill you all, I will." She thrashed from side to side under the netting.

"Just give us a few minutes. Please calm down. No one wants to hurt you, but we sure as hell are going to protect ourselves until you can feckin' behave!"

A female, maniacal laugh addressed the warehouse speaker system, "Now, now, Dakota – there's no need for threats. You'll have your day."

"Chyort, the Priestess!" Ludovic shouted. "She's here!"

"Tsk. Tsk. Tsk. Ludovic, is that any way to greet me? Come now, *please* introduce me to all your new friends." She lingered on the "s" sounds a little too long. "But that won't be necessary for most of them, now will it?"

A shroud covered the hangar doors as three dragons stood side by side across the entrance.

Crap, we're trapped!

Without a warning, Briggs created a brume of protection around us. Khaldon slashed through the netting and grabbed me off Briggs. Khaldon heaved and pulled us down onto the floor. I couldn't see anything. I knew this was Sheridan's only chance.

"Torchy, get Sheridan out of here! *GO!*" I screamed through the fog and prayed they heard me.

The brume's murkiness was thick, but I could hear what seemed like hundreds of boot steps around us. We pushed forward through the haze as I tried to make my way to where Dakota was caught under the nets.

"Dakota! *Run!* Get away – do anything, don't let them take you again!" I screamed in terror. I heard her screech. I felt her struggle against the snare as she pulled on the ropes we had just dropped on her. Briggs had released Dakota from his back and sidled in behind Khaldon and myself forming a wall around the soldiers.

With the hangar doors opened, the fog dissipated quicker than I expected. Fifty or so young men wearing red and black cloaks surrounded us, dangerous weapons in their hands. I assessed the situation and concluded we were in deep shite.

The voice spoke over the intercom once again with a wicked laugh. I knew that voice, but I couldn't quite put my finger on it. I looked up at Khaldon and noticed his jaw set firm. Amicula stepped into view as if she were on a catwalk.

"Amicula, be careful. The Priestess is here." Even though I didn't care for her, or her evil Aunt, I heaved an immense sigh of relief knowing backup had arrived. "Is Lord Stovall with you?"

That haunting, evil laugh cascaded from Amicula's mouth once again, accompanied by that practiced smile of hers.

The blood drained from my face.

Unholy hell! Stovall isn't with her. She's the priestess!

"Here, here, now my, dear Khaldon." We both stepped backward a few paces. Dakota continued to flail against her bonds. "You have done me well." We backed up into guards as she reached out to grab his chin. "Bringing back not only Dakota, but her beloved sisters, too. You are such a hellishly good little boy." She smacked lovingly at his face. "I shall reward you handsomely, my dearest lover." She winked and blew kisses at him in the most alluring way.

I looked up at Khaldon and cocked my head in curiosity. Instinctively my body stepped away from the man who'd apparently just sold us all down the river.

"Cheyenne, don't. It's rubbish. Don't believe it, she's crackers." Khaldon reached out for me. "These are all lies. I promise you – it's not true."

I blinked at him. The love of my life, the man I planned to spend forever with – had this man played me for a fool the whole time?

Have I truly been that blind? This can't be true – what would Lady Caz do?

My blood boiled. In that instant, I felt every last ounce of torment, pain, anger, and loathing for these *monsters!* I refused to comprehend or believe the betrayal my ears heard. I felt as if my heart was ripped out of my chest and my guts exploded into infinite bits. My entire body shook from adrenaline. My fangs extended as I crouched ready for battle. This bitch was going down!

Amicula stood, laughing at me, encouraging the other vampires to laugh out loud, as well.

"Dakota, *fly!* Get out of here!" I screamed.

Dakota struggled against her bonds. I could see her wings were healing, but they did not appear strong enough for her to fly. As the guards tried to remove the netting, she attacked three of them and ripped their bodies apart. Arms, legs, and intestines burst into the air as if she sent them through a rip saw. Dakota ate the guards as fast as they could approach her.

"Protect her, you fools!" Amicula shouted.

I bolted toward Amicula. I was going to kill her for what she'd done to all of us. As soon as I was a breath away from snatching her in my hands, she jumped up into the air as if she were the Caped Crusader with a fancy tool belt. She left me to dive into her dust motes. I tried to jump after her but failed miserably. I saw Ludovic hide inside a metal locker.

"Pathetic." She laughed at me. "Why my aunt is hell-bent on you three, I'll never know." She bellowed, "Guards, take them!"

She is truly a mad mental.

Immediately Khaldon turned into the fighting machine that I'd only experienced in the game. I didn't know he could actually fight. With his bare hands, he fought the men who held swords, axes, and knives. Why would he be fighting against them if he had aligned with them?

I didn't have time to think. I ran after Amicula as she raced down the second floor corridor. I wasn't letting her get away. I took the flight of stairs three, four at a time. We halted our chase as she stood at the top of the stairs and I stood at the bottom. We were alone, but we were able to see onto the main floor below us.

Dakota screeched as the dhampir guards continued to approach her. She struggled to escape the net and chomped her way through the thick nylon cords. The dhampir henchmen pulled glowing silver bindings from beneath their cloaks. They wore thick leather gloves to protect themselves.

As Amicula watched them, I inched my way toward the wall one step at a time.

Dakota devoured her fourth victim as she stepped out through the hole in the nets. She pulled her wings back into place and crouched to jump toward Amicula.

I advanced one step closer, wishing I had any kind of weapon at all. I put my hand in my pocket to feel for my keys.

Dhampirs used their bows and arrows to shoot silver bindings into the air. The arrows had a boomerang effect and flew around both Dakota's legs, entangling themselves. She moved forward and tripped over the bindings.

"Stop – no don't – the silver!" I screamed. Amicula snapped her head and stared daggers into my eyes as I sprayed her with my vampire repellent Dakota had given me the night of Halloween Scream night.

She screamed as she scratched at her face and bent over from the pain. The pepper spray might not be a real vampire repellent, but it still hurt like hell. I kicked her in the ass and attacked her with my fists banging into her back, her head, and face. My blows seemed to have zero affect on her. Her strength was unlike anything I'd ever experienced. She was much stronger than Mr. Flower Delivery guy. Amicula backhanded me, and I felt my teeth fly across to the other side of my mouth. Her one hit sent me flying through the air towards the steel rail. The momentum of the blow toppled me over the railing with a sickening crunch as I crashed on the cement floor, at Dakota's feet. It hurt to breathe. Something cracked in my ribs.

"Chey ... Cheyenne?" I heard Dakota whisper to me.

In the distraction, several guards threw a silver cloak onto Dakota.

"Nooo – *Stop!*" I cried as I stood up holding my ribs and yelled at the dhampirs.

Dakota stopped screeching and fighting. Instead, she sighed in marked relief. The silver seemed to mend Dakota, not burn her. The silver drape thrown over her settled her as if it were mom's quilt on the couch.

Everyone else in the hangar also stopped. Briggs continued to chew on a guard as a black cloak hung out the side of his mouth. A collection of broken swords and other weapons lay at his feet.

Khaldon had gained a katana from somewhere and mowed down the dhampirs as soon as they were in range.

Amicula sauntered down the steps and over to Dakota as she kicked dead dhampir away as if they were trash at a Mardi Gras parade. Her face looked burned from the pepper spray. Her beautiful makeup smeared - hair disheveled. To me this facade revealed the hideous monster that actually lived inside her.

I moved in closer.

"Don't worry, Cheyenne, we'll give her all the adequate care she deserves. She's quite a remarkable creature, you know. A rare beauty, indeed. We'll be sure to teach her the way of the Vampyre."

"Stay away from me, you bitch." Dakota looked up at Amicula and slapped her in the face with her tongue. "I want nothing to do with the Vampyres. You are nothing but demon fodder to me."

Amicula's eyes shot wide open. She looked as shocked as the rest of us.

Oh hell, yeah! Go Dakota!

Howling came from the distance. It sounded as if packs of wild dogs had piled around the building.

Harris! Yes, he's here with his packmates.

The dragons roared outside setting flames around the back door perimeter, trapping us further inside the building. Smoke quickly filled the entire structure; it wouldn't be long until this place was gutted.

Everything happened at once, as if it were in slow motion.

Amicula ordered, "General Nicholi, enough of this! Grab Dakota and get her into the dragon cage. It's time we returned her to her rightful guardian."

Werewolves crashed through the doors. Torchy and Sheridan followed behind them and back into the building.

Dammit, Sheridan why are you here? I told you to stay safe!

General Nicholi nodded. "And the sisters?"

"We'll get them some other time. I have the oocytes that I need for now from Sheridan." Amicula sneered at me. "The sisters are always accessible to us. We'll pick them up again when we need them."

I jumped at her again, but Khaldon pulled me back. "C'mon, the building is on fire. We have to get Dakota!"

"Wait, Priestess, where do you want me?" Ludovic shouted as he slithered out from the wall locker. "We have to put out the fire! What about all your breeders? What shall we do with them?"

"As far as I'm concerned, you shall die at the hands of the men you helped bring into this world," Amicula hissed back at him. "And I can always obtain new breeders."

"But I called you. I told you they were bringing Dakota back. I've got all three of them here for you now."

I saw three dhampir heading towards Ludovic. He was as good as dead.

Choking on the smoke, I barked at Sheridan, "Get the hell out of here. Grab Torchy and find somewhere safe now. Stay low."

She turned to leave. I grabbed her arm. "Wait! Try the medical supply room where they keep the blood. There's a ladder to the roof in there. Torchy can fly you to safety. *GO!*"

She nodded and hugged me fast. She whispered into my ear, "I'll forever love you, little sister."

The last I saw of her was a flash of red hair skirting around the corner through the smoky maze of black and red robes.

Briggs tried to douse the flames with his water spray as quickly as the fire dragons re-engulfed the building again. It was a draw, but there were more fire dragons than he could handle all by himself.

I ran towards the dhampirs who had Dakota. A hulking, sandy brown, curly haired wolf ran up beside me with snarling fangs. I ducked, thinking it was getting ready to attack me, when the wolf jumped over my head and landed on the three guards behind me knocking them over as if they were bowling balls. The wolf chomped one dhampir by the neck and shook it violently. One of the guards grabbed his katana and raised it for a death strike against the wolf. I jumped over the werewolf, grabbed the katana in full swing, and reversed its direction and chopped off the dhampir's head instead. The last dhampir was caught under the back end of the wolf. The guard pulled out a knife and repeatedly stabbed the wolf in the back. Without hesitation, I skewered the bastard, and his knife clamored to the floor. I grabbed the knife and shoved it under my belt.

Dakota plucked several more guards up in her gaping jaws. It helped that they had cloaks, they were easy to snag as they tried to run away.

An energy vortex surrounded Dakota as she was entrapped inside a cage with no walls. Her body floated up and away from us and out the hangar doors. I ran toward her but more guards fought against us blocking our path. Dakota was loaded onto the back of a green dragon which spewed forth flames torching everything in its path. The guards began to retreat and follow the dragons outside.

The wolf nudged at my hand.

"Harris? Is that you?"

He woofed at me.

"C'mon. They just took Dakota." We ran after them. I shouted, "She's wrapped in silver bindings. Be careful!"

We ran, cutting down dhampirs with almost every step. Khaldon was right beside us trying to catch up to her as well. Briggs swiped his massive tail to take out more of the guards and ease our path to the other dragons. We finally made it out past the hangar doors.

They were securing Dakota onto the dragon's back as she screamed out my name. "Cheyenne, Cheyenne, help me! I can't get out. I don't want to go!" she screeched and thrashed her body against invisible bonds.

I knew my little sister was in there. "I'm coming Dakota, hold on! Try to break out of those bindings."

"I can't. They're locked onto me," she cried back.

I ran towards her. Amicula and the general were already on top of the other dragons.

My head slammed into the ground as my feet were pulled out from underneath me. A dhampir sideswiped me as I fell into the grass. I crawled up on top of the jerk and bit his throat. He flipped us. I landed on my back. I felt the air in my lungs explode out of my chest.

The dhampir punched my face. He was about as strong as the flower delivery guy, and I threw him off. I pulled the knife I had sheathed into my belt and slammed it into his heart.

Torchy flew overhead as Briggs took off. I prayed they would be able to catch them and free Dakota.

Harris jumped at the tail of the green dragon. The wolf's sharp teeth gnoshed on to the dragon's fleshy tail as they lifted off the ground. The dragon roared. They were airborne.

Khaldon jumped in the air after them and missed Harris' paw by a mere hair. He fell back to the earth and landed in the marshy lake.

We had lost her as quickly as we had found her. I stretched my hand out to the starry sky – *Dakota!*

Chapter Fifty Six

"Hold on, Harris!" I yelled up at him. The dragon vigorously swished his tailed back and forth. Harris flew off and must've fallen over two hundred feet out of the night sky. I heard him yelp. He landed with a splash into the swampy mud. The dragons flew off with Dakota, Amicula, and the rest of the dhampir soldiers.

I ran to Harris and found him face down in the water. He'd already shifted to human form. I grabbed him and gently turned his head to get his face out of the water without risking damage to his neck. His backside was covered in deep knife slashes across his back and buttocks. With so many hearts wildly beating around me, I had trouble distinguishing his. I laid my head against his back to listen closer. His pulse was weak, but he was alive. His cuts were healing before my eyes, and I noticed a chunk of green dragon flesh by his head.

Way to go, Harris. Tore a chunk right out of the dragon's hide!

Snarling werewolves padded up around me. I was surrounded by dozens of glowing eyes. Did they think I was the one who hurt Harris? Now I had a different threat to deal with. I protectively covered his bleeding body with my denim over shirt.

"Harris is my friend. I'm Cheyenne O'Cuinn. Do you understand me? I need to get him to a doctor. Who else in the pack is hurt? We need to help each other. I don't know how many more vampires are coming. Please, we need to work together."

A blonde werewolf cocked her head up at me in a sideways glance and morphed into human shape. She wore a jeweled crown made of sticks and moonstones in her blonde waves. I couldn't remember ever seeing such a beautiful naked woman before. Obviously not shy about her lack of clothing, her hair draped down cascading over her body.

"I am Naomae, werewolf pack leader of the Southeast region. Harris called upon us for assistance against the vampires. How am I to know you are who you say you are?" she huffed.

"Can't you smell her? She stinks to high heaven." Harris smiled at me and turned over.

I looked down at him and hugged him to my chest. "Oh thank the Goddess you're all right!"

He licked my cheek.

"Ewww."

I stood up and put my hand out. "Thank you, Naomae. Thank you for your help and assistance. I apologize for what has happened here. Your help is immensely appreciated, and we hope to find a way to repay your kindness one day."

Naomae looked me up and down and huffed at me again. "All right, troops, let's secure the area. Pull together the bodies, and determine if we've lost anyone."

"Here's the last of them," shouted Khaldon from a distance. He pulled himself out of the marsh, dragging Ludovic behind him by the ear. "Caught this one trying to get away at the boat ramp."

I looked at Khaldon, not sure of what to say. I was still seriously confused by everything that just happened between him and Amicula. "Naomae, this is Khaldon. Khaldon Seters. And this idiot is Ludovic. The reason why you were called here to help us." I spat on him. "Why aren't you dead?"

Naomae nodded to Khaldon with a wry smile on her face.

He acknowledged her with a guilty glance. "Ahh, yes ... we've met before," he said.

They each took a slight step backwards away from one another.

Are you feckin' kidding me? Another one? Who hasn't this guy been with?

Khaldon dangled Ludovic like a sack of old rotten potatoes. "We have to keep him. He's the only one who can help find Dakota again. If we kill him, we'll never find her."

A couple of towering figures swept through the moonlight overhead. Briggs and Torchy were on the ground and immediately by my side. In an instant, they had transformed back to human form.

Briggs grabbed Ludovic by the shirt and roared in his face, "I'd rather eat him and use his bones to pick my teeth."

No one made a move or said a word. Ludovic's heart rate doubled.

Briggs continued in a controlled, but deadly tone, "But I'm a patient man, and if he's our only connection ..." Briggs pulled him closer until they were eye-to-eye. "I'll wait until after we have her back. Then I'll eat him." Briggs threw him back to Khaldon. Ludovic landed in a pile at Khaldon's feet.

Harris stood up and wrapped my shirt around his waist. "So what happened?"

"We lured Dakota back, the plan worked. But Ludovic tipped off the Priestess somehow and now Amicula has stolen Dakota away. She's gone again!" I turned to Ludovic and kicked gravel at him as he stood up. "Why didn't you tell us Amicula was the Priestess?"

"Who? Amicula? I honestly did not know her name. She has always been the Priestess to us. She comes and takes the newborns. I can't believe she left me to be killed by the very men whom I helped birth." He looked around at us. "Look, she betrayed me, too. She promised me I could leave the breeding facility and all this mess if I handed you all over to her. I want nothing more of this."

I smacked his face. He stood there looking at me. The face smack wasn't nearly as satisfying as I wanted it to be, so I punched him hard in the mouth, and that sent him to his knees.

Sheridan ran up to us with a fire extinguisher clutched in her hands. "I've been able to keep the fire away from the last of the breeders left in there. I found a ventilator fan and cleared out the smoke. Their machines seem to be working, but we'll need to check on them again soon. I need Ludovic to help make sure they're stabilized."

Torchy walked over to Sheridan and offered to hold the fire extinguisher.

She looked down at her hands as she handed it over to him and gave him a half smile. "What happened with the dragons? Torch, Briggs – where did they take her?"

Briggs looked down at his feet. Torchy looked away out over the water.

"Briggs?" I pushed.

"I don't know, Chey Chey." He looked down at me and touched my arm. "It was like, one minute they were in front of me and the next minute – they were gone."

"It was insane," Torchy added. "No scent trail. No nothing. The sky opened up a hole, and they flew right into it. It closed behind them. They were just ... gone! I'm so sorry." The look in his eyes pleaded with us for forgiveness.

Sheridan and I looked at each other, both of us on the edge of tears. "It's not your fault, Torchy. You did your best." I heaved over and put my hands on my knees. My ribcage still ached.

Naomae asked, "Who are these guards?" She gestured to the bodies the werewolves piled alongside the building.

"These are the dhampir soldiers," Ludovic explained. "This is what the breeding facility is about. The Vampyre Queen is creating an army. But now she wants super soldiers so she can wipe out the rogues. That's why she is taking Dakota."

"That's genocide." Khaldon grabbed Ludovic by the shirt. "Why would the Queen go through with such a ridiculous plan?"

"It's not crazy as far as she's concerned." Ludovic tried to wriggle out of his grasp. "She feels the rogues are a blight on society and need to be eradicated."

"But why?" I pressured.

"She's afraid there isn't going to be enough food supply soon at the rate the rogues are reproducing. There's too much nuclear activity on the planet. She's preparing for an apocalypse."

"Nice! I like this Queen." Naomae laughed. "Anyone willing to get rid of a few more vampires in this world is fine by me. But what worries me is what will she do with this army after she purges her rogues. Will she attack the Were Community next? I need to contact Queen Ayame about this. Come, boys, let's get out of here and let them sort out their own problems. Harris, we'll need to talk later. Keep us informed." She turned and morphed back into her blonde wolf form once again and fled into the darkness. The rest of the pack followed her into the night. We could hear them howl as they faded from sight.

"I'm sorry, Chey." Harris hugged me. "Naomae can be a little, intense."

"So what's next? What do we do now?" Sheridan asked.

I kicked a dead dhampir with my toe and looked at my sister. "I guess we plan for a baby."

Everyone stood silent for a few moments.

"I don't know," I finally said, "We need to find some way to locate where they've taken Dakota. I wish I had thought to tag her with a GPS device. She called out for help when they were taking her away." I turned to look at everyone. "Did anyone else hear her cry out for help?"

"We all heard her, Cheyenne." Khaldon stepped closer to me and put his arm around my shoulder.

I shrugged him off. "No matter what she's turned into, she was frightened and didn't want to go."

"Other than obvious, what's wrong, Cheyenne? Are you hurt?" Khaldon stepped back with a look of surprise on his face.

"What's wrong? You have the balls to ask me what the hell is wrong, loverboy?" I stepped into his face and poked my finger hard into his chest. "Reward you later? So pleased you have delivered all of the sisters ... does any of that ring a bell?"

"But I told you that was all lies. You can't believe what she said?"

"I don't know what to believe anymore." Overcome by grief, I finally had to let it out. "How could you be in cahoots with this ... this weasel?" I pointed to Ludovic. "How could you be lovers with Amicula? How could you do this to me, to us? Why would you betray your race?"

"What? I don't understand." He winced. "I didn't know anything about this, Cheyenne." Khaldon grabbed my arms and tried to pull me in close. He lowered his voice to almost a whisper. "You have to believe me."

"Oh, do I now, really?" I exploded out of his grasp.

"Cheyenne, I can explain." His palms up in surrender. "Or I think I can explain. I'm just as shocked as you are about this. Honestly, I am."

"Why is that? Because she outed your relationship?" I said with a sneer. Disgusted, I turned my back on him and to hide my bloody tears.

"No, not at all. I told you that first night, in complete transparency, that we were once together, but that was over three hundred years ago."

I bit my lower lip and started to walk away. "What does that have to do with me and my sisters and how you have betrayed us?" I yelled out at him.

"Bollocks, Cheyenne. I didn't want to have to tell everyone this, but Amicula drugged and raped me the other night."

I one-eightied on my heels, and everyone else looked up at him. The collective look on our faces reflected my shocked surprise.

"From what I understand, it's the second or third time she's done it to me, and I had no idea that it had happened." Khaldon ran his hand back through his hair and rubbed his neck. He looked at each of us. "That's the only reason why I can figure out how Sheridan is pregnant with my ..." he swallowed hard, "my children."

Sheridan made the "T" sign with her hands. "Time Out! What the hell are you talking about?"

"Okay, there's a lot to tell you, but you gotta hear me all the way out, okay? You can't jump to any conclusions – do you understand?" Khaldon took another deep breath. "Regardless of what I'm going to say – we need to keep in mind that we're dealing with sick, lunatic vampires." Khaldon pointed at Ludovic.

Ludovic looked at the ground.

Khaldon continued, "We all know that Amicula works for her Aunt, Queen Civetateo. The Queen is located in the Amazon Rainforest somewhere. They keep her hidden for her safety against other supernatural beings who would like to dethrone her."

"And this Amicula chick, the Priestess, is her niece?" Briggs asked.

"Yes, that's right," Khaldon continued. "That night when I didn't return from Mordez Moi, I didn't tell you the complete story. Amicula drugged me and took me to her beach house out on Cocoa Beach."

A hard lump began to grind inside my throat. I didn't like where this was going.

"At the bar, she did tell me about the Queen's plan to purge the vampyric race, but that wasn't all she revealed."

"I'm sorry," I stammered. "I don't understand why it caused you to be alone at her beach house."

"Cheyenne, you need to hear the whole story." Khaldon grabbed my hand, but I wrenched it away. He furrowed his eyebrows at me.

"It's all right, mate. Just tell us what the mental bitch did to you." Torchy touched his shoulder.

"She slipped the lunar blood to me at the bar. Once she drove me out to her place, she bound me up with silver bindings – arms and legs to the four posters on the bed." Khaldon breathed in a huge breath and exhaled forcefully. "All I can figure out is that she must have given me more of the Solunarae lunar blood, just enough to make me lose control. When I woke up, she was gone. I found myself tied with one arm to the bed, and I had been ... ridden." He looked at me sideways. "She left this note on the table."

Khaldon pulled a crumpled piece of violet stationery out of his pants pocket. The letter reeked of her perfume.

I crinkled my nose from the pungent spice.

Harris sneezed.

"Basically it says, thanks for the little swimmers. I'm off to go take care of the sisters."

"Fuck me, I dinnae expect that!" exclaimed Torchy.

"Are you fuckin' with me, bro?" Briggs snorted. "You mean the bitch slipped you a roofie and milked you dry with a cock pump?"

"What the holy fuck?" Harris grabbed both sides of his head and nervously pulled at his hair. "She seriously raped you?"

I looked at Khaldon for a long breath and began to laugh out loud. I pointed at him in my hysteria. "You ... you honestly expect me to believe that? That you, a man, could be raped? You know you had me buying your story for a minute." I laughed so hard, it made my ribs ache. Nobody else joined me in my doubtful laugh.

"Fine, whatever, Cheyenne. You know I'm sick of this bullshit myself." Khaldon raised his voice, and bitterness stamped every word. "Bloody hell, I sure as fuck don't need this kind of shite from you, or anyone else, 'cause I didn't ask for it!" he screamed at me. "It is what it is and that's it." He poked his finger hard at me but didn't touch me. His furious energy exploded all over the rest of his words. "I don't like this any more than the rest of you. You can refuse to believe my rape if you want. But the truth remains ..." he pointed at Sheridan, "she is pregnant with my progeny, and there's no telling how many more eggs they took from her, mated them with my sperm, and impregnated those other women we rescued last night with our children!"

Everyone stood still as a statue. I looked at Sheridan, Torchy, Harris, Briggs, and then finally at the only person who might have answers.

Ludovic stepped towards me with his palms up. "Cheyenne, I am very sorry."

"Sorry? You lousy piece of shit. Do you see what you have done to all our lives? Can you possibly imagine the sheer amount of grief and pain you have caused in thousands of people? How do you live with yourself?"

"I don't. I've been numb for an awfully long time. That is why when I met Dakota, she changed something in me. I want to make things right, but I don't know where to begin. But that is not the issue right now." He swallowed hard and pulled an electronic tablet from his back pocket. The one he used to access the breeder's records. "Regardless of what I've done, Khaldon speaks the truth. The Priestess records the video samplings and sends them to us for the chain of custody. The specimen containers are numbered and labeled for when they arrive here at the lab, along with the videos."

"You honestly expect me to believe this crock?" I shook my head in disbelief. "Why would she do this?"

"Here, watch it." He swiped on the screen and navigated to the breeding facility intranet website. Ludovic handed me the small tablet. "You'll understand when you see it."

My eyes widened with horrific shock at how this insanity could possibly be true. I looked at Khaldon. He didn't meet my eyes. Everyone gathered closer to watch the video.

"She tells us how much Propofol she uses on each donor." Ludovic continued to describe the procedure as if he saw this every other day. "Then she tells us how much of the lunar Solunarae blood she used to keep them conscious, but still wild. They have no memory of what they do."

Illuminated on the screen was a still image of Amicula and a test tube. I pressed the play button and what Ludovic explained was exactly what happened. Khaldon was tied to a vertical rack with a bench in front of it. His eyes glowed red.

I took in a deep, rushed breath.

Khaldon looked down at the ground and walked away from us. I stole a glance at him as he stared up at the sky. I had to finish watching this video. I had to understand.

My knuckles turned white as I held on to the tablet. Amicula placed a vacuum pump onto Khaldon and turned on a timer. Within seconds, the orgasm release was over. The pump sucked the semen and deposited it into a test tube. Amicula wrote on a sheet of paper. 'Next deposit in seven minutes.' There were two entries already on her list with exact times next to them.

"How many times has this happened?" Sheridan asked.

I looked over at Khaldon and then back at Ludovic.

"This was his second time, but there are two more videos. The latest one was three days ago when she drugged him at the bar," Ludovic explained. "But he isn't the only one. She does this to men all over the world."

"Are you feckin' kidding me?" Torchy exclaimed. "Blimey, how long has this been going on?"

"How many deposits does she normally collect when she does this?" I shook with fury.

"They have been doing this for close to five years now. Normally there are about four deposits per vial she sends." Ludovic swallowed again. He looked over at Khaldon and pointed. "Khaldon is lucky. We've seen videos where the donor doesn't have much to offer. Let's just say she gets angry. We have videos of castration because the donor could not please her enough. The guy never knew what hit them. They would either die or wake up castrated. But they're all on video."

Khaldon had squatted with his head in his hands.

"Do not destroy this." I handed Ludovic the tablet back.

"On second thought, give that back." Sheridan snatched the tablet from Ludovic. "I need to know who is the father of whom and what. We need to try and help these guys as much as the women. They are all victims. I can't believe how inhumane she is to people."

"That's because she isn't human, Sheridan," Torchy added. "She couldn't care less what she does to them."

I looked at Khaldon, uncomfortable and horribly angry with myself. I'd had defiled him in front of our best friends. He risked his life for me. There was no telling how many men he had killed here tonight to help rescue Dakota. He'd had been a pawn in this woman's wicked games longer than any of us had.

What a terrible jerk I've been. I doubted him in his most vulnerable state.

I walked towards him, knowing that whatever I said most likely wouldn't matter. I could never repair the damage between us now. He stood up, turned his back on me, and looked out over the water. I reached my hand out to touch his shoulder but retracted. He took a few steps away.

I'll be surprised if he ever talks to me again. How could I be so damn unkind? Why didn't I trust him?

I reached out again and gently touched his shoulder. He grabbed my hand and pulled me in closer to him.

"I'm so sor..."

He turned around and shushed me with his finger. "Shhh ... m'lady. Don't. I would have done the same thing."

He leaned down and put his forehead to mine. Tears escaped my eyes and dripped down my nose.

"I'm sorry, too. We'll find a way to get through this." He grabbed my shoulder and reached to lift my chin, forcing me to look into his green eyes, his face covered in his own tears. I wiped his cheeks and tried to smile through my trembling lips.

I put my hands on both sides of his face and pulled him in to kiss me. He lifted me off the ground and held me tight. I cried out at the pain in my ribs, and he released his grip. We kissed with more passion than I had ever dreamed of in all my nights of gaming with him. Our salty, coppery tears mingled with our tongues as grief, relief, and exhaustion flooded through me. I wanted him so very much in my life. I couldn't imagine life without him.

One day, I will kill Amicula and everything she has done to us!

***

After we checked on the breeder women inside and determined they were still safe, we looked around at the cleanup.

"What do you want to do with all these dead bodies?" Harris asked.

"There are two choices," Khaldon answered. "We can call in the cleaners, but most of them are busy with taking care of the women we rescued yesterday. Or, we can call the ghoulies to come and take them away. Whichever way, we need to take care of them soon."

"Won't they just disintegrate when the sun comes up?" I asked.

"Not knowing who their vampiric fathers are, we have no idea about their dynamics or sun sustainability. If we don't cut off their heads, or have the ghoulies disassemble them, the city of Orlando is going to have a murder of revenant vampires let loose on the population."

Harris, Briggs, Sheridan, Torchy, and I turned to look at Khaldon. We couldn't have timed our shock any better than a rehearsed Gregorian chorus. "REVENANT VAMPIRES!"

Chapter Fifty Seven

The Penthouse

Thanksgiving Day

"Do you mind if we turn off the TV for a while, Chey? I can't keep listening to these global catastrophes. It's nothing but fear porn." Sheridan grabbed the remote and muted the CCNN channel.

"I know, but since we don't have a clue about where Dakota is or if she escaped from that wicked wench, I've been scouring the headlines looking for where she might be attacking people for food. I want our little sister back. I miss that brat."

She hugged me and patted my back. Her baby bump pressed up against me.

"I even have the headline news ticker on my phone to alert me if more than two bodies are found mutilated somewhere." I pulled out my phone to show her. "ExsanguiNation pings me if it finds any blood demons, or if any case lots of Solunarae blood are being sold through the Super Market."

"Listen, Chey, we'll find her. It won't be long now. If you keep watching this stuff though, you're gonna turn into a paranoid fear junkie."

"*Oookay*. Whatever. You'd be amazed at how many humans are killed every single day on this planet. It's surprising we aren't extinct."

"Seriously, Chey? That can't be healthy."

"You're right. It's not good to bombard my brain with so much negativity, but I don't know how else to find her. You've got your ways, and the guys have theirs." I heard Beano kick over his empty food bowl in the kitchen. "Any one of us is bound to find a trace of her."

Beano trotted into the living room with Stormaggedon on his heels. They sat at my feet.

"I guess you're hungry huh, big fella? And you too, toots?"

Stormy lifted a paw to shake.

"You know, Cheyenne, we were supposed to take Daddy out to the Cracker Barrel for Thanksgiving dinner today. Do you still want to go, or do you want to make something at home?" Sheridan looked at the circled date on the wall calendar.

Beano pulled the sad puppy dog eyes on me. "C'mon, Sher, let's go to the grocery store. I need to get the pups some food anyway. We should start some new traditions with the new family. Why don't we invite the guys over and have a nice dinner?"

"Sounds fabulous. Let's go. I need chocolate."

I grinned at her and grabbed my car keys.

An hour later and we had the fixin's for a Thanksgiving feast that would make our mother proud. I never had a reason to own a formal dining room table, so Sheridan and I pulled out the old ping pong table that hadn't seen the light of day since I moved. We draped a pair of white sheets over the top, added flowers with fall leaves for decorations and called it good. We now had a space large enough for all of us and the food.

One by one, the guys arrived and took their well-earned position at our humble table. We put everyone to work serving up the food. We loaded platters with smoked turkey and spiral ham. Torchy brought out the rosemary garlic mashed taters while Khaldon took out the green bean casserole and sweet potato pie. Daddy was right behind him with a steaming pot of grits and greens and a loaf of French bread. Briggs hogged the giblet dressing while Harris dished out the orange juiced yams. I completed the spread with my mother's ambrosia recipe passed down from many grandmothers before her. Everything looked and smelled delicious.

I clinked my spoon on the wine glass to gather everyone around. "I'm not sure how you guys have done Thanksgiving in the past, but in the O'Cuinn household we each go around stating what we're thankful for this year. There are a few obvious ones, of course, and this is the first Thanksgiving we've had without Dakota since she was born." A silent, crimson tear threatened to cascade down my cheek, but I held it back.

Already familiar with this little tradition, Harris started. "I'm thankful that everyone is alive, no matter in what capacity."

"I believe I have found a new purpose in life." Torchy raised his glass towards Sheridan. "And a new family if they'll adopt me."

Sheridan blushed and raised her glass to meet his toast and request.

"What are you thankful for, Briggs?" I asked.

"Old friends, new friends, and treasured times to come. Next year Dakota will be sitting right here next to me."

I smiled at him.

"I'm thankful we uncovered a global plot and can hopefully put an end to the madness," Khaldon said and he kissed my cheek. "Not to mention that I finally have m'lady here, live and in the flesh."

"Good recovery, Khaldon." Harris elbowed him in the ribs.

Daddy leaned over the back of his chair before he sat. "I'm thankful all my daughters are alive and there's a grandbaby on the way."

I patted Sheridan's growing bulge.

Everyone's eyes were on Sheridan. "Wow – that's a tough one for me this year. I have a lot to be thankful for, but to be painfully honest, I'm thankful to be able to wake up. I've been afraid to fall asleep for fear of the coma again."

I squeezed her hand and tipped my head towards her.

"What are you thankful for, missy?" Sheridan tipped her head back toward me.

"I'm thankful for each of you. Without you, we wouldn't be sitting here today being thankful for anything."

"Hear, hear!" Khaldon raised his mug.

We took our respective turns clinking everyone's bottle, glass, cup, and mug. I didn't own a twelve place setting of china or stemware either so our beverage assortment matched the ping pong table perfectly.

"I would like to hold a moment of silent prayer that our beloved Dakota will be found and will come home soon," my father said and grabbed the hands of Torchy and Harris beside him.

The rest of us followed suit holding hands around the table.

My prayer was simple.

I pinky swear promise I will find you again and bring you home. May the Gods and Goddesses, above and below, give us all strength.

"Okay – let's attack!" I grabbed the steaming plate of buttery mashed potatoes in front of me and spooned a monster size portion onto my plate.

Sheridan sat with her hands in her lap. "Ya know, three weeks ago, I never would've believed in supernatural creatures that walk among humans, much less thought I'd be pregnant. I'm still trying to wrap my head around this craziness. How did this happen to us?" She reached out to pluck the turkey leg off the platter as Harris whisked it away.

"I know, right?" I took a piece of bread. "Never in a million years would I have believed the Red Man from my dreams could change me forever."

"There's something that I need to tell you girls and I just can't seem to pull it up out of my mind," my father said. "I dream about it almost every night, but when I wake up - it's gone."

"It's all right, Daddy," I said. "Maybe one day you'll remember. Don't let it worry you."

He grimaced and shrugged. "Can you pass me the sweet potatoes?"

"Has anyone thought about how we're going to find Dakota?" Briggs scooped up the grits and greens. "Can you pass the hot sauce, please?"

I handed him the bottle.

"Thanks. We should set up a battle plan soon," Briggs said.

"You're right. I've been going over different scenarios in my head, but we should write it down."

Torchy reached for the cranberry sauce. "Could we map it out in a simulator? There's an API program that will enable us integrate with Google Earth's 3D renderings, and we can recreate where she's being held."

"That's a perfect idea, Torch. After we digest, let's work on that tonight. We can create various scenarios to determine how to infiltrate different types of places. This time we won't be fighting a Battle Kroc of Doom, but rather more dragons. You guys will be instrumental in helping us prepare for the unexpected."

Khaldon set his glass of pomegranate bloodwine on the table. "I've been practicing with Ludovic. Hopefully, he'll improve at communicating with her. If Amicula had her way, he'd be toast, and we'd be SOL in finding Dakota. Whether we like it or not, we have to keep him safe and keep him close. We have no idea when Amicula will send dhampirs out to get him or any of us. We need to start training everyone in weapons and combat."

Briggs added, "I don't think we should share our plans with Ludovic, though. I don't trust the bastard, especially after he ratted us out."

Harris squirreled a spoonful of stuffing in his cheek before he spoke. He pointed towards the kitchen with his fork. "How much longer are we going to keep Ludovic tied up in the chicken coop?"

I shrugged. "Not sure. Until we can secure a better place to keep an eye on him, that's where he stays put." I reached for the salt and pepper. "This way Padme has complete surveillance on him at all times and we can be notified immediately if he moves. Plus, it's a little satisfying, don't ya think?"

Sheridan grinned and passed the ambrosia salad to me. "What I want to know, Cheyenne, is when did our virtual game become such a reality?"

***

Meanwhile, deep within the Amazon Rainforest...

Queen Civetateo reread the emessage from her niece. She drummed out an irritated cadence on the window sill with her fingernails. Abruptly she turned to her trusted councilor. "Aisling, if I had known your daughters were going to be this troublesome, I would have captured them myself. Find a way to clean up this mess, before I do!"

<<< >>>

References
Novels

Dragonriders of Pern
by **Anne McCaffrey**
Ballantine Books May 12, 1986

The Island of Dr. Moreau
by **H.G. Wells**
Heinemann, Stone & Kimball 1896

The Exorcist
by **William Peter Blatty**
Harper & Row 1971

Interview with a Vampire
by **Anne Rice**
Alfred A Knopf 1976

IT
by **Stephen King**
Viking September 15,1986

Movies

Star Wars: Episode IV – A New Hope (1977)
Lucasfilm (as a Lucasfilm Limited Production)
Twentieth Century Fox Film Corporation

Fatal Attraction (1987)
Paramount Pictures

Final Destination (2000)
New Line Cinema

Psycho (1960)
Alfred Hitchcock
Shamley Productions
Paramount Pictures

Frenzy (1972)
Alfred Hitchcock
Universal Pictures

Lifeforce (1985)
Golan-Globus Productions
The Cannon Group
TriStar Pictures

Silence of the Lambs (1991)
Strong Heart/Demme Production
Orion Pictures Corporation

Jurassic Park (1993)
Universal Pictures
Amblin Entertainment

Underworld (2003)
Lakeshore Entertainment
Screen Gems

Alien (1979)
Brandywine Productions
Twentieth Century-Fox Productions

When A Stranger Calls (2006)
Screen Gems
Columbia Pictures

My Fair Lady (1964)
Warner Bros

You've Got Mail (1998)
Warner Bros.

My Fair Lady (1964)
Warner Bros

Television

The Six Million Dollar Man (1973)
Universal TV

World's Dumbest Criminals
Meetinghouse Productions
truTV

Artists

Edward Munch
The Scream (1893)

Diego Velázquez

Venus at Her Mirror (1647)

Steve Hanks (Contemporary)
Greenwich Workshop

Music

Celebration
by **Kool and the Gang** (1980)
Album: Celebrate!
Label: Mercury

Can't Get Enough of Your Love, Babe
by **Barry White** (1974)
Album: Can't Get Enough
Label: 20th Century Records

Danger Zone
by **Kenny Loggins** (1986)
Album: Top Gun Soundtrack
Label: Columbia Records

Born to be Wild
by **Steppenwolf** (1968)
Album: Steppenwolf
Label: Dunhill RCA

Dirty Diana
 by **Michael Jackson** (1988)
Album: Bad
Label: Epic

In Your Eyes
by **Peter Gabriel** (1986)
Album: So
Label: Geffen Records

Bitch is Back
by **Elton John** (1974)
Album: Caribou
Label: MCA, DJM, Rocket/Phonogram

Crocodile Rock
 by **Elton John** (1972)Album: Don't Shoot Me I'm Only the Piano Player
Label: MCA

Friends in Low Places
by **Garth Brooks** (1990)
Album: No Fences
Label: Capitol Nashville

Restaurants

Larry's Deli & Sandwich Shop
Land O' Lakes, Florida
*For the BEST Cuban
Sandwiches – EVER!

www.ingramcontent.com/pod-product-compliance
Lightning Source LLC
Chambersburg PA
CBHW031556240626

47153CB00002B/532